The
STAR SOCIETY

The STAR SOCIETY

A HISTORICAL NOVEL

GABRIELLA SAAB

HARPER **MUSE**

ISBN 978-1-4003-5132-9 (epub)
ISBN 978-1-4003-5130-5 (TP)
ISBN 978-1-4003-5131-2 (HC)
ISBN 978-1-4003-5133-6 (downloadable audio)

HarperCollins Publishers, Macken House, 39/40 Mayor Street Upper, Dublin 1, D01 C9W8, Ireland (https://www.harpercollins.com)

Library of Congress Cataloging-in-Publication Data

CIP data is available upon request.

Art Direction: Halie Cotton
Cover Design: James W. Hall
Interior Design: Chloe Foster

Printed in the United States of America

25 26 27 28 29 LBC 5 4 3 2 1

For my two little sisters, who keep me smiling, laughing, and endlessly proud. I love you both so much!

CHAPTER 1

New York City, 1943

ADA

Performing was first essential to her art; now, to her survival.

Years at Arnhem's Muziekschool had taught the young woman how to tell a story through movement, instilling her with a discipline that rivaled that of the German soldiers who had overtaken her homeland during these last three years. When a ballerina takes center stage, she dances with levity and elegance, defying the way her body burns and bleeds, enduring the pain. Masking everything that must remain hidden. Every step and turn influences what the audience perceives and what they conclude.

Tonight, a quiet Manhattan street is her stage, she the soloist. And she must perform.

A chilling wind sweeps over her; she does not slouch against it, does not flinch when a distant *crack* sounds too much like a gunshot, does not beg a nearby street vendor to spare a morsel for the woman who has been too thin for too long. She presses onward, shoulders back, chin lifted. She has walked for some time, banishing the unsteadiness in her legs following her journey overseas, settling into her performance. Into the woman she has come here to be.

The Dutch girl she has been for the past twenty-one years has fallen. Another casualty of war. Now she is Ada Worthington-Fox: a proper British woman, according to both her new identification papers and the accent she developed from years in a boarding school in Kent. A woman who has come to New York City with nothing from her old life. Only its disciplines. Its pain.

And the documents tucked inside the novel hidden beneath her overcoat, pressed against a heart pounding in rapid contrast to her measured pace.

Across war-torn Europe, across the ocean, all the way to America. Ada is here at last, safe. Far from those who must not find her.

From an open apartment window, a newborn's wail breaks the quiet. She passes a well-dressed couple sharing drinks outside a bar, then a bedraggled man huddled on a stoop. At last, Ada glances over her shoulder. This street is abandoned, so she turns down a narrow alley.

Damp air, heavy with rot and filth, seeps into her skin. With shaking hands, she pulls a set of matches from her coat pocket and extracts one of the documents tucked inside the novel. Then she strikes a match, watching the golden flame dance with all the effortlessness of a ballerina en pointe. An effortlessness that, in fact, requires far more effort than one might expect. Ada should know.

This flame will take her past, protect her from its truths, its pain, its memory, and leave her with her new role. No, she must not think of it that way any longer. Not a role, not even a performance. Her new life.

Ada Worthington-Fox touches the eager flame to the paper. It succumbs, and she stands alone in the dark, quiet alley, watching it burn.

* * *

Three Years Later
Hollywood Hills, 24 August 1946

When Ada planned this evening's celebration, Gordon had insisted a champagne tower was necessary. Now, as the sparkling liquid descends from the tower of coupes to fill each glass, Ada cannot deny that her agent was correct. Every celebration deserves a little extravagance. And Gordon Sharpe's home in Hollywood Hills is just the place for such a party.

After accepting a glass, Ada lifts it to the actors, filmmakers, and various members of the entertainment industry gathered around the backyard pool. "To the dear members of my Star Society: May our careers be long and our drinks be strong!"

Cheers rise while guests raise their coupes in response. Someone starts the gramophone as Ada sips her champagne, watching the moonlight glittering over the pool.

"Spectacular, as always." Gordon repositions his horn-rimmed spectacles and appraises the dress hugging her slim figure. "Gold lamé, fitted bodice, sweetheart neckline, shining like the Oscar that is certainly in your future. A perfect complement to your toast, if you hadn't left out the most important part: 'We're celebrating this evening because I, Ada Worthington-Fox, rising star represented by the esteemed Gordon Sharpe, signed a contract for my first lead role in a film.'"

"Esteemed?" She flashes a teasing grin. "Did you mean arrogant?"

"Always tout your own excellence, kid. By the time I'm finished this evening, everyone will expect this role to send you to the Academy Awards." As she chuckles, Gordon taps his glass against hers. "Congratulations. Now, if you'll excuse me, I've got some bragging to do."

"Not too much. Casting is confidential until the official announcement, remember?"

He sighs. "Fine, although it's hardly fair that the papers get to break the news and I don't."

A rush of warmth courses through Ada as he joins a few men—members of the Screen Actors Guild Board, she recalls. Her parties are always lavish affairs, yet right now she is present only to the summer evening's warmth and the champagne tickling her throat. After three years working between New York City and Los Angeles, at last she has secured her first lead role in a major motion picture. And for Abe Sternberg, the director who selects promising actors and transforms them into stars. When Gordon mentioned Mr. Sternberg was seeking a lead for his upcoming film noir, that was all she needed to hear before she snatched the script. Then she left her audition with the same indescribable feeling she had found when, as a girl of six years old, she first stepped onto a stage for a ballet recital.

Performing feels the way champagne tastes—thrilling, a bit dangerous, yet too addictive to resist.

As for why she hasn't made the announcement as Gordon expected, well, it *is* confidential. And because being cast in a lead role does not make her worthy of praise yet, not until she lives up to the responsibilities, the expectations. There is still plenty of time to fail.

She swallows the last of her champagne, letting it wash away such doubts. Tonight is for indulging in her accomplishments, in this role that will secure her place in Hollywood. She is Ada Worthington-Fox, for God's sake—Hollywood's Vixen, as christened by the gossip rags, hostess of the ever-so-exclusive Star Society, and soon-to-be household name when this role propels her to stardom. A delighted little shiver runs down her spine.

When the gramophone strikes up a lively swing dance, Ada grabs the nearest fellow—who, if she's not mistaken, happens to be Fred Astaire. Ada's gatherings might be invitation only, but sometimes even she is impressed by her own guest list. Mr. Astaire, here at her party despite his recently announced retirement, which Ada hopes won't last; the industry needs talent like his.

She slips her arm through Mr. Astaire's. "Come along, darling; you look like a fellow who knows how to dance."

The teasing remark wins a laugh. He leads her beyond the pool and onto the dance floor set up on the lawn. There Ada loses herself in movement, in believing she is, at last, almost where she wants to be in this new life she's found for herself, with the old one firmly behind her.

* * *

"Will you please go to bed?" Ada calls to Gordon long after the final guest has departed. He emerges from the pool, wraps a towel around his hips, and uncorks a chilled bottle of champagne. "You promised to run lines with me tomorrow, so stop drinking so ambitiously."

"Too late for that, my dear. And the Star Society was your idea."

It all started after signing with Gordon and moving to California. Beyond the all-female boardinghouse where she resided alongside other aspiring entertainers, Ada wanted to connect with industry professionals. Why not host a party? Gordon, being a wise agent and dear friend, readily agreed. One party developed into another until the frequent gatherings earned a nickname from the gossip rags. Now that she's exchanged the boardinghouse for one of Gordon's spare rooms, she intends to make them an even more regular occurrence.

While Gordon smooths a hand over his graying mustache, Ada offers him two glasses. "Thank you," she says as he pours. "For always letting me host parties here. And for believing in me."

"The star of the Star Society and of the great Abe Sternberg's upcoming picture—which I can say now that we're alone, so you can't chastise me for spoiling it before the papers do." With a cheeky grin, he waves the bottle in farewell. "Turn off the lights, will you?"

While he goes inside, the warm summer evening prompts beads of moisture to form on Ada's cold glass. Without the party noise, the night is quiet. Almost too quiet.

Much like the last time she performed in a starring role. Except then she danced the lead in a ballet, *Giselle*. Then, she performed to no music, no applause, no celebrations, nothing that might attract the soldiers occupying her country. Then, any noise might have gotten her killed.

Ada stifles a trembling breath with a sip of champagne. She always imagined that the next time she played a lead, she would celebrate surrounded by everyone important to her. That was before she learned what war is. What it does. War takes and takes and so rarely returns.

Darling, I need you to trust me.

The refined lilt is so sudden in Ada's head, the champagne sours on her tongue. She had trusted Mother until she could trust no one anymore, not even herself. And now Ada is here. Where Mother is, she does not know anymore. As for whether it would be easier if she knew, Ada is not certain of that, either; perhaps it would have been more difficult to detach from something known rather than something unknown.

Before the growing pinch can fully form in her chest, one signaling the deeply buried pain, regret, and guilt, Ada silences Mother's voice, the memories, the war. She cannot dwell on the girl she no longer is. She is Ada, just Ada. A woman with no one and nothing, a woman whose past is hers and no one else's.

After finishing her drink, Ada turns off the lights, passing through the various rooms until she reaches the small office Gordon allows her to use. The place where she can most fully connect to who she is rather than who she was. Inside is a desk, a bookshelf, a small chaise longue, and a few film posters and newspaper clippings.

Soon she will have new posters to add to this wall, ones that will read: *Starring Ada Worthington-Fox.* A shiver travels across her skin. The first article she ever framed discussed her role in a picture that released two years ago, in 1944, and the piece was featured in *The Dish*, the gossip rag responsible for naming her parties.

FROM THE GREAT WHITE WAY TO TINSELTOWN
by Minnie Musgrave

Actors often make their way from Broadway to Hollywood, but none quite like Ada Worthington-Fox, as poised as a duchess yet as sultry as the vixen in her name. The twenty-two-year-old captured attention in *Read the Fine Print*, playing a businessman's daughter who seduces the leading man, part of an elaborate plot to dupe him into a foolish deal. A minor yet bewitching role. Acclaimed talent agent Gordon Sharpe recently discovered the British actress, who was a dancer and chorus girl on Broadway, and now represents her. When asked why he felt the part was fitting for his newcomer, he said: "America has her sweethearts. What she needs is her siren."

And thanks to Mr. Sharpe, Hollywood has her: Ada Worthington-Fox. Every woman wants to look like her and every man wants to take her to—well, dinner, of course. Why, what did you expect?

Ada rolls her eyes at the last paragraph. She had initially considered trimming it out, but enduring Minnie Musgrave's drivel is key to surviving this industry. Best to start practicing right away. Since this article, Ada's roles have steadily improved—bigger parts, more lines, better scenes. And now, at last, a lead.

As she closes the office door, a knock reaches her ears. She glances at the hall clock—well past midnight. Company at this hour? Perhaps someone from the party forgot something.

Stifling a yawn, Ada strolls down the hall, past the foyer's elegant curving staircase, and opens the front door.

No one is there.

She presses her lips together as she steps beneath the portico and stares past the four sturdy columns, across the redbrick motor court, and toward the dark street. One of the neighborhood children must be having a bit of fun, though it's far too late in the evening for pranks. Gordon needs to put up that gate he's been mentioning. She's about to close the door when something catches the moonlight.

An envelope rests on the doormat—no address, only a name. *Ada Worthington-Fox.*

Fan mail, perhaps? No fan has ever hand-delivered a message—or discovered her residence, for that matter. A prickle steals over her neck. Definitely time for a gate.

Once she pulls out the letter, she unfolds it—except it's not a letter. It's an otherwise blank page containing a name.

Aleida de Vos.

A gasp chokes in her throat while Ada presses a palm to her stomach. The hand clutching the letter trembles. Surely her eyes are playing tricks on her. Too much champagne and too little food.

No, the name remains. Aleida de Vos.

Only a few people could have written that name.

But one of those few must be dead. She had promised to write, to assure Ada she was safe, and she never did. They never broke their promises to each other, so this note cannot be from her, because she cannot have survived.

Ada grips the note tighter, fighting to steady her breaths. She swore to forget everything that happened in Arnhem, the severity of her failure. To forget the fury igniting with the memories. To forget the past.

She should have known that the past would always find her.

CHAPTER 2

Arnhem, 1940

ALEIDA

Two sharp claps echoed around the Muziekschool's dance studio, interrupting the accompanist at the piano and causing Aleida and her fellow dancers to pause mid-pirouette. By the mirrored wall stood Madame Bellamy—tall, elegant, and frowning at her students.

"No, no, no! *Mon Dieu*, where are my graceful young ballerinas? You're fumbling about like infants learning how to walk." When a few dared to giggle, her piercing gaze silenced them. "What do I always tell you? To dance you must *feel* the music."

Even Aleida sometimes found it difficult not to wither beneath such a scrupulous gaze, yet her years of training with Madame Bellamy had revealed the instructor's passion for ballet, translating into the deepest respect for the art and the highest standards for her students. And when Madame Bellamy caught her eye, Aleida knew precisely what the look meant.

Her heart leaped in terrified yet eager anticipation while a small collective sigh rose from the girls who had been spared this time. They withdrew to the outskirts of the floor, leaving Aleida to demonstrate the choreography so Madame Bellamy could dissect every step, mention everything wrong, use one student as an example to challenge the entire class toward improvement. A challenge that always ignited something irrepressible within Aleida, giving her the courage to perform the way she had once feared she would never perform again.

"I don't want to go to Kent," she had wailed to Madame Bellamy before class one day more than ten years ago, when she was seven years old and lamenting Mother's intention to send her and her twin to boarding school. "What if I forget how to dance?"

"Your mother will enroll you in dance lessons there, will she not?"

"It won't be the same."

"Nor will it be so different. You will learn from your new instructor, practice on your own, and take lessons with me every time you come home."

Yet from the moment she had stepped shyly into her first dance class a few years prior, Aleida had known no instruction from anyone else except this stern Frenchwoman who was, in fact, not always so stern. She could not lose her lessons, even temporarily, from the trusted ballet mistress who had taken her from uncertain pupil to confident ballerina eager to learn, to improve, to dance professionally someday.

Madame Bellamy knelt to her eye level and gently brushed a tear from Aleida's cheek. "Write to me at the Muziekschool. Tell me about your lessons and your new instructor, ask me questions, anything, and I will answer. Then I will be here when you come home. You will not fall behind, I promise." She gave the little girl's shoulders a reassuring squeeze. "You have no need to fear, Aleida, and you are far too talented to give up. Promise me you will keep dancing."

Aleida had taken her advice. Despite boarding school, she had studied, trained, learned, and stayed in touch with her instructor when she was not home to take classes from her, and she had not fallen behind.

Now, as Aleida came to the end of her demonstration, Madame Bellamy did indeed tear apart the performance before concluding with a few praises, then a nod.

"Overall, good enough. But I trained you to be your best."

"Yes, madame," Aleida replied, resisting a small smile. Pleasing her instructor was the most motivating challenge of all.

Before the other girls could resume their places, a sound came from the doorway. A man clearing his throat. Concern built in Aleida's chest. The Netherlands fell in early May, hardly a few weeks ago, yet she was still unaccustomed to the green-uniformed Ordnungspolizei patrolling the streets. Ones like the young man entering the room.

"Girls, you are dismissed," the ballet mistress said calmly before addressing the policeman. "Good afternoon, may I help you?"

Pointe shoes clacked across the parquet floor as the dancers gathered their belongings. Aleida removed her shoes slowly, watching the Orpo officer.

"Pardon the interruption." He spoke in polite, German-accented Dutch. "Please ensure this building is open tomorrow so all signage can be updated. The Dutch signs will remain as well for those who require them."

He handed her a document, likely a notice of the changes. What a foolish order, adding German signs to every building. As if the soldiers were here to stay. This occupation was temporary, though. It had to be.

While Madame Bellamy accepted the paper, Aleida watched as the officer glanced briefly at the tiny gold Star of David around her neck. A harmless observation, so Aleida couldn't explain why the knot in her chest tightened. Then he tipped his cap to her and smiled at the dancers, leaving a few girls tittering, staring after his retreating figure.

One girl sitting near Aleida leaned closer to another. "The soldiers are nothing like I thought they would be—all so civilized and friendly. And young. And *handsome*."

"My parents say there's nothing to worry about," her companion replied. "If Jews have to register here like they do in Germany, what's the harm? All it means is that the government knows how they worship."

Before Aleida could ask how they would feel if such laws impacted them instead of their Jewish neighbors, or if they were really so confident that supposedly civilized behavior would not develop into something more sinister, the girls vacated the building. Then only Aleida and her instructor were left.

Madame Bellamy sat before the piano, her back to her remaining student. She placed her fingers on the ebony and ivory keys and played a piece Aleida recognized by Chopin. She listened, feeling the music as Madame Bellamy always instructed. When the final note ended, the ballet mistress sighed, rose, and startled when she turned.

"Forgive me, I thought everyone was gone. Did you have a question about the class?"

"No, I . . ." Aleida glanced at the policeman's document resting on the piano bench, then looked to her instructor. "I wanted to ask how you are."

A foolish question to ask a Jewish woman during such uncertain times, especially when Aleida could do little to help. Still, Madame Bellamy's eyes warmed briefly with gratitude before a hollowness returned, one leaving Aleida's own chest feeling hollow. The elder woman had never looked at her in such a way.

"Without you, the little girl who took her first ballet class here would have lost herself and her passion for dance in boarding school, and she would not have grown into the young woman and ballerina she is today. You always supported me when I needed you most. Please tell me how I can support you."

The ballet mistress picked up the notice. "Many of my friends expect matters to worsen. Some wish to leave—which requires funds, papers, and more. Until we develop a way to acquire such resources, there's little to be done." She placed a hand on Aleida's arm. "Yours is a kind offer, likely a dangerous one."

Dangerous. An unsettling realization. In occupied Arnhem, a simple offer to help a friend was now considered dangerous.

As she picked up her bag, Aleida stared at the pointe shoes tucked inside. Perhaps the solution was simpler than it seemed. Dangerous or not, they had to try.

"Let us help—your dancers. Those who can be trusted, anyway." She gestured to the empty room. "We can perform to raise money for Jews who need assistance."

Madame Bellamy arched a brow while Aleida's heart pounded. Something to be done. A way to feel useful until this war was over. Maybe some saw no reason to worry about the occupation, but how could Aleida sit by while her countrymen suffered?

After her instructor promised to consider the suggestion, Aleida left the Muziekschool and, outside, found the June sky painted in a sunset as vibrant as the warmth in her chest. Perhaps her idea would help to assuage Madame Bellamy's concerns, the same way her instructor had once assuaged Aleida's.

Before she could walk to her family's house on Jansbinnensingel, she noticed the young Orpo officer lingering outside the building, finishing a cigarette. Suddenly Aleida's mouth tasted like ash, even though she pretended not to see him. She would be cautious and not make her disdain for the invaders obvious, but unlike the girls from her class, she had no interest in befriending them. Not when their presence posed a threat to all Dutch citizens, particularly Jewish ones, if Madame Bellamy's worries proved valid. Maybe the soldiers had been relatively civil since the invasion. Maybe they would not always be.

"You are one of the dancers."

Aleida jumped when the young Orpo officer's voice sounded behind her. "I am," she replied shortly, then bit her lip when he stepped in front of her. She stopped, unable to pass.

"My sister takes ballet classes. But she is only six and not very talented yet, I'm afraid." He laughed, then cast a fond gaze at the Muziekschool, perhaps lost in thoughts of home. If this was an attempt to endear himself to her, it would not work. He blinked, returning from the reverie, and doffed his cap in introduction. "Wachtmeister Julius Hochheimer. May I walk you home, Fräulein?"

"I know the way, thank you."

"Please, I insist."

Her eyes fell instinctively to the gun at his hip. Did she have the power to refuse? With a small nod, she consented and led the way down Boulevard Heuvelink even as her heart raced. He chatted amiably and did not seem to care if she answered, so she stayed quiet.

More of this supposedly civilized behavior would not make her forget the brief shadow that had overtaken his countenance when he noticed Madame Bellamy's Star of David necklace, nor would she dismiss her instructor's fears. If Jewish people felt unsafe, Aleida would do whatever she could to assist them until Arnhem belonged to the Dutch again.

When they reached her front door, she forced a smile and spoke with attempted lightness. "Thank you for accompanying me home, Herr Wachtmeister." A poor effort; she heard the tension concealed within her tone.

"Of course." Then, as she reached for the door, he caught her arm. "A word of advice: When choosing the company you keep, choose wisely."

Somehow she did not think he was referring to himself. Everything inside her bristled in protest. Was this because her ballet mistress was Jewish, because she had lingered to speak with Madame Bellamy beyond class time rather than leaving when the other girls did? He had no right to deter a pupil from associating with her instructor. Still, it did not sound like advice. More like a threat.

Aleida did not move, did not breathe, not until he released her, tipped his hat with a charming smile, and watched as she slipped inside. Once the door was firmly closed, she placed a hand on her chest, attempting to slow the heart that had pounded the entire way home.

"Everything all right, darling?"

At Mother's prompting, Aleida joined her in the living room, where she was sitting on the sofa, brow creased in concern. Aleida sat beside her and rested her head on Mother's shoulder the way she did so often as a girl—whether seeking comfort or listening to the calming cadence of Mother's British accent or simply enjoying each other's company. One by one, Mother removed the pins from Aleida's bun until her dark hair fell about her shoulders, then she ran her fingers through it, steady and rhythmic and soothing.

No, everything was not all right. She could not sort out if Hochheimer had threatened her or not, nor could Aleida speak of her intentions to help Madame Bellamy. If doing so would be dangerous, she could not put Mother in jeopardy, certainly not before she knew what the work would entail or the risks it would impose.

"I'm afraid, Mother," she whispered at last, because that much was true. Even if the other dancers were right and the occupying soldiers had not done anything yet beyond instate their own laws. But worry had found its way into her heart when Arnhem fell, then more strongly with every passing second after the Orpo officer's visit and the look on Madame Bellamy's face, the concern in her eyes, the worries she had expressed.

Mother kissed the top of her head. "Oh, my dear girl . . . How I wish I could take those fears. But I will keep you safe no matter what happens. I promise."

Aleida wondered if such assurances were within Mother's power to give.

CHAPTER 3

Washington, DC, 1940

INGRID

A late summer breeze spurs the young couple onward through the dark night, their paces brisk, hands intertwined. Since stepping off the train, the young woman has not slowed her steps, although she feels the pavement through her thin soles. They have spent so much of this journey on foot. Walking through woods, concealed in trucks with deliverymen bribed to slip them across Nazi borders, taking refuge in empty barns, boarding a ship, then a train, and now here.

Theirs had not been much of a plan, really. Only to go. To escape a country overtaken by fascists.

Her hand feels so small in her fiancé's grasp. So much thinner now compared to when they started this journey—weeks ago? A month? More? She cannot remember. Her mind is too clouded with fatigue, with hunger, with the urge toward safety that has sometimes been the only thing sustaining her.

Another couple strolls by, casting a curious glance at the young couple in torn, tattered garments. Along their journey, they carried little more than whatever food or water they managed to find and obtained changes of clothes when possible, but it had rarely been possible. Now, all she wants is a hot meal and a bath. Once she feels like herself again, she will believe they are safe. Free.

That is why this was their chosen destination, because of what this country promises. Democracy. Liberty. Everything her grandfather once spoke of with such a wistful look in his eyes. She swallows hard, pushing thoughts of him aside before they overwhelm her. She cannot think of him, of anyone from home, because that place is not home anymore. This is home now, where they can work and live and be free from the oppressive powers that stole their former country and made it a land she no longer recognizes.

The man's English is heavily Dutch, the woman's heavily British, yet they are now Lars and Ingrid, Americans. By this time tomorrow, Mr. and Mrs. Van Essen—or, if not tomorrow, as soon as possible. The thought nearly brings tears to her eyes, but not yet. Not until they are safe.

They reach their destination, a small apartment building, where they knock on the door. It opens to reveal another young couple, who allow them to enter. Only once the door closes and the woman pulls Ingrid into her arms does Ingrid let out a breath and allow the tears to come.

All these weeks, one hand has spent nearly every moment gripping her fiancé's while the other has clutched the pistol in her skirt pocket. At last, she loosens her hold on both.

This is home, the land of liberty and democracy, and this is where their lives can begin—far from the war, from Arnhem, from those she was eager to escape and those she wishes, more than anything, she had not left behind.

* * *

Six Years Later
Washington, DC, 12 August 1946

Arriving on time for work, for luncheons, for any engagement is not so difficult. One commits to being somewhere at a certain time, then takes the necessary measures to fulfill that commitment. People who are perpetually late are ones Ingrid rather hates. That is why, over the last six years, not once has she been late to the office.

This morning, after reviewing the newspaper article about the upcoming November elections and the candidates' positions on fighting Communism, she goes about her usual routine with the piece heavy on her mind. Since reading about Prime Minister Churchill's speech at Westminster College cautioning against a totalitarian regime in a postwar world, Ingrid has spent every spare moment learning more, as she once sought to understand the threat of fascism. And, since escaping occupied Arnhem, she has never taken a moment of freedom in Washington, DC, for granted.

She adjusts her cloche and picks up a tube of lipstick, painting her lips pale pink before rising from her vanity and dancing around her husband as he steps toward the dresser.

Lars ties his necktie and gestures to the apartment door. "Go. You look fine, *schatje*. Even if you didn't, it's a work meeting, not one with President Truman himself."

Meeting at nine o'clock sharp on Monday was all Crenshaw said when Ingrid left the office last week. She can't be late, nor can she arrive looking like an absolute wreck. A woman in a male-dominated field must look her best, do her best, only to be passed over again and again—but God forbid she do anything less.

Half an hour later, after reaching Crenshaw Investigative Services a few minutes early, Ingrid slips into the meeting room, finds an open chair, and smooths her pale cerulean skirt and jacket. Others gradually trickle in while Howard Crenshaw takes his place at the head of the long table, where he drops a large stack of files. Ingrid sits taller, her heart already racing as she anticipates the purpose of this meeting. Something serious, judging by those files.

"Let's get right to it," Crenshaw says. "We've been tasked with an investigation into Communism on behalf of the House Un-American Activities Committee."

Ingrid scribbles notes—partially because it's her job at these meetings, partially because she would take them anyway for her own benefit. As she writes the word *Communism*, she clenches her jaw. Churchill's recent concerns aside, she has been in America for six years and has worked in private investigation long enough to know a rise in Communism has been an ongoing concern. Still, the confirmation of an increased threat leaves her mouth dry.

She left one country when its potential new government did not suit her. Where will she go if forced to leave this one?

That summer evening in 1940 lives so clearly in Ingrid's mind, when she and Lars left Arnhem once it fell to the fascists. What might have happened if they stayed? And what happened to those unable to escape the Battle of Arnhem, the starvation, the suffering?

"Which brings me to our task."

At Crenshaw's announcement, Ingrid startles and looks up. Did she permit her mind to wander? She is at work; this cannot happen at work. Biting her lip, she refocuses on her notes.

"Hollywood, the Commie capital of the United States."

Rather exaggerated, Ingrid thinks, but Crenshaw is always one to emphasize a point.

"Our primary focus will be Communist influences within labor unions and the entertainment industry, so I'll be sending some of you to California to investigate the identified targets."

As he goes through his list of actors, directors, producers, screenwriters, musicians, entertainers, and more, Ingrid jots them all down—some familiar, others not, mostly men.

"Next is Ada Worthington-Fox," he says after he's been droning for some time. "Age twenty-four, British, has worked in New York and California and is now based in Los Angeles. A few years back, a gossip columnist said her parties were"—he consults a document and reads aloud— "'a veritable constellation of stars, an entire society of celebrities.' Rumor has it a version of the description is now used every time she throws a party, which is often. And which could mean nothing, or could imply Communist ties, given the star symbolism and the many union members who attend. That's for you to uncover."

"Anything for the safety of our country." Archie Stribling, who sits beside Ingrid, folds his hands behind his head and leans back in his chair. "If that includes parties with a dish like Ada Worthington-Fox— well, a fellow's got to do what he must."

A few chuckles and murmurs of assent join his suggestive smirk. Ingrid returns to her notes, stifling the ever-present urge to retort. Such efforts tend to be futile. Holding her tongue is the most prudent course of action, although someday when she's been promoted beyond the role of glorified secretary, she will not be prudent. For now, she presses her pen too hard against the paper, causing the ink to bleed. She's not familiar with the actress, but apparently the men will be grappling over who gets assigned to the poor girl.

One man sitting near Crenshaw picks up the dossier. He scrutinizes the actress's headshot, then his brows lift. "Say . . ." He glances from the photo to Ingrid, who stares back even as her jaw clenches with uncertainty. No one ever acknowledges her in these meetings. "If you changed your hair, maybe lost a little weight, you two would almost look—"

"Up next," Crenshaw interrupts, picking up the next file and silencing further talk. Her coworker leaves Ingrid with a final look, then he shrugs and tosses the dossier onto the table.

Ingrid touches a self-conscious hand to her auburn chignon and grinds her teeth together to contain a retort. No need to waste another second considering whatever irritating comment her coworker was going to make. Probably something like *you two would almost look—actually, never mind, Ingrid would still look like Ingrid* or a similar remark to win a laugh. Her looks are hardly what they are in this room to discuss.

Crenshaw mentions more names, including those he intends to dispatch to Hollywood. Archie's among them; Ingrid's absent. As usual. She writes down the investigators with one hand and drives her fingernails into her palm with the other—another frequent occurrence to keep from voicing fruitless protests.

What will it take to encourage Crenshaw to assign her to something more? Maybe he won't allow her to investigate someone important, but why not someone he considers minor? A lesser-known composer or the newest Screen Writers Guild member, perhaps. The least important task for the least important of his employees, or so the logic would go in his mind. Better than nothing. Such is the game Ingrid must play, even if she so rarely wins.

Once the meeting is over, she waits until the room empties before rising. "Mr. Crenshaw, might I have a word?"

He's already gesturing to the array of documents. "Put these on my desk, Mrs. Van Essen."

Her supervisor departs without awaiting her reply. So much for her intended proposal.

Sighing, she gathers the documents left in disarray. While her colleagues depart for Hollywood to thwart potential threats, she will be here. Organizing papers, compiling research, anything that relegates her to a desk.

Ingrid has nearly finished sorting and alphabetizing when she picks up the next document—and almost drops it again when she notices the face peering back at her.

Something stirs deep within—something that cannot be, because it is not possible.

Swallowing past the knot in her throat, Ingrid pats each jacket pocket, the usual places for her reading glasses, before she notices them by her briefcase at the opposite end of the table. Her heels clack against the parquet floor. Like her mother's heels against the wooden floor six years ago, when she had burst into the bedroom: *Wake up, the war is on.* Moments later, the streets of Arnhem were flooded with soldiers.

Ingrid shakes her head and snatches her glasses. The war is over. Everything—and everyone—from that time is gone. What she suspects cannot be true. But she can't ignore the tightening in her chest as she peers at the image more closely.

This is a photograph of the actress Crenshaw mentioned, Ada Worthington-Fox. A woman with chiseled features, dark hair styled in romantic waves, refined looks. A woman whose face Ingrid has seen every time she has closed her eyes these last six years.

Each breath sharpens as she reads the document slowly, awaiting the name from a time and a life long forgotten. A name that will confirm her suspicions.

A name that no longer exists, because that woman is dead. She must be; otherwise she never would have broken her promise.

Ingrid reads the document once, twice, seeking an alternate birth name, an alias, anything. But no, nothing. No evidence of the name she anticipated. Except Ingrid does not need a confirmed name to recognize the face she will never forget.

It is her. Alive.

She's alive.

An unsteady breath catches in Ingrid's throat. She sinks into the nearest chair, removes her glasses, and rubs a trembling hand over her eyes, as if the gesture will help her to make sense of it all. There will be time for the many questions swirling through her mind. For now, she clutches the paper to her racing heart.

Communist ties. Crenshaw's suspicions can't be true. Still, if this actress is engaging in subversive behavior, Ingrid will talk to her, will encourage her to listen. Not Archie, not anyone else, Ingrid.

This assignment will be hers. It must be.

She marches into Crenshaw's office and sets the documents before him. "Sir, I'd like your permission to investigate Ada Worthington-Fox."

He laughs. "Why? Because she's a kindred spirit from jolly old England?"

"I'm from Holland." How many times must she explain herself? Her accent is due to attending an exceedingly proper boarding school in Kent, one formerly attended by her exceedingly proper British mother—that dreadful woman. "The actress is my age, neither of us are from America, and I'm certain I can do this."

"There's far more to this job than commonalities. You're a hard worker, and someday you might be ready for a task like this, but I have men who have gone undercover, earned trust, gathered information. Everything you've never done." Crenshaw leans across his desk toward her. "You think you can do better than them?"

"Yes, I do." She holds his gaze. "Women don't trust men. We trust women."

At this, Crenshaw chews on the ear of his spectacles. The file mentioned that Ada is incredibly private; such a woman will never speak candidly to men like those in this office. With Ingrid, though, she might be more willing.

Connecting with this actress is the easiest and fastest way to sort out whatever trouble she's gotten into with this Communism business—if Crenshaw's concerns prove valid—and to keep Ingrid's coworkers occupied elsewhere. Otherwise they might ask questions that will lead to truths Ingrid has kept close for so long. Her colleagues cannot take this case. Not when Ingrid knows this woman better than any of them.

The silence stretches like the quiet following a gunshot. Expectant, awaiting the next bullet, yet desperately hopeful that the *crack* will not come and that, for now, the silence will extend into calm.

"I will send you to Hollywood to make contact." Not even Crenshaw's scowl robs those blessed words of their beauty. "If you lose the ring."

Guarding her feelings and reactions is essential in the workplace; yet as he nods to the gold band and diamond encircling her finger, the absurd, infuriating request nearly makes Ingrid forget to control herself. Even her marriage is a strike against her?

"How does my ring affect my ability to complete this task?" she asks with only the faintest hint of irritation.

"Think of the headlines if the tabloids see a married woman flirting with all the male celebrities. I need you to be invisible, not to get your face splashed across the papers."

No use explaining that she has no intentions of flirting with men who are not her husband. But he has a point: Being a married woman will draw attention from anyone seeking a bit of gossip.

Whatever she must do to secure the assignment.

"No ring, then," she concedes, despite the knot in her throat. The married male investigators will surely not be required to abide by this stipulation.

Perhaps Crenshaw had thought the condition would deter her, but he gives no reaction and continues. "The actress is rumored to be involved in an upcoming film, and Archie Stribling will be investigating its director, so you will share anything of relevance with him. You will contact me at regular intervals and compile a detailed report for your FBI handler—Klaus Stieber, who will make contact with you in California. And if you don't give me anything useful within a week, I'm replacing you. Is that clear?"

"Yes, sir, though I assure you it won't be necessary."

She departs before he can change his mind, though she hears him grumbling about how he'd better not regret this. Maybe she has to work alongside Archie; maybe she has to report to a handler; neither can eliminate the thrill pulsing through her veins—a combination of relief and eagerness she hasn't felt in so long.

As she passes through sparse hallways smelling of stale coffee and too much cologne, Ingrid almost smells the tulips in Arnhem, almost feels the wind tugging her skirt as she rides her bicycle toward home. How joyful those times were before Dutch laws were replaced with German ones.

She shoves the memories back into the deeply concealed place where she keeps them locked away, then returns to her desk and places a phone call.

"Federal Bureau of Investigation," announces a brisk voice on the other line. "How may I direct your call?"

"Skip the formalities, Hattie, it's just me."

"Well, good morning to you too, Ingrid," comes the laughing reply, one that brings an immediate smile to Ingrid's face.

Darling Hattie, Ingrid's dearest friend from boarding school who married a fellow and moved with him to America. Only a few months later, they opened their home to Ingrid and Lars when they, too, arrived in America and Ingrid wrote to Hattie desperately seeking refuge.

"Will you research a couple names for me?" Ingrid asks, then she drops her voice. "I'll be traveling with a coworker on assignment—"

"Assignment?" Hattie interrupts with a squeal. "Well done! I know better than to ask what it is, but it's about time you got to have a little fun."

"As much fun as one can have when forced to work with Archie Stribling. I expect everyone in my office is clean, but if you could provide some reassurance, I would appreciate it. And there's one more—my FBI handler, Klaus Stieber." Ingrid drops her voice again. "Was he one of them?"

Given the name, the man is certainly German, but not every German was a Nazi. The thought of working with one sends nausea twisting in Ingrid's stomach.

"Archie might take me a little more time, but I've spent the morning organizing new agent files, and I could swear I saw Stieber's name among them," Hattie replies. "Let me check."

Ingrid waits, casting an instinctive glance around to make sure no one is eavesdropping, tapping her heel against the floor in anticipation. Moments later, Hattie returns to the phone.

"Yes. Just desk work, but yes," she says, distaste apparent in her voice.

Ingrid bites her cheek to contain a curse. When Hattie told her of former Nazis being recruited to work for the American government in exchange for pardons, she did not believe it at first. Now she will have to report to one. To a man whose party forced her to flee from everyone and everything she had ever known. She curls her hand into a fist until her wedding band presses into her skin, battling memories she cannot consider because she cannot afford tears.

"I don't know if I can do this," she says at last—although Ada's face returns to her mind. Someone *will* be investigating her. If the responsibility is to fall to Ingrid, she has no choice other than to report to a former Nazi.

Hattie sighs. "Nothing to do except make the best of it, I'm afraid, if you want the job. Although I don't like it any more than you do."

"I know you don't," Ingrid replies gently, wishing she could pull her friend close.

When the Blitz broke out in England, Hattie's husband, Ian, had insisted on going home to enlist and begged his wife to stay in America, since returning to her parents' home in Birmingham might have subjected her to bombings. Following encouragement from Ingrid, Hattie had moved in with her and Lars. And while living in their spare bedroom, Hattie received the news that her husband's plane had been struck down and his body never recovered.

"After I lost Ian, I didn't think I could do anything ever again," Hattie murmurs. "You assured me I could, and you were right. I found work, I went back to living on my own, and I'm happy. So it's my turn to assure you: You can do this, Ingrid. And I'll be there for you the same way you were there for me."

The encouragement softens the tension in Ingrid's chest. "You have been there for me from the moment I reached America, and long before."

Hattie promises to be in touch after she researches Archie, then they hang up. Ingrid settles back. Hattie is right. Even if she must work with a former Nazi as her handler, she can do this. She must.

CHAPTER 4

Arnhem, 1940

INGRID

A prosecuting attorney's office was an unusual place of refuge, yet it was the one Ingrid had sought ever since she was a little girl. She was not a child anymore, but she still came here at every opportunity, and nearly every day since early May. Since Holland had succumbed to the Nazis after only five days.

Five days. Every time she remembered that tiny number, her heartbeat climbed as it had when she sat at her bedroom window, listening to planes roaring overhead, watching enemy troops swarming the streets. Her country's sense of security had been eroding while the war swept across Europe, yet to have succumbed after a mere five days left her painfully aware of how strong the invading forces were. At least Lars was home from the front, although she was not certain he would be any safer here.

She toyed with the diamond ring on a chain around her neck, usually worn beneath her clothing—the engagement ring he had given her after returning from the service. A secret she kept from Mother, since Mother disapproved of him simply because Lars was a Dutch military man, not a wealthy British aristocrat worthy of her daughter.

"What if this occupation is not temporary, Opa?"

Ingrid had always clung to the assurance that it would end soon, but here, in the security of her grandfather's law office, she allowed fear to emerge just this once. Opa looked up from behind his desk, where he had been quietly working. He peered at her through his spectacles, smoothing his gray mustache.

"Will an occupation change your beliefs?" he asked.

"No."

"Then there is your answer. If it endures, the only difference is you might need to find a place where you are free to maintain such beliefs."

Ingrid nodded slowly. Every time Opa spoke of freedom, his eyes ignited with curiosity and longing. Despite his commitment to Dutch law, he had always spoken admirably of American democracy. Once, when Ingrid was ten years old, she had come home from boarding school and hurried to Opa's office, where she told him about her studies, then turned the pages of his American history book.

"Would you ever go to the United States?" she had asked.

He shook his head. "I am too old, too settled. But it would be fascinating, would it not? To be there to study its constitution, its laws, its elections. What a remarkable country it is." He nodded to the massive tome. "And you, Ingrid? Would you go to the United States?"

"Not without you," she replied, to which a faint smile appeared beneath his bushy mustache.

That had been eight years ago. Now Ingrid glanced at the American history book on Opa's bookshelf. She could not abandon her country, her loved ones, yet the idea of freedom was certainly appealing.

A knock sounded on the door, then it opened to reveal a man in a green uniform. Ingrid knew that shade of green even before he fully entered the room. Orpo officers were everywhere, overtaking the city. She sat taller, heart racing, and glanced at Opa, whose expression remained neutral while the young officer tipped his hat and offered her grandfather a document.

"A notice for attorneys and government officials. Effective immediately, laws instated by the Third Reich are to be enforced. Should you have questions, my name is Wachtmeister Julius Hochheimer."

Ingrid gripped the arms of her chair as her temper threatened to flare. They could not force her grandfather to do this. Still, if the Third Reich was enforcing its laws, then this occupation might not be as temporary as she hoped.

Slowly, Opa accepted the paper, then removed his spectacles. "Ingrid, go home."

His voice was calm, yet suddenly Ingrid felt like she had received the harshest, most undeserved reprimand. He had never ordered her away before. A lump found her throat, a combination of hurt and confusion she could not ease.

Before she could decide between protesting or obeying, Hochheimer held up a hand. "Any questions can be addressed in front of her."

A muscle along Opa's jaw tensed. He glanced at Ingrid, a look she could not decipher, then handed the notice back. "As an attorney, I cannot in good conscience practice under any laws other than those of my country."

Despite her lingering confusion and uncertainty, a flush of pride warmed Ingrid even as the tension in her chest increased so much, she could hardly breathe. So far, Hochheimer had been polite and official. Now, a slight hardening overtook him like a storm brewing in the near distance, seconds from being unleashed.

"These orders are to be followed, and you will follow them."

Opa remained as he was, offering Hochheimer the document. Ingrid sat perfectly still, blood rushing in her ears while neither man wavered.

"You will not adhere to any laws except those of your former government?" The Orpo officer jerked his head toward Ingrid. "Does she feel as you do?"

"She is a girl."

Implying such matters would not interest her or, even if they did, she was a woman, a girl with no right to an opinion. Opa made the remark for Hochheimer's benefit, she knew. Her grandfather was the one who encouraged her to expand her knowledge and form her own thoughts. She still fought the urge to protest. The officer seemed to agree, though, judging by the dismissive glance he gave her, to which she exercised all her control to keep quiet.

"Your colleagues, then? Do they agree with your beliefs?" Hochheimer seemed to take Opa's silence as confirmation. "Tell me the names of those who share your views, and you may keep your position. Refuse and you are dismissed, effective immediately."

Ingrid sprang from her chair. "No, you can't forbid him from working!"

"Hold your tongue, or I will arrest you both."

Arrest them for what? For being forced to name others who shared Opa's views? For losing his career if he didn't? For Ingrid pointing out the unfairness of such a demand?

Opa had already risen to his feet and placed a restraining hand on her. "I will collect my belongings, and the space will be vacated by this time tomorrow." He stepped from behind the desk, holding Ingrid's arm firmly, and led her past the Orpo officer.

She could do nothing except walk beside him, her mind whirling too much to make sense of what had just occurred. Only once they had safely exited the building and proceeded to the next block did he release her, and she whirled on him.

"He can't do that to you! It's not right."

Gently, he took her shoulders. "If I cannot be proud of the work I'm doing, then I don't want to be doing that work. My career is not worth my integrity."

She looked into his bright blue eyes, warm and kind and matching her own. She had never known her father, but knowing her grandfather felt like knowing Papa in a small way. Except Papa had left. Opa had not.

Ingrid wrapped her arms around his neck, infusing all her love and pride for him into her embrace. He kissed her cheek, then released her and nodded her along, since Lars was waiting on the corner to accompany her home. She hurried toward him, every step fueled by the temper she could never seem to control.

"It's wrong. It's all so terribly wrong," she announced when she reached her fiancé.

Then she poured out the whole story. A good, kind man who had been a dedicated attorney for decades had lost his job over refusing to compromise his beliefs. Because no one in Arnhem was free to do anything anymore.

When she finished, Lars brought her into his embrace, where her heartbeat finally slowed. Opa was her comfort, but so was Lars.

"Your grandfather is a brave man, and you, my love, are a brave woman," he said. "All we can do is defend ourselves, even when it isn't enough."

Always so calm and reassuring and everything she needed. He brushed her dark hair from her face and kissed her cheek, then she threaded her arm through his as they began their walk. For the past two years they had been inseparable—ever since one summer afternoon when she had swerved her bicycle to avoid a vehicle stalled in the road, nearly crashing into the handsome blond fellow attempting to fix it.

Once at home, they paused outside the door, where she brought his mouth to hers. She was not even free to do this, to kiss the man she intended to marry, because if Mother opened this door she would put a stop to it. Ingrid didn't care. Mother could attempt to take her fiancé, and the Third Reich could attempt to take her freedom, but Ingrid would cling to both with everything she had.

After leaving Lars with a final kiss, Ingrid went inside. She closed the door softly, then pressed a palm to her chest, feeling the tiny ring hidden beneath her clothes.

"Ingrid? Where have you been all day?"

She pressed her teeth together. She was already on the precipice of unleashing every emotion tangled inside her, letting it all out in a flood of tears, of rage, of she did not know what. One single provocation from Mother was all it would take.

Mother entered the foyer, eyebrows already furrowed in disapproval. "Have you been with that boy? You know how I feel about him."

"I also know how *I* feel about him," she retorted with a rush of satisfaction when Mother bristled. "Opa approves of him."

"Your grandfather is not your mother; I am." Then she sighed. "Darling, I only want what's best for you."

Ingrid and Mother had very different opinions of what was best for her. Mother hailed from England and envisioned a posh aristocrat in her daughter's future. Was it wrong to want someone else? Mother would sigh about Ingrid's strong-willed nature, saying it had come from her father. Was it wrong to speak her mind? Mother would encourage her away from politics and toward more ladylike pursuits. Was it wrong to take an interest in important matters?

"An Orpo officer dismissed Opa from government work. All because he doesn't agree with their laws. Are you pleased, Mother? Is that what you and your friends wanted?"

"Me and my—?" Then Mother stopped, realizing what Ingrid was implying. "How many times must I explain it? I believed the promises, the lies . . . So many of us did back then. Will you punish me for it all my life?"

It was childish and unfair of Ingrid to resort to such a jab. When the war began in Europe, Mother had tearfully professed repentance of the beliefs she had held in the 1930s. Right now, though, Ingrid was too angry to care. There were no Wehrmacht soldiers or Orpo officers here for her to blame for the fascism overtaking her life, so she could only lash out at the woman who had once upheld the same views. Neither was Ingrid so sure she could trust Mother's change of heart after she had spent so many years supporting the party.

Although she tried to push past Mother, a hand found her shoulder, then arms encircled her. Ingrid lost the strength to resist, the will to argue, the need to do anything except succumb to tears and fury and her mother's embrace. She did not want them to fight as often as they did; it just seemed to happen. For this moment, though, she could pretend it did not. She could cry on her mother's shoulder. Mourn the injustices her grandfather suffered. Fret over the rumors circulating about what this occupation might mean for Jews. Long for the life she wanted with a fascinating career in politics or law and a loving husband by her side.

A life she would never have until they found freedom.

CHAPTER 5

Hollywood Hills, 24 August 1946

ADA

Ada stands outside Gordon's front door, clutching the paper that reads *Aleida de Vos*, and looks toward the tall hedges that could easily shield someone in this darkness. She hears nothing aside from the blood rushing in her ears.

If whoever left this note hasn't gone, she might as well face them.

"Go on, then," she calls out, fighting to keep her voice steady. "Show yourself."

Silence. Then footsteps. Swallowing past her dry throat, she closes one hand around the doorknob, prepared for a hasty escape if necessary.

From behind the thick hedges, a silhouette appears. A woman's. Ada cannot see her features, cannot hear anything but the light thud of her feet against the motor court as she approaches the two-story white brick mansion. Yet as she nears, something irrepressible flares in Ada's chest.

When the figure steps into the light from the two flickering sconces, Ada grips the doorknob tighter. The woman's hair is pulled back and almost as red as the front door, and her face is one Ada can still envision as clearly and distinctly as the last time they stood before one another like this. But surely it cannot be her.

Except it is. Without a doubt. Yet Ada can only stare, unable to believe this woman is standing before her. At last she finds her voice.

"You changed your hair."

"You changed your name." The other woman gives a faint teasing smile. "Am I still allowed to call you my twin sister, or have you changed that too?"

Everything inside Ada breaks free, emerging in a cross between a laugh and a sob. "Ingrid." The name is a prayer of thanksgiving upon her lips as she captures her sister in her fiercest embrace.

Six years have been lost to them. No need to lose another moment more.

Ingrid immediately clings to Ada in return, neither loosening her hold. A fit that feels as right as it always has, no different than when they were girls. So much of Ada longs to discard everyone and everything from her old life. Everyone and everything except her sister and this moment. Theirs is an embrace unburdening every fear, every worry, every concern each has carried for the other since they parted; now they are both here. Together, as they should be.

At last, they loosen their holds, wiping tears while Ada manages to voice one of her many questions. "How did you find me?"

"I recently saw your photograph, so of course I realized it was you, and nothing could keep me away." Ingrid brushes a final tear from Ada's cheek. "I've missed you terribly, Leidje."

The old nickname should be comforting; instead, it stirs the worries, the pain, the silence, everything she has suppressed for so long because dwelling on it changed nothing. Except now the change—the truth—is standing before her. Ingrid left Arnhem and ventured into a world ablaze with war, traveled for God knows how long to God knows where. The sister Ada remembers would not have left her with silence, with nothing except the fear that Ingrid had not survived such an arduous journey.

"You promised me." Ada's voice trembles, sharpens. "You promised to write when you and Lars were safe."

"I *did*—dozens of times, and you promised to write back. None of which would have been necessary if you'd come with us." Ingrid's own voice sharpens in return, then she sighs. "When I never heard from you, I was afraid you hadn't survived . . . I suppose my letters never reached you. I'm sorry."

Here is the sister Ada once mourned, alive. How Ada wishes nothing had ever changed between them, yet so little remains the same. Then they were girls united by the bond of sisterhood; now they are women torn apart by war, sisters in their bond yet strangers in their experiences. What Ingrid endured, she does not know. What Ada endured, she fears she will never find the strength to share.

The woman formerly known as Aleida stayed in Arnhem to help those who needed her, to fight for their homeland. Ingrid fled with her fiancé. Their paths have diverged. Ada often considered what it would be like if Ingrid had survived, if their paths led to each other again, yet she did not anticipate the ache now consuming her insides, nor can she pinpoint its cause or why this sudden darkness is fighting against the light of relief and joy.

The war buried Aleida alongside all her pain and created Ada, the most vibrant, alluring act of her career. If it has done the same to Ingrid, they do not know each other as well as they once did.

"I'm sorry for leaving a note . . . I wanted to see who answered the door in case it was someone other than you. All this would be rather difficult to explain to a stranger." Ingrid gives a sheepish smile, then nods to the note in Ada's hand. "It's late, so I won't keep you, but will you meet me tomorrow night around five? I wrote down my hotel and room number."

Ada glances at the paper, confirming the information at the bottom of the page. She hadn't noticed it before. Of course they will talk. Once they do, this strange discomfort inside her will cease, surely.

Perhaps the broken promise is what has unsettled her so. It's not fair to be angry with Ingrid if she really did write, yet it doesn't change the gaping absence of these last years. And with her sister's presence comes a past no one can know—not even Gordon, certainly not the press.

By stepping into the spotlight, she had assumed the risk of being found. A woman with every reason to hide would not become a public figure, would she? Which is precisely why Ada did. The war took ballet from her; she would not let it take performing too.

Still, she has been found by Ingrid. Perhaps others will follow.

Ada pushes down the thought before it can overtake her, agrees to meet Ingrid, and bids her good night. Ingrid retraces her steps across the motor court. Moments later, a car rumbles to life and fades into the distance. Then Ada goes inside and stands by the door, waiting for her breaths to steady, clutching the note from the sister who was once dead and is now very much alive.

CHAPTER 6

Arnhem, 1940

INGRID

Ever since Opa's dismissal from his position as a prosecuting attorney, Ingrid had spent the last couple of weeks assisting Aleida with her plan to raise money to aid Jews. Aleida had shared her intentions in an eager whispered conversation one night in their bedroom, so of course Ingrid had volunteered her assistance. She wanted to do something helpful, not to feel as helpless as she had that day in Opa's office.

Madame Bellamy had prepared dances for the trusted students lending aid while anyone sympathetic to the cause was invited to attend. Now, the night had arrived. The Muziekschool's first clandestine performance—a blackout performance, they called it. The studio was filled with chairs for the guests while Ingrid stood by the door, accepting donations and pointing each attendee to a sign listing the rules: total silence. No talking, no applause, no music for the performance. Noise might alert the occupiers.

Once the guests were seated, Ingrid placed the donations into a box and found her seat between Lars and Opa. She and Aleida had agreed not to mention their work to Mother—for her safety, and because Ingrid maintained her doubts about Mother's political loyalties. She had invited Lars, though, and one of Opa's colleagues had invited him, despite Ingrid's worries for his safety since the Orpo officers had already identified him as anti-Nazi, which was why Ingrid and Aleida had refrained from mentioning it to him in the first place.

"I will not be deterred from supporting a worthy cause or seeing my granddaughter perform," he had insisted when Ingrid expressed her fears, so that was the end of the discussion.

Tonight's performance was a selection of original pieces choreographed by Madame Bellamy, and Aleida was first. Illuminated by a single light, she stepped onstage wearing a pale pink leotard, white tulle skirt, and flat ballet shoes, since those were quieter than pointe shoes. Then she began, stepping gracefully into an arabesque—if Ingrid remembered the correct word for the step—before proceeding into a series of turns and extensions, fast and slow steps, large and small jumps. Her grace, strength, and the little smile toying around her lips and igniting her eyes made each movement appear effortless, yet the effort was apparent in every visible muscle contracting and rippling.

Ingrid watched, captivated. She had seen Aleida dance countless times, but something was different about tonight. About watching her sister pursue her passion in support of an important cause. When the dance ended, Ingrid sat on her hands to remind herself not to applaud while Aleida took center stage and curtsied. When she straightened, she found Ingrid in the crowd. Ingrid grinned, hoping her sister felt every bit of her pride and love.

Beside Ingrid, Opa's eyes crinkled around the edges as Aleida found him next, and he gave her a tiny nod, communicating his own delight.

The evening continued in a reverent, respectful silence more thunderous than any applause. When the performance concluded, the guests filed out, one by one, while Ingrid returned to the door to collect any additional donations. Once finished, only she, Aleida, Lars, Opa, and Madame Bellamy remained, and all evidence of their event was gone. Ingrid returned the collection box to the dance instructor, who nodded, granting permission to speak quietly now. When she accepted the box, her eyes widened.

"It is far more than I expected," she murmured. "And it will help considerably."

"Then we should schedule the next performance," Aleida replied with a grin before wrapping her arms around her grandfather's midsection. "I'm delighted you came, Opa."

"And I will be at every performance." He kissed her cheek, then Ingrid's. "I'm so proud of you both."

He bid them good night while Ingrid caught her sister's eye. For the first time since the occupation, a little flame of hope had ignited inside her. They were making a difference, and if they continued to do so, perhaps this occupation would end after all.

When Madame Bellamy removed the funds from the box, Aleida reached for them, but she shook her head. "No, I will make the delivery. Someday the task might fall to you. Until then, I will not endanger you any more than necessary."

"A frivolous girl walking home from dance class draws less suspicion than an older, wiser Jewish woman," she teased before sobering. "It will be easier and safer for me. Let me do it, please."

The ballet mistress hesitated, then she gave Aleida's arm an appreciative squeeze and agreed. Aleida tucked the funds into her pointe shoe, then Madame Bellamy drew her aside to give instructions privately.

The twins walked home with Lars while the warm evening air, the lingering rush of joy from watching her sister onstage, and the success of the endeavor left Ingrid feeling almost as giddy as she had when Lars proposed. At last, a way to do some good.

They detoured so Aleida could deliver the funds—although she would not allow anyone to accompany her for the last few blocks, unwilling to endanger them or burden them with knowledge of the contact. Despite initial protests, Ingrid conceded and waited with Lars. Her heartbeat did not slow until Aleida came into view—unharmed, humming a carefree tune, swinging her dance bag as though she was indeed an oblivious girl, not a young woman partaking in clandestine resistance work. She gave Ingrid a sly wink, to which she chuckled, then they proceeded on their way.

"We should do something tonight to celebrate the evening's success," Lars said. "Any ideas?"

"None that involve having my sister with us."

While he chuckled in response to her suggestive grin, she gestured for Aleida to hurry—half a block behind them, lagging to admire shop windows. That girl, so easily distracted. At last she caught up, and the three were passing a pub when the door swung open, bringing noise, the stench of alcohol, and a stumbling figure whom Lars failed to intercept before he barreled straight into Ingrid. Gasping, she staggered and would have been sent sprawling if Aleida hadn't steadied her.

"I beg your pardon," she snapped, whirling to glare at the offender—a uniformed man. Further rebukes died, replaced by a knot in her throat. Wehrmacht.

Ingrid sensed Aleida's grip on her arm tightening. Lars held one man upright—presumably the one who had collided with her—while another supported him on the opposite side.

"Good man, helping a soldier of the Reich," the unsteady one slurred, flashing a giddy grin at Lars. "A wise position to take now that we have your country. Next we'll have your men in our military and your women in our beds."

Ingrid stilled. Had she heard him properly? At once, Aleida dragged Ingrid along and grabbed Lars with her free hand, urging them down the street. As if removing Ingrid from the situation would make her forget the taunt that, empty or not, had left her heart racing.

"What did he say?" she demanded, craning her neck to look at Lars, whose face was red with suppressed outrage. "About the military? Our men? Is it true?"

"Keep your voice down," Aleida replied, but Ingrid pulled free and stepped in front of Lars, bringing them to a halt.

She needed to hear it from the man who had given her the ring she wore around her neck and soon, God willing, around her finger. Unless the answer stripped away the opportunity, took him from her a second time. This time, perhaps, not to return him.

"Are you going to be conscripted? Were you honestly not going to tell me?"

Crushing silence magnified her own shaking breaths as she held his steady gaze. Lars passed a hand over his jaw.

"Nothing has been confirmed, but it . . . It is possible."

She knew what *possible* meant. Considering the Netherlands fell, hadn't history and politics taught her to expect this? Yet here she was, vacillating between shock and grief until fury consumed both while he continued.

"You and Aleida needed to stay focused on tonight's performance, so I didn't want to distract you or ruin the evening. I was going to tell you tomorrow."

"I don't need to be protected from this war. You know that, know *me*. And instead of my own fiancé telling me the truth, I had to hear it from the bloody Wehrmacht."

She announced the last bit far too loudly, considering they were on a public street. She didn't care. With a look to warn Lars not to accompany them the rest of the way home, Ingrid proceeded down the street, her breaths sharp. Moments later, she sensed Aleida beside her.

To the front again. To face death again. Except she knew Lars; he would desert before he conceded to fight for the fascists. A choice that felt far more dangerous. A transgression for which, if caught, he would be killed. She was at a greater risk of losing him than ever.

At the house on Jansbinnensingel, all was quiet. Mother must have gone out, thank God, or she was in the back garden. This night had been trying enough without Mother demanding to know where the twins went or whose company Ingrid kept this evening. Inside, something on the foyer wall caught her attention. She stopped.

The photograph was not a family portrait. Long before the twins had been old enough to remember Papa—a Dutch baron in name only, absent the money Mother had expected—he had left home, so Mother had thrown out all evidence of his existence. This photograph was from 1936 and depicted their mother, Constance de Vos, in Nuremberg, where she attended the Reichsparteitag—the annual National Socialist German Workers' Party Congress. There, surrounded by throngs of Nazis, Constance shook hands with a dark-haired, mustached man: the Führer, Adolf Hitler.

A few years ago, a painting had replaced the photograph. Apparently Mother had decided to hang it again. Not surprising, really. Ingrid had always expected the distasteful thing to return. Mother had never done anything to convince Ingrid she was no longer a fascist. No vocal support of Queen Wilhelmina or Dutch leaders, no discussions with Opa about law, no political talk except when instructing Ingrid to develop an interest in something else. Still, the photograph left a knot of disappointment in her stomach. For all her doubts, she wanted to believe Mother. Yet this proved she had been lying all this time. She had never changed and never would.

Aleida, too, paled at the sight of the photograph. Ingrid glared at it a moment longer, then pressed on, so her sister followed.

Upstairs in their bedroom, Aleida placed a new pair of pointe shoes and satin ribbons on her bed. As her sister rummaged for her sewing kit, Ingrid clenched her shaking hands.

A mother who likely still supported the fascists, as evidenced by the

Reichsparteitag photograph. A fiancé who would be forced to fight for them unless he deserted. A grandfather who was dismissed from his position due to his opposing views. A Jewish dance instructor who was so concerned for the future, she was raising funds to help those like her escape. Arnhem was dangerous now. It would not be safe again until the war ended.

"Lars can go underground," Aleida said as she threaded a needle. "Madame Bellamy has contacts who will help."

"Right, underground, where I can't see him, can't communicate with him, where God knows what will happen if he's caught? No, he can't stay here, *we* can't—" Ingrid broke off with a bitter laugh. "God, I'm such a hypocrite."

Too cowardly to stay in her occupied homeland and see the fight against fascism through. And she called herself an advocate. Yet despite her eagerness to help, the situation was beyond their control. Arnhem was no longer a place for anyone who stood against the Nazis.

"You're not a hypocrite; you love him," Aleida replied softly. "And you're right, leaving is best. I'll keep Mother from finding out."

Aside from Opa, Aleida was the only person Ingrid had trusted with the news of her engagement to Lars. Throughout their relationship, Aleida had been immeasurably helpful in orchestrating moments for Ingrid to spend with him or in keeping Mother from discovering where she was. Her sister's willingness to protect Ingrid's relationship always left her heart warm. This time, though, she frowned. How did Aleida expect to distract Mother when she would be going with them? But when Aleida didn't look up from her sewing, a coldness settled over Ingrid, sharpening her voice.

"No, you are absolutely not going to—"

"I have a needle, and these shoes have quite a hard box, and I'm not afraid to use either if you pester me."

With an exasperated breath, Ingrid sat beside her, though she was wise enough to keep her hands to herself. "You can dance anywhere, but you can't stay here. Certainly not with her."

Neither could Ingrid face such a possibility. Not when the thought of being apart from her sister was unfathomable.

"You saw the photograph," she persisted. "If you stay in a fascist household—"

"This has nothing to do with ballet or Mother." At last Aleida stopped sewing. "Aside from Madame Bellamy, I'm the only one who knows who our contacts are, and I'm not Jewish, so if matters worsen and the laws limit her more severely, she'll need me even more."

"*I* need you."

"You don't. Not the same way the work needs me or Lars needs you."

She was right; if Aleida stayed, Lars would never ask Ingrid to abandon her sister for him. Nor would he flee for his own safety while Ingrid remained in an occupied country. She couldn't let him stay or bear the thought of being apart again. But to leave Aleida? Just the possibility made her feel sick.

"You're always saying the war is temporary. Isn't that all this is? Temporary." Aleida took Ingrid's hand. "Be with the man you love. Marry him. You can't do that freely here."

"My sister or my fiancé, then?" Ingrid swallowed hard, blinking past her hazy vision until Aleida gently wiped an escaped tear. "Please," she managed, meeting her sister's steady blue-gray gaze. "Please don't make me choose between you."

"You're not. I'm choosing your happiness—and my own, because I can't be happy knowing you'll be miserable if you stay."

They had spent nearly every moment of their eighteen years of life together—from this childhood bedroom to the boarding school in Kent to this war. She had to change Aleida's mind. And she had to protect Lars.

Then, all at once, she knew exactly where they would go: America. The United States. A place far from the war overtaking Europe and where they would be free to live as they wished. The idea was almost tempting enough to make her concede. Yet even with Aleida's blessing, doubt and confusion wrestled inside her. She could not leave her sister.

A tap sounded against the window—a pebble lightly striking the glass, indicating Lars was attempting to be discreet, since Mother would order him away if he knocked. Aleida stepped to the window and waved, meaning Ingrid would be down to see him. Then she faced her sister.

"You know I'm right, Inge," she said softly. "It's the only way to protect him, so do it, please. For him and for me."

Ingrid swallowed hard. She could not deny that the possibility of freedom had fanned the spark of hope inside her to a full flame, even as the thought of being separated from her sister threatened to douse it entirely.

Outside, moonlight illuminated his silhouette beneath the shadows of the old chestnut tree, their usual meeting place. The hasty swish of her footsteps through the grass carried her closer to him, narrowing the distance even as they constantly faced the endless distance of separation.

"I had to see you were home safe," Lars said when she was within earshot. "I know I should have told you sooner, and that I don't need to protect you from this war, but are you honestly angry with me for *wanting* to protect you? For wanting to enjoy our time together without it being ruined by—"

She silenced him with a fierce kiss while the tension coursing through his body shifted into a different intensity as he held her close. Maybe she didn't need protection. Neither could she ever resent him for giving it to her anyway.

"Darling, we're all right," she murmured before meeting his gaze, his eyes shining silver in the moonlight. "Aleida and I have an idea."

After she relayed it to him, his eyes brightened with irrepressible hope, then he took her hands. "Are you certain this is what you want? I don't want to cause a rift between you and your family."

The rift between Ingrid and Mother had existed long before Lars. This was what they had to do, the only way to avoid losing him. Even if being separated from her sister for a time—only a time—already felt like losing a part of herself.

* * *

The next evening, after Mother retired to bed, Ingrid gathered her belongings—a few clothes, bread, and a canteen of water. Anything more would be too conspicuous and cumbersome, and she didn't have time to delay. If the rumors of conscription proved true, Lars needed to get out of Arnhem before he received his orders, so they were leaving tonight. These were her last moments with her sister, who had spent all day diligently helping Ingrid prepare and not saying a word about their impending separation.

"I understand why you want to stay," Ingrid said quietly as Aleida offered her a folded blouse. "I couldn't be prouder of you, truly. But there's time to change your mind."

Aleida responded with a wistful smile, crushing the hopes Ingrid knew better than to permit. Then she tugged on the chain around Ingrid's neck, freeing the engagement ring. The small diamond sparkled in the lamplight.

"You're going to be the most beautiful bride, Inge. And I'm going to miss you terribly."

The ache that had lingered in Ingrid's chest all day intensified even as a pulse of energy joined it. Bride. Once they were settled, she and Lars were to be married. On that day, the first of a lifetime with the man she loved, her sister would not be there to celebrate with her. She covered Aleida's hand with her own, seeking words, finding none.

Aleida cleared her throat and stepped back, adopting their mother's pursed lips and judgmental frown before imitating her crisp, refined lilt. "Ingrid, Ingrid, where did I go wrong? That girl has always been too much like her father."

Despite immediate giggles, Ingrid shook her head in protest. "Don't make me laugh; that's not fair."

Aleida's cheeky grin failed to eradicate the heaviness in her eyes, though her voice was steady. "Once you're safe, write to me at the Muziekschool. Mother won't be able to intercept the correspondence, and Madame Bellamy will give me the message. Promise me."

"I promise. Write back the moment you receive it." As Aleida nodded, Ingrid took her hands. "Lars and I are forever indebted to you. And I will see you soon."

"Of course you will." Aleida quickly escaped Ingrid's hold and shoved the bag into her hands. "Go, don't keep him waiting."

True, they needed to make the most of the evening hours, yet Ingrid paused at the bedroom door. Quiet settled, broken by her resolute breath. This was it, then. A new life and a time apart. Her opportunity for freedom and happiness deformed by the gaping wound she would carry with her.

She turned and caught Aleida in an embrace, blinking past tears as Aleida's fierce grip and shuddering breaths matched her own. For this moment nothing else existed—not the war, not their choices, only her sister.

Their time apart would be temporary.

Except war held the power to take what was temporary and make it permanent.

CHAPTER 7

Los Angeles, 25 August 1946

ADA

Most never receive the miracles they await. Ada has: Ingrid is alive.

Then why, as she stands before the Biltmore Hotel in downtown Los Angeles, does an unbearable coil of tension seize her stomach?

A warm August evening breeze sweeps over her, carrying the steady rumble of street traffic. The last note Ada received from Ingrid was a final farewell tucked into her pointe shoe, found the morning after Ingrid left Arnhem. She carried that scrap of paper with her until she stood in a dark alley in New York City one night. If she were going to be Ada, she could not possess a note addressed to Aleida from a woman who was surely dead. Tears pricked her eyes as she watched the fire consume her sister's handwriting, and their names along with it.

Drawing a breath, Ada pushes away the chill of that night and the heat of its flames, then passes through the lobby with its vaulted ceiling and elegant staircase. She takes the elevator to the seventh floor, where she finds the proper room number.

After working on her script all day with a cantankerous Gordon—Ada did warn him not to drink so much last night—she told him she had dinner plans but made no mention of Ingrid. It felt too delicate to mention the sibling he didn't know she had, as if doing so would take her sister away again. She can't explain everything she's kept from him—for his safety and her own.

When the knot in her stomach tightens, Ada combats it. She will not allow her past to interfere with the thrill of spending this evening with her sister. The reminder settles her and silences the memories, so Ada raps her knuckles against the door. In seconds, it swings open.

There she stands, proof that Ada's memories from last night were not a champagne-induced hallucination. When Ingrid steps aside, Ada crosses the carpeted floor and looks around. A bed, a nightstand, a dresser, a small desk, and simple curtains open to a view of downtown. She removes her large dark sunglasses and headscarf—useful disguises when attempting to avoid the public—then faces Ingrid, who brushes a stray auburn lock from her forehead.

Ada awaits permission to cling to the reality before her, and the assurance that, if she does, it will not slip through her grasp.

"I just can't believe you're here." Ada sits on the bed, almost feeling as if this room is their shared bedroom in Arnhem. "How have you been? Are you still with Lars?" She sees no ring, though, and her mouth runs dry.

Ingrid notices her staring and waves a dismissive hand. "We're fine, don't worry. I left the ring at home for safekeeping."

Leave it to Ingrid to be so concerned about her most valued possession as to take extreme measures not to lose it. Combined regret and warmth rush over Ada. Her sister is married, and she was not with her to partake in such a wonderful occasion.

"Did you travel directly to America from Arnhem?"

"To Washington, DC. We stayed with Hattie for a time—you remember her, from boarding school."

"And you've been well? Happy?"

Ingrid nods without meeting Ada's gaze. She has not sat down beside Ada, as she might have in the past, nor is she conversing the way they usually do. This woman is nothing like the one she encountered last night. Nothing like her sister. Ada swallows hard, suddenly feeling unwelcome. Except Ingrid invited her here, so why is she so disengaged? Distance stretches between them as if they remain oceans apart.

Still, as she watches Ingrid cross and uncross her arms and smooth her skirt, Ada senses unity in their uncertainty, in this awful discomfort that has never been between them before and should not be there now.

This is her sister, her *twin* sister. Being together should feel as natural as it does to perform. Instead, Ada feels as if she stands alone in center stage, and when a single spotlight falls on her, none of her meticulously memorized lines come to mind.

"Did you come all this way only to want nothing to do with me?" she asks, although her tone is more wounded than accusatory.

"No, no, of course not, I—" Ingrid's voice falls. "Like I told you, I was afraid you never wrote back to me because you hadn't survived. But then I thought perhaps you chose not to write . . . because you resented me for leaving."

Silence follows the confession. Had Ada resented her? Perhaps, alongside the hurt and pain and guilt of those years, there is the smallest kernel of resentment. Not because she consciously decided to hold Ingrid's decision against her—after all, it was Ada who encouraged her to choose Lars. And yet, if not for Lars, Ingrid never would have left.

Now, hearing Ingrid's fears expressed, she releases the tiny kernel. She clings to so much from that time. This, though, she can put to rest.

"When I told you to go, I almost begged you to stay. Purely for selfish reasons. But, more than that, I wanted your safety and happiness, and it is such a relief to know you found it. I never would have wanted you to endure what took place in Arnhem."

At this, Ingrid's eyes darken with sudden worry, seeking the answers Ada cannot give. Not yet.

Ingrid seems to realize it, though, so she simply nods. This time, the silence is closer to the way it used to be.

At last Ingrid draws a breath. "Care for a drink, Miss Worthington-Fox?"

Lately, Ada has grown more accustomed to that name than the one bestowed upon her at birth. Still, hearing it come from Ingrid's mouth leaves an unexpected weight in Ada's chest. A reminder that she is no longer the girl her sister once knew.

Ingrid pours two glasses of champagne from the bottle chilling in an ice bucket, then sits in the desk chair across from Ada. "I've heard all the rumors. You're an actress—one of Hollywood's hottest, if speculations regarding an upcoming big break are to be believed. You host excellent parties. And . . ." She leans toward Ada in that conspiratorial way from their youth. "You are an absolute bitch on set."

Such a label is to be expected when a young actress, new to Hollywood, refuses to sleep with the director in exchange for a few extra lines. Men and their silly wounded pride. Pathetic, really. Mr. Sternberg carries no such reputation, however, so working with him in *Lady Bella Donna* will be a far more pleasant experience.

Ada pretends to ponder the gossip. "Rising actress, party hostess, and absolute bitch . . . all lies, I'm afraid, save for the last one." She lifts her glass to Ingrid, who taps her own against it in a congratulatory toast.

The sound of clinking glasses dislodges the smirk from Ada's lips. Such a coy reply is one she would give in an interview. This is not an interview. After so many years in this industry, Ada is no stranger to hearing others tell her who and what she is. Hearing Ingrid voice each statement—each one, in fact, true—suddenly leaves her feeling hollow. Why is Ingrid asking her about gossip when they have so much more to discuss?

"The Star Society . . . is that right? Highly elaborate, invitation only, as grand as the rumors claim?"

"Grander." The simple response is all Ada can think to say.

They should be discussing their lives, sharing stories and laughter, enjoying each other's company. To be fair, rumors are a part of Ada's life, but the sister Ada remembers would care about getting reacquainted with the real woman, not dissecting the persona she projects to the world.

Distant chatter comes from somewhere in the hall while Ada draws a breath, inhaling notes of bergamot, vetiver, and jasmine from the perfume lacing her skin. "Your work?" she asks, attempting to redirect the conversation.

"In an office—services related to legal or personal matters, although mine is secretarial work, mostly. Nothing that would interest you in the slightest."

Ingrid takes a long sip of her drink, then shifts in her seat. Reluctant to share more. Normally Ada is the one steering conversations or interviews away from personal matters and back on course, never descending beneath the surface, hence her reputation for privacy. The tactic is not one she expected her sister to use, certainly not with her.

Ada should not allow the realization to pierce her core as fiercely as it does. Perhaps they are too different now for everything to feel as it always has. Perhaps it will never feel that way again. Not when so much has happened. Still, sisters should be willing to sort through any awkwardness or uncertainty, should be trying to break through the surface immediately rather than remaining safely above, refusing to push deeper.

Maybe, after spending all this time fearing Ada's resentment, Ingrid fears her rejection if she exposes who she has become over these last years. The same way Ada fears her sister will reject her if Ada can ever bring herself to reveal everything that happened in Arnhem. Such a heartache is one Ada can't bear to risk. Nor can she bear to lose this opportunity. The war took so much. She will not let it take this too.

"I'm still me, Inge," she says gently. "Beyond the new name, the career, the gossip, and the glittering lights of Hollywood, I'm still me."

The lines around Ingrid's mouth soften. Maybe she needs time to sort through how she's feeling, so Ada will not stay and overwhelm her further. She excuses herself, but she only makes it a few steps down the hall before she hears the door open and feels a light tap against her shoulder.

When she turns, Ingrid is looking at her the way Ada remembers— like the sister who knows her, not the stranger interested in gossip. "I know you're still you, and seeing you happy, with a career, a life . . . nothing makes me happier. And I'm still me too."

"Are you?" Ada lifts a teasing eyebrow. "Ingrid van Essen, interested in Hollywood gossip?"

Ingrid laughs, her cheeks flushing. "I'm sorry, I was trying to make you comfortable. Don't you Hollywood types discuss those sorts of things?"

"Of course we do, but *you* don't—you, the girl who once told me about every single one of Opa's cases, certain you could convince me to develop an interest in such matters. And if I hear the word *rumor* from my charming, intelligent, exhaustingly persistent sister ever again—"

"Exhaustingly persistent? As opposed to you, always begging me to enroll in dance classes?"

Warmth finds Ada's chest amid their shared chuckles. This is what she wanted, what she missed. This is Ingrid, her Ingrid. When the laughter fades, Ingrid glances toward her hotel room door, as though reluctant to return.

"How long are you staying?" Ada asks.

"I haven't decided, really." She pauses, considering. "You wouldn't happen to need a temporary personal assistant, would you? So I can have an excuse to stay, one that might encourage my employer to grant me a brief leave."

"Don't lose your job for me, and what about Lars? Of course I want you here, but—"

"Lars will understand, and even if my boss doesn't hold my position, I can find another. I just don't want to tell him it's a family matter keeping me . . . He might ask for details I'm not willing to share."

Ada can understand that more than anyone, and Ingrid is right. If she can simply tell her boss she's pursuing a temporary opportunity, both their privacies will be better protected.

"Well, then, the position as my assistant is yours, although I won't really make you work," she says with a grin.

Ingrid grins in return, then Ada departs, her heart suddenly fluttering. They still have so much to discuss, but will she be able to discuss any of it?

Years have passed since she last spoke to anyone from her life in Arnhem. The heat searing her skin and breath sharpening in her lungs are signs of the life that belonged to Aleida de Vos. Buried for so long, now fighting to claim her again.

The life Ada Worthington-Fox must forget. The life Aleida de Vos reminds her she cannot, *will* not forget. Not after how severely she failed.

* * *

Back at Gordon's house in Hollywood Hills, Ada changes into a bikini and beckons Mr. Sowerby, her Yorkshire terrier named after Dickon Sowerby in *The Secret Garden* by Frances Hodgson Burnett—a novel Ada purchased from a quaint, ivy-covered bookshop in Kent while in boarding school. Together, they retreat to the backyard to enjoy the fading sunlight. She stretches out on a lounge chair and tosses a ball to her delighted pup, whose golden and slate-gray coat gleams as he darts across the grass. This is what she needs to unravel the tangle of nerves after visiting with Ingrid and the recollections of Arnhem it stirred, ones she cannot think of when she's about to star in a film.

Ingrid is here, though. That much is enough to settle her. And Ingrid will not pressure her to discuss anything before she is ready.

"Cast announcements are this week, so you've got an interview Tuesday morning."

Gordon's voice prompts Ada to pause with her arm raised before Sowerby's impatient bark reminds her to throw the ball. "Casting for the film?"

"No, for who's playing Ada Worthington-Fox in the biographical picture about your life. Yes, for the film." Gordon shakes his head as he sits in the chair beside hers. "The biggest role of your life, and it's the last thing on your mind."

"Not true, although it's rather difficult to focus on work out here." She gestures to the pool—Gordon's favorite part of his home. The compliment wins the pleased nod she was hoping for, then Sowerby returns and drops his ball at Gordon's feet.

The biggest role of her life, indeed—playing fierce, unapologetic Stella Fairchild, otherwise known as Bella Donna, leader of the Fair Ladies, a notorious group of female criminals. When her own sister is found dead, she will not rest until the murderer is brought to justice.

"Who's conducting my interview?"

"Minnie Musgrave, of course, and she will ask you nothing about the project and everything about your personal life, and then you have my permission to tell that devil woman to go back to where she belongs." When she laughs, his lips curve in a fiendish smirk as he tosses Sowerby's ball. "No, it's with a fellow from the radio. I left a note with the details on your desk."

No roles for *Lady Bella Donna* have been revealed yet—despite the rumor circulating of Ada's involvement, to be confirmed during the announcement. As for the male lead starring opposite her, nothing of substance has leaked. He will play Detective Gregory Merrick, who has tried and failed to take down Stella's crime ring and whom she convinces to go undercover as her lover to help her solve the murder—glory and recognition for him, justice for her. If they don't betray each other first.

Ada sits up while Gordon lights a cigarette. "Any news on my costar?"

"When have I been known to keep my mouth shut the moment I'm privy to a juicy bit of industry gossip?" Gordon purses his lips around the cigarette, a sign of his own disappointment. "If I knew, so would you. There are no secrets between us, kid."

As her agent leans back and unfolds a copy of *The Hollywood Reporter*, Ada gets up, suddenly unable to be next to him, to this man who, as he said, never keeps secrets from her.

She, on the other hand, keeps so many from him.

When she sits with her legs dangling over the pool's edge, cool water sweeps over her skin. She turns her face toward the sturdy palms climbing skyward and inhales a breeze carrying the sweet fragrance from the nearby rose garden. Meanwhile Sowerby, tired of his game, curls up on the chair she vacated. She cannot think about the past, about her secrets, about any distractions. She has a film to make.

"Are you listening to me? I said the cast will be published Tuesday morning in the papers, but Sternberg wants you at his party tomorrow night—showing you off to his producers and investors before the announcement is public." Gordon wades into the pool and faces her. "I bought you a dress—don't ask, you'll love it—and the tailor will bring it first thing in the morning. Significant alterations shouldn't be needed. The car will pick you up at four, and the event is at the Biltmore."

"Are you coming?"

"I leave for New York tomorrow, remember? A couple weeks of meetings and shows, and I've got a party meeting in the morning while you're getting fitted."

A Communist Party meeting, the ones he never pushes her to attend, though the invitation is open. Ada can think of nothing more distasteful than meetings about politics.

Why Gordon takes such an interest in the party, she isn't certain, other than knowing he favors it socially and economically and does not believe—as some do—that foreign Communist governments will infiltrate America and threaten freedom and democracy. Similar concerns of Communist influences have slowly started rippling across the film industry. Whispers of Communist writers inserting such influences into scripts, although propaganda would never make the final cut, considering how many people review every aspect of a film before it reaches its final product. If a writer or producer or actor tried to insert personal views, someone would catch it. So Ada will leave them to it and keep herself out of it.

"Ada." When she feels his palms against her knees, she blinks. "You are not the chorus girl I saw on Broadway anymore. You are a Hollywood star. *My* star. And you will dazzle them."

He's taking her silence as nerves, she supposes, and settling them as he does so well.

"Must you always be such a dear?" She kisses his cheek. "I do hope to make you proud."

"You already have."

"Shall I throw a party to welcome you home after your trip?"

"I'd be heartbroken if you didn't." He gives her cheek an affectionate pat, then embarks on leisurely laps across the pool while Ada fetches her towel. Gordon's paper remains on the lounge chair, open to the article he must have been reading: "Wilkerson Names Names."

Names names? What sort of phrase is that?

The article describes an exposé condemning members of the Communist Party of the USA and mentioning them by name, including their card numbers. Ada doesn't blink, doesn't breathe, not until she has read every name twice, confirming Gordon's is not among them. Only a slight relief as she marches to the edge of the pool—especially because her director, Abe Sternberg, *is* among them. When Gordon comes up for a breath, she waves the paper.

"What the bloody hell is this?"

"Can you believe it? Wilkerson has been drawing attention to suspected Communists for more than a month, and when he finally confirms some, he doesn't include me. That bastard."

"This is not a joke, Gordon, and certainly not the sort of fame you should hope to attract." When he emerges from the water, she follows him to his lounge chair. "If Communism is worrisome enough to warrant exposing people like this, then is it wise to attend party meetings? For God's sake, my director is listed here, and what if film publicity turns into political disputes?" As he reaches for his towel, she snatches it. "Can't you be serious?"

"Why worry? For those named, the only difference it makes is that people know how they vote." He takes both the paper and the towel from her. "Columnists and politicians can clamor to remove us from the industry and from America all they want. They can't force it to happen. Sternberg has never kept his affiliations private, so if he was hired to direct your picture anyway, then that means your studio heads aren't worried about him. This won't hurt you or the project, I promise."

True enough; industry professionals are certainly aware of Mr. Sternberg's Communist leanings, so perhaps the public exposure is not as damaging as she fears. Neither is such talk as harmless as he makes it sound. The last war showed the world the power of rhetoric. Of what it caused. Words are never just talk, never just noise, never just gossip; words hold meaning, sway opinions, prompt action.

He pats her shoulder in reassurance, then makes his way to the house.

Ada sits and places Sowerby in her lap, seeking the little dog's comfort to steady herself. Fascism brutalized her home country. If Communism seizes hold of this one, it might be another extremist government. Gordon might believe in the party, or what he believes it to be, but surely he would not support extremism. Neither is he the threat this fear of Communist sympathizers might make him out to be. Where such a fear might lead, though, she does not want to imagine.

She will not get involved. No good comes from political disputes. Ada learned that as a girl fighting for Arnhem only for everything to go wrong. She can't do it this time—not if it might lead to another failure, and not if it awakens her past.

Hollywood is a powerful entity. If these political clashes escalate, she's one of Sternberg's leading ladies. Assuming her film is a success, studio heads protect their valuable assets, so she hears. With this role, she will step into a position that will allow her to experience such protection, surely. Neither Ada nor those close to her will be affected by this turmoil. No need to worry.

Her event is another matter. For that, she will permit herself some worry.

A party tomorrow night. At the Biltmore Hotel. Where Ingrid is. She can seize the opportunity for another visit, although thoughts of the war still loom over her, waiting to descend in a way she has not permitted since leaving Arnhem.

The same urge that seized Ada after the Orpo officer visited her dance studio finds her again, prompting her to act. To let the memories resurface—not to plague her but to drive her toward justice. She entertains the urge for a single moment. Then she quiets it, lets it return to the recesses from which it emerged, buried by patience and warnings that the risk is too great.

It *is* too great. For now. That is why the past must remain there. But if Ingrid discovered Ada is alive, those she escaped might have discovered the same. If so, the past will find her.

Unless, with Ingrid's help, Ada can find the past first and silence it.

CHAPTER 8

Arnhem, 1940

ALEIDA

The morning after Ingrid fled with Lars, one sound made Aleida's heart thud: her mother's heels clacking against the hardwood floor. A sound she had known would come soon enough. Time to perform.

The theater had been a part of her life since she'd been a girl. Ballerina, actress, entertainer. She was prepared for this, wasn't she? She needed only to keep to her role.

A gentle rap, then the door opened, accompanied by Mother's sigh. "My darlings, you're late for breakfast."

A fashionable aubergine skirt and jacket hugged her tall, thin frame while her dark hair curled into a neat chignon. She stilled, looking from Aleida to the empty, neatly made bed across from her.

"Where is Ingrid?"

"Downstairs, I suppose. She was gone when I woke up. Haven't you seen her?" When Constance de Vos pressed her small mouth together—a look her daughters always tried to avoid—Aleida sat up straighter. "My class starts in an hour. If she isn't home by the time I come back, I'll look for her."

Mother lowered the open window, centimeter by calculated centimeter, silencing the trill of birdsong. It clicked shut quietly, deliberately, almost making Aleida wince.

"Find your sister and bring her to me straightaway. Her and that boy . . . I will not allow Ingrid to behave like a common whore."

What a terrible name to call anyone, particularly one's own child—and certainly not a name Aleida would allow anyone to apply to her sister. Of course Mother assumed Ingrid had spent the night with Lars. Still, she almost felt Ingrid's hand over her mouth. Rebuking their mother was not part of the act.

When Mother passed a hand over her eyes, the venom left her tone. "Forgive me, it's . . . well, that child has never been easy, has she?" She placed her hands on Aleida's shoulders, eyes glassy. "Please find her. Bring my daughter home."

Aleida resisted the urge to look away or shift beneath her touch or blurt out that Ingrid was fine, honestly—unless she and Lars had been caught, a notion Aleida refused to contemplate. It was one matter to tell Mother harmless little stories. Ingrid went shopping, Ingrid met friends for lunch, Ingrid took her bicycle to remedy a flat tire, all while she was actually with Lars. From such outings, she always returned after a few hours, so Mother never knew the difference. Ingrid never disappeared in the middle of the night, certainly not for days, weeks, months, however long she would be away.

It really was cruel to worry Mother like this. Still, it was safer for everyone, her included, if she didn't know the truth.

After a shaky breath, Mother cleared her throat. "Do be home in time for dinner. We're having company. Dress properly, act like a lady, everything just as I've taught you. It's—" An indiscernible look passed over her while something in her tone shifted. "It's quite important."

Aleida nodded. Best not to ask about the unexplained dinner guest.

"You know how much I love you. And your sister." The unusual edge lingered in Mother's voice. "Darling, I need you to trust me. And do not ask questions. Not under any circumstances, no matter what happens, until I tell you otherwise. Do you understand?"

Again, Aleida nodded, although the tension in her mother's grip set her heart pounding even more than the strangeness in her tone. Mother held her gaze a moment longer, then slipped out and closed the door softly behind her.

Whatever Mother meant, perhaps she would find out later, although Mother had never looked at her that way before. For now, Aleida brushed her curiosity aside. So far, all was carrying on according to plan. After ballet class, act 2 of this play would commence, in which she would play the distraught sister in a performance worthy of an Academy Award. Returning home, acknowledging Ingrid's continued absence, embarking on her fruitless search for her sister, then frantically bursting into the house, delivering choked lines through tears: *I looked everywhere, Mother. I simply couldn't find her.*

Ingrid and Lars must be far from Arnhem by now. Aleida certainly prayed they were, because if not, then this whole charade had been for nothing. She couldn't bear the thought that her sister might have been caught. Or worse.

* * *

The rest of the day progressed as expected, and Aleida played her role spectacularly. Remaining in character was much easier than she thought it would be. Despite the guilt brought on by Mother's obvious worry, Aleida focused on Ingrid, on her promise to help, and did not succumb to the urge to allay Mother's concerns.

"I know what this is about," Mother said after Aleida had poured out her story and her tears. "I know precisely what she's doing. This is because of—" She stopped, swallowing hard, but Aleida knew what she had been preparing to say.

Because of the Reichsparteitag photo having been returned to the foyer. The uncomfortable silence was broken only by Aleida's lingering sniffles. She did not like the photograph any more than Ingrid did, nor did she understand why Mother had hung it up again. Mother was not a fascist anymore—despite what Ingrid feared, and despite the little flicker of uncertainty that threatened to take root every time Aleida walked by the image. But given Mother's recent instruction not to ask questions, she resolved not to pry until she had been granted permission.

"Ingrid is punishing me, isn't she? All to prove a point, just like he would do . . . That child has always been too much like her father."

Aleida's final little sob hid a giggle. The expected reaction, precisely why she had predicted it last night. Her imitation of Mother always made Ingrid laugh. A sound Aleida wanted to capture, to return to time and time again when her sister was no longer here to laugh with her.

Mother sighed, then she kissed Aleida's cheek. "Not to worry, darling. Ingrid will come home soon enough."

As Aleida went upstairs to change for dinner, a tight ache found her chest. Until now, she had not entirely considered what life would be like without her twin. It was as if one of her own limbs were missing. A sensation to which she would never grow accustomed. But once she heard from Ingrid, knowing her sister was safe would ease the ache. Someday they would find each other again.

Once ready, Aleida detected faint voices. The guest must have arrived. Tardiness would warrant a reprimand, so she smoothed her dark locks, hurried downstairs to the foyer, and froze.

There, Mother stood with an SS officer.

Was he here because of the blackout performances? Because of the Orpo officer who had walked Aleida home and warned her against associating with Madame Bellamy? Because Ingrid and Lars had been caught? Yet as Aleida's heart slammed, she realized this did not appear to be an official visit. This man appeared to be Mother's dinner guest.

Constance had once been an ardent fascist: This Aleida had known ever since childhood, when Mother had vocally supported Hitler. Along with her sister, Aleida had learned enough about her own country's government and ideals to know she did not want a life under German rule, adhering to fascist ideology. Unlike her sister, she had turned to music, dance, theater. The arts were her escape from the world and her defense of all she held dear.

Perhaps Ingrid was right. Perhaps Mother remained a fascist after all. The photograph was the first indication, and now this. At this very moment, she heard Mother regaling the SS man with the story behind the image, to which he was nodding in approval. Then they caught sight of her, unmoving at the bottom of the stairs. Her grip on the banister tightened.

Mother gestured for her to come closer. "Darling, I'd like you to meet Gregor Dietrich, Schutzstaffel and Police Leader here in Arnhem. Herr Polizeiführer, my daughter, Aleida."

As she approached, Aleida studied the man—perhaps her mother's age, wearing a decorated field gray uniform. His cap was tucked under one arm, revealing a thin crown of light brown hair, neatly combed, peppered with gray. Thin lines surrounded his pale blue eyes. Yet it was his neck that held Aleida's attention. A scar stretched just above his uniform collar, as if someone had attempted to slit his throat. When she reached him, Aleida felt as if she had a knife pressed to her own throat.

Dietrich took her hand and bowed. "A pleasure, Fräulein. You are as beautiful as your mother."

She wanted to snatch her hand away, to scrub off the feeling of his clammy lips brushing against her skin. But this man oversaw both the SS and police forces—green police like the Orpo, secret police like the Gestapo, and any others responsible for maintaining order. If he suspected she harbored anti-Nazi sentiments, he held the power to inflict whatever punishment he saw fit.

Instead, she gave a small, polite nod in response to his compliment, then followed the officer and her mother into the dining room.

Over the meal, Aleida spoke only when addressed while the nausea twisting inside her stomach made eating impossible. She forced down a few bites. If only Ingrid was in the distressingly empty place across from her. Someone to endure this dreadful meal with her. Someone whose ankle she could lightly kick to catch her attention every time Mother leaned closer to Dietrich or brushed her fingers across his arm. Someone who would echo Aleida's request to excuse herself in search of privacy.

Upstairs, she closed her bedroom door, opened her window, and pressed her palms to the sill, gulping breaths of fresh air as if her lungs would never be satisfied.

She should have fled with Ingrid and Lars. Why hadn't she fled?

Because if not for the war, they would still be here. Jews like Madame Bellamy would not need help. The sooner the war ended, the sooner Arnhem would be safe again. Until then, she would await news of Ingrid's safety and commit to her reason for staying behind.

I need you to trust me, Mother had said. Could she? Aleida was not certain of anything anymore—unless Mother had issued the order to protect her daughter the same way Aleida kept her own secrets to protect Mother. Except Aleida's secrets did not involve welcoming the enemy into their home. Had the officer invited himself and left Mother no choice other than to comply? Or had Mother extended the invitation? Aleida shivered at both prospects.

Still, if Mother continued to bring Nazis home, the men's conversations might reveal their intentions for the Jews. Useful information for her to relay to Madame Bellamy.

This was a new role, nothing more. A part in a play.

* * *

For the next few months, Aleida engaged in blackout performances, kept her work secret, and did not ask questions while Mother entertained. Luncheons, dinners, parties, all for Nazi supporters or SS men or Ordnungspolizei. And that Dietrich fellow was always among them.

All while Aleida listened. All without a single letter from Ingrid.

One would come, surely. Perhaps it had taken Ingrid and Lars much longer to settle on a destination and travel there than anticipated. Ingrid had promised to write, and she would.

At last, one evening after Dietrich alone had joined them for dinner, Aleida excused herself early, blaming exhaustion on a rigorous day of dance classes. Dietrich was a dull man who never spoke of his work; no need to remain in his company any longer than necessary.

Upstairs, after readying herself for bed, Aleida was stretching her sore muscles when she heard two distinctive sets of footsteps—one a heavy pair of boots, another a dainty pair of heels.

Dietrich's low voice. Mother's airy chuckle. The steps receded; bile rose to Aleida's throat. They could not be moving in the direction she thought. She held her breath as the steps ceased. Then her mother's bedroom door clicked shut.

Aleida clapped a hand over her mouth to keep from shrieking a protest, then flung herself into bed and buried her head beneath her pillow. If God was indeed merciful, let Him spare her from hearing anything else.

Even as she impatiently awaited sleep, Aleida's heart pounded in her ears. *A common whore*, Mother had spat when she thought Ingrid had slipped out to be with Lars. How dare she condemn her own daughter—especially now that she was in bed with a Gestapo agent.

Mother had always been far too critical of Ingrid. And if being with a good man like Lars made Ingrid a common whore, then being a collaborator made Mother something far worse.

CHAPTER 9

Los Angeles, 26 August 1946

INGRID

After last night's conversation with her sister, Ingrid has not yet notified Crenshaw of her success, despite the condition placed upon her investigation. For a time, their reunion is theirs alone. Now that she has made contact, the real work will begin—inserting herself into Ada's world, meeting Ada's friends, exploring every rumor, securing an invitation to Ada's Star Society, uncovering the truth about the organization. Everything she is determined to do to protect her sister from the threats overtaking her industry. Everything Crenshaw believes she will be unable to do.

Tomorrow the one week he permitted her to make contact will be over, so she calls the office. After the secretary connects her, Crenshaw's smug greeting follows.

"Need a flight home?"

"On the contrary, sir, I wish to remain in California until my investigation is complete. Miss Worthington-Fox was in need of a personal assistant, and I have secured the position."

Silence. What a pleasing sound. She pictures him leaning back in his desk chair, chewing on the ear of his spectacles, mulling over this un-expected news.

"Given she's highly concerned about her privacy, it will be im-portant for me to maintain her trust and make her feel supported and protected. I will report back to you with more information—meetings, appointments, associates, and her parties of course."

Ingrid relishes his discomfort as he fumbles for a reply. For once he just might pay her a compliment, although that's probably expecting too much.

"Eight weeks," he says at last.

Eight weeks. Enough time to uncover Ada's loyalties, surely, and cer-tainly much longer than Crenshaw anticipated keeping her here, which is almost even more satisfying.

When the phone call concludes, a knock sounds on Ingrid's door. No one responds when she asks who's there, so she peers through the peephole, finding a middle-aged man dressed in a nondescript suit. Be-fore she can tell him he's found the wrong room, he knocks again.

"You are wasting my time, Mrs. Van Essen. Open the door."

This man speaks German-accented English and knows her name. Cautiously, she obeys, leaving the chain attached. He doffs a brown homburg and flashes something, so she scrutinizes the item. A badge.

This must be her handler. Mr. Crenshaw did say her handler would be making contact in California, although Ingrid had expected him to arrange a meeting, not to show up unannounced.

"Terribly sorry, sir." She unlatches the chain, then the man—a former Nazi—barges into the narrow vestibule.

A former Nazi. Ingrid hastily pushes the distasteful thought aside. She cannot allow her aversion to his previous position to interfere with her work.

"Klaus Stieber, Federal Bureau of Investigation. Have you made con-tact with your assignment?"

She clears her throat, doing her best to look him in the eyes and avoid picturing him in an SS uniform. "Yes, sir. I will be working as Miss Worthington-Fox's assistant, so I'll have access to her home and personal spaces as well as her calendar and schedule, to know where she's going and whom she's meeting. I have no proof regarding whether she runs a Communist front organization yet, but I'll build her trust and find out."

Although Ingrid had asked Ada about her Star Society, she refrained from expressing interest in attending herself. Bringing up the rumors had been uncharacteristic enough, and of course Ada pointed it out. Requesting an invitation to a Hollywood party would have been even more unusual. The idea for Ingrid to attend must be Ada's, then Ingrid will allow herself to be coerced. Nothing unusual about that.

The corners of Stieber's eyes crinkle with—dare she call it approval? Though the look disappears, a tiny smile finds her lips.

"Compile a thorough report, and I will be in touch."

Not quite an expression of total faith in her, but certainly more than expected.

Once the brief visit concludes, Ingrid steps to the window overlooking downtown Los Angeles. She draws a breath. She did not fail yet, and she has eight more weeks to ensure she won't. And no matter what else happens, she found her sister.

Aleida is now Ada. The performer Ingrid never doubted she would become. Even if Ada had indeed resented her all this time and refused to speak with her after their initial contact, knowledge of her sister's safety and happiness would have been enough for Ingrid.

Her sister is no Communist, though. Surely not. Of that Ingrid is almost entirely certain. It won't take her long to prove, she expects. Her task is simple: Identify threats within the entertainment industry, protect Ada from them, and prove Ada can be trusted.

Because she can be, can't she?

A little whisper of doubt and uncertainty threatens the edges of Ingrid's mind, the way it did every time she was around Mother—the parent she should have trusted, wanted to trust, but never could. But Mother was a proven fascist. Ada never supported fascism, nor does Ingrid have any reason to believe she supports Communism. Until she knows the truth, she will have faith. Whatever the truth is, even if Ada or her associates have Communist leanings, she will do everything she can to educate and redirect them.

Ingrid left her sister to fend for herself in Arnhem; she will not do so now.

* * *

After a swim in the hotel pool, Ingrid takes a hot bath, pulls on a bathrobe, and produces the wire recorder she planted underneath the desk in her hotel room prior to Ada's visit. While preparing for the investigation, Archie had taught her how to use various devices, though at the time she did not entirely trust his instruction. It would have been just like him to teach her certain methods and then supply her with equipment requiring techniques she hadn't learned. Prior to leaving for California, she had checked her assigned equipment and was pleasantly surprised to find devices and models like those Archie had shown her, so she understood exactly what to do when using the recorder during her sister's visit, even if doing so led to nearly the most unnatural conversation she's ever had. She hopes her own discomfort is not apparent in the recording as she begins to listen.

Ada's questions about Ingrid, noticing Ingrid's unusual behavior, which Ingrid attributed to worries about Ada resenting her—true worries, yes, though not the entire reason for her nerves. Knowing the recorder was listening had made her painfully aware of every word spoken, every inflection, anything that might betray that she and Ada know each other. How desperately Ingrid wanted to converse with her as they always did. But she needed to provide evidence of her work, so she had attempted an air of professionalism and distance long enough to get a few useful snatches of conversation to submit to her superiors.

As she listens, she glances at her bare hand, picturing the ring that should be there. Despite Crenshaw's order to remove all signs of her marriage, her ring is with her, tucked safely among her jewelry. Lars would have understood if she had given her reasons for removing it—as much as she could, given the confidentiality of her work—but it was an explanation she didn't want to give. Yet kissing her husband goodbye, meeting Archie at the airport, then removing her ring aboard the plane feels like betrayal of the cruelest sort.

She closes her eyes, blurring the images. It's for the job, nothing more. When it's done, she can tell Ada and Lars the entire truth.

"Care for a drink, Miss Worthington-Fox?"

Her own voice on the recording captures Ingrid's attention. Professional yet friendly, just as two women making each other's acquaintance would sound. Good. She was careful not to slip in the old, familiar *Leidje* during this part of their conversation, despite how wrong it felt using the new name. What follows is a bit of business, convincing and natural. Ingrid is building rapport with the celebrity she just met, not reacquainting herself with the sister she hasn't seen in years.

Because if Crenshaw discovers they share blood, he will never let her finish this. She cannot have that—for her sake or Ada's.

The beginning of the recording will be easy to trim out before she submits it, as will the end, when Ada reminded Ingrid she was still herself.

The line will come soon, although Ingrid has no desire to hear it again. Once was enough. The hurt in Ada's eyes, the confusion regarding why Ingrid brought up those ridiculous rumors. Ingrid had nearly blurted out the whole truth then, that this was for a recording and she was not trying to be distant, to seem shallow, to push Ada away when all she wanted was to pull her close. So when Ada left, Ingrid followed her into the hall, where they could speak freely and she could suggest working as her assistant. A perfect excuse to give Crenshaw and Stieber regarding how she was so easily welcomed by the private, reserved Ada Worthington-Fox.

A sharp rap sounds on her door, followed by an urgent voice.

"Open up if you're in there, Inge."

Ada is here. At once Ingrid stops the machine and shoves it back into the valise under her desk. Surely her sister did not overhear anything. After Ingrid unlatches the door, Ada slips inside.

"Forgive the rush—I was afraid someone would notice and follow me. I can't very well stay out of sight in this." She gestures to the floor-length gown, understated yet elegant emerald silk draped over her slim figure.

Not even the beautiful ballet costumes from her youth had ever made Ada look like this. A glamorous gown, her dark hair expertly styled, diamonds glittering against her earlobes. She looks—well, like a film star.

Ingrid glances at her own white robe and touches the towel wrapped around her still-wet hair. "You're rather overdressed."

"Pardon? Oh, this . . . I've got a little party downstairs, so I can't stay." Ada smooths a dark, wavy lock draped over her shoulder and sets a small handbag on the bed. She remains standing, though, as does Ingrid.

Her sister is the same yet entirely different. Refined and elegant yet, beneath it all, reticent and tormented. The flickering flame that was once Aleida de Vos was overtaken by Ada Worthington-Fox, a blaze so terribly, painfully bright, distracting from ash and wreckage and ruin. Except Ingrid sees beyond the brightness to the destruction, to whatever imparted this look in her sister's eyes, one Ingrid has no power to take away.

"My life is . . . different. People take pictures of me, write about me, speculate about my public and private lives. Ada Worthington-Fox does not speak of anything personal. Ever." Ada fidgets with the gold bangles around her wrist. "Do you understand?"

"No one knows you have a sister." Ingrid nods, though an inexplicable knot forms in her throat. "You want it to stay that way."

"Dragging you into the public eye isn't fair, not when I chose this and you didn't."

Indeed, Ingrid wants nothing less than the attention Crenshaw feared she might attract. Dodging cameras will be hard enough when mingling with celebrities, much worse if the press realizes she's related to one.

"We differ enough in appearance. I don't expect it to be a problem, especially if we aren't seen together."

"Please don't misunderstand. We'll spend time together, of course; we just might have to be clever about it. And if your employer believes you're my assistant, we can tell others the same. Then it won't be a lie." At the word *lie*, a little flush of guilt courses through Ingrid while a momentary look so distant and haunted crosses over Ada's face before she draws an unsteady breath. "During the war, after you and Lars left . . . it was worse than anyone expected."

Worse than what little Ingrid had heard of the starvation and suffering in Arnhem? Worse than being the daughters of a Nazi supporter?

Too much like her father, Mother often said about Ingrid. The father she can't recall but would have adored, she's always thought, if they are so much alike. Perhaps that was why she was so drawn to Opa, because he was the connection to Papa she had always been missing. *I did not raise my son to abandon his family*, Opa once said with a shake of his head, yet he had become a paternal figure adored by both twins, and Ingrid in particular.

She wrote to him too, and never heard back. Perhaps Ada knows what happened to him. She swallows hard, unable to find the words to ask.

"No one knows about Aleida de Vos, or about Mother. No one can, especially not with my upcoming film. If the press finds out she was a fascist in the 1930s—"

"*Is* a fascist, assuming she's alive. Not *was*."

"You don't know that, nor do I, and the point is you know how gossip works. One scandalous tidbit and that's all anyone will talk about, even if it's something completely out of my control. Then Minnie Musgrave will write an article about me with one of her ridiculous headlines—something like 'Hollywood's Siren or Hitler's Spawn?'"

Ingrid has never paid enough attention to the gossip rags to know if Ada is being serious. When her sister doesn't laugh, she concludes such headlines must exist in her strange world.

The air in the room is dense, the silence thorny as Ingrid shifts from foot to foot. Of all the distasteful conversations. Ada should know that Ingrid will be the last person to mention anything to anyone about Constance de Vos. Her sister witnessed every clash between Ingrid and Mother. Over politics, over Lars, over *everything*. She crosses her arms as if to protect herself from the onslaught of memories, from the heat they bring to her veins. She never told anyone about Mother's political views, either, and Lars knows only because he was there to witness it.

"I need our past and the war to remain between us," Ada continues. "And since I can't do anything discreetly without someone finding out, I need your help. Plenty of government people live in Washington, DC, don't they? People who might help me locate someone." She clenches her jaw for a moment of tight silence. "An SS man named Gregor Dietrich."

Every muscle and nerve inside Ingrid seizes. How could she have left Ada? She should have stayed with her—no, forced her to flee with them. Instead she and her fiancé found safety and security while her sister remained in Nazi-occupied territory. With their fascist mother.

And, perhaps worse, something happened between her sister and an SS man. Something that has left Ada wondering, worrying. Even after all this time.

Ingrid can barely speak. "I swear to God, Aleida, if you don't tell me what this is about—"

"You have succeeded. In your studies, your career, your marriage. I have failed. In my aspirations to become a professional ballerina, in my resistance work, maybe in acting if this film is poorly received. But finding Dietrich . . . I owe this to our home, to everyone in Arnhem, to my—" Ada breaks off and takes Ingrid's hands. "I cannot fail. Nor can I succeed without you."

Ingrid stares into her sister's eyes, large and deep gray. She must focus on uncovering Communism, not distracting herself with fascists, but she cannot reveal her true purpose to Ada; she is under strict orders of confidentiality. And she cannot work on a separate case without Crenshaw's consent.

Yet whatever happened to Ada in Arnhem led to this request. To that brief tortured look on her face. None of which would have happened if Ingrid had convinced Ada to leave, given her no choice in the matter. The courageousness of Ada's decision and worthiness of her cause didn't prevent whatever she suffered.

How easily the old web of guilt captures her. Ingrid did not protect her sister then. She owes her this much now.

She nods.

"I will tell you everything soon, I promise," Ada says softly. "If Dietrich is alive, he will believe I took something from him."

"And did you?"

"Yes."

Then, without further explanation, Ada slips from the room.

Ingrid nearly chases after her to demand more. Instead she draws a breath, pushing the information aside for now. A party downstairs, Ada said. Well, then, it seems Ingrid has a party to attend.

Beyond the understanding of politics and law necessary for her work, this is what drew her to private investigation. Opportunities to emerge from behind a desk, to gather information, to piece elements together until the truth is revealed. The sort of work that would have made her grandfather proud. She imagines him in his office, his blue eyes warming in approval as she tells him of her persistence, of how he inspired her toward this career, of overcoming the obstacles in her workplace, of defending the values they both admired about this country. Of helping her sister. The image is soothing, calming, even as her throat tightens with lingering worry over whatever it is Ada has carried since leaving home.

She dresses in a simple skirt and jacket, hides as much of her damp hair as possible beneath a headscarf, puts on her glasses, pulls the camera from the valise containing her equipment, and grabs the false badge a fellow in the office made for her, identifying her as a reporter. Enough of a disguise so long as she doesn't get close to Ada, who will have no trouble recognizing her. Satisfied, she makes her way downstairs.

Members of the press are lingering outside the Biltmore's music room, so she joins the crowd. Moments later, the doors open for them. Drawing a breath to settle the eager shiver racing down her spine, Ingrid follows the others inside.

The beautiful space is filled with women in fashionable gowns, men in suits, a quartet playing jazz, tables draped in white tablecloths with floral centerpieces, waiters carrying silver trays of hors d'oeuvres. Ingrid has entered Ada's world, glamour and elegance and excitement. The infectious energy pulses through her as she follows the press toward a podium, where a man prepares to address them. Cameras flash as eager press members photograph everyone and everything, so Ingrid follows their example, documenting as many guests as possible.

Once everyone is in position, the band ceases. Near the podium, Ingrid finds Ada—drink in hand, calm and focused.

Even as she watches the actress with her winning smile and stunning gown, Ingrid imagines her sister's face from her hotel room moments ago, feels the tightness of her grasp. Telling of darkness, of difficulty, of a past that Ingrid, too, might come to know.

If she finds the information Ada requested about Gregor Dietrich. And if Ada reveals what she took from him, and what led her to hunt a Nazi.

CHAPTER 10

Los Angeles, 26 August 1946

ADA

The war is over. Everything from that time is over. By God, Ada has tried to forget it, changed her country, her name, her life, everything to separate herself from what Aleida de Vos endured. Except she can't detach, not entirely. The war is a brand seared upon her skin. Even if she cuts it off, its scars will remain.

Perhaps she can't forget because she has spent these past years knowing, if he is alive, Dietrich will be looking for her. For what she took from him. She feels the book against her chest with the documents tucked inside, smells the charred, burning letter from her sister as she stands alone in a filthy New York City alley on her first night in her new country.

Aleida de Vos would have been far more likely to disappear than to become Ada Worthington-Fox. Still, if he is seeking her, of course he will likely see through her attempt to fool him. Initially, Ada resolved to forget about Dietrich, but reuniting with Ingrid has prompted her to reconsider. She should find out what happened to him before he has a chance to find out what happened to her. Then, with Ingrid's help, she will hold him accountable for every war crime he perpetrated and leave that time firmly behind her. The past will not, cannot distract her from her career.

Downstairs, she proceeds down the galleria with its elaborate frescoed ceiling and intricate oak-paneled walls. She's nearly reached the music room, where the event is to take place, when she's intercepted by the familiar flash of a camera bulb and an eager male voice.

"Miss Worthington-Fox! In light of the upcoming November elections, care to share your thoughts on Communism?"

Ada never treats invasive journalists any differently: Keep walking, offer a brief smile, single remark, or polite "no comment" until she's out of sight or they stop harassing her. This one nearly makes her falter.

They ask about her career, love life, industry gossip. Never has one been so bold as to ask about her political opinions.

She considers a clever reply to avoid a real answer but refrains when a member of hotel security hastily intervenes. She walks without looking back. The light from the chandelier overhead is suddenly too harsh.

Ada has seen enough of divisive politics, witnessed everything an oppressive government could do. If one comes to this country, she knows too well what might follow. Last time, though, her efforts to combat it led to loss. Her best was not enough.

With a breath to banish all distractions, she enters the music room with its herringbone floors and colorful glass ceiling panel glittering like a massive jewel. This is no time to worry about anything except her job. She spent three years working and hoping for a role like this one. This is her opportunity to prove herself before she must do so for the camera. To flatter the guests, charm the producers, leave everyone confident in her ability to lead. Including herself.

"Pardon me, are you Ada Worthington-Fox?"

The question comes from an attractive dark-haired man in a tailored suit lingering near the elegantly carved doorframe. Someone involved in the film, perhaps? She awaits him, hoping her smile hides her nerves.

"I've heard a lot about you—your talent, your parties, your beauty." Although she laughs, the approving look he gives her quickly disappears when he steps closer. "And that you turned down an anti-Soviet film in 1944. Why did you refuse the part?"

She remembers the job clearly; she was tempted to accept it. But a role in such a film meant engaging in politics and war after she had fled a country torn apart by both. Doing so would have transported her back to that time, might have left her shattered and shaking in the middle of the shoot, and then the new life she was curating would have fallen apart. So she said no, gave some excuse as to why the part didn't appeal to her.

What sort of producer or investor—if this man is either—would ask such a question now? This is not the time to discuss past career decisions. His light brown eyes are focused too intently on her, but she gives a dismissive chuckle.

"You mean the part playing a soldier's wife? You tell me, darling: Do I strike you as a convincing girl next door?"

In truth, Ada has nothing against housewives or playing one, but a subtle reference to the sultry past role that earned her acclaim is certain to distract. Instead, her companion persists.

"Answer the question, miss. All I want is an explanation, then you can enjoy your party."

His East Coast accent—New York, perhaps—indicates he's not from here. Ada glances around. Plenty of people fill the room, though she and this man stand away from the crowd. Attracting attention discreetly will be impossible if she needs assistance, and she doesn't wish to disturb the event. She can only hope he'll go quietly.

"This is a private event." She lifts her chin, holding his gaze. "Unless you have a right to be here, you may leave, or I will ask for your removal."

He says nothing. Very well, then, if he won't leave, she will. Yet when she turns, a grip finds her forearm. Suddenly this man's grip is the one that found her in Arnhem when the cold burned her lungs, when the air once fragrant with tulips now smelled of blood, gunsmoke, death. A time she cannot, will not remember. Certainly not tonight.

"Being a star requires winning the hearts of your public. The public wants a true American, not a Red." The stranger tightens his hold, emphasizing his point. "Be careful, Miss Worthington-Fox. Of the company you keep and the roles you do or do not accept."

Her blood races. To anyone else, he probably looks like a man leaning close to be heard over the din, not one threatening her for reasons she can't fathom. Like that June day in Arnhem when the Orpo officer cautioned her against associating with her dance instructor.

The grip relaxes. She pulls free while he tips his hat, as if this were a cordial exchange, then slips out.

Ada stares after him, her cheeks burning. Had this man accused her of being anti-American because she had turned down a job opportunity?

Drawing a breath, she steadies herself. Past roles, past lives, and strange conversations with strange men will not disturb her when so much relies on this evening.

A featherlight touch brushes against her shoulder. A young woman—hotel staff, judging by her uniform—regards Ada with the adoration often directed toward celebrities, a look Ada is experiencing more often now that the public is taking increased notice of her. Venturing a generous guess, Ada supposes she can't be more than eighteen. The girl makes no attempt to school her face into something more professional. Instead she beams, blushes, looks down, and offers a small envelope.

"A message for you, Miss Worthington-Fox."

Nodding, Ada accepts it. Perhaps Gordon called to wish her luck and express his regrets over missing the evening. She breaks the seal, extracts the paper, and reads.

You cannot hide.

Nothing more. No name, no signature, nothing. A single typewritten note. She looks at the envelope again, confirming the name typed on the front is hers. Her breaths sharpen, just as they did the last time she found an envelope with her name and a message addressed to Aleida de Vos.

It was not him that time. This time might be different.

The employee is already exiting, so Ada rushes after her and touches her arm. When she turns, that same mixture of terror, elation, and disbelief crosses her face; this is hardly the time to behave like the self-appointed president of Ada's fan club.

"Did someone deliver this in person?" Ada demands. "Did you ask for a name?"

The girl blushes. "No, ma'am, I . . . well, I guess I got distracted watching all the celebrities arrive for this event. I just moved here from down South and it's my second week on the job, but I want to be in show business, so—what I mean is, I found the note on the desk. I didn't notice who delivered it." Her lip quivers; any moment now, she's bound to burst into tears. "Is something wrong? Whatever it is, I'll fix it, and I'll pay more attention next time. Please don't tell my boss."

Next time hardly does Ada any good. And if this aspiring actress wants a speaking role in anything other than westerns, she's got to smooth out that twang. Still, recently Ada was a starstruck girl fighting for her place in Hollywood. She tucks the envelope into her handbag, settling the current racing through her.

"No, you needn't worry. Everything is quite all right." Once the employee departs, Ada feels like every word from the note is burned into her chest.

She is hiding so many things. And whoever sent this note is aware.

She must not jump to conclusions after she's already been interrogated about her political views and criticized for turning down a previous job. The article Gordon was reading about exposing Communists returns to her mind. Are others similarly concerned about Ada's views? She looks around, seeking someone who might settle the uncertainty in her chest, until she locates a portly, middle-aged fellow—Russell Hendrix, head of Hendrix Productions, the studio behind her upcoming film. When she joins him, he beams.

"Miss Worthington-Fox, don't you look ravishing?"

"Only the best for you, Mr. Hendrix," she teases while he takes her hand and kisses it, then she drops her voice. "Sir, I've noticed the industry has taken a growing interest in certain . . ." She searches for a way to phrase it delicately. "Political matters. I've been questioned about my own views, so if this is a concern of yours too, or something I should—"

"Not at all, my dear, not at all." He pats the hand still in his grasp. "If the public has a problem with me, my pictures, or the people working on them, the theaters won't show my films, so I take public opinion very seriously. These matters will settle soon, but even if they escalate, you are the prettiest face in Hollywood, and the new face of Hendrix Productions. I protect my assets." He winks, then wraps his arm around her waist, bringing her closer. "Be the woman the public expects—elusive, alluring, and a damn good actress. Keep quiet about politics. Make me money. Do that for me, and I will keep you and those important to you safe."

The tightness in Ada's chest releases. So the rumors are true. Studio heads protect their stars, and now she is one of them. She can focus on doing her job and not concern herself with anything else.

After thanking Mr. Hendrix, she excuses herself. From her handbag, she produces a long cigarette holder, places a cigarette on the end, lights it, and takes a deep, calming drag. At last, she can begin to enjoy this party.

First, the bar.

Near the luxurious fountain against the far wall, a long table is laden with bottles of clear and amber liquids, various wines, sparkling crystal glasses, and fresh garnishes. As she approaches, a gentleman does the same. Ada freezes. Though his back is to her, an aching familiarity couples with an unusual rush spreading across her skin.

In an industry so big, everything is actually so small. Everyone works with everyone else, knows everyone else, makes it their business to know everyone else's business. In spite of it all, somehow it's been almost two years since she last saw Vince Hart in person. Since—well, everything happened between them.

Ada steps to his side, though he fails to notice as he awaits the busy bartender. "This would be quite the opening scene for a film: a man and woman meeting at a glamorous party."

Vince turns. Almost as if he has been expecting her. As if this exchange, this moment, has always been inevitable: the moment they would see each other again. Something seizes her insides—what it is or what it seeks, she does not know, even as it urges her to continue.

"The two stand side by side, then a brief exchange reveals they are not strangers. They are former lovers." A pause for dramatic effect. "Will they spurn one another? Accuse one another? Fall into one another's arms?"

Ada holds his steady gaze, heart thudding, uncertain what she awaits or if his response will lead to whatever it is.

"None of those things," Vince replies slowly. "They will say no more, do no more, be no more except what they are: two who were and are no longer."

Countless people in this room, yet none. The truth laid bare before them is all that exists. Ada's heart constricts. Maybe she hoped for an expression of his forgiveness, though she doesn't truly need it because hers was the proper decision and remains so. Still. Even proper decisions are not without pain.

Vince clears his throat, breaking the tense silence. "Such a film opening has been done before, I suppose."

"I thought we were off to a decent start."

The din surrounding them fails to prevent his words from echoing in her ears. *Two who were and are no longer.* No anger, no resentment, no bittersweet fondness, simply a fact. Perhaps the indifference of such an observation is what prompts Ada to tighten her grip on her handbag.

There is no pain quite like indifference.

As the bartender approaches, she catches his attention. "Cognac for Mr. Hart, neat."

"And a martini with a twist for Miss Worthington-Fox." Then his voice softens. "You remembered."

"So did you."

"Two years or two hundred, I will never forget."

A small sign of no ill will. Heat blossoms faintly against her cheeks. As the drinks appear, Ada finishes her cigarette and Vince offers the glass to her—cold and clear with a bright strip of cheerful yellow lemon peel bobbing in its center.

"Enjoy your evening, Ada."

She almost leans closer, anticipating the brush of his lips over her cheek. How easy it is to fall back into old habits. Now that she has seen him after so much time apart, she will put this unusual bout of nerves to rest and focus on the reason she ended things, and the purpose of this evening: her career.

"Ah, there are my stars!"

The booming voice belongs to a lanky man with a thin mustache and hints of gray in his light brown curls—the director, Abe Sternberg. It is only then, as Mr. Sternberg kisses her cheek and shakes Vince's hand, that she realizes she never considered why Vince is at this event. A reason she now understands with full clarity. A knot of tension forms in her stomach.

The film. *Her* film. Her unannounced male costar.

She vaguely hears the confirmation as Mr. Sternberg mentions their roles, then she glances at Vince, his gaze infuriatingly steady. Indifferent, even. If the revelation regarding her involvement surprises him, he does not show it.

Neither does she, instead offering a pleased smile. She will not reveal her true feelings, not after years of keeping her sister's secrets, of silently hating Mother's dinner guests, of carrying out clandestine resistance work, of being Ada, of *acting*. When her role is assigned, she plays it.

"I'm allowing the press ten minutes to take photographs to include with tomorrow's casting news," Mr. Sternberg says, taking Ada's arm and motioning for Vince to accompany them. "Mr. Hendrix will say a few words, then I'll follow him, then you, Ada. Vince, stand by, don't react too much. Fans and press will be eager to see how you two get along, given your history, so don't give everything away."

As she walks, Ada sips her martini, letting the cold gin mingle with the heat pulsing through her. A role that should win her respect and credibility—if she plays it well—reduced to ridiculous former relationship drama. Headlines like those that read "Silver Screen Siren Snags Hollywood's Hartthrob" when she and Vince were first seen together—he a leading man who had garnered various nominations and accolades, she new to Hollywood and fighting for her place.

But he is not the one speaking this evening; she is. She will not focus on him, on how the press will frame the narrative, on anything other than her chance to address the public for the first time about a life-changing role.

As hotel staff members open the doors, the press floods inside, cameras and recorders at the ready. While they assume their places, Mr.

Hendrix steps to a small podium, calls the room to attention, and begins, discussing his company and its successes before introducing Mr. Sternberg. Ada waits in her designated position near Vince. He really does look every inch the leading man, with his single-breasted navy chalk stripe suit, chestnut hair, intense blue eyes, charismatic smile. Damn him.

Fortunately, she, too, looks like the leading woman, dressed in this spectacular emerald gown. Thank God for Gordon Sharpe.

After introducing the film and naming its stars, Mr. Sternberg steps aside, so Ada takes her cue. The moment she reaches the microphone, the room erupts in flashing bulbs. *Let them admire you*, Gordon always advises, so she does. Gossip about her and Vince won't detract from this film's potential, nor can she allow it to distract her.

"Good evening, ladies and gentlemen. Now, if you intend to ask me for confidential details about my role, I must kindly ask you to refrain. I'd rather not lose my job before I start it." She casts a slight smile at the director amid laughter rippling over her audience. "While I can't share much, I believe in this story both as an artist and as a woman, and I'd like to extend my gratitude to Mr. Russell Hendrix, everyone at Hendrix Productions, and Mr. Abe Sternberg for choosing me to partake in this spectacular film. I am utterly delighted to work with you alongside my costar, Vince Hart."

Vince acknowledges the statement with a brief nod while the onlookers erupt. More flashing cameras as Ada thanks the crowd, then she and Vince pose with Mr. Sternberg and Mr. Hendrix for photographs. After pictures and a few questions, hotel staff usher the press from the room. As Ada watches them go, a glimpse of color catches her eye, so quick she can't make it out.

Or perhaps she imagined the flash of red hair.

* * *

Hours later, as her chauffeur takes her home, Ada closes her eyes to fight the spinning in her head—a sensation she wishes was from too many drinks rather than seeing Vince Hart.

Theirs was a brief relationship prior to the release of *Read the Fine Print*, a role that first won her acclaim. The recognition prompted her to realize she wanted her career and any accolades she earned to be hers alone. Not granted due to her association with Hollywood's favorite actor.

With him starring opposite her in *Lady Bella Donna*, she will always wonder if the success she hopes to achieve will be due to her, him, or both.

Sighing, Ada rubs her eyes and settles into her seat. Vince can't understand why she ended things so abruptly—partially because she never explained her reasons, partially because he is not a woman in show business.

Even their first meeting in early 1944 was the result of her failure and his success—she finding her way to Ciro's on Sunset Boulevard after a horrendous audition for a minor part, he after booking the lead for that same project. The nightclub was popular among celebrities. Maybe she would never be one of them, but at least she could socialize with them. As she sought a place to sit, she considered a table or red silk sofa near the bandstand, then settled on the bar and nursed a martini.

"This would be quite the opening scene for a film, wouldn't it?"

A young man with bright blue eyes appraised her the way an artist studies a painting, capturing her attention the same way she had obviously captured his.

"A young lady alone at a nightclub, where a jazz band entertains the patrons. She is quiet. Pensive. Sipping a martini with a twist—a strong, elegant drink, indicating she must be a strong, elegant woman. As the camera focuses on her face, casting her features in light and shadow, the audience notices the lack of spark in her eyes." He looked from the glass to her. "Hers is not a celebratory drink, but a despondent one."

"And as your muse, I expect to be cast as the lead once you sell that script. It's about time I booked something worthwhile."

"Ah, a correction: Our heroine is British, alone in a foreign country . . . If I sell such a script someday, you'll be my first call—although currently my work is in front of the camera rather than behind it."

"You should write. You clearly have the interest, and from what little I heard, you seem to have the skill."

"Someday, maybe."

Whatever his reasons for hesitating, he did not elaborate, although Ada detected a slight waver to his confident air. A feeling she recognized; growing up, she had played the piano and performed in a few plays, but not with the same confidence she had when dancing. Now she was focused primarily on acting, which had forced her to work through such insecurities—even though failed audition after failed audition left her wondering if she really did have a future in this business.

The actor's momentary hesitation vanished as he sat beside her. "Did you come from an audition?"

"A dreadful one, and thus I'm drowning my sorrows." Never mind that just yesterday Ada had begged her landlady for an extension on her overdue rent, so this frivolous spending was hardly wise. "I heard Vince Hart was asked to lead the same project." She met his vibrant, blue-eyed gaze. "Do you know him?"

"Not as well as I'd like to get to know you." He lifted a hand to the bartender while warmth rose unbidden to Ada's neck. "Another for the lady, my good man."

"And the usual for Mr. Hart," she added.

Perhaps Ada had not been in California long, but the moment he joined her, she knew this man was Hollywood's Hartthrob, as the gossip rags dubbed him. Vince Hart was in countless popular pictures, his face on every magazine, his dashing good looks the talk of every aspiring actress. When a sly grin turned her companion's lips, she rolled her eyes.

"Oh, don't look so pleased. Lucky guess."

"No doubt you recognized me by my dazzling charm rather than my face splashed across the tabloids." He offered her a hand. "And you are?"

"You'll find out soon enough. Once I manage to get my face splashed across the tabloids."

A day that would come sooner rather than later, Ada hoped. After numerous small parts granting her a single line of dialogue if she were lucky, she had recently wrapped a role for an upcoming film, a minor speaking part in which her character seduced the lead as part of a larger ploy. Those on set had been impressed with her performance, so perhaps the public would be too.

As the bartender brought their drinks, Ada lifted her glass. "Well, thank you for the consolation prize, and congratulations on your upcoming lead."

He nodded in acceptance of the compliment. The sourness that rose to her mouth was not jealousy, only bitter resentment at how much easier this life was for him than it would ever be for her.

No use sulking, though. Today was not her first failed audition, nor would it be her last. Such was the business.

Vince took a thoughtful sip of cognac, his eyes never leaving her. "Have you been to the Cocoanut Grove? It's a nightclub inside the Ambassador Hotel on Wilshire Boulevard. Will you meet me there tomorrow night?"

"Perhaps, if I have time. I've still got to find work, you know." Ada offered him a coy smile. "Glad to hear I've made an impression."

Flattering though it was to have a famed actor's attention, tomorrow was a new day. If an unexpected audition came along, she needed to be available and prepared, not distracted by a handsome man—even if that man was Vince Hart. If she found her schedule open, well, that was another matter.

"Your face will be in the papers," came a sudden remark, so quiet Ada almost didn't hear. "Of that I have no doubt."

Not advice from an established success to a newcomer, not an arrogant proclamation, simply encouragement from one artist to another. Not much, yet just enough.

Still, the question of success plagued her, filling her mind with every critique she had placed upon herself from her childhood ballet performances to today's audition. To the casting director's declaration that she was entirely wrong for this part.

"Everyone in Hollywood wants to succeed. What makes you so certain I will?"

"Because, at the risk of sounding cliché . . ." He looked her up and down, as if confirming his opinion and bringing heat to her cheeks. "You understand that believing in your ability is only the start. This job will decimate you time and time again. But those rare occasions when it doesn't? Those make it worth it. So you're willing to fight for what you want, even when everything else has gone wrong."

"Well, Mr. Hart, that's rather bold of you to assume *everything* has gone wrong." She looked him over in return, a slight smile curving her lips. "One thing today went right."

His clear blue eyes held hers as she left him with his half-finished drink. Perhaps she would stop by the Cocoanut Grove tomorrow, perhaps not. For now, she would allow Vince—and herself—to wonder.

FORMER FLAMES ATTEND FILM FETE

by Minnie Musgrave

Tinseltown was abuzz Monday night as stars gathered at the Biltmore Hotel in downtown Los Angeles, where award-winning director Abe Sternberg shared more about his highly anticipated upcoming motion picture, *Lady Bella Donna*, set to film in a few months and releasing soon from Hendrix Productions. Sternberg is notoriously secretive about his projects until an intimate pre-filming party, where he reveals his leads to exclusive members of the press before the public announcement follows. Little is known about this project, although the gossip has been swirling: Many speculated that his leading lady would be Ada Worthington-Fox, and indeed the rumors proved true. She is Lady Bella Donna herself alongside the male lead, Vince Hart, in an as-yet-undisclosed role.

Yes, *the* Vince Hart. Our siren's former beau.

Both have been disappointingly private about their previous romance and about what broke them up in 1944. Did the flame fizzle out? Did another woman steal Miss Worthington-Fox's fellow away? Did Mr. Hart's lady find herself unwilling to be tied down? And if you have those answers, give your old friend Minnie a call. Inquiring minds and all that.

No noticeable ill will came between the two at Mr. Sternberg's party. As pictured, Miss Worthington-Fox gave a brief speech while Mr. Hart stood by, then they posed for photographs with Mr. Sternberg and studio head Russell Hendrix. More to come from these two as filming and press commence. Will their love rekindle, or will there be blood?

Mr. Sternberg was not available for comment, so we must impatiently await additional details. Whatever sort of film this will be, it's bound to be a good one—assuming Mr. Sternberg keeps his Commie politics from painting the silver screen red.

CHAPTER 11

Los Angeles, 27 August 1946

INGRID

I f anyone catches her reading the gossip rags she picked up in the hotel lobby, Ingrid will never show her face in public again. Do people actually read this nonsense by choice?

The things Ingrid does for her investigation.

Today *The Dish*, the paper written by that Minnie Musgrave woman Ada mentioned, features her sister. She reads the article again, jotting relevant information onto a notepad. She writes the name *Abe Sternberg*, the director Archie is investigating, then adds *Communist* and underlines it. According to various articles, Sternberg has never denied his affiliations, and a recent exposé in *The Hollywood Reporter* included his name and party number—the article mentioned naming names, which reminded Ingrid of the Orpo officer who had come to Opa's office with a similar tactic. The fact that the *Reporter* had so readily exposed others sent a chill through Ingrid's blood. Fighting Communism and defending democracy can be done with respect to basic rights and freedoms. It's the approach Ingrid has always taken—the proper one.

How anyone could favor a government that will inevitably lead to suppression will never make sense to her. Then again, others have never fled from such a government. She has. Which is precisely why her firsthand experience makes her qualified to caution against such views. Still, Sternberg's beliefs will only make Crenshaw and Stieber more convinced of Ada's, although Ingrid will not allow anyone's views to influence her own opinions of her sister.

She looks to the photographs—Ada speaking, then posing with the studio head, the director, and her strikingly handsome costar. Ingrid scrutinizes them as she taps her pen against the paper.

Working alongside a Communist does not make Ada a Communist. Nor does it prove she is not one. Pinpricks traipse across Ingrid's skin until she dismisses the sensation. Nothing is proven, and this is a start. She has the photographs and notes she took at the announcement party too, plus her recording and her position as Ada's assistant. Still, something directly from Ada about her political loyalties and the Star Society's purpose would reassure both Ingrid and her employer most of all. She looks from her notes to *The Dish*, an idea taking root. One her sister will hate, so Ingrid will simply have to convince her. She calls the phone number listed at the bottom of the article, encouraging readers to place anonymous tips.

"What have you got for me, love?" comes the middle-aged woman's voice on the other line. Abrupt, as if she's in a hurry, yet cloying in a way that makes Ingrid's teeth clench.

"Mrs. Musgrave, I presume? I have a question regarding—"

"Dish it or ditch it, doll. This is a tip line, not a fact checker, so give me something to print or I'm hanging up in five . . . four . . ."

"Regarding your interest in a proposed piece," she finishes, already more than a little irritated. "An exclusive interview—"

"Three . . . two . . ."

Can this woman not allow her to finish a sentence? "As I was saying, an interview with—"

"Listen, doll, you don't get to be where I am by falling for every actress who calls this line thinking she can give me false promises in exchange for payment. I don't pay until I have a story in my hands, and since you already called this a 'proposed' exclusive, that tells me you have nothing, so you don't get to continue wasting my time and I don't get my gossip. Do call back if you come up with anything useful." Yet she allows Ingrid no time to come up with anything useful, to speak, to comprehend that this conversation is over. "One."

"With Ada Worthington-Fox! I work for her, and I can get you an interview."

The anticipated click on the other end doesn't come.

"The most private woman in Hollywood hired—what? An assistant?" Although the question is dubious, she seems intrigued enough to stay on the line. A muffled clatter and ding, evidence of a typewriter. "Prove it. Do you know what happened between her and Vince Hart? Or is she as red as Sternberg?"

"I just started with her, so I can't speak to either matter, but I can tell you—" Ingrid stops.

Everything she wants to say to prove she knows Ada are things Ada would never reveal to the press. She's a trained ballerina who raised funds for the Dutch resistance. She always requested her favorite dessert—chocolate cake—on their birthday. She once challenged Ingrid to a bicycle race, proposing the loser would do everything the winner said for an entire day, then complained of her unjust fate when she lost. At boarding school, she improvised a spontaneous one-woman play, leaving a room full of homesick girls doubled over in laughter with their sorrows forgotten. When the headmistress reprimanded them for the noise, not even the punishment that befell the instigator dulled the spark in her eyes. Such memories are ones Ingrid cannot share, the facets of Ada no one else knows.

"I can tell you something soon, once I know her well enough to convince you," Ingrid tells Mrs. Musgrave instead, her voice tight as she fights the lump in her throat.

Swallowing hard, she stares at the words *Communist* and *Sternberg* in her notes. If Ada will be working with him, what of her sister's reputation should the film come under criticism for its director's views? She's here to help Ada, isn't she? Crenshaw and Stieber need confirmation that she isn't a threat, so Ingrid will uncover undeniable proof.

"If you'll give me some time, would you be willing to publish an interview with Miss Worthington-Fox? About her opinions on Communism in the entertainment industry?"

Mrs. Musgrave laughs. "You don't read my paper, do you? That girl never talks about her private life or personal opinions."

"I'll try to convince her, and I think it's important for her to make her position known. This is not an effort to sell you a fake story. I'm not asking for payment in advance, only your patience."

A beat of silence. Ingrid feels both her own anticipation and the columnist's desire for such a story seeping through the receiver. "Convince Ada Worthington-Fox to give me an exclusive, and I'll run it. Disappoint me, and I won't play nice."

Then the line clicks dead.

Ingrid updates her notes, and seeing it in print makes her breathe more easily. A published article for the world—and Ingrid's superiors—to read. A public profession of Ada's views printed by a columnist who is a known anti-Communist. Just the thing to discredit any talk of Ada participating in subversive behavior. And if Ada is indeed running a Communist front organization, well, this gives Ingrid plenty of time to dissuade her before the interview.

After putting away her work, Ingrid checks the time—nearly three o'clock in Washington. If she were home, she might meet Lars for dinner later at their favorite tavern, dine on roast beef, then walk to their apartment. There she would kick off her black oxfords and open a window, allowing in the late August breeze smelling of impending autumn, while he would mutter about needing to inspect that window since it squeaks too much. Then they would listen to the radio before falling into bed. A rather boring night by certain standards, compared to the one she could be having here, where nightclubs teeming with celebrities promise raucous music, bodies slick with sweat and spilled liquor, evenings of revelry and mischief.

Except on this or any night, it's not about what she is or isn't doing. It's the spark in his eyes brought on by his incessant need for projects. The way he's chosen restaurant tables by the window ever since their first date in Arnhem, when she mentioned those are her favorite. It's offering him a lighter before he's even reached into his coat pocket for a cigarette. The way she traces her finger along the narrow scar on his shoulder, brought back from the war. It's about who she is with him, who he is with her, who they are together.

She glances at her bare ring finger. With it comes the ache from all those years ago, awaiting her mother's approval of her relationship, though she never expected it to be granted—nor was it. Awaiting cherished moments of privacy with Lars. Awaiting him after he joined the Dutch Army and Ingrid assured him her affections would not fade in his absence, then wondering when or if he would come home.

The ache is different now, somehow heavier.

She can't call him, not when he isn't permitted to know where she is, what she's doing, or when she's coming home. A fact both understood and accepted, though it makes the separation no easier. When she picks up the telephone, she does not call Crenshaw or Stieber either. She'll mention the possible exclusive to them once she has been here longer and can use the assistant job as proof of established trust between her and Ada.

Moments later, the operator connects her with her sister.

"Are you busy?" Ingrid asks. "Or do you have time to come by?"

"Better. I'm sending a car."

A car? Whatever for? Ingrid opens her mouth to ask, but Ada has already hung up—meaning she knows Ingrid will object to whatever she has in mind, so she's leaving no opportunity for refusal.

* * *

The car takes Ingrid along a winding journey up a steep hill, where she steps out at the top. In the distance, a large white building stands sentinel, its three dark domes glinting in the sunlight. And a familiar figure in a headscarf is already climbing out of a second car and hurrying to meet her.

"What are we doing here?" Ingrid asks.

"Being tourists, because that's precisely what you are." Ada gestures to their surroundings. "Welcome to Griffith Observatory."

A public tourist attraction, where anyone might see them? Even if Crenshaw hadn't warned Ingrid to keep her face out of the tabloids, she and Ada agreed to avoid provoking attention. True, they aren't identical, and Ingrid's change of hair color makes their similarities not quite so noticeable; still, they remain noticeable enough. Already the conversations around them feel louder and every person becomes a member of the press eager to snap a photograph.

Ingrid drops her voice. "Are you mad? What happened to keeping anyone from knowing we're sisters?"

"What if you're my cousin from Kent as well as my assistant?" A sly smile curls Ada's lips, the same way it did when she developed lies to tell Mother—stories, she called them, since it was a nicer word. "Nobody here is paying attention to us. Even if they were, or if the press does find out about you, a cousin is far less interesting than a sibling, and it will explain our similarities."

If someone as private as her sister believes the risk is minimal, perhaps there's no need to worry. Ingrid's pounding heart slows. Here they can spend a day outdoors like the many they spent in Arnhem.

"Did I still attend that dreadful boarding school where Mother locked us up?"

"Of course. And if anyone wonders why we look so much alike, we'll say it's our mothers who were the twins."

The mischievous gleam in Ada's eyes leaves Ingrid nodding her consent. Ada dons her sunglasses, then offers Ingrid a second pair. It can't hurt to obscure her features a little, so she accepts them.

The observatory is aglow in the bright afternoon sun while people of all ages lounge in the lush grass. Ingrid follows Ada toward the perimeter overlooking Los Angeles. A breathtaking view—greenery and cityscapes, rolling mountains and vibrant colors, land and sky meeting and mingling.

Ada points to a group of houses, so distant and small they look like miniature figurines. "Gordon's house is somewhere over there, in Hollywood Hills. You're staying somewhere over there." She indicates distant structures that must be the buildings downtown. "I'm afraid I can't get any more specific, considering I'm rubbish at geography."

Ingrid laughs. "It's a lovely view. And this was a lovely idea." To that, Ada lifts her chin in pride as they begin a leisurely stroll around the grounds. "How was your party last night?"

"Fine, I suppose, other than some strange man who pestered me about a job I declined years ago, implying my decision was un-American." Ada shrugs. "Because they see us on their screens, people assume they know us and have a right to say whatever they please—though I didn't expect that my turning down a film was such public knowledge."

A stranger who uncovered what Ada thought was private, asking her about work and politics. Ingrid buries her fingernails into her palms. She has a feeling she knows exactly who that man was. The other person from Crenshaw Investigative Services who expressed a keen interest in Ada Worthington-Fox—albeit for entirely different reasons than Ingrid's. The one whose target was at the same party, so he seized the opportunity to undermine Ingrid's investigation, and now God knows what Archie will do with whatever information Ada gave him.

What her sister is dismissing as a trivial matter is not trivial at all.

As they begin their ascent to the observatory rooftop, she catches Ada's forearm, stopping her on the narrow staircase. "Did you tell him if your decision was politically motivated?" she asks—rather too harshly. Tempering her words has never been her forte. "Haven't you been paying attention to the rumors of subversive influences in your industry? You can't talk about politics with a stranger who might twist your words."

"Stop fussing. Answering prudently and evasively is my specialty. I didn't say anything that might be misinterpreted."

The only thing that can't be misconstrued is explicit clarity. Which Ada never gives, not when she wants everyone to stay out of her business. Ingrid should berate her for dismissing this matter so easily, should mention the exclusive she promised Minnie Musgrave—but Ada won't concede if she feels pressured.

"I've heard the rumors, and of course I'm taking them seriously. I asked Mr. Hendrix—my studio head—about them, and he promised not to let any of this reflect negatively on me."

"If he can't keep that promise? You can't rely on him to protect you." Ingrid bites her lip to keep from telling her to avoid Archie, from saying he's an investigator, as is she, and she's here to prove Ada is not an insti-gator of subversive behavior. Breaching confidentiality is a certain way to get her assignment revoked. Then Ada will be facing all this alone. "This is not a rumor about a romance or an upcoming role. These are serious, concerning matters that could hold serious consequences," she says instead. "I should know. I spend more time immersed in politics than you do."

"And I spend more time in Hollywood than you do. I appreciate your concern, but I can handle myself."

The silence is charged, tense. Ingrid draws a breath, fighting to cool the heat in her veins. Maybe she can't expose Archie, but she can do her best to keep him away from Ada. At last Ingrid takes the lead up the stairs. She did call Ada for a reason—originally, to broach the possibility of the exclusive. A subject that will have to wait, since it seems Ada is in no mood to discuss such matters.

"Something else happened at the party," Ada says when they reach the rooftop and proceed to a less populated corner overlooking the view. "I received an anonymous note saying I can't hide, and I think it might be from—" She stops, adopting that same look from last night when she briefly mentioned the SS man who, according to Ada, will be seeking whatever she took from him. The next word is hushed, barely more than a whisper. "Him."

Everything inside Ingrid stills. But they cannot simply assume the note is from Dietrich, not without evidence.

"Are you certain? Maybe a reporter is trying to encourage you to be more vocal about your private life. Why would Dietrich leave you such a note?" Even his name makes Ada flinch, a realization that brings the heat back to Ingrid's skin. When she doesn't reply, Ingrid crosses her arms. "What am I supposed to do if you won't help me understand? Ask everyone in Washington to look for this man for reasons I don't even know?"

War crimes, likely, the specific nature of which Ada has yet to divulge. Thus of little help to an investigation.

A warm breeze tugs on their skirts as Ada looks toward the distant mountains. Away from Ingrid. Ada, who chose her sister's happiness, who remained in an occupied country to help persecuted Jews, who was eager and willing to aid her country, now withdrawn, isolated, reluctant. Due to the failure she believes is hers, to whatever Dietrich has done, to everything she won't share. Not even with her sister.

Ingrid takes off her sunglasses, then turns Ada until they face one another and removes hers. Her sister's gaze is heavy, weighed by responsibility, determination, and something unsettlingly close to terror.

"You are not alone anymore. And you are the bravest person I know."

"The girl you knew in Arnhem might have been. I'm not her anymore, am I?"

"Because you became so much more. You resisted and survived a war. We established lives and careers in America. And we have each other." Ingrid returns the sunglasses, which Ada folds. "Avoid speaking to anyone about politics unless you're clarifying your views in an appropriate setting. Tell me what I need to know about Dietrich. And let me help. Please."

"I will," Ada replies quietly. "It's not you, it's just . . . difficult." Then she meets Ingrid's gaze. "But since you arrived, the idea of facing it has gotten easier."

The reassurance is comforting, although Ingrid wishes she could emphasize just how important her sister's honesty is, wishes she could be fully honest herself. Working under the strictest confidentiality is proving more difficult than anticipated.

"I've got to get home to study my script, but how do you feel about a little party next Saturday night?" Ada grins, her spirits already brightening. "As you've heard, I have a bit of a reputation for them."

Ingrid holds back a laugh; this is exactly what she knew would happen. Ada has extended the invitation, she will expect Ingrid to be reluctant, and she will persist until Ingrid concedes. So Ingrid stays quiet to encourage Ada to go on, though Ada has never needed encouraging in that regard.

"Our group has become known as the Star Society—celebrities, stars. Group gathering, society." Ada shrugs. "Minnie Musgrave will give a terrible nickname to just about anything, though I've grown rather fond of that one."

Ingrid's heart thuds. Her opportunity to determine whether these gatherings are a Communist front organization or not. To determine whether Ingrid should not trust Ada.

The thought has surrounded her all this time, constricting one moment, loosening the next. Now it collides with her the same way a Wehrmacht soldier once did. If Ada is engaging in subversive behavior, Ingrid must convince her to change before the damage is irreversible. Before her superiors find out. Because if it comes to that, there will be little Ingrid can do.

And if Ada refuses to alter her ways, or sees no harm in such activities, then what? Ingrid can't give a false report, so she will have to tell the truth: that Ada is indeed subversive. Untrustworthy.

Could she bring herself to tell the truth? Or would she lie in her report, or else breach confidentiality to tell Ada of her efforts, then protect her sister no matter Ada's views or the cost to herself?

She pushes the terrible notion aside. It will not come to any of that. Of course Ada is trustworthy. Maybe some of her friends are Communists, but surely not her. It would be just like Ada to concede to hosting their gatherings even without participating in political matters. If so, Ingrid will caution her against such reckless decisions. Once she reveals the truth of the society to Crenshaw, and if she can encourage Ada to clarify her views through an exclusive, neither he nor his HUAC contacts will doubt her investigation's success.

"A party?" She lifts a brow. "Sounds rather exclusive. Celebrities only."

"Exceptions can be made for those related to the hostess. And don't worry about the press. It's a private event, and my friends will be discreet."

A party among Hollywood's elite. This is the organization she is here to understand, and the prospect of mingling with so many from the entertainment industry has left her heart pounding. While Ada waits, Ingrid pretends to contemplate. At last she sighs.

"Very well, *cousin*," she teases. "I'll come."

Her sister isn't the only one who can act a little.

* * *

Once Ada drops Ingrid off at the Biltmore, Ingrid refrains from reaching for a cigarette. She wants nothing to calm her, nothing to quell the reprimands or rebukes, because she'll be damned if she refrains from telling Archie Stribling exactly what's on her mind.

Instead she lets every lingering concern, frustration, and worry mingle when she reaches her floor, and every step propels her to the end of the hall, where she slams a fist against the door.

When it opens, Archie stands in a robe, his dark hair wet and mussed while the smell of chlorine hits Ingrid's nostrils, indicating he's come from the hotel pool. Her colleague doesn't look surprised to see her, chuckles when she pushes past him, lifts a brow as if prompting her to speak and entertain him further. All of which makes her long for something to throw at him.

"Did you threaten Ada Worthington-Fox at the film event last night?" she demands.

"Threaten? I prefer the term 'caution.'"

Interfering with her investigation. Her sister. Yet revealing the entire truth would not alter the way he's regarding her, indifferent to her frustration, her fury. As if both she and her work are of less importance.

"Leave Ada to me. Why were you looking into her work history?"

"I went to Lucey's Restaurant across from RKO and Paramount Studios, met a casting director, claimed to be an aspiring actor, and got him talking about Sternberg—confirmed Red, according to the casting director and the *Reporter* exposé, if you missed it. Then he went on about all the directors he'd worked with or actors he'd auditioned or wanted for parts, her included." Archie picks up a bottle of whiskey and pours two glasses. When she doesn't accept hers, he swallows both, then clears his throat. "Last night, outside the event, I saw the actress, didn't see you to give you the tip, and thought I'd help you."

"If I need your help, I will ask for it." Alcohol might not be such a bad idea after all. Ingrid snatches a new glass, pours her own serving of whiskey, adds ice, and drinks, letting it burn her throat the way the next question burns her tongue. "What did she tell you?"

"Nothing specific. Which means she's hiding something."

Indeed she is, far more than Archie knows.

"A woman hiding something from a man she doesn't know who decided to *caution* her?" Ingrid scoffs. "I can't imagine why she wasn't willing to talk to you."

"*Archie, you bloody menace,*" he replies, pitching his voice up and adopting her accent.

Outright mockery? She would toss the rest of her drink at him if she didn't want it for herself. Instead she presses both palms against the glass, focusing on the cold rather than the intensity of the flames heating her neck. In the workplace, some men ignore her; some are kind to her; most are indifferent. Archie clings to her like a rash—always irritating, occasionally even painful.

Without an audience to appreciate the imitation, he sits on the bed, frowning. "Ease up, Britain, can't you take a joke? *Holland,*" he corrects quickly to avoid what she's bound to say next. "Despite what you think, my reasons for talking to Ada had nothing to do with making you mad. She's a nice, talented girl, and if she's not already a Commie, I'd hate to see her ruin her career. Someone needed to tell her to be careful."

"That's my assignment, not yours."

"Just trying to be a good friend to you, Ingrid. And you can be a good friend to me by sending her to my room every once in a while, now that you two are going to be spending time together." A sly grin brings a salacious spark to his eyes. "One favor in exchange for another."

How easily and how often women are relegated to playthings, to bartering chips, to favors. If they were in the office, Ingrid would bury her fingernails into her palms to keep from retorting. Here, thousands of miles away, when the little whisper reminds her to be prudent, she tells it to shut up.

"Subject her to you? No woman deserves such an unfortunate fate." When he places a hand over his heart, as if wounded, Ingrid finishes her drink and crosses to meet him. Enough of his antics, his flippancy, his interference. "This job is everything I've worked toward for the last six years, everything you've been permitted to do from the moment you started. We are here to work, not for you to treat every woman like a conquest. Certainly not the one who is my responsibility." For once he holds his tongue as she shoves her empty whiskey glass into his palm. "Stay away from Ada."

His look of genuine surprise would be laughable if not for the anger and whiskey and, at last, candidness bolstering each step as she leaves him sitting there and returns to her quarters. When she's back in the office, maybe she won't refrain from speaking plainly anymore. Prudence be damned.

CHAPTER 12

Los Angeles, 30 August 1946

ADA

A few days later, after a dress fitting for the outfit she plans to wear at next Saturday's Star Society gathering, Ada visits the Biltmore to invite Ingrid downstairs for a drink. In a far corner of the bar, they find a secluded leather banquette, where each sips a French 75 on an afternoon as normal as any between sisters. As if they had never parted.

"Politics and law," Ada says, breaking the comfortable silence. "Some things never change."

Ingrid nods, chuckling. "To Mother's great disappointment, if she were here to know as much." Then she looks to her drink, as if to find the confidence to continue. "Do you know if . . . if she . . . ?"

No need to finish. Ada shakes her head.

"I'm not certain."

When Ada fled, Mother was alive. She doesn't know what happened to her throughout the war's remaining years. Perhaps she never will.

How strange it is, contemplating what happened to someone who might not deserve her sympathy or concern. Yet so often people are misguided; they face choices that are not real choices at all, do what they feel they must. People can change. Perhaps Ingrid is right about Mother's fascist leanings, or perhaps Ada is right to cling to hope, to believe Mother wanted to do the right thing even when her choices seemed to reflect the opposite. Maybe she was just trying to survive, the same as everyone else.

"And Opa?" Ingrid continues, her voice barely a whisper.

"Arrested in May of 1942 for his anti-Nazi views," she replies quietly. "I never heard more."

Ingrid swallows hard, so Ada takes her hand, providing what meager comfort she can. It is one of the worst parts of survival: not knowing the fates of those most dear. After a moment, Ingrid smooths an errant lock of hair before attempting to speak more brightly.

"Are you still dancing?"

"If the part requires it. Not ballet anymore."

"No? Ballet was your favorite."

Indeed it was; part of her misses it terribly. The rigorous training, the elegant movements, the power within her own body. Another part can't bring herself to step into pointe shoes. Not since Arnhem.

The silence, once comfortable, now feels like pinpricks across Ada's skin. Ingrid, too, shifts in her seat.

"You really haven't told anyone?" Ingrid lowers her voice. "About your past? Not even your agent?"

"Him least of all," Ada replies, matching Ingrid's tone. How could she risk destroying such a lovely relationship? "Have *you* told anyone?"

"Nobody cares about my life. I'm not in the public eye, so it doesn't matter as much. You're a celebrity. Everyone wants to know everything about you, and if we hope to find"—Ingrid pauses—"*him*, I thought you might have mentioned something to your agent about it, in case word gets out."

Finding *him* is even more reason to keep the truth from becoming public knowledge. If the press finds out Gordon represents a woman who spent the war in a household of fascists, hers will not be the only ruined career. Which is why Ada and Ingrid must handle it quietly.

"It's not a bad idea, you know. To address your views regarding certain matters." When Ada sighs, knowing exactly what her sister is implying, Ingrid leans closer. "I'm asking you this because I care about you, so please answer me honestly and don't get angry: Are you a Communist?"

Ingrid's eyes are bright, filled with something more intense than concern. A genuine fear Ada has so rarely seen in her. Ada glances around to ensure no one is eavesdropping.

"This really is not the place to discuss such things," she whispers. "No, I am not. Now can we please change the subject?"

Visible relief sweeps over Ingrid. "Well, then, it's simple: Give a statement to clarify your political opinions. You don't have to talk about the war, but remember the man who asked you about the role you declined? Out of concern for your reputation, you should eliminate cause for speculation."

"People will speculate no matter what I say, so why bother?"

"For your sake, not theirs. Yes, people might form their own theories, but they will also listen to you."

Despite a sigh, Ada can't prevent the warmth brought on by her sister's words. Leave it to Ingrid to be worried about how politics might affect her. Concerns of Communist influences have overtaken her industry; Ada is well aware. And Ada does not like the idea of speaking about her private life simply because of public pressure.

Ada Worthington-Fox has built a reputation for privacy so she can avoid such topics. No one will wonder why she's keeping quiet. But Aleida de Vos watched suspicions and accusations tear through her community in Arnhem. If speculations begin to circulate, her carefully curated persona cannot protect her from everything. Certainly not from the man who might have found her, who might have sent her the anonymous note at her casting announcement party, who will be seeking to take back what she took from him.

"Until any of this gets worse—if it does—there's no need to say anything, nor will it even make a difference if I do," she says.

"Do you want to be mistaken for a Communist, or for people to assume you're a sympathizer?"

"I told you, the studio and those in power are the ones who control the narrative in Hollywood. Mr. Hendrix already told me to keep quiet and he'll keep me away from controversy. If I disobey him, he can easily put me in the middle of the controversy instead."

"Don't let fear silence you. Maybe the studio can protect you from certain issues, but if concerns about Communist influences spread, the government will get involved, and then what power will the studio really have?" Ingrid takes Ada's hand. "A statement would be wise. Promise me you'll think about it?"

Clarifying her position will hardly make a difference in the eyes of those who control her career, and if the government does indeed get involved, perhaps the studio would be powerful enough to keep her safe from them too. Perhaps not. Either way, it won't matter as much as Ingrid seems to believe. What matters is whether anyone in Hollywood wants her to continue working, so she must focus on making the best film possible to ensure she is too valuable an asset to lose. Yet that look in Ingrid's eyes—fear, true fear—leaves her inclined to do anything to assuage the one person who knows her, past and politics and all, to keep that look from overwhelming her again.

"For you, my dearest sister, I will think about it," Ada says, then she finishes her drink while Ingrid flashes an appreciative smile. "Well, I'm afraid I must rush off, but this was lovely. And don't forget about next Saturday."

After Ingrid nods, Ada proceeds toward the exit. Ahead, a man steps around another patron. When she glimpses his face, she stills. That nosy fellow from Mr. Sternberg's party, the one who asked her about the anti-Soviet film.

Did he follow her? Whatever this is with him and her career, she's not going to tolerate it a moment longer. She pursues him as he crosses the galleria and passes through the archway, then heads down the bronze staircase, across the lobby with its travertine walls and elaborate arched ceiling, and through the heavy bronze door.

Outside, clouds impede the sun's warm rays. Ada catches up to the man, who turns at the sound of her approaching footsteps.

"Do you want to know why I turned down that film? Is that why you keep coming around? Because if you want an answer, I don't owe you one." She doesn't break his gaze as she steps closer. "Leave me alone."

"Says the woman who came to the hotel where I'm staying and followed me outside."

His homburg remains low over his face, but not low enough to hide the eager spark in his brown eyes. Undeterred. Confronting him has not yielded the results she intended. It appears she's only led him to recognize a new opportunity. When Ada turns, he moves to block her path.

"Listen, doll, I have ways of finding information, the sort preferably kept quiet. About you. Your agent. That gorgeous redhead you were visiting." He dips his head toward the Biltmore. "If I can't find something useful, I can—embellish, let's say, if you catch my meaning."

Ada glares even as her blood stills. Is he resorting to threats simply because she avoided his question about a past job opportunity? Yet this can't be a bluff. He found out about her previous career decisions somehow. He could find out much more. About Arnhem, even. Or he could fulfill his threat. *Embellish* is nothing more than a pretty word for *lie.*

The only thing more ruinous than a lie is the truth.

"Let me attend your next Star Society gathering—just one, unless you wish to extend future invitations, should you find my company irresistible. Or it's your reputation, Mr. Sharpe's, and Mrs. Van Essen's."

She can't risk refusing; she's about to star in a film, for God's sake. If he's threatening to start rumors—or uncover worse than rumors—about her, Gordon, Ingrid, she can't allow it. And, as Ingrid said, if she's going to assuage concerns about her loyalties, it should be through a public statement. Information fed to a stranger can be too easily warped and altered.

"If you attend, you'll leave us alone?" she asks. "And you won't pester my friends or make a nuisance of yourself?"

"You have my word."

That leaves her with little confidence. Still, whoever this man is, she can't afford to make an enemy of him.

"I will send an invitation with all the details," she concedes at last. "Bring it with you to be permitted entry. Do we have an agreement?" She extends a hand, which he accepts.

"Archie Stribling. Now you know the name to add to your guest list." Mr. Stribling kisses her hand before she can snatch it away. "Until then, Miss Worthington-Fox. I have no doubt you'll show me an excellent time."

Then he continues down the street, whistling a jaunty tune while Ada hails a cab and slips inside, where she closes the hand that shook his into a fist.

Whatever Mr. Stribling wants can't be worse than the harm he threatened upon her loved ones. Yet as the car begins its journey, the deal she's made stretches over her like the clouds stretching across the sun above. Soon to envelop it completely, to snuff out the light, to wash the world in darkness.

The public wants a true American, not a Red, he warned her at Mr. Sternberg's party. If Mr. Stribling suspects her of Communist leanings, perhaps he's a reporter or someone hoping to expose her. Maybe Ingrid made a valid point; maybe she should clarify her views before any rumors begin. Except, if she defies Mr. Hendrix's instructions, how will he retaliate? If she goes against his wishes before filming has even begun, he would have time to cast a replacement, could even slander her name to prevent her from working anywhere else. If she keeps silent, his promised protection might or might not prove authentic. If she speaks up, she relinquishes the option entirely.

All she can do is put her faith in Mr. Hendrix, do her best on her film, and hope he meant what he said: He protects his assets. Until then, she's protected herself, Gordon, and Ingrid from Mr. Stribling's threats. For now. Yet she feels no different than she did the last time she tried to shield a loved one from harm.

As if she herself brought evil to their doorstep.

CHAPTER 13

Arnhem, 1941

ALEIDA

Blood thrummed through Aleida's veins when ballet class ended and she stepped to the mirrored wall, complaining of a hairpin driving painfully into her scalp. While dancers filed from the studio, removed pointe shoes, and pulled bandages from blistered feet, Madame Bellamy assisted her and freed a single hairpin. The one around which Aleida had wrapped a slip of a note, which her instructor discreetly tucked into her own bun.

Thursday evening was what she had written. An indication of Mother's next dinner party. Madame Bellamy usually took the opportunity to stage a blackout performance, since dinner provided a guaranteed distraction for the Gestapo agents, SS men, and Ordnungspolizei in attendance.

"Our next performance will be on Thursday," Madame Bellamy said the next day when she called a resistance meeting at the dance studio. "Aleida, will you conduct rehearsals this week?"

She nodded. "And I'll bring a report after my mother's dinner— names of those in attendance, information they reveal about Jews or subversive activities, whatever I can gather."

"Good. All of you, spread the word to those who wish to donate to our cause and forget the war for a short time. And remember: No music, no applause, nothing to alert the soldiers to our presence, so those attending must agree to abide by the rules."

Heads bobbed in a collective nod, though a few dark looks found Aleida. Over the last months, she had attended countless resistance meetings, during which the same proposal often arose: If so many SS men would be gathering at Aleida's house, why not stage an attack against them? Yet Madame Bellamy insisted the information Aleida provided was too valuable; therefore ambushing the De Vos home was not worth risking her exposure.

Sometimes Aleida wished Madame Bellamy would approve the attack. After months of evenings with Mother, Dietrich, and their friends, listening to the conversations and seeking information even as she feigned disinterest, Aleida was running out of strength.

If exposed, she no longer had to pretend. If exposed, perhaps Mother's act—if it was one, as Aleida so desperately wanted to believe—could end too.

She could not run out of strength, though. Until the war ended, she had a role to play. Her silence was protection—and not just her own.

As the meeting adjourned, the door to the Muziekschool burst open.

Footsteps pattered down the hall toward the studio, keeping time with Aleida's heart as she and the other dancers gathered their belongings, as if finishing a late rehearsal. Hopefully the Gestapo would consider it an acceptable excuse, if they were the ones who had rushed inside.

A noticeably pregnant woman entered the room. Aleida breathed more easily as she recognized Madame Bellamy's daughter, who had attended dance classes prior to her marriage and pregnancy. Usually she participated in these meetings.

"Maman, you must come quickly," she said, then continued in rapid French.

Aleida watched as Madame Bellamy stilled. The look of a woman who had received news too devastating to grasp.

Even as her heart raced with concern, Aleida joined them. "Go. And tell me how I can help."

Madame Bellamy's eyes were vacant, one hand pressed against the piano as if for support. "My son . . . He was attacked by a group of soldiers. Not because he violated a law, simply for being Jewish, and he . . . his injuries are extensive."

Aleida could hardly breathe. Violence against Jews had increased since the occupation, but this could not be happening, not to this woman—both strict and gentle, eloquent and courageous, a woman who treated her students like her own children. No one deserved this, she and her family least of all.

Suddenly Aleida wanted to go home, to throw Dietrich out, to curse him for the hatred and violence his regime perpetrated.

"Go to your son, madame," Aleida said, gently but urgently. Her instructor seemed too dazed to comprehend anything, so Aleida steered her toward her daughter, who took the elder woman's arm. "Be with your family for as long as you need. I'll make sure the blackout performance goes well, and I'll deliver the funds."

Madame Bellamy shook her head. "Let someone else deliver them— someone you trust, and tell them what to do. You'll be missed if you aren't home in time for your mother's dinner."

"Then I won't be late."

Maybe she trusted her fellow resistance members, but there was no need to share information with them unless it was essential. Those who knew little could not compromise the work as severely if caught and interrogated by the Gestapo. In time, they would need to delegate tasks and information more broadly. Jewish citizens were increasingly persecuted, having their jobs taken and rights stripped, and as the resistance work expanded, it was becoming too much for Aleida to be the only one sharing full awareness with Madame Bellamy. For now, though, Aleida was enough. She could stage the performance, deliver the funds to their contact, and be home without Mother missing her and without putting her fellow resistance members at an unnecessarily increased risk.

Leaving Madame Bellamy no time to protest, Aleida departed, mounted her bicycle, and pedaled down Boulevard Heuvelink toward home, her blood pumping hard and fast.

For every month she spent engaging in resistance work, it felt as if the next brought more hardship. First the occupation, then harm to Jews. Nothing worse would be next, surely. But if it were to come, she was certain to hear about it at one of Mother's parties.

The men came. They drank. God willing, they talked. And Aleida listened.

If only Ingrid were there to assist her—though Ingrid would never have the patience to sit through a dinner party, nor would she keep her opinions to herself or her temper in check.

A cool late-afternoon breeze swept the painful thought away. More than a year since Ingrid and Lars had left, and still Aleida had not received news of their safety. But she did not permit herself to think of what might have happened to prevent her sister from contacting her. She *would* write. Until then, Aleida would remember why she had stayed.

For Ingrid, her twin sister. For the Netherlands, her country. For Madame Bellamy, the Jews, and the resistance. And for herself. Because someday this war would end, and she and her countrymen would be free.

* * *

Someday felt more distant than ever as the months dragged by and 1941 transitioned into 1942. Even Mother had been forced to make some adjustments throughout the winter's strict rationing, despite Dietrich providing her with more than the allotted rations. Aleida's countrymen suffered, all while the occupiers indulged and wasted every resource.

Yet, to Aleida, Mother never spoke about Dietrich, Ingrid, or the war. So Aleida never spoke to her about those topics either. The truth was obvious enough, she supposed. That Mother was everything Ingrid feared she was. Or maybe, just maybe, if Aleida was living a story, perhaps Mother was too.

Perhaps Aleida was not the only one pretending.

The possibility was too delicate to discuss, however, so Aleida never did. They were simply two people existing within the house on Jansbinnensingel, going about their lives, keeping their secrets. Mother had said to trust her, to not ask questions. Just like Aleida kept information from her fellow resistance members for their safety, she prayed Mother was doing the same for her daughter. Because if Mother truly did support Dietrich and everything he did, Aleida would never forgive her.

One evening, Mother was hosting another dinner, so Aleida hurried home immediately after ballet class to help her prepare, as she usually did. She found Mother in the living room with Dietrich, who was smoking and reviewing a few documents. Aleida refrained from attempting to steal a glimpse. Dietrich kept his work in Papa's old study, and it was always locked, the key always on his person. Instead she sat beside Mother, relaxing before the evening's festivities while Mother took down Aleida's bun. A gesture that always reminded Aleida of her childhood, when they would sit together and discuss her class while Mother removed the pins and brushed her dark locks.

"Darling, what's this in your hair?" Brow furrowed, Mother held up a pin with a tiny slip of paper wrapped around it.

Aleida's heart stilled as Mother removed the message—one she had forgotten to deliver to Madame Bellamy. She had been late to class, having stopped on her way to check with a contact planning to smuggle a family out of Arnhem tonight, then she left early to make it home in time for Mother's dinner and forgot about the note.

Mother unfurled the paper. "'Tonight, R. W.,'" she read aloud. Nothing damning unless one knew it meant a family would be escaping this evening, escorted by a contact whose initials were R. W. Still, it was not information she wanted in anyone else's hands, certainly not Dietrich's. Already, he was puffing slowly on his cigarette, watching while Aleida took the note with a forced chuckle.

"Oh, this was just so I wouldn't forget about dinner, and the initials are for Richard Wagner. I want to practice some of his pieces so I can play the piano this evening. The men always enjoy the music, don't they? And isn't the hairpin clever? The paper would have gotten lost in my bag, but this way I'm certain to remember everything." She was explaining too much, she knew, so she sprang to her feet and gathered her belongings. "I'll change so I can help you before the guests arrive, Mother. What are we serving for dinner? I'm famished."

She did not listen to the answer, her heart pounding too much as she felt Dietrich's eyes following her toward the stairs. Only once she was in her bedroom with the door safely closed did she tear up the paper and let out her breath.

She could not afford to be careless. Maybe none of the information she had written had been obvious, but she might not be so fortunate next time.

Dinner proceeded without incident, and it was late when the last guest finally vacated their home. A warm summer breeze swept through the living room window when Aleida opened it to air out thick clouds of cigarette and cigar smoke, then she collected scattered glasses and emptied the ashtrays. As the one who never partook in the reveling, the task of cleaning often fell to her.

From the dining room, she heard a shattering glass followed by Mother's peal of raucous laughter. She bit her lip to contain a curse.

Mother never laughed over ruined finery. Meaning she was terribly drunk.

Red wine and crystal fragments spilled across the table, glinting in the light. Aleida picked up a white cloth napkin to clean the spill. She hoped the wine would ruin it. Then, every time she looked at that stained napkin, she would imagine it was Dietrich's eyes turning blood red when one day—*one* day—this war ended. On that day, when he no longer held power over them, she would tell him everything she truly thought of him.

"A Jew still works there," Dietrich was slurring as Aleida cleaned around them.

She cleaned more slowly. After almost two years of living here, Dietrich had never spoken of his work, not even when drunk, even though his companions often did. Tonight was finally the exception.

"At the Muziekschool. Have you allowed your daughter's dance training to come from a Jew? Dancing under a subversive influence, carting cryptic messages back and forth, then what will be next? Defying the Reich in the middle of your next dinner?"

She almost dropped her cloth. No, not this, not the resistance or the Muziekschool or Madame Bellamy. There had always been a chance this time would come, but now that it was here, she pictured her kind, devoted instructor dismissed from her position, or led from the dance studio in handcuffs, or beaten and bloodied. What would they do to her? And then what would become of their little group of resistance members?

Was this because of her note? Did Dietrich really believe Aleida and Madame Bellamy were engaging in subversive behavior, or was he simply drunk and overly suspicious?

"Cryptic messages?" she repeated with a faint laugh. "Herr Polizeiführer, the notes are just a little system I devised to help my memory because I'm far too forgetful. And it works, it really does."

Dietrich made a little sound of acknowledgment—one that did little to indicate whether she had convinced him—while she returned to cleaning as if nothing was wrong.

"And the instructor?" he pressed. "If a Jew remains, she must be replaced."

Aleida had no escape, nothing except the shards of crystal pricking her skin when she pressed her palm against the table. Keeping her opinions to herself, despite her silence benefiting the resistance, already felt like enough of a betrayal to the Jews and those like her grandfather who defied the Nazis outright. She could not, *would* not betray them with her words.

"Darling, isn't Madame Bellamy married to Dr. Janowitz?" Mother asked while she tapped a manicured finger against the table. "I suppose she would be registered as Mrs. Janowitz, then . . ."

For God's sake, what was Mother trying to do? The Janowitzes were registered. They wore yellow Stars of David on their clothing, ever since the order became effective in the spring. They complied with every law. Yet something struck Aleida's core, staining these assurances the way the wine stained the cloth gripped tight in her white knuckles.

"Answer your mother, Aleida." Dietrich's blue eyes were narrow and hazy with drink, although they never left Aleida as he swallowed another sip. The scar across his neck bobbed and stretched.

She picked a crystal fragment from her palm, stared at the drop of blood left behind. "She's an excellent instructor, Herr Polizeiführer. Who is not subversive and follows the laws," she added, because she wouldn't allow her defense of Madame Bellamy to cost the woman her job. Or worse.

Pleading for her friends was hardly grounds for Dietrich to accuse her of resistance sympathies. Even if he did, she no longer cared.

"Madame Bellamy has been at the Muziekschool for years, has trained me since I was a girl. There's no need for that to change."

Not when she didn't deserve this persecution, not when she was doing so much good for so many. Ingrid was already gone. Aleida could not lose Madame Bellamy too. She caught her mother's hand.

"Please, Mother, tell him. Tell him she's not a threat."

If Mother cared for her, truly cared for her, regardless of her political loyalties, she would not allow Dietrich to take this from her daughter, would not let him destroy an innocent woman's livelihood.

Mother was already rising unsteadily to her feet. If she had heard Aleida's request or felt her touch, she gave no indication. Her attention was entirely on Dietrich as she leaned close and caught his chin. "Come, darling, I'm not finished with you."

Wood scraped and shrieked across the floor as he pushed his chair back and followed Mother upstairs. Aleida gripped the edge of the table so hard she thought her fingernails would puncture the wood.

In February 1941, a strike protesting the occupation and subsequent Jewish persecution had been quickly and brutally suppressed. Madame Bellamy's son had been attacked for his faith. Jews were being sequestered in specific neighborhoods, so it was only a matter of time before Madame Bellamy was ordered to move. Every day, the situation worsened, and those working directly against the Nazis would certainly face harsh punishment if caught.

Maybe Mother and Dietrich were drunk. Maybe nothing would come from anything they said. But she could not wager lives on *maybe*.

When the bedroom door closed, she fled. However much time she had, she needed every minute.

She traveled on foot through the woods and fields; a bicycle on the streets, though faster, included the risk of being spotted by nighttime patrols. Fortunately, her destination was not far. When she reached the small house, she knocked.

"Madame, it's Aleida de Vos. Let me in," she urged as loudly as she dared. "Please, you must—" Her words were cut short when the door opened.

"What are you doing here at this hour?" Madame Bellamy stood in a nightgown with Dr. Janowitz beside her. "Have the soldiers hurt you?"

Aleida was already hurrying down the small hall toward their bedroom. With shaking hands, she opened a dresser and pulled out neatly folded sets of clothes. This was not the time for questions, explanations, anything other than action.

A pair of hands caught her shoulders.

"Look at me, Aleida." At last she met her instructor's light brown eyes. "What is the meaning of this?"

"You and the Muziekschool, that you're Jewish, and Mother and Dietrich . . ." She couldn't form coherent sentences, couldn't think until she sucked in a breath, then the elder woman nodded for her to go on. "He doesn't approve of me dancing under a Jewish instructor. They were drunk, so he might not remember, but I came as soon as I could because he also knows about a note I forgot to give you today. I told him it was nothing, but I don't know if I convinced him . . . He was carrying on about subversive behavior, and now if I've compromised your safety—" She couldn't finish, because she couldn't bear what it might mean if she had.

Madame Bellamy's expression did not change. Rather, she glanced at her husband, who also appeared resigned to the news.

"You must go." Aleida fought tears as they burned and blurred her vision. "If he asks, I won't tell him anything, but he will find you with or without me, so you must go."

"You will do as he says without protest." When Aleida tried to argue, Madame Bellamy held up a hand. "You cannot be foolish when you live in the same house as that man."

Though the words weren't meant as an accusation, they stung as fiercely as a blow. She was a prisoner in her own home, subjected to the will of the fascists—and even if she did not bend to it by choice, did that matter when her circumstances could force her into feigned collaboration?

"And you?" Madame Bellamy pressed. "If he found your note, are you safe?"

She nodded. "They will blame you for influencing me, if it comes to that, but I can always feign repentance." She was not entirely certain it would work, but her safety did not need to be Madame Bellamy's concern.

The elder woman glanced at her husband, visibly grappling with what to do. When Dr. Janowitz nodded, Madame Bellamy drew a resolute breath, then turned to Aleida.

"Without me, the resistance will need you. For your safety and that of the work, you must not betray your loyalty. Promise me."

Aleida nodded, shaking too much to speak. For the work. She had to protect the work. She was still Madame Bellamy's second-in-command, the one who knew their contacts, the one who collected information from her mother's parties. This was why she hadn't fled with Ingrid. Because she was needed.

"I should have prepared for this months ago and pretended I'd quit the Muziekschool, anything to draw his attention away from you. I insisted you followed the laws, told him you did nothing wrong . . ." She swallowed a choked breath. "An apology will never be enough. But I'm so sorry."

Madame Bellamy cupped Aleida's face between warm palms, her gaze absent any resentment, any animosity. The look of reassurance she had once given a little girl who feared boarding school.

"This night, you have saved two lives by risking your own." Madame Bellamy kissed her on both cheeks. "Thank you, dear girl. And may God protect you."

She was trying to save two lives, anyway. Such efforts could hardly be considered valiant when she was the reason those lives were at risk.

CHAPTER 14

Hollywood Hills, 7 September 1946

ADA

Building a Star Society event requires meticulous planning and careful execution. First, the details. Formal or informal attire, game night or pool party, themed costumes or masquerade ball, and the food, music, and decor to accompany the particular soiree. Then a carefully curated guest list. Finally, embossed invitations coordinating with the theme, designed by Beverly Tolbert—fellow actress and another of Gordon's clients whose flair for artistry is much better than Ada's, which is why Ada asked her to take on the responsibility upon the group's inception.

This night calls for simplicity. Best not to overwhelm Ingrid with Ada and her friends outdoing one another for best dressed. When preparing the guest list, writing her sister's name had sent a thrill down Ada's spine. She does so want Ingrid to enjoy herself.

After donning the pink sundress she chose for the event, Ada hears the door swing open. She rushes downstairs, and Gordon has hardly set down his luggage before she throws her arms around him and kisses his cheek.

"Oh, I've missed you terribly. And I've got lots to tell you, but you're going first. How was New York?" Before he answers, something catches the light from the glittering crystal chandelier—a purple and yellow discoloration beneath his eye. Slight, as if it has been healing for a while, but certainly noticeable. Frowning, she brushes her thumb over the spot. "What's this about?"

In all the years she's known him, Gordon is hardly the sort of person who comes home with inexplicable black eyes.

"A few unwelcome guests got into our party meeting. Haven't you heard? Communists are a massive threat to national security and must be eradicated at all costs." With a sigh, he smooths a hand over his mustache. "Never get your face in the way of a fist, kid."

A short while ago they read the exposé naming members of the Communist Party, when Gordon thought her concerns for him were unfounded. Now it's come to this—to physical attacks. Her agent's prior lack of concern suddenly seems as bruised and discolored as his skin.

"Are you all right?" she asks softly.

"I was better before a loudmouthed son of a bitch tried to knock off my mustache." Heaviness weighs down the jest, adding to the heaviness in Ada's own chest.

"No one should take their concerns to such extreme measures, and I'm sorry it happened," she says. "Does it worry you, though, knowing people fear your party?"

He replies with bravado, as if conducting an interview. "I'm here with notoriously private actress Ada Worthington-Fox. Tell me, miss, how do you vote? Are you seeing anyone? Why did you end your relationship with Vince Hart?"

She frowns. "That's hardly the same thing."

"If you can criticize my position, I can criticize yours. I'm listening to concerns on all sides, so I will thank you to do what you do best and keep quiet."

Her retort dies on her tongue even as his scowl softens.

"Goddamnit, I didn't mean that."

Despite her efforts to avoid controversy, she can tolerate criticism—expects it, even. In this industry, it comes from everyone. Not from Gordon. Not from the one person who has cared for her, supported her, never hurt her.

"Pay no attention to your agent. Cranky old bastard," Gordon mutters, although the quip is half-hearted. Then he sighs. "None of this will settle down as easily as I hoped, will it?"

With each passing day, Ada fears the same.

A high-pitched bark prevents her reply as Sowerby scurries into the foyer to welcome Gordon home, so he picks up the dog and coddles him. Ada's eyes return to the faded bruise.

After fleeing from Arnhem, she could have gone anywhere in the world. She chose this country, made its values her own, yet the choice might not be enough for the public to accept that she is not the anti-American Mr. Stribling accused her of being. Maybe the public needs direct reassurance. Surely they will trust her if Ada Worthington-Fox breaks her commitment to privacy and clarifies her position.

Which is exactly what she has been forbidden from doing. Mr. Hendrix wants her silence and mysteriousness, not her openness and honesty.

Whatever the public wants, however, he will give to keep his films in theaters, so perhaps circumstances will change his mind.

Tomorrow she will worry about what should or should not be done. Tonight she is Star Society hostess, and she must focus on the infiltrator who will be in their midst: Archie Stribling. Whatever his reasons for wanting to attend, she will find them out.

A knock sounds on the door. Ada answers to allow Ingrid inside and flashes a sly smile at Gordon, whose eyebrows arch while his eyes dart between the two women.

"Gordon Sharpe, meet my cousin, Ingrid van Essen—for public purposes, my temporary assistant. She's visiting from Kent. You don't mind that I invited her over a little early, do you? Ingrid, meet my dear friend and agent. And this"—she scoops up the terrier, interrupting his inspection of the newcomer—"is Mr. Sowerby, or just Sowerby for short. A Yorkshire angel like his namesake."

"By God, there's two of you." Gordon offers Ingrid a hand. "My dear, have you considered being in show business?"

"I'm afraid there's little I would despise more," she replies with a faint smile. "No hard feelings, I hope."

"Not unless you change your mind someday and I find out someone else represents you."

After kissing Ingrid's hand, Gordon excuses himself to change and takes Sowerby with him, then Ingrid hands Ada a small wrapped parcel.

"For you," she announces. "A little hostess gift."

After untying the royal-blue ribbon and tearing off the elegant gold wrapping, Ada opens the box. Inside is a porcelain figurine—a robin redbreast with bright black eyes, its head tilted curiously to one side.

"Like the one in your book, *The Secret Garden*. No, I haven't read it," Ingrid adds, since it's the question Ada always asked her when they were girls. "I never forgot the way you talked about it, though. Ever since we parted, robins have reminded me of you." Her voice dies, likely lost in the memory of that time, before regaining its strength. "When I was out shopping the other day, I saw this one and had to find it a nice home."

The little bird that was so dear to irritable, lonely, unloved Mary Lennox, then to Ada, now to Ingrid. Ada blinks back sudden emotion as she kisses her sister's cheek.

"It's lovely, Inge. And I know just where to put it."

Ada leads her through the house, past hired staff preparing for tonight's event, and into the library, where she places the figurine on a bookshelf near the mantel. They step back to evaluate it, then Ingrid nods.

"He looks quite content there." Her eyes drift upward, admiring the shelves. "You live here, then? With your agent?"

"You've nothing to fear. Gordon is entirely professional and perfectly harmless, and one of the kindest people I've ever known."

Never mind that Ada is not quite Gordon's type. She refrains from saying as much, though, even to her sister. Some secrets are not hers to share.

Ada much prefers Gordon's company to boardinghouses with their lack of privacy and countless pairs of prying eyes, so she was not entirely devastated when she was late paying rent—again—and the landlady tossed her out. Gordon offered her a spare bedroom, so she accepted, then she stayed, heedless of rumors that might circulate about an actress living with her agent. This home is a quiet, secluded sanctuary ideal for a notably private woman, and anyone who knows her or Gordon knows the arrangement is innocent.

Ingrid circles the room, then casts an expectant look over her shoulder. "This is when you're supposed to offer me a tour." She purses her lips in feigned disapproval. "Shirking your duties, Star Society hostess?"

"Hostess with the power to throw out guests who criticize her," Ada warns, to which Ingrid gives an innocent smile, her eyes bright with eagerness and curiosity, before steering Ada from the room.

Chuckling, Ada relents. She really should be focusing on event preparations, but for Ingrid, she can make time for a tour.

* * *

When the party has started and Ada finds Archie Stribling near the pool, he's with a small group of guests. Among them is Mr. Sternberg. Maybe that's why Mr. Stribling is here, to confront everyone about their political leanings or to threaten their reputations like he did with Ada. The champagne turns bitter on her tongue as she hurries to intervene.

"Might I steal this gentleman?" she asks, then she pulls Mr. Stribling into a dance and offers her most flattering, threatening smile. "Care to tell me what you're really doing here?"

"Can't a fellow enjoy himself without ill intentions?" They sway in time to the music, keeping up appearances for any onlookers. "All I'm doing is satisfying my curiosity."

"Is that supposed to make me feel better?" While he spins her under his arm, she catches his faint chuckle before he pulls her close again. Then she grabs the hand that strays too low and places it higher on her back, arching her brow in warning. "This wouldn't have anything to do with what you mentioned at Mr. Sternberg's party, would it?"

Although her tone is light, her heart races. If he threatens her to force an answer about her political leanings, she will have to give it regardless of Mr. Hendrix's instructions or Ingrid's warnings about placing such information in a stranger's hands.

"Do you mean am I going to ask you or your guests about past jobs or personal opinions?" He draws her close, bringing his lips to her ear. "Don't worry about me, Miss Worthington-Fox. You upheld your end of the bargain, so I'll uphold mine."

She's not certain if she should believe him, but it's a possibility she never considered. That's all this was, then: a bluff. At Mr. Sternberg's party, he proved his ability to gather information so she would believe him when he threatened to do the same outside the Biltmore, all to coerce his way into a Star Society invitation. A lot of bravado for nothing. All of which sours her opinion of him further while providing slight peace of mind.

Her career is safe from Mr. Stribling, as are Gordon's and Ingrid's. His threats were fabricated. As for the other threats sweeping through her industry, those might not be. But, for now, her guests are safe, so she can relax and enjoy her own party.

Ada is sipping her third glass of champagne when she notices Vince Hart and nearly chokes. He stands across the pool, wearing dark trousers and a short-sleeved white button-down, accepting a drink from Beverly Tolbert. No one gets past security without an invitation, so how did he get here?

When Beverly wanders away, Ada catches up to her and threads their arms, leading her on a leisurely stroll toward the back garden.

"Did you invite Vince?" she asks, keeping her voice low.

"Why wouldn't I? Now that you're costars and all. I assumed you accidentally left him off the guest list, so I printed an invitation for him."

Leaving Vince out had been quite intentional. Beverly never strayed from the preapproved list of names, so when she returned the completed invitations, Ada never bothered to check them prior to sending them out. If she had, she would have noticed the extra invitation and promptly extracted it. Being Vince's costar is one matter. Welcoming him back into her circle of friends is entirely another.

When Ada stays quiet, Beverly frowns. "Didn't you tell me all is well between you?"

"It is—that is, we harbor no ill will toward one another. Working together should be about our film, not our past, so I don't want to give people any ideas, that's all."

Not that Ada is hoping to rekindle anything with Vince, of course, but naturally everyone will be suspicious when they start filming. No need to contribute to speculation by spending time together outside the workplace.

Beverly laughs. "Darling, *everyone* will be talking about your past. Might as well accept it."

With that, she slips from Ada's grasp and hurries toward the waiter carrying a silver tray of finger sandwiches. Ada walks through the back garden with its abundance of roses and citrus trees until she reaches the tennis court, where she breathes the fresh night air. She should find

Ingrid. She meant to keep close to ensure she was enjoying herself. One conversation with a guest led to another, and before she knew it, she lost her sister. Tonight is for spending time together. Tomorrow will be for worrying about work and past flames.

"Care for one?"

No matter how much time passes, she will always recognize that voice, and it will always send an unbidden spark of energy through her. Vince had the same idea as she, apparently. He crosses the tennis court, offering her a pack of cigarettes. She accepts one and allows him to light it, then inhales deeply.

A sliver of moonlight peers through the dark sky overhead. When Vince's cigarette flares orange, she glances at him. He looks into the distance, his free hand tucked into his pocket.

Once he would have wrapped his arm around her waist. Once he would have tucked his own cigarette between her lips, trading puffs between kisses. Once he would have looked only at her, rather than anywhere except her.

Though there is no ill will between them, perhaps it would be easier if there were. Then they would know to hate each other, ignore each other, resent each other. Instead it's as if neither one knows how to feel.

"This has always been a quiet place to get away, hasn't it?" she asks.

After their first meeting at Ciro's, then a night at the Cocoanut Grove nightclub, their next night together had been at one of her first Star Society parties. Ada slipped away from the noise as she sometimes did and found that Vince had done the same, both ending up at the tennis court.

"You'll sell a script someday," she said that night. "Many scripts."

He chuckled. "How would you know when you've never read anything I've written?"

"The same way you know my face will be in the papers: because neither of us will accept anything less." As the faint, distant music slowed, she stepped to the middle of the court and reached for him. "Dance with me?"

Vince pulled her close, one hand against the small of her back, the other in hers, his grip warm and assured. He was quiet, the way he was when, Ada was learning, he was absorbing every sensation and stringing them into words, the same way she transformed hers into music and movement.

"The next scene in your script, the one in which I am your muse? Our captivating British heroine meets a charming, handsome American. He fascinates her, and he never leaves her wondering who he is. What he wants. As for what she wants, well, I should think the audience has little doubt." She studied the curve of his lips, then met his eyes, bright as the moonlight, withholding nothing from her. Her heartbeat steadily climbed as he traced her jaw, lifted her chin, drew forth her breathless question. "And then?"

"And then . . ." Vince pressed his mouth to hers, eager yet lingering, intentional yet unrestrained, awakening parts of her no one else had found before. Then he spoke against her lips. "End scene."

Just the ending she wanted—wrapped in his arms, his lips against hers, swaying to the music. An ending that, she felt certain, was the start of a beginning.

"Some party."

Ada blinks while Vince gestures over his shoulder, the music and chatter muffled by the distance. They are not in each other's arms now, as they were then. They stand by the net, smoking, uncertain how much distance between them is too much or too little.

She takes a drag of her cigarette to fill the silence. "Have you done any writing lately?"

"A little."

God, she needs a much stronger drink. Should she attempt conversation? Find an excuse to leave? Wait for him to go? She can't determine how this encounter should proceed any more than she can decipher his feelings about it. Even though their feelings were once so profoundly clear about one thing: each other.

Two dancers once perfectly in time, now out of step; a script once neatly written, now crossed-out scenes on pages tossed aside.

Vince taps ashes from his cigarette. He stares beyond the court toward the distant hills. Not at her. If they intend to work together, they've got to do something about their inability to look at each other.

"When you signed on to the film, did you know I was rumored to be involved?" she asks quietly.

"When a director like Abe Sternberg calls because he wants you for his upcoming project, you take it."

True enough, despite not answering her question. She waits. He offers nothing further. If this is their last opportunity to speak before the work begins, she can't lose it.

The lively faraway music slows to a ballad.

"There will be talk and rumors," Ada says quietly, resolutely. "You know that as well as I do. And I don't give a damn about what anyone says or thinks or expects from me because this job means more to me than anything I've ever done."

She takes a drag to calm her pounding heart until Vince looks at her, his eyes dark in the evening blackness. Vince, who should be impossible. Every feature and muscle and bone perfectly placed, eyes that betray glimpses of the most fascinating mind even as they maintain careful reservation. No man should be permitted to look like that. To look at *her* like that. To make her recall the way flutters once rippled across her stomach when they moved as one across this court.

"My focus is the work, Vince. Only the work."

"As is mine. I sure as hell don't want to be the actor who disappoints Mr. Sternberg. So as long as we're in agreement . . ." He finishes his cigarette and extinguishes the embers. "See you on set."

As Vince returns to the party, Ada finishes her own cigarette while the tension in her chest lessens. Thank God the air is somewhat clearer.

Now to find poor Ingrid, who will be certain to gripe about being left alone among countless members of the entertainment industry. For that conversation, Ada will need more champagne.

CHAPTER 15

Hollywood Hills, 7 September 1946

INGRID

Everywhere Ingrid looks, someone is eating, drinking, laughing, dancing, swimming, even kissing. One couple is in the pool, clothes and all, lips pressed together amid a smattering of cheers.

Too many drinks, by far.

For the best, really. With everyone so distracted, no one is paying attention to Ingrid, and she lost Ada a while ago. Thanks to the house tour she requested, she knows exactly where to go.

Inside, the bedrooms are quiet. She slips into Gordon's room first, then Ada's, neither of which contains anything useful for her investigation, so she proceeds into Ada's office. Sowerby is napping on the chaise longue, although he rouses to greet Ingrid. She scratches his chin affectionately. If anyone finds her, she can say she came to pay the little dog a visit. After Sowerby curls up on the chaise again, Ingrid approaches Ada's desk.

From her handbag, she produces a pack of cigarettes—which instead contains a Whittaker Micro 16, a new style of subminiature camera she picked up from a shop after Ada invited her to this event. All night, it's been easy to discreetly photograph the partygoers, since she fashioned holes into the cigarette packet so the camera can remain tucked inside, undetected. Now that she's alone, she extracts it from the packet, replaces the used film with a fresh cartridge, and photographs the room, then searches the desk. Nothing there to prove or disprove Communist leanings for either Ada or her Star Society, which is a relief, yet also frustrating. Ada said she is not a Communist, so of course Ingrid believes her, but Crenshaw and Stieber will need more proof than her sister's word.

After a few more photographs of the desk materials, she moves on to Gordon's office. Film and theater posters and pieces of art decorate the walls. Once she locates client files, she photographs each one, lingering on Ada's—again, nothing to prove or disprove anything—then returns the items and notices a day planner. She flips through the entries until one catches her eye: CPUSA. Communist Party of the United States of America.

Swallowing hard, she takes a picture of the entry, which includes a time for the meeting. A party meeting. If Ada's agent is a confirmed Communist, it will only reinforce Crenshaw and Stieber's fears about Ada surrounding herself with Communist influences. Her director and her agent are Communists; therefore Ada herself must share their views and assist them with her front organization, they will assume. Unless Ingrid can prove otherwise before her allotted eight weeks are up.

Ingrid closes the planner, then eases open a desk drawer and is sifting through it when something seizes her arm—a grip, a tight one, and she gasps, tensing while a man's accusatory growl finds her ear.

"What the hell do you think you're doing?"

Even as her frantic mind seeks an explanation, she knows that voice. Panic gives way to irritation, and she drives her elbow into the man's ribs.

"Let go of me."

"God, that was fun." Chuckling, Archie releases her and jerks his head toward the faint music and laughter beyond the slightly open door. "Hell of an event, isn't it?"

How did he secure an invitation? Already, she feels it—the verge of unrestraint, that place she sometimes has no more control over now than she did as a hotheaded girl, and she glares. "I told you to stay away from Ada."

"Relax, I'm here for Sternberg, not her. Since his views are confirmed, I need to find out how involved he is with the party and who his associates might be, so I needed her to get me in tonight." Archie studies Ingrid. "You know, you two favor a bit."

"And you resemble a much less appealing Clark Gable, but you don't hear me carrying on about it." To her chagrin, he brightens—she should have chosen someone less attractive than Clark Gable. It's true, though, so hopefully he will accept a resemblance between her and Ada and spare her from having to explain further.

Archie nods to the drawer he caught her searching. "Document evidence if you find any. And if you haven't planted listening devices—"

"I know how to do my job." Then, drawing a breath, she puts away the tiny camera and speaks more evenly. "I'm doing everything that needs to be done, and I'm taking my work seriously."

"I never said you weren't. I'm not the enemy, remember? Now find out if this is a Communist front, or Crenshaw and Stieber will have your ass."

Archie doffs his hat in farewell and slips out. Maybe he's here for Sternberg, but having him this close to Ada leaves Ingrid feeling as she did moments ago when he startled her, tense and afraid something is about to go terribly wrong.

After settling her nerves, she casts Archie from her mind. She has been gone too long, and maybe no one has noticed, but if they have, she needs to mingle before she arouses suspicion. Various conversations meld together as she rejoins the guests, then a voice reaches her ears—Gordon's, she surmises. She finds him in the living room with a few men and women, all holding cigars, cigarettes, and drinks.

"I'm telling you, it will get worse. I didn't think so before, but now I do," Gordon is insisting. "Those in the entertainment industry are falling under primary suspicion. Everyone was talking about it at my last meeting."

A Communist Party meeting, most likely. Thick clouds of smoke fill her lungs while Ingrid takes another discreet photo, then steps closer.

"Mind if I join you? I can't seem to find Ada."

"That girl is impossible to keep up with at these events." Gordon pats the seat cushion beside his. "Are you enjoying your visit?"

"Well, Los Angeles is rather different from Kent." The remark secures a laugh from the group, which is almost as pleasing as having remembered the story Ada developed. Ingrid accepts a cigarette from the woman beside her and looks at the surrounding faces. "I must say, I feel like I'm the only one not in show business. Does anyone here do anything else?"

"Of course. You'll find waitresses, secretaries, bartenders, salespeople . . . It's merely a coincidence that every single one is trying to make it in show business at the same time," the woman with the cigarettes says, followed by more laughter. She seems a few years older than Ingrid, with short blond hair styled in soft, playful curls.

"Mark my words, Bev, you won't be serving at Lucey's much longer. Not after your television pilot airs," Gordon says before taking a puff of his cigar and looking to Ingrid. "Show business is all about who you know, what you want, and how far you're willing to go to get it."

"Sounds awfully similar to politics." Ingrid draws on the cigarette and releases a slow stream of smoke. Surely someone will take the bait, will direct the conversation back to whatever they were talking about when she found them.

"Darling, so sorry for wandering off! Have you been enjoying yourself?"

At the sound of Ada's cry, Ingrid bites her cheek. Just when she was nearly getting somewhere. She suppresses the desire to shoo her sister away as Ada joins them.

"Care to properly introduce me to these friends of yours?" Ingrid asks.

"Right, of course, that was my fault," Gordon says, tapping a finger against his temple. "Allow me. Everyone, this is Ada's cousin, Ingrid."

"Van Essen. Not Bergman, lest you confuse us," she adds, to which those in the circle laugh.

Gordon introduces everyone else while Ingrid commits the names to memory. If her suspicions are correct, at least a few will likely be registered members of the Communist Party of America.

Crenshaw will certainly be pleased, yet this is not proof of the entire group being a front. Only of at least one Communist, Gordon, discussing his party with others who may or may not be members. She lets Ada lead her away even as her heart races. Is Ada aware that such conversations occur at her events? She will certainly be irritated if Ingrid questions her now. Or worse, she'll ask why Ingrid is so interested in what sorts of discussions are taking place here.

Or perhaps not. Perhaps she is just drunk enough to not be bothered.

"Leidje?" Ingrid prompts, although she keeps her voice down. Ada immediately shushes her despite a giggle and a glance to make sure no one overheard. Indeed, just drunk enough. "Why did you start throwing these parties?"

"For fun, of course."

"Nothing to do with politics?"

Ada wrinkles her nose. "Invite my friends over to discuss politics? Sounds dreadful—I'm not you. Only teasing, only teasing." She threads her arm through Ingrid's. "You know I adore you, silly interests and all."

As they walk, Ingrid bumps her hip against Ada's in playful admonition, though her steps remain weighted with concern. According to Ada, the Star Society is not intended to be a front organization, but considering her sister's current state, Ingrid can't accept anything with complete certainty. When Ingrid convinces her to make her statement, she will advise her to clarify the purpose of her gatherings so these parties can be just that.

"Paul, tell Gordon to let you put up that privacy gate you mentioned," Ada calls out as she drags Ingrid toward a distinguished, middle-aged Black gentleman. "Between us, we can convince him to protect all your hard work, can't we?"

This man must have built the house, then. He can't be who Ingrid thinks he is—except of course he can, because nearly everyone here is someone she never expected to meet.

"Paul Revere Williams, architect to the stars?" she clarifies. He grins.

"The very one." He shakes her hand before turning to Ada. "We'll get the gate up one of these days. Maybe after you hire me to build you the biggest, most extravagant mansion in Hollywood Hills."

"Sooner rather than later, darling." Ada winks, then kisses his cheek and pulls Ingrid along.

Ingrid looks back as Mr. Williams greets a remarkably attractive young man—Vince Hart, the renowned actor, Ada's former beau.

"My, don't you have famous friends?"

"Paul is lovely, isn't he? You're not going back to your hotel tonight," Ada announces. "We'll have fun, and I'll give you all the industry gossip: who has thrilling, unannounced roles, who plans to leave her husband, who's having affairs with whom, all of it. You'll drink as much as you want, and you'll stay here with me."

As they step outdoors, Ingrid pushes aside the weight in her chest. Enough work for tonight. She's in a stunning mansion attending a ridiculously lavish party among Hollywood's elite, for God's sake. Might as well enjoy it.

* * *

Morning brings the splitting headache Ingrid hoped to avoid. Somehow conceding to a single refill of champagne led to another, then another, until she lost count. Ada can be quite persuasive.

Gordon left early to meet a friend for breakfast, so Ada makes omelets and buttered toast for two, then sits at the breakfast table across from Ingrid.

"Come now, don't be cross," she says as Ingrid glares at her from over her water glass. "You had fun, and you needed it."

She did, admittedly. Once the work was finished, it was nice to forget for one night. To not think so much about missing Lars or telling her sister half-truths. The headache, however, is far from nice.

"Well, now I can count myself among those worthy of attending a Star Society gathering."

"And I fully expect to see you at the next one." Ada smears a generous portion of cherry jam across her toast.

Ingrid gingerly takes a bite of her omelet, testing the strength of her stomach after last night. "I'll be there, although I'll need to go home eventually. And if I'm going to help you locate Gregor Dietrich, it will be much easier to do that from home than to discuss it with my contacts over the telephone."

At the mention of Dietrich, Ada clenches her jaw while her grip on her knife tightens, prompting Ingrid to set her own utensil down.

"You promised to tell me more. I understand if it's difficult, but if I'm going to help, I've got to know."

She waits while Ada sips her coffee and seems to wrestle with her decision. At last she clears her throat.

"The day after you and Lars left, Mother invited company for dinner."

"Dietrich?" When Ada nods, Ingrid leans closer. "Mother entertained the invaders?"

Ingrid shouldn't be surprised—and, in a way, she isn't. But the abject horror coursing through her veins leaves her unable to say more.

"Do you remember the work we started with Madame Bellamy, my ballet mistress at the Muziekschool? We continued performing to raise money for the resistance, and since I was around Dietrich and his men so often, I communicated any information I overheard, names of those who attended Mother's dinners, whatever might help."

A strange mixture of warmth and cold spreads over Ingrid—pride for her sister yet pity for everything she must have endured. Fortunately, Ada has always been able to hold her tongue better than Ingrid. Ingrid never would have made it through one of those dinners without telling Mother's guests exactly what she thought of their politics. She places a hand over her sister's, but Ada rises from her chair.

"I dined with them, spoke with them, played the piano for them, over and over and over, all while feigning indifference to the war and everything they were doing to our people and our country." When her voice wavers, Ada presses her fingertips to her eyes, resisting tears. Ingrid stands, wanting to pull her close, to reassure her. More than anything, she wants to change everything about that night when she embraced her sister for the last time.

She and her new husband spent the war in America, happy and safe. Her sister lived through hell.

"Dietrich was the SS and Police Leader in Arnhem," Ada continues, a distant look in her eyes. "He lived with us."

"Lived with you? Meaning . . . ?"

"Meaning our mother was sleeping with him." Ada sinks back into her chair. "I know what I saw, what she did—it was wrong, of course it was wrong, but what if Mother was living a lie just as I was? When the war started in 1939, that's what changed her mind about fascism in the first place, remember? She told us herself."

Ingrid remembers the renouncement well. At the time, it had

brought her slight relief, even though she had spent too long witnessing her mother's support of fascist ideology to easily forget, to move forward, to forgive. Ada, on the other hand, had stepped into this new chapter of Mother's reformed ways, eager and willing to pretend the old ways could stay behind them. And although Mother claimed to have lost interest in politics, Ingrid had waited for something more, solid proof beyond Mother's word, which was enough for Ada but not for Ingrid.

"She told me to trust her," Ada says almost desperately, as if wanting so fiercely to believe it. "Before introducing me to Dietrich. To trust her, to not ask questions, and that she loved us—you too, even though you weren't there. What if she thought it was the only way to protect me? Maybe she had no choice, or thought she had no choice . . . and I still hated her for it, hated *him*. She brought that man into our home, a man whose job was to kill and torture . . ." She props her elbows on the table and cradles her head as a single sob escapes. Ingrid stays where she is, unable to move.

If Dietrich was involved with the Gestapo and police forces, and if Mother was his mistress, Ada must be hunting him to hold him accountable for every war crime she witnessed.

"I'm so sorry. I'm so, so sorry, Leidje."

Such was the life Ada had known. For years. Ingrid had abandoned her sister to a fate neither of them could have imagined. An apology is so meaningless, so trite, so powerless. It's not enough. Nothing ever will be.

After the invasion brought the Reichsparteitag photograph back to their foyer in Arnhem, Ingrid had believed this feeling now stirring inside her would never be rekindled. The truth is often just what it looks like. Even if it tries to hide. Even if cause for speculation remains. Until the truth is professed with utmost clarity, it can't be entirely known.

Still, for the first time in so long, Ingrid allows the possibility to linger.

She might be wrong about their mother's ability to change, despite the appearances she kept up during the war. Perhaps Ingrid has spent these last years judging Constance too harshly. Sometimes a mother faces a choice that isn't a choice at all.

When she calms, Ada stands. "Come with me."

She leads Ingrid into the library. There she removes the little robin figurine from the shelf and pulls a stack of books aside. Tucked behind them is a tattered copy of *The Secret Garden*, the one Ingrid remembers Ada reading countless times throughout their childhood. The distant look overcomes her again. As if she's back in Arnhem, reliving that time.

After a moment, she opens the book. "As the years went on, everything worsened. Starvation, the treatment of the Jews, the crushing of the resistance. The Gestapo was relentless. Dietrich kept his work in Papa's study, which was always locked." She pauses until Ingrid nods her encouragement. "I took some of his files."

The weight in Ingrid's chest lifts. Dear, brilliant Leidje. This is just what Ingrid needs. Without files, there's little she can do even if they locate Dietrich, unless the FBI uncovers evidence of his crimes. With files, she's much closer to having a legitimate case.

From inside the book, Ada pulls out a collection of photos, negatives, and folded papers and hands them to Ingrid.

"The pictures are from Papa's study, which Dietrich decorated with Nazi propaganda and a plaque with his coat of arms. His family crest includes a . . . a skeleton key." Ada's voice tightens. Before Ingrid can determine why, she nods to the documents. "I also photographed those same records. Lists of Jewish names in Mother's handwriting, proving her involvement, even if under duress. Jewish deportations and massacres. Police files of prisoners, most of them resistance. Dietrich's name is all over those pages, signing orders. And if he survived, if I'm right about him being here and looking for me, I feel certain these crimes are not known to the public. Otherwise I can't understand why he would be allowed in America."

"Well done," Ingrid says, returning the items. "We can use these once we find him."

"And?" Ada prompts, because of course she knows there's something Ingrid isn't saying.

"And . . ." she continues slowly, "it might be enough. Or it might not." When Ada opens her mouth, Ingrid holds up a hand. "The FBI has brought former Nazis into service—blackmail, usually. Work for America against Communism and we'll ignore your war crimes; don't and go to prison."

"You can't be serious."

"You hear things in DC." Ingrid's own handler is one of those former Nazis brought into service, although she refrains from saying so. "My point is, if Dietrich is in America, there is a chance he entered the country under similar terms, or could use those terms to negotiate a deal, assuming your evidence exposes crimes he didn't disclose. Even if we find him, I don't want you to get your hopes up."

"Will it help if I testify? If that's what it takes to convict him, I'll do it."

Ingrid fights an exasperated breath. Difficult to hear or not, her sister must be fully aware of what they're facing. "That's what I'm trying to tell you. Even with evidence and a testimony, we might not win a case. Or if the government sees an opportunity with Dietrich and wants him badly enough, they might make a deal with him."

Ada shakes her head, pacing as the realization overtakes her. "No. No, they can't make a deal! He doesn't deserve a deal."

"None of them do, but it's a government decision, not ours. He might even deflect responsibility by arguing that he was acting under a superior's orders, so unless we have indisputable proof of—"

"I am the proof."

Suddenly Ada begins undressing. First her blouse, then her brassiere, both coming off before Ingrid can ask why in God's name she's stripping off her clothes. Her lower body remains covered, though, then she indicates her bare right breast and a mark above her nipple.

There Ingrid notices a scar—except it's no ordinary scar. It's a horizontal image, perhaps five centimeters across. Distinct slashes form an intricate bow featuring multiple interlocking circles, a barrel, a double-notched bit—not the result of a heated iron, but of a blade. Someone carved this image, cut after meticulous cut, to form a skeleton key.

A symbol that is part of Dietrich's family crest.

Ingrid presses a hand to her own chest, aching as if it bears a twin mark. Ada has been branded.

CHAPTER 16

Arnhem, 1942

ALEIDA

After two years in this house with Dietrich, Aleida could bear no more. It had only been a few days since Madame Bellamy's disappearance, yet each relentlessly plagued her with thoughts of how to escape. Where she would go, Aleida did not know. Underground, perhaps, so she could continue aiding the resistance. If surviving underground proved impossible, or if Dietrich hunted for her, she would flee to protect the work. It would continue with or without her, and she would instate someone else to lead the Muziekschool's group.

Except she could not abandon Mother, not if she, too, felt trapped. She had to convince Mother to join her—but if she tried, and if Mother proved loyal to Dietrich, they would not let Aleida leave. Not when she knew too much.

Perhaps a solution regarding what to do would come to her this morning during dance class. The new ballet mistress, appointed by Dietrich, was supposed to arrive today, so Aleida had already warned her resistance group that their blackout performances might be impossible until they found a way to continue without getting caught.

When she reached the Muziekschool, two Ordnungspolizei stepped from their vehicle and approached.

"Halt, Aleida de Vos."

The harsh command immediately set her heart thudding, although over these last years of occupation, she had been stopped for various inconsequential reasons. Surely this would be no different. If these officers already knew who she was, maybe they had been to one of Mother's gatherings.

She handed them her papers, ones stating her real name. Unlike most resistance members, she didn't carry false documents, not when so many SS men and Orpo officers attended Mother's events and might recognize her. As she waited, she kept her manner light, polite.

"May I ask what this is about? If there's something I—" She fell abruptly silent when one officer caught her chin in a viselike grip.

He said nothing, yet the look in his eyes indicated another word would make him raise a hand. She drew a shallow breath, flinched when the second officer caught her arm, yet she didn't move, couldn't move.

Not until she felt the round, solid mouth of what could have only been a pistol against her back—enough pressure to make her gasp and force her to take a stumbling step forward, then another, closer and closer to the waiting car.

* * *

When Aleida shifted positions to give the woman beside her more space, it only brought her closer to another woman shoved into their small cell. She had been imprisoned in the Oranjehotel, as it had been nicknamed by those who had the misfortune of being sent there, for the past—two days? She didn't know, nor did it matter.

Time did not exist in this place. Only moments.

In this moment, she was in her cell. In the next, she might be in an interrogation room.

Aleida drew a shallow breath; any deeper and the smell of blood from the woman beside her would be too overwhelming.

More of a girl than a woman, really. Sixteen, maybe. She lay still. One eye was swollen shut; the other stared at nothing. Aleida had no water to offer her, nor any to quench her own parched throat. Instead she tore a fragment of her skirt, suddenly grateful she had not had time to change into dance clothes prior to her arrest.

Where to begin? The blood covering the girl was mostly dried black, so Aleida pressed the cloth to a seeping forehead wound.

At her touch, the girl flinched, then her shoulders heaved as a breath passed over her dry, cracked lips.

A pathetic offering, this scrap of fabric for a girl who had been taken from their cell and returned almost unrecognizable. Not for the first time, Aleida cursed her own helplessness. Her eyes fell to a bloodstain on the girl's clothing, low on her right breast. Each of her cellmates had returned in various states betraying the severity of her interrogation, yet all bore a similar bloodstain. Aleida could not bring herself to consider what might have caused it.

The next few moments were no different from what she had come to expect. Booted footsteps nearing. The creaking cell door. A guard barking the next woman's name.

"On your feet, Aleida de Vos."

Her own name.

Performing onstage was a singular experience binding movement and emotion into one. Aleida had never found that rush of intensity or focus or feeling anywhere else until now. Hearing her name, feeling the strong hands dragging her from the cell, staggering down the hall, smelling blood and antiseptic in a cold interrogation room. Each linked her mind and body not through the exuberant passion of performance but through sharp, gripping terror.

The guards shoved her into a chair across from Polizeiführer Gregor Dietrich.

Of course he knew she was here. The clang of metal accompanied one guard who handcuffed her wrists to the chair. More than ever, she needed to play her role, to settle this matter, to protect the work. So she scowled as if this were all an inconvenient misunderstanding.

"Why am I here, Herr Polizeiführer? Could this matter not have been resolved at home?"

No reaction. She glanced at the two guards, who stood at attention behind Dietrich. Three of them, one of her. She could not do this, could not withstand what those girls in her cell had endured if the same awaited her—except she had to find the strength somehow. After all these months of resisting in silence, she would not let Dietrich force her to betray anyone.

"Constance told me about your twin," he began. "You profess no interest in the war effort. Yet you are the sister of a staunch anti-fascist, and you continued your dance training under a Jew's guidance."

"My mother never forbade it. I've wanted to dance ever since I was a girl, so why should the war change anything?"

"After you learned of my intention to replace her at the Muziek-school, my men found her and her husband gone and the house in disarray."

That would have been the morning after Aleida warned them to escape. It would have looked as if someone had pillaged the home while attacking, kidnapping, even murdering the Jewish couple who lived there. Not as if someone had advised them to flee.

What a brilliant woman Madame Bellamy was.

Except Dietrich was a cunning man. He might see through the lie.

"One must wonder if the dance instructor was attacked. Or if the note you had around your hairpin was a message; therefore you are both involved in subversive behavior. In which case she might have escaped."

Understanding settled over Aleida, cold and aching. It had been too much to believe he would dismiss the note as nothing, would be too drunk to act on his observations from dinner. He suspected Aleida had helped Madame Bellamy to flee, that they had been involved in the resistance together.

Though her heart thudded more with every second, she combated the rise in her voice. "Am I being accused of breaking the law, Herr Polizeiführer? I don't know anything about Madame Bellamy or subversive behavior, and Mother will be worried, so I'd like to go home."

Dietrich chuckled—a chilling, callous sound. "One of Constance's daughters ran away. Why not the other? Perhaps I found you unharmed. Or I found you left for dead. Or I did not find you at all."

The perfect excuse: Ingrid. If Aleida did not return, all Dietrich had to say was that she must have run off like her sister. Even if she *did* return, it was an explanation for her absence: She had run away, perhaps gotten attacked by thieves or partisans, thus resulting in whatever injuries he intended to inflict upon her now if she did not cooperate.

Would Mother believe him? Or if Aleida told her the truth, would Mother believe her? With profound, sudden sorrow, she realized she did not know the answer. But she would give him nothing—not her knowledge, not her fear, not a single word or tear or plea.

A moment of terrible silence, then Dietrich rose and left the room. The guards moved Aleida's chair back and the table aside while her wary gaze shifted between them and the door. Would they torture her before Dietrich returned? Or had he gone to fetch his instrument of choice so he could do it himself? She did not have long to wonder. The door swung open again, bringing Dietrich's voice as he ordered someone else into the room—another prisoner. A bruised, bloodied, middle-aged woman.

When a cry burst from Aleida's chest, the woman's rich brown eyes met hers, widening with immediate recognition before she whirled to face Dietrich.

"Let her go—she's just a girl!" Then, although her hands were cuffed behind her back, Madame Bellamy dropped to her knees beside Aleida's chair, meeting her at eye level. "Protect the work and yourself," she said, her voice low and strong despite swollen cheeks and bloodied lips. "However you must."

How was Aleida supposed to do either when she had already failed at both? She had led Dietrich to uncover a resistance message, had told Madame Bellamy to flee, and they both had been captured. This was entirely her fault.

She had no time to reply before one guard dragged Madame Bellamy away. Once the two women were facing each other, Dietrich forced the ballet mistress to her knees, then he drew his pistol and leveled it at Aleida.

She was to be the instrument of torture. The bile raging in her stomach refused to settle while Madame Bellamy stared in disbelief before Dietrich touched the cold metal to Aleida's temple. The elder woman drew a sharp breath while Aleida's cuffs bit into her skin. He would do it, would shoot her, then he would lie to Mother about everything.

"Did Aleida advise you to flee?"

Madame Bellamy's jaw tightened, her eyes on the pistol. "Yes."

He shifted his aim to her, and Aleida's stomach jolted again. He was using them both.

"Aleida, are you part of this woman's resistance organization?"

Her mind was too clouded with terror to answer, so she only managed a sob. "It's all my fault. I'm so sorry . . ."

For letting a message be discovered. For sending Madame Bellamy into the Gestapo's hands. For whatever Dietrich forced her to confess, even if she avoided betraying their colleagues, limited the information to matters that affected only her and Madame Bellamy because it was too late for them anyway. He would torture them, kill them, and nothing she said would prevent him.

Dietrich seemed to take the apology as confirmation. He gripped Aleida's chin, lifting it until she met his gaze, her breath shuddering so much she could hardly hear.

"I will let you live. In return, you are mine. You will continue working with the resistance. And you will report all members, contacts, and activities to me."

She blinked past her tears. He was turning her role entirely on its head—from reporting on the fascists to reporting on the resistance. She glimpsed Madame Bellamy, whose eyes were wide with horror.

"That is my offer." Dietrich released her and aimed his weapon at the elder woman again. "Refuse and I will shoot her."

Madame Bellamy remained frozen while a wave of lightheadedness threatened to overtake Aleida. How could she agree? Reporting on resistance activities would lead to arrests, likely murders. But she could not let him shoot the woman who now had a gun against her head.

"Make your decision, or I will shoot you both."

Madame Bellamy's own fractured breaths joined Aleida's, because they both knew her choice was not a choice. If she betrayed the resistance, they lived; if she refused, Madame Bellamy died. If she did not make a choice, neither one would survive.

Aleida opened her mouth, unsure if she could force words past the tears or the urge to be sick, but when Dietrich cocked the weapon, the sobbing shriek rushed free.

"I'll do it! I'll work for you, I'll do it . . ." Then she choked on words, on tears, on her own betrayal while Dietrich lowered the pistol.

One guard uncuffed her and she sank to the floor, pummeled by gut-wrenching wails, unable to meet the tears in Madame Bellamy's gaze. Saving their lives would cost countless others, because now she had agreed to work for the Gestapo.

After Madame Bellamy was escorted out and Aleida had exhausted her supply of tears, she lay on the cold floor, shaking, until hands brought her upright to face Dietrich.

"Ours will be an auspicious partnership. But I can't allow your past mistakes to go unpunished." A chill pulsed through her body, leaving her unable to look at him yet unable to look away. Then he issued his next order. "Strip her."

Newfound energy surged through her, and she struggled until pain exploded against her stomach. The blow sent her to her knees, gasping, then fire ignited along her shoulders as one man forced her arms behind her back and pulled her upright again, then they were pulling, tearing, yanking every piece of fabric—her blouse, her skirt. Her undergarments. The sour taste in Aleida's mouth intensified. No amount of struggling or protesting would be enough.

Dietrich would let them have her. Torture her. Lie to Mother about what really happened over the last few days.

Instead of forcing her over the table, as she expected, they pressed her back to the cold cell wall, secured her wrists in thick metal cuffs on either side, closed heavy chains around her ankles. Then the guards stepped away.

The room felt too quiet, too still. Her chest heaved in shallow, chok-ing breaths while the men studied her, every part of her. She could only stare in return; nothing would release her, cover her, spare her. She was exposed, trapped, helpless. Completely and entirely alone.

Dietrich drew a thin dagger and unfastened his tunic and collar, exposing the long line across his neck. "This scar is from the Great War, when the Allied soldier who sliced my neck open didn't cut deeply enough. Some might call my survival a miracle."

She neither spoke nor struggled. All she could do was imagine the many ways he might be preparing to use that dagger.

"Do you know what I've realized?" He brushed his thumb across the skin above her nipple, prompting her whimper. "That soldier wasn't trying to kill me. He wanted me to live. To spend every day with a reminder of that moment when my life belonged to him."

His eyes were as cold and sharp as the dagger in his grip. Then Dietrich pressed the blade into her breast, slicing through her skin as effortlessly as the pain slicing through her body, drawing a piercing shriek from the depths of her being as he began to carve.

* * *

A few hours later, the men left Aleida in the interrogation room. For how long, she did not know. Only that every breath ached and smelled of blood and fear.

When the guards returned, they brought her new clothing. The sight should have been reassuring, but nothing could reassure her anymore. Once she was dressed, they led her down the halls. Where they were going, Aleida did not know, and she did not resist.

What did she have left? Ingrid had been gone for years. Madame Bellamy was in custody. No one in the resistance would be safe when Dietrich extracted names and information from Aleida. And she no longer wanted to exist within this body of hers and what it now bore.

Outside, a cold wind swept over her; she shivered but marched forward. Maybe they would go somewhere out of sight, where she would be shot down like a diseased animal. One quick bullet to put the wretched creature out of its misery.

Instead they stopped outside the gate, where a car waited. Despite the bright sunlight obscuring her vision, Aleida recognized the elegant woman who stepped out.

"Mother?" Her voice was roughened by the screams that even now echoed in her mind.

"Oh, my darling, I've been so worried. When you didn't come home from class, I went by, and one of the girls said she saw the men who came for you. Gregor hasn't been home for a few days; otherwise I would have come sooner, but I contacted every one of his colleagues until I found where they had taken you." Gently, Mother cupped Aleida's face. "I notified him and arranged for your release, so I've come to take you home."

She was free because of Mother? Aleida wanted to curse her for bringing that horrible man into their home, but everything inside her was warped and twisted and she didn't know how to untangle any of it. A sob racked her body, and she stepped into Mother's arms.

"There, there." Mother shushed her, coddled her as if she were a small child. "You've had a fright, but all is well now."

"An unfortunate misunderstanding. I've identified those responsible for the confusion, and they will be punished to the full extent of my power."

The new voice sent a chill through Aleida far harsher than the cold wind whipping around them. A misunderstanding. So that was what he was going to call it for Mother's benefit, pretending this had not been the result of his orders, had not led to interrogation or threats or torture. Simply a harmless, mistaken arrest.

"Aleida, please accept my apologies on behalf of the entire Ordnungspolizei and Gestapo," Dietrich said as he reached them. "Such carelessness will not be tolerated under my command."

Mother placed a grateful hand on his cheek while Aleida fought a fresh wave of nausea. Mother had no idea what that man had done. And when he nodded for them to get into the car, she had no alternative. So she sat between Mother and Dietrich, still and silent, while the driver took them home.

Once there, she professed a desire to bathe and rest. Then she retreated upstairs, closed the door, and vomited into her washbasin.

She heard nothing more over the sounds of her own heaving, not until she wiped her mouth and a booted footstep sounded just outside her door.

Nowhere to escape, no way to prevent whatever he might do. As Dietrich allowed himself inside, Aleida backed away until she found her bed and could back away no more.

"I'll scream. I'll tell Mother everything."

He lifted a mocking brow as he eased the door closed. Because if she fulfilled her threats, he still had Madame Bellamy in custody. He could give Mother an excuse, blame another guard for harming Aleida without his knowledge, then punish her for speaking out by retaliating against Madame Bellamy.

"Provide me with a list of resistance colleagues. If I don't have your list by morning, and if any leads are false, I will hold your dance instructor accountable." His eyes drifted over her, lingering on her breast, then he met her gaze. "This time I brought you home; next time, I will not."

Dietrich waited until she had nodded her assent, then he departed, and she heard her mother's bedroom door gently close. A list by morning. He was leaving her no time to warn anyone, to do anything except comply.

She grabbed the thin dress the guards had given her. With shaking hands, she pulled it over her head and stared at her naked body reflected in the floor-length mirror.

Untouched, save for one place. Now she knew why the girls in her cell had returned with matching bloodstains on their breasts. Because Dietrich must have interrogated them too.

She stared at the red slashes, the sharp lines forming the key from his crest.

Then she turned back to the washbasin and vomited again.

Aleida was alive. Alive with the reminder of when her life had belonged to him. She gathered the dress but lost the strength to put it on. Instead she held the garment against her chest, sank to the cold floor beside Ingrid's bed, and wept.

She needed to warn the underground resistance, to save herself from becoming an informant, to gather funds to bribe a guard into releasing Madame Bellamy tonight because they could not delay any longer. For the right price, surely a guard could be persuaded to break out a prisoner. For now, though, she could only sob.

In moments like this, her sister would calm her, reason through everything that had happened, promise her that she was safe. Now she had no one to calm her, to reason with her, to assure her that she was safe. Because she was not. Not here in this house or in Arnhem or as herself.

Being Aleida de Vos was no longer safe. She had to become someone else.

CHAPTER 17

Hollywood Hills, 8 September 1946

ADA

In the middle of Gordon's library, Ada stands half naked, exposing that dreadful mark that has violated her body for the past four years. She watches as her sister's face contorts—first with confusion, then open-mouthed shock as she presses a hand to her own chest.

Such a reaction is not unexpected yet confirms what Ada already knows: No one, not even her sister, will view her the same way after knowing her body has been desecrated at a Nazi's hand.

This was a mistake. To involve Ingrid in her past, to show her this scar, all of it.

At last Ingrid speaks unsteadily. "Dietrich did this to you?"

"To the other women in my cell too. Likely many more." Ada looks down, suddenly unable to meet Ingrid's gaze. "When Mother arranged my release, Dietrich told her it was a misunderstanding. She believed I was held, nothing more."

"Mother arranged your release?"

The surprise is apparent in Ingrid's voice, but the usual scowl at the mention of Mother is not present. Mother did try to be a decent parent at times, even if Ingrid never expected as much.

"I couldn't contradict Dietrich, so I never corrected his lie to tell her what really happened. I've never told anyone until now." The silence is crushing. Ada dresses, her eyes downcast, then she continues with a wry chuckle. "Thank God it's not somewhere obvious. Between my brassiere and makeup, it's always covered, even around my dressers on set. And I only allow them to dress or undress me up to a point."

Ingrid is quiet, absorbing the information. At last, a gentle hand finds Ada's.

"Never be ashamed of a sign of your resilience. Your survival. And I'm so sorry I wasn't there for you."

After returning from the Oranjehotel, it was all she wanted: reassurance and comfort. All these years later, she has it, despite every unwarranted fear to the contrary. She gives Ingrid's hand a grateful squeeze before releasing her. Perhaps no one else will ever know of this scar. The fact that her sister does somehow makes the weight less crushing.

"When you were together, did Vince—?"

"That is hardly your business." Such a rational question doesn't deserve the snap that comes out unbidden. Indeed, Ingrid startles in response, then Ada looks away. "We never . . . I never . . . let him."

Even now, the reminder of her greatest struggle during her time with Vince brings heat to her cheeks. Every kiss, every touch, every caress left her aching for more. Yet every time *more* became a possibility, she felt the scar as acutely as if it were being seared into her flesh again. And every time, it led to some excuse to keep him from anything further.

Perhaps that was partially why she ended things. Because he deserves someone who can love him and be loved by him in every possible way.

"Right," Ingrid says softly. "Well, with your documents and"—she falters, as if seeking a way to phrase it delicately—"and this, and potentially other women who had similar experiences, we might have enough for a case."

Ada nods, breathing a little more easily. It's a start, anyway.

"Do you need copies of the documents? Take them, if so, then return the originals once you're finished. I don't want anything submitted to the authorities until we're certain something will be done; otherwise my documents will end up in some forgotten file. Don't show them to anyone without my consent."

Ingrid agrees, so Ada excuses herself to fetch an envelope from her office, Sowerby following at her heels. This is the first time she's spoken so openly of the past to anyone. Now she can almost sense the ache in her feet after a blackout performance, feel the resistance funds as she tucks them into her pointe shoes, smell the crisp night air as she delivers the money on her way home.

She will never know if Madame Bellamy survived. The night of her release, she went underground and explained her circumstances to trusted contacts, who immediately sent a hefty bribe to a willing guard at the Oranjehotel. She waited for a few hours until she heard Madame Bellamy had been smuggled out, then she could afford to wait no longer. As for whether her former instructor survived beyond that night, she does not know. Such a weight will never grow lighter, shouldered by a strength and endurance it is her responsibility alone to find. There are worse things to live with than uncertainty.

When she reaches her office, she stops. The door is ajar. Last night she left it closed—didn't she?

"Am I going mad, Sowerby?"

The little dog cocks his head, as if pondering how to phrase his opinion tactfully.

With her heart suddenly pounding, Ada eases the door open. Nothing is amiss. The artwork is on the walls, her desk organized, her script for *Lady Bella Donna* open to the scene she rehearsed yesterday.

Then she notices something on the pages—a sealed envelope. Like the one she received at the Biltmore. She extracts the message as everything inside her grows heavy.

I know your secret.

Someone found her first at the Biltmore, then here. Someone who claims to know her secret—perhaps her true identity or what she took from Arnhem.

With the note and the envelope for Ingrid in hand, Ada returns to the library, her heart aching against a chest that tightens with every step. Unless an uninvited guest breached security to leave this note, only two people from last night were new additions to the group: Ingrid and Archie Stribling.

Her sister couldn't have done this. What cause did Ingrid have to leave menacing notes? She's never been shy about asking—or demanding—answers when she wants them. Not Ingrid. She does not make sense.

Archie Stribling, on the other hand, might.

"Do you remember the man from the announcement party who asked me about the role I declined?" she asks when she rejoins Ingrid. "He bullied his way into last night's party, and I just found this."

Ingrid takes the offered note, then reads it silently. "Might he have been a reporter? If your politics have become a topic of interest among the press, perhaps he was seeking information and got cunning with his methods. Parties are an excellent opportunity to pry unnoticed." She indicates the note. "Maybe he believes you're a Communist but has no proof, so he's trying to frighten you into an admission."

It's a possibility. But a stronger possibility has taken root in Ada's mind ever since the note from the announcement party. Mr. Stribling threatened his way into the event; of course there was a reason for his eagerness, something beyond a simple bluff.

"If someone sent him?" she asks quietly.

Surely Ada would have noticed Dietrich himself at the Biltmore event, certainly in Gordon's home. But if Dietrich is alive, he might have hired Mr. Stribling, might have sent him to both the Biltmore and Gordon's with messages meant to frighten her. To let her know he had found her. Perhaps even to steal the evidence, though clearly Mr. Stribling did not find it if he was looking for it.

Guilt presses upon her chest, shortening her breaths. Her past might have brought evil to her agent's house, just as she did to her dance teacher's in Arnhem. She can't tell Gordon about Dietrich, though, certainly not with the uneasiness present in his warm brown eyes ever since the incident at his party meeting. Ada can't have him worrying about her too.

She takes the note back from Ingrid. These are efforts to frighten her, to silence her, to control her, the same as he did in Arnhem. No more. She has protected her new life with everything she has, but if fear controls her, she will be no freer now than she was then.

"I want to make a public statement. About my views regarding the industry."

Ingrid stares at her. "You do?"

Ada nods. "Not until filming is over so Mr. Hendrix won't replace me." Her gaze falls to the note again. "A statement won't make a difference in my career, I don't suppose, because the industry controls how I'm portrayed, so there's only so much I can do to influence such matters. An offensive image can be rehabilitated, or a spotless one can be ruined, all depending on what those in power decide. If the film does well, Mr. Hendrix will want me, so he'll forgive me for going against his advice even if he's not happy with me. Or conversely, even if I obey his every whim, the film could fail, or he could decide not to sign me on to anything else. So I might as well do what I want."

Ingrid considers a moment, then she nods. "I realize this isn't a decision you've made lightly, and I'm proud of you. If you don't want to speak to anyone directly to make the arrangements, I'll do it. As your assistant," she adds with a faint smile.

"That would probably be best. If I call a reporter to arrange a statement, they won't let me off the phone until I give it." Ada chuckles, then she draws a steadying breath. "Speaking freely in Arnhem meant getting yourself or your loved ones killed, so we resisted in silence. But the war taught me I'm never as protected as I think I am. Whether I speak out or I'm silent, if someone wants to hurt me, he will. And I'm tired of letting him keep that power over me."

Ingrid's brow furrows. "What are you saying?"

"Being more open to the public will show Dietrich I'm not trying to hide from him. If he can't keep me silent, he'll come for me and the evidence I took."

"No, you can't bait that man. Let me talk to my contacts, then we can lure him into a controlled setting."

"He won't be predictable enough for something like that. We have the evidence, don't we? That's our case. All we need is him." She places a reassuring hand over Ingrid's. "If these messages are from him, he already knows where I am, doesn't he? He could confront me at any time. The only reason he hasn't yet is because it's more fun for him to taunt me first."

"Right, antagonize the man who tortured countless women and did God knows what else. Brilliant idea," Ingrid retorts sarcastically, turning aside as she begins to pace.

"Isn't the advantage of being a public figure to make a difference with my influence, my position, my celebrity? If I expose him as a war criminal, he can't disappear. Even if nothing comes of it, or if the government offers him a deal, I'll have shown the public and my fans who I really am, and who he is. That will be stronger than any statement."

Ingrid's jaw clenches, but she seems to realize Ada is right. "Hattie works for the FBI. I'll see if she can find any information about him. And if there's anything else I should know that might help, please tell me."

Ada nods, then she tucks the evidence into the envelope and offers it to Ingrid—her hands steady, unlike the night when she held these documents for the first time.

Following her arrest, Dietrich had made one critical mistake: He left her alive. That night, after her release, she lay awake, listening until long after the sounds of his and Mother's lovemaking grew quiet. Then she rose, changed into a dress, and slipped into their bedroom.

There, they slept soundly, their clothes on the floor. He lay on his back, his head toward Aleida. Any moment now he would open his eyes, catch her, finish what he started in the Oranjehotel.

Her bare feet muffled her footsteps, then she knelt beside Dietrich's trousers and slipped a hand into each pocket. Nothing. She moved on to his tunic and felt it—a solid piece of metal.

A key.

Dietrich shifted.

Aleida didn't breathe, didn't move, didn't release the key. Not until his breathing regulated. Then she returned to her bedroom, grabbed a small bag of belongings, her coat, shoes, and her copy of *The Secret Garden*, and proceeded downstairs to the study, where she unlocked the door and stepped inside.

Through the darkness, she crept to the desk drawers and file cabinets. No time to delay. She opened one, rifled to the bottom of the stack, and examined the documents. She stifled a gasp. Orders for a mass execution of Jews that, according to the date, had been carried out a few months ago. Too late to prevent, she realized with sickening dread. She grabbed a few more slips of paper, then found a list of names in Mother's handwriting.

At this, she paused. What if he had forced Mother to betray people the same way he had ordered Aleida to list resistance members? Mother might not have had a choice. But if Mother was posing as a Nazi supporter to earn Dietrich's trust, leaving evidence of Mother's guilt would indicate Aleida did not want to incriminate her, perhaps even did not believe her actions were authentic. To keep her protected, Aleida had to pretend she believed Mother was a fascist.

Except she did not know what she believed anymore.

So she took the list.

One last drawer, then she could afford no more time. There, she found a camera.

Aleida took pictures of the office and her documents, pulled out the film cartridge, replaced it with a new one, and returned the camera. She left everything exactly as she found it, tucked the papers and film into her copy of *The Secret Garden*, and hurried to the front door, where she pulled on her coat and shoes. With shaking hands and painstaking movements, she eased the door open, certain the creaking hinges would awaken the two upstairs. When the gap was wide enough for her to pass through, she looked around her childhood home one last time, hid the book under her coat, and slipped out into the night.

Perhaps she should have left the documents; the camera film was enough. But she wanted Dietrich to notice the missing paperwork someday. To know someone had proof of his crimes no matter how this war ended. To live in fear.

To know that, as long as she had evidence, his life belonged to her.

CHAPTER 18

Los Angeles, 8 September 1946

INGRID

With a headache that is only marginally improved after last night's Star Society party and Ada's admission regarding what happened in Arnhem, Ingrid steps from her cab and onto the corner of Hollywood and Vine. Streetcars and automobiles rumble down the busy street, the noise doing little to ease the pounding in her temples.

Melody Lane is buzzing with patrons as Ingrid enters the restaurant where her meeting is to take place. She follows the curving bar counter toward a small round table and leather banquette in a secluded corner, where Agent Stieber is halfway through his breakfast—a stack of thin hotcakes glistening with butter and golden maple syrup. Steam wafts from a cup of black coffee, joining the buttery sweetness that hits Ingrid's nostrils as she takes her seat.

Following a "good morning, sir" and a cursory glance at the menu, she orders black coffee and a glass of water. The eggs and toast Ada prepared for them have settled well enough, but the greasy sweetness lingering in the air leaves her no desire to tempt fate.

"Did you confirm the Communist front at last night's Star Society gathering?" Agent Stieber asks.

A bright-eyed waitress brings Ingrid's coffee, sparing her from an immediate reply. Soon enough she will have to mention Gordon's political affiliations, but that can wait until she has something better to offer regarding Ada's.

"Nothing to confirm yet. I have photographs of the attendees and will conduct further research. I found no evidence that Miss Worthington-Fox is a Communist, but I've advised her to make a public statement to address her views. This morning, she agreed to do so."

"A statement? In which she might lie?"

Not quite a reprimand, although it brings heat to her cheeks. Still, if Ada saw the wisdom in the idea, surely Stieber will too.

"Let's say she claims she's not a Communist, and meanwhile I confirm the Star Society is a front. She will be exposed as a supporter of subversive behavior. But if I confirm the Star Society is *not* a front, if no evidence indicates Miss Worthington-Fox is subversive, and if she states she is not a Communist through an anti-Communist publication, then we have no reason to doubt her. The truth will be uncovered, your office will have all the necessary information to protect our country, and the public will remain adequately informed regarding which actors they support."

"And she is willing to do it, despite never speaking publicly about such matters?"

"She is, although she wants to wait until her film shoot has ended. I will be contacting Minnie Musgrave from *The Dish* to offer her the story."

Nothing changes in Stieber's face as he chews the last bite of his breakfast. "A statement, then. Have it in place before your eight-week deadline, keep me informed, and bring me a printed copy." The small indication of approval is all Ingrid needs until he continues. "Some-one with a reputation for privacy is someone with secrets. Find out hers."

Tension wraps around her throat, preventing a reply, so she nods. She had expected a statement made through an anti-Communist publication to be enough for him, but apparently she will need some-thing more—proof of existing associations with anti-Communists, perhaps. She will certainly find a variety of political leanings among the Star Society's guests, then she can investigate Ada's past working relationships to identify other connections.

Agent Stieber seems convinced Ada is hiding something. Which she is, technically, but Ada's secrets have nothing to do with his purposes. Ingrid cannot say as much, though, so she will simply do what she came here to do: uncover the truth and protect her sister.

* * *

The next day, after spending her morning updating her file with every-thing she learned from the Star Society, including the names from Gordon's circle of friends who were—most likely—discussing their politics, Ingrid proceeds to her next destination: a tall office building with a curved facade on Sunset Boulevard.

She finds the proper office, knocks, steps inside, and is greeted by a cloud of cigarette smoke.

Minnie Musgrave is everything Ingrid expects her to be—a woman with a face caked in layers of makeup, wearing a bright blue floral dress, beaded necklaces and bracelets, and a flat-brimmed yellow hat with obscenely large peacock feathers jutting at various angles.

"Good afternoon, Mrs. Musgrave. We spoke on the telephone. I'm Ingrid van Essen."

Mrs. Musgrave holds a cigarette between lips painted a gaudy pink and doesn't accept Ingrid's outstretched hand. Instead she gestures for her to sit.

So much for formalities.

"Pleasure," Ingrid continues as if such rudeness were not terribly irritating. "I mentioned the possibility of—"

"An exclusive with Ada Worthington-Fox, and you called this morning to say she's agreed, so I said get your ass over here." An impatient edge laces the words as the gossip columnist drops her cigarette into a coffee mug and leans across the desk. "Dish it, doll."

Best to get right to the point, then. She pulls a few items from her handbag, brought with Ada's approval to satisfy Mrs. Musgrave and prove Ingrid's claim of their working relationship. First, an old entry from Ada's day planner, then a note from Ada herself: *Minnie darling, this is all rather excessive, so I expect you and I will get along splendidly. Now do please take poor Ingrid at her word. Kisses, A. W-F.*

"Miss Worthington-Fox would like to offer you an exclusive interview focusing on Communism in the entertainment industry," Ingrid says while Mrs. Musgrave reviews the submitted material. "She would like to make arrangements and run the article after she finishes filming."

Mrs. Musgrave arches a brow. "I'll agree to run the interview after filming if she gives it to me now. And I reserve the right to the next exclusive."

Ingrid doubts there will be a next exclusive, but Mrs. Musgrave has a point about the interview. Ada will be busy when filming begins, and the story needs to print as soon as possible—for both Ada's sake and Ingrid's—so it might be best to conduct the interview while she has the time.

"Deal. I'll consult Miss Worthington-Fox's schedule and be in touch to make arrangements."

When Ingrid leaves Mrs. Musgrave's office, she takes a deep, cleansing breath while a rush of pride and relief surges through her. The exclusive is in place. It's too soon to call this a successfully completed assignment, but she is certainly much closer. And after this, surely her sister will be much safer.

After a quick lunch, Ingrid makes her way to Schwab's Pharmacy. The drugstore on Sunset Boulevard is a popular spot for Ada, her friends, and other members of the entertainment industry, or so her sister once said. Indeed, as she wanders through the aisles of medicine and miscellaneous essentials before stepping to the soda counter, Ingrid could swear she spots a woman who looks just like Ava Gardner. She's not here for autographs, though, simply to listen. To observe. To do what she's been sent to Hollywood to do.

Ingrid is finishing a hot fudge sundae, sipping a cherry soda, and listening to two writers discussing a script when a blond woman assumes the seat beside hers. As she gives a sidelong glance to acknowledge the newcomer, she pauses. Haven't they met? Her companion narrows her eyes, as if trying to remember why she recognizes the red-haired woman, then brightens.

"Gordon Sharpe's house—the Star Society party. I'm Beverly Tolbert, another of Gordon's clients, and you're Ingrid, right?"

"Quite right. Lovely to see you again. Are you meeting someone?"

"No, I've got plans later, so I stopped in to pass some time. You? Is Ada on her way?" Before Ingrid can reply, Beverly's eyebrows shoot up with a look that can only mean she's spotted a handsome fellow. "Well, this is turning into quite a little gathering of my new friends," she says, waving the person over.

When Ingrid turns to introduce herself to the man holding a half-finished chocolate malt, she resists a frown. Must he be everywhere?

"Afternoon, Miss Tolbert." Archie tips his hat, bringing color to

Beverly's cheeks. "I was told the best chocolate malts in town are right here."

"You were told correctly. Archie Stribling, meet another first-time guest from Saturday's party, Ingrid van Essen—who also happens to be Ada's cousin."

Everything inside Ingrid runs cold while Archie stops with his hand halfway extended toward her.

Damn it all.

The cover story. A perfect solution to their resemblance, to any questions regarding why Ada's temporary assistant looks like her. A cover story she hoped her fellow private investigator would not hear since she had instructed him to stay away from Ada, and a resemblance she hoped he would accept as an uncanny similarity. She should have expected him to force his way into a Star Society party, to get close to Sternberg and Ada's circle of friends and hear the story, and now he's bound to realize she's investigating her own relative.

"Ada's cousin?" Archie's face breaks into a wide grin. "No wonder you two favor so strongly."

"So we've been told." She quickly shakes his outstretched hand, hoping he doesn't notice how clammy hers has become. "You and Beverly met at the party, did you?" Not that changing the subject will make matters any better.

"Yes, Mr. Stribling is an aspiring actor, so when he met Ada at the Biltmore one afternoon, she invited him. Although one must earn Ada's trust before being welcomed into the Star Society, which is no easy feat. Dare I ask how you convinced her to accept you so readily?" Beverly raises a flirtatious brow at Archie, who says something equally irritating, although Ingrid can hardly focus on the exchange.

If Beverly keeps prattling, Ingrid won't last in this seat a moment longer. She almost snatches Archie's malt to cool the heat scalding her skin. She can't listen to these two, can't think about what Archie's going to tell Crenshaw, can't do anything but wait until she's free to sort this out with him before he has a chance to act first.

She waits, tense and doing her best to seem engaged, until Archie brings this dreadful encounter to an end.

"Well, I'm off. Good to see you again, Miss Tolbert, and to meet you, *Miss* Van Essen." She doesn't miss his wink. "This turned out to be my lucky day."

When he departs, she watches to see which way he turns down the sidewalk, waits for approximately fifteen seconds, then gives an excuse about an errand, gets up before Beverly can reply, and rushes from the pharmacy.

Everything around her fades—the street noise, snatches of muffled conversations, a distant whistle, everything except the breath rushing in her ears and hurried footsteps thudding against the pavement. She prepared for this, didn't she? She only needs to catch him, and she's rounding the corner when she nearly collides with the man lingering there. Gasping, she stops, then is met with his familiar sneer.

"You're fucked, Cousin Ingrid."

She shields her eyes against the bright afternoon sunlight, glaring as she steps into the shade beneath a storefront awning, where Archie joins her.

"And don't give me some bullshit about not knowing that investigating a relative is a conflict of interest, because you're not that stupid. Although apparently you're not as smart as I thought."

"It's not like that. I'm trying to find out the truth, and I won't let you interfere. Ada won't be honest with anyone else. She knows me, trusts me—"

"Why wouldn't she? A cousin on the inside helping her cover up her front organization?"

A statement like that to Crenshaw, and Ada's exclusive will be rendered useless, then Ingrid will be promptly removed from Hollywood and imprisoned behind a desk, or she might even lose her job. Every breath comes faster, impeding her efforts to harness her thoughts even as her tone sharpens.

"Shut up and listen to me, you absolute prick—" She breaks off when he steps closer, then her back is against the building, her eyes locked with his steady dark gaze.

"You're getting loud, and our job is to be discreet, so remember that before you make more of a scene." He braces one forearm against the wall, leaving her no space to wriggle aside. "Relax and smile—you do know what a smile is, don't you?"

To any onlookers, they look like two lovers eager to steal a private moment on a busy street, although Ingrid will take the utmost delight in kicking him if needed. Still, he's right; they can't create a disturbance, not when their job is to blend in. And if he believes he has the power in this situation, it will be all the more satisfying to dash his expectations. So she stays where she is until she feels a palm against her waist. She promptly slaps his hand, even though it doesn't budge.

"I'm married."

"Not in Hollywood, you're not." He arches a brow, then shakes his head to silence her retort. "God, you're uptight. Now here's what we're going to do: I've got a car parked down the block. You're coming with me to visit Agent Stieber, and you will admit to working a conflict of interest. Or I'll tell him for you."

Those who believe they have the upper hand are always the same: eyes alight with a triumphant gleam, with certainty that nothing will steal this victory from them. Yet being the one who is overlooked, the one considered inferior, disposable, powerless, has taught Ingrid exactly how to be none of those things. To be everything those like Archie believe she is not.

And if he threatens her sister, her career, she will ensure he regrets it.

She pushes his hand off her waist. This time, he releases her. "Fine, tell Stieber, tell Crenshaw, tell whomever you damn well please." Then she shoves against his chest, forcing his step back. "You certainly won't mind if I tell them about New York."

The faintest flicker of uncertainty passes across his face before he scoffs. "What about it? That I was raised there? That I graduated from NYU in 1940? All the things they already know?"

"Of course not. I mean all the things they don't." She watches him, studies the way he studies her, the way the veins in his temple pulse in anticipation. This will be fun. "Such as 1937, when a pro-Communist rally took place in the city. You wouldn't know anything about that, would you? Or anything about a photograph taken during the event, later published in a newspaper article?" As Archie visibly bristles, she offers a little smile. "Quite a good picture of you, isn't it? Very clear."

After Ingrid was assigned to work alongside Archie and Stieber and she asked Hattie to investigate them, her friend managed to uncover more than Ingrid ever hoped to find—evidence of an article that was likely swept aside after a convincing word or deed from Archie to whoever ran his background check.

Except nothing is ever destroyed. Not entirely. One never knows when such tidbits might be useful, so Ingrid filed it away for a moment precisely like this.

Archie stares as if unable to comprehend what he's hearing before he glowers. "It was one rally, then I never associated with the party again. Kids are stupid, make mistakes, and that's all it was, and if you think I'm going to let you tell Crenshaw or—"

"You're getting loud, and our job is to be discreet." She really should throw his own words back at him more often, judging by the glare it wins her. "You should know I do have the proof. And I won't be telling you if it's with me, hidden, or with a trusted source. As you so kindly pointed out, I'm not that stupid."

He might think she's bluffing—which she's not, because of course she collected the proof. All it takes is calling Lars, explaining where she keeps the sealed file at home, and requesting that he not ask questions but please deliver it to her employer. Every bit of insurance counts.

Archie gives a half-hearted laugh, then he passes a hand across his jaw. "You bitch . . . you're not going to ruin my career over a harmless mistake made years ago. You don't have it in you."

"Shall we find out?" She waits, letting him squirm. Because she's going to make him say it, not her. "Unless you convince me to reconsider. Assuming you ask nicely."

This time she is not going to be the one fighting to keep her place. This time, for once, it will be him. Let him implore her not to share his secrets with their superiors, let him fight for his career the way she fights for hers every single day.

"Don't give your proof to the bosses. Don't mention it to anyone. Please," he relents at last. "If you keep your mouth shut, so will I. Nothing to anyone about you or Ada."

Only then does Ingrid realize her racing heart has never slowed, not until she hears those words. She doesn't show as much, though, simply dips her head before extending a hand, which Archie accepts. She pumps his in a single vigorous shake, then she doesn't release him.

"I really don't care if you like me, or if you want me here, or even if you trust me, but I am committed to this job. The same as you are. At the Star Society party, you reminded me you weren't the enemy, so let me remind you: Neither am I."

No snarky retort, no sexist remark, nothing beyond the twitch of his jaw before he releases her and continues toward his car. Not much. Not enough. But a start.

CHAPTER 19

Hollywood Hills, 16 September 1946

ADA

Inviting Minnie Musgrave to snoop around Gordon's house felt like a terrible idea, so Ada opted for conducting her interview within the confines of Minnie Musgrave's office, which felt only marginally better. Now that the day has come, she and Ingrid proceed down the halls of an office building on Sunset Boulevard while Ada's racing heart refuses to settle.

Is she really going to break her reputation for silence, go against Mr. Hendrix's advice, trust a gossip columnist to keep her word and not run the story until Ada finishes filming? Still, despite her concerns, a quiet certainty bolsters her forward. She is using her voice. Whatever comes of it, she will not regret her decision.

When they reach the proper door, Ada draws a breath, so Ingrid finds her hand.

"You can do this," she murmurs, to which Ada nods. Then she knocks on the door.

When a voice calls for them to enter, they step into a small office filled with cigarette smoke. Behind the desk sits the gossip columnist, nearly prompting Ada to reach for Ingrid's steadying grasp again.

Ada has encountered Minnie Musgrave from a distance among members of the press, or for a moment of small talk at an event. Environments in which Ada has always had a convenient excuse to get away, to avoid spending time with a woman so openly willing to pry. This is entirely different. This is her domain, and Ada has entered of her own volition. Here, words flow freely and time is of no consequence.

"Nowhere in our terms did I agree to an audience." Mrs. Musgrave directs a pointed stare at Ingrid. "Run along, doll."

Ingrid's mouth forms a hard line, a visible effort to control her temper. Ada was counting on her sister's presence to keep her calm, settled, reassured. She could insist on having her remain, but most actresses would not allow their assistants to linger. Even if they did, Mrs. Musgrave seems adamant.

Ada tells Ingrid to meet her at home, then Ingrid departs, despite her eyes igniting with the urge to protest. The door closes, trapping Ada inside. Leaving her alone.

She endured years of Nazi occupation, resistance work, a Gestapo interrogation, a journey to America, and the creation of a new identity. She can manage an interview.

"Ada Worthington-Fox, here in my office." A slow grin spreads across Mrs. Musgrave's features, as though she's won first prize and Ada is her trophy. "Have a seat, doll."

Normally Ada would flash a winning smile, offer a clever quip, tease with a vague remark. This time, she does not.

"Before we begin, allow me to reiterate the terms of our written agreement. Under no circumstances is your exclusive to run until I finish filming. You will provide me with a copy of the draft, and I reserve the right to request edits. In exchange, I will not give this story to anyone else and will offer any future exclusives to you, and you may run teases ahead of the article's printing. If these terms are violated, the entire agreement is off. Do you understand?"

"I signed our agreement, and I will abide by the terms, so don't ruin the fun part with business talk, or I can take away the image you have spent so long crafting. And then Ada Worthington-Fox goes from beautiful, charming, elusive star to untalented hopeful, to irritable brat, to jealous bitch, to whatever I want." Mrs. Musgrave lights a cigarette and leans forward. "Trust me, love, you want me on your side. Keep me happy, and I'll keep you happy."

Ada studies the elder woman with her overly painted face and large brown hat covered in netting, velvet ribbons, and multicolored jewels. Threats will not daunt her into silence. And she will not allow Mrs. Musgrave to turn this exclusive into frivolous gossip. Her serious pieces might be rare, but this must be one of them if Ada's words are to be accepted.

"I am under no illusions regarding our positions in this industry, Mrs. Musgrave. This statement is important to me, so if we can respect the terms we defined, I see no reason for this to go poorly for either of us." At last, Ada sits. "Shall we begin?"

"I'll ask the questions." Mrs. Musgrave offers Ada a cigarette, which she accepts. "Everyone shows the world a version of themselves. This form or that one, never the full picture. Especially you Hollywood types. For the purposes of this piece, I can maintain enough of your image while also convincing readers they're getting the real woman. To do so, I need you. The real you."

Ada lights her cigarette and inhales, although it does little to calm her pounding heart.

"My ex-husband divorced me because he wanted me to be a serious journalist, and I wanted to have fun. To let people escape from their dull lives into a world of glamour and scandal. When I found a press willing to take a chance on me, a woman with nothing beyond the idea for *The Dish*, my husband was so embarrassed, told me it would never amount to anything . . . God, I wish I could see that bastard's face now." She winks. "And I won't be ashamed of embellishing stories or using people like you to bring satisfaction to ordinary people, because that's what you agreed to do when you stepped into this industry, isn't it? To entertain."

Mrs. Musgrave has certainly done well for herself, and Ada can't help being impressed by her determination. Even if her justification of her methods leaves Ada shifting in her seat.

"Your turn: Why did you become an actress? The real answer, not some standard one about childhood dreams or discovering potential. Off the record."

If the answer is off the record and won't be included in the article, Ada could tell her about how ballet made her think of Arnhem, so she couldn't do it anymore, nor could she bear to give up performing entirely, so she turned to acting and other styles of dance. But the purpose of this exclusive is not to share everything, only the important things. To give enough of herself to reveal the woman behind the image.

"Why did I become an actress?" she repeats slowly. "To hide. To escape. To become anyone other than the girl I was, because I was too ashamed to be her anymore."

She has never admitted as much aloud. It's disconcerting but, in an odd way, also rather a relief, even as the hand holding her cigarette maintains a slight tremor.

"There, not so hard, is it?" Mrs. Musgrave situates a fresh sheet of paper into her typewriter. "Let's begin."

Not so hard, if only she can get through it. And she will, because she must.

* * *

When Ada returns home, she follows the sound of a faintly crackling radio program, which leads her to the living room. There she finds Ingrid lying on the sofa, eyes closed, methodically stroking Sowerby's ears while the little dog sleeps beside her. When Ada sits near Ingrid's feet and the cushion settles beneath her weight, her sister's eyes flutter open. She sits up while Sowerby crawls into Ada's lap.

"All right, then?" Ingrid asks softly.

Theirs had been a more open, honest conversation than any of Ada's previous interviews. As for how Mrs. Musgrave will alter the piece for her readers, she will soon find out, but it's done.

She pulls a document from her handbag and hands it to Ingrid—a copy of the first teaser, which will publish soon within an article yet to be determined. Ingrid accepts the paper, and Ada reads over her shoulder.

> Now for the juiciest tidbit of all: a special message from Hollywood's Vixen.
>
> "Hello there, readers. I'm Ada Worthington-Fox, Abe Sternberg's leading lady, and if there's one thing you know about me—well, it's that you don't know much about me at all, do you? Shall we change that sometime soon? I have a few things I'd like to share—and trust me, darlings, you'll want to hear this."
>
> Pick up your jaws off the floor, dolls. A possible glimpse into Ada Worthington-Fox's personal life? If the most private woman in Hollywood spills her secrets, I'm buying each of you lovely readers a drink at The Frolic Room.

CHAPTER 20

Hollywood Hills, 11 October 1946

INGRID

The bright California sun warms her skin as Ingrid relaxes beside Gordon's pool, reading the first draft of Ada's exclusive. And not a moment too soon, considering Ingrid's eight weeks are almost over, so she's running out of time to ensure a satisfactory piece. She pestered Mrs. Musgrave multiple times about when they might expect the draft, then conceded to waiting impatiently after she was told to *ease up, doll, or I'll write an exclusive about the most annoying assistant in Hollywood.* This morning, Mrs. Musgrave called to relay its completion, so Ada's "assistant" picked it up and brought it over. After reviewing the piece and making a few notes, Ada returned it to Ingrid for her approval.

Next to Ingrid, Ada is clad in a bikini, stretched out on a lounge chair, reading the latest issue of *Vogue*. She looks up briefly to wave at Gordon's gardener, who waves back as he passes by after tending the roses.

This mansion has countless rooms, gardeners, housekeepers, cooks, even waitstaff when necessary—though none live on the grounds because, according to Ada, Gordon prefers a home to himself. Not to mention parties with celebrities Ingrid once knew only through the cinema. What an unusual life her sister leads.

When Ingrid finishes reading, it takes all her self-control not to rush inside to call Agent Stieber and relay her success. Perhaps he was hesitant to trust an exclusive, but such a clear, honest piece will surely ease his doubts.

"It's wonderful, Leidje, really. Make sure you mention the Star Society too, just to avoid confusion. These days, even the most innocent of gatherings can be suspected of being a front."

"Very well, if you insist." She sighs. "I suppose we'll find out if this works."

Whether she means to convince the public of her views or to encourage Dietrich to emerge from hiding, Ingrid does not know. Both, perhaps.

"Must you leave next week?" Ada asks as she flips the page in her magazine. "It's been so lovely having you here."

"It's been lovely being here, but I do miss Lars. And you start filming soon, so you've got to be prepared." Ingrid adjusts her swimsuit strap and tucks both hands behind her head, narrowing her eyes against the bright sunlight.

"Filming will be fun, won't it? Film noir has been so popular lately. *The Blue Dahlia* with Veronica Lake, *The Big Sleep* with Humphrey Bogart and Lauren Bacall . . . Can you imagine making a film with your spouse? Of course they weren't married yet during filming, but acting alongside someone you love must be equally as thrilling as it is peculiar."

"You'll be making a film with your former beau. Are you concerned about working with Vince Hart?"

Ada's laugh is somewhat strained. "We're on fine terms, really. Even if we weren't, it's a job, so we would treat it as such. And I do hope being here hasn't cost you yours."

"My what?"

"Your job. The temporary leave." Ada sits up and removes her sunglasses. "The moment you realized who I was, you came all the way here, spent weeks away from your husband, risked your career . . . No one has ever done anything so kind for me, and I'll never forget it."

Suddenly Ingrid can't bear the light shining in her sister's eyes. "You would have done the same for me." Then she holds up the exclusive. "Shall I take this inside so we don't get it wet?"

Without awaiting a reply, she springs to her feet and hurries toward the house.

This little prickle of guilt over Ada's gratitude is unwarranted. Of course Ingrid would have come the moment she realized Ada was alive, not just because she was sent here for work. She has no reason to feel as if her sister's appreciation is undeserved. And she will explain once she has permission to speak of her other reasons for being here. Surely Ada will understand why Ingrid couldn't be honest right away and will appreciate Ingrid's efforts to protect her.

She swallows a hitch in her breath, then she takes the exclusive to the spare bedroom where she left her bag containing a change of clothes and a few pieces of equipment tucked beneath her belongings. She finds the cigarette packet concealing her Whittaker Micro 16, photographs the piece, then returns the camera and drops the article off in Ada's office. Once finished, she closes her hands into fists, settling a slight tremble.

Soon. Soon she will tell Ada everything.

She cannot delay any longer, so she hurries back to the pool. At the sound of her approaching footsteps, Ada looks to her, brow furrowed.

"Everything all right, Inge?"

"Yes, fine." Ingrid doesn't take her seat, though, and instead steps to the pool's edge and dips one foot into the water, giving herself an excuse to avoid Ada's gaze. "Make us drinks, will you? Something fruity and tropical with lots of rum."

"Not until you tell me what's bothering you."

"Nothing, I ..." As Ada joins her by the pool, Ingrid sighs but doesn't face her. "I'm going to miss you terribly, that's all."

"Not until next week," Ada says briskly, although Ingrid recognizes that false brightness from years ago before they parted, when her sister was so calm and encouraging, containing her true feelings for Ingrid's sake. "You're right; a drink is just what you need. I'll be right back, so cheer up, darling."

Before Ingrid can reply, a shove sends her over the pool's edge, where she hits with a splash before the cool water swallows her. She stays under as time suspends and shock transforms into bliss, then bobs to the surface and finds Ada retreating toward the house, although not without throwing a cheeky grin over her shoulder.

"You are an absolute child!" Ingrid calls after her as their joined laughter floats across the lawn. She flips onto her back, absorbing the sun's warmth while the cool water washes over her.

Ada is right; they still have time, and Ingrid has nearly finished what she came here to accomplish. The November elections will take place in a few weeks—results that will either give more power to HUAC or revoke it—and her investigation has done enough to help the committee, surely, and to erase concerns regarding her sister. On her next visit, work can be forgotten.

* * *

After returning to the Biltmore, Ingrid cleans up from her afternoon by the pool, then calls Agent Stieber to request a meeting. When he arrives a few minutes prior to their agreed time, she welcomes him into her hotel room, then immediately offers him the roll of film.

"Photographs of Ada Worthington-Fox's exclusive regarding her views on Communism. The article won't be printed for a few months, but this shows the edited draft."

He accepts it with a curt nod.

"I was at her agent's house today and recorded a conversation between Miss Worthington-Fox and Mr. Sharpe. It will be included in my report, of course, but I thought you should hear it now." Ingrid plays the recording—a bit of meaningless conversation, then a rustle of paper followed by Gordon's voice, indicating Ada had offered him a document.

"What's this?"

"The exclusive I gave to Minnie Musgrave about my views on everything happening in the industry. I'm going to request a few small changes, but I thought you should hear about it from me before it runs in a few months."

"Why didn't you tell me you wanted to make a statement? I would have arranged it."

"Because I didn't know what you would say, or if you would agree with Mr. Hendrix about staying quiet to maintain my image."

"To hell with your image and Hendrix and me, for that matter. It's your career, Ada. Do what you feel is best. I'll give you my thoughts or advice, but the ultimate decision is always yours. And I'll always support you."

A little sigh of relief, then Ada's soft voice: "I've learned neither words nor silence can truly protect me. But I've also learned to do what I feel is right. This time, for myself and my fans, I want to be honest."

Faint rustles, the click of a lighter, then an exhale, indicating Gordon had lit a cigarette. "After the Depression, when I was a young man, the party was against fascism and advocated for social welfare, which appealed to many during such a difficult time. Such causes remain important to me, of course, but those made it easier to overlook the flaws in the party's implementation as seen in history and other countries." Pensive silence. "Don't let anyone tell you what to say or why you should say it. Don't be afraid to say how you feel either. Your words might encourage someone else to think. As you did for me."

The recording ends. Stieber fears Ada will lie in her exclusive, but this is the proof he wanted. Verbal proof in the privacy of her home, sharing her honest opinion with a man she trusts. Ingrid turns off the machine, watching her handler's face even though it never betrays him.

"The agent is a Communist?"

Ingrid resists a scowl. Was that all Agent Stieber got from the conversation? "He has reconsidered his views, due in part to her encouragement. Details will be in my full report, which I'll submit to you and Mr. Crenshaw when I return home. But after spending these last weeks with her and uncovering evidence such as this, I can confidently say Ada Worthington-Fox is not a Communist, and there is no reason to believe the Star Society is a front."

Stieber offers the camera film back to her. "Complete the report. I want the names of all Communists, union members, and subversives, confirmed or suspected, and all who attend her gatherings so final determinations can be made." When she accepts the film, he does not release it, so she meets his gaze. "You've done well, Mrs. Van Essen."

In her shock, Ingrid almost forgets to thank him. She can't remember the last time anyone from work complimented her so directly—if anyone from work has ever complimented her at all. Now she has shown she is indeed a skilled private investigator. Most of all, she has helped her sister.

Once the exclusive goes to print, surely both their careers will be safe.

CHAPTER 21

Hollywood, 27 November 1946

ADA

O n set in ten, Miss Worthington-Fox," calls an assistant from beyond her dressing room door.

Ten minutes. Ada stands before a full-length mirror. It's remarkable what a bit of costuming, hair, and makeup can do. The woman staring back at her is the cunning leader of an elusive ring of criminal women; with dark eyeliner sharpening her gray eyes and a black dress hugging her figure, she certainly looks it. Silver threads run through the fabric, shimmering when they catch the light.

Stella Fairchild: an ambitious woman, passionate, protective of herself and her secrets. A woman Ada has little trouble understanding.

When someone knocks, she permits entrance. Vince steps inside, dressed in his suit and tie for the scene.

"Mind doing me a favor?" He holds up a photograph—Ada's headshot. "A friend wants to surprise his wife for her birthday. She's an admirer of yours."

"A girl with taste, is she?" Ada autographs the image in bold, looping script, then offers it to him.

"People will be talking about you when this film releases," Vince says as he accepts it. "Everyone on set already is."

The praise should be reassuring; instead her skin prickles like it did when she was a girl after her dance performances, piano recitals, and plays. A reminder that there is always something she might have done better. She does not want to be praised for anything until she deserves to be. And she does not want such praise from Vince.

Now it's as if the room itself feels her pulling away from him, the same way she did when she so briefly permitted him to love her.

"Do you still find it impossible to accept a compliment?"

At Vince's wry remark, she blinks. Filming commenced only a few days ago. So far they've managed to be professional, to not let their past interfere with their work—perhaps because they haven't had a scene together yet. But the word he added to his question, that one word: *still*.

Two who were and are no longer.

He is her costar—her friend, even, despite everything. His support should be important to her. Instead she faces the mirror to wipe away an imaginary smudge of lipstick, avoiding his gaze. She does not want to be defined by his celebrity, by his praise, by anyone but herself.

She clears her throat. "We're due on set." Then she hurries from the dressing room.

How well he remembers everything about her, even still.

Ah, that word again.

When she reaches the soundstage, Mr. Sternberg is rushing this way and that, barking orders to sound and lighting. The scene takes place on a set made to look like a run-down alley, where an abandoned building with a boarded door leads to Stella's headquarters.

Off camera, an assistant is tying a blindfold around Vince's eyes, so Ada joins him. She pushes their conversation aside, concentrates on the scene. Her first with him.

No need to be nervous; her scenes have gone well so far, and in the past she's worked alongside plenty of other actors—everyone from newcomers to esteemed professionals. This actor is well established and a brilliant talent, yes, but he's Vince. Former flame and friend.

Maybe she has to kiss him in later scenes, but she's kissed plenty of men for work, hasn't she? This will be no different.

A hand finds Ada's arm—not painful, yet firm, breaking her concentration. "Miss Worthington-Fox, a word."

She looks up at Mr. Hendrix, who scowls as he leads her to the outskirts of the set. She has little time to ponder what he wants before he releases her and holds up a copy of *The Dish*.

"Explain this." He jams a finger to the end of an article, displaying the first tease about her exclusive. "Did I not tell you to maintain privacy?"

Ada has been preparing for this moment, of course, since Mr. Hendrix was bound to notice when mention of her exclusive went public. Still, preparation can't prevent her heart from racing. She gives an airy laugh and places a reassuring hand on his forearm.

"Not to worry, sir, I remember our discussion. The press was prying more than usual, so I thought I'd have a little fun to indulge them. Teasing is harmless, isn't it?"

As Mr. Hendrix relaxes, Ada leaves him with another winning smile and hurries back to her place even as her heart refuses to slow. This was only a glimpse of how worried and irritated he will be when he realizes she really did give an exclusive. There is an excellent chance she has ruined all future opportunities to work with him.

As she rejoins Vince to await their cue, she glances at him, trying to forget the severity of Mr. Hendrix's frown and focus on their roles. Detective Gregory Merrick is haunted by a previous failed attempt to arrest Stella, but now that Stella's sister has been murdered, the two characters have struck a tentative agreement. He will act as her lover, giving her an excuse to bring him into her criminal ring since she believes the unknown murderer is someone close to her. He gets credit for solving the case; she gets justice. Except Stella plans to frame him as an accomplice to her own crimes, causing him to lose his job so he can never arrest her in the future, while Merrick intends to destroy her network.

Following Stella's proposition and Merrick's acceptance, she brings him to her headquarters, which is the scene they are preparing to film. When Mr. Sternberg calls action, Ada grabs Vince's arm, presses a prop knife into his back, and leads him into the alley and on camera.

"Relax, Merrick," she says as they step into the frame. "We're already here. That wasn't so bad, was it?"

When she releases him, he removes the blindfold and looks from the crates and debris to the boarded building. "Quite a headquarters you've got here. Nothing like a feminine touch to spruce up a place."

"Save your quips for the fellows in your office, Detective. It's just through that door."

Before he can proceed, Ada catches his tie, slips the knife beneath the loop, and cuts it from around his neck. A snap releases, making the action appear convincing. Then she presses his back to the building and the knife to his throat.

Vince doesn't flinch as his eyes lock with hers. She feels his pulse pounding, smells the faint freshness of his aftershave lotion mixed with sweat from the heat brought on by the set lights.

"There, that looks much better." Leaning closer, she lowers her voice. "Remember, when you meet my girls, you're not a detective; you're a man who is crazy about me. Act like it."

"Will you act like a lady?"

Silence falls while Ada feels herself slipping out of character for an instant. And for that instant she is simply Ada, and he is Vince, and she wonders if her lips would tingle if she pressed them against his. If he would slip his thumb beneath her chin and draw her into him. If kissing him would feel like it did before.

"Cut!" Mr. Sternberg calls. "Line, Ada! Where's your head?"

Where, indeed? *I always do*, she's supposed to say in response to Vince's question, complete with a coy smile as she intensifies the blade's pressure. Flirtatious yet dangerous, tempting yet cautionary. Instead she stood there.

It's not until Vince clears his throat that Ada realizes she hasn't released him. She steps back, her heart thudding as it did during the scene. Her career and her security rely on her acting, on the film's success, on pleasing Mr. Hendrix. And right now she cannot focus on anything except her history with Vince and Mr. Hendrix's confrontation, all of which will lead to the poor performance she cannot afford.

"Mr. Sternberg, might I have a moment?"

Though he frowns, he jerks his head in assent. "Ten minutes while we reset, and you'd better come back and give me a flawless take."

She nods, then retreats to her dressing room, fingernails buried into her palms. She knows better than to let one conversation with her studio head or the pressure of acting opposite Vince rattle her.

Footsteps indicate he's following her. She can't decide if his presence will focus her or leave her more agitated. When they reach the room, he removes his suit coat and tosses it onto the dressing table, then leans against the closed door. Casual, not flustered by anything, certainly not their ruined take or their shared past.

Sighing, she sinks into a chair and pinches the bridge of her nose. "A bit off today, I suppose."

"So you missed a line." He shrugs. "Happens to all of us."

Still, with only a few days of shooting complete, there's time to cast a replacement if she fails to deliver the performance Mr. Sternberg and Mr. Hendrix expect.

"Talk to me about the scene. That might help me find the proper mindset." She shifts to face him. "Where is Detective Merrick's head?"

Vince crosses his arms, considering. "No noteworthy cases to his name. He blames Stella for his shortcomings since she evaded him, so this is his chance for redemption. Your character seeks justice for her sister, so there's a more selfless aspect to her motivations. For mine, it's about his own wounded pride—entirely selfish."

Years ago, when they ran lines together for various projects, he did this with each script: analyzing every character, every scene, every purpose for every stage direction. Thinking not simply as the actor he is but as the writer he hopes to be. Such discussions bring him to life the way dancing center stage once did for Ada.

"Think about Stella's sister more in the scene," she agrees with a nod. "And Merrick's dedication wins her respect. It's a quality they share, despite their differences. In a way, she's attracted to him, but their worlds will never coincide, so he's . . ." Suddenly her throat gets tight. "He's not worth the risk."

A beat of aching silence stretches between them. Vince looks beyond Ada, somewhere far away as he contemplates the characters.

"And he's attracted to her, sure. She's a mysterious, powerful woman. Dangerous. Beautiful." At last he meets her gaze. "But he won't let himself acknowledge that attraction. Not after the way she damaged him, because she could easily do so again."

Ada nods slowly, then distracts herself with her reflection, checking her hair and makeup. This discussion will not eliminate whatever this is between her and Vince, these reminders of their past that will continuously interfere unless they move beyond them. How, she doesn't know; they've tried everything.

Except . . . not everything.

"Shall we do it, then?"

One look at Vince indicates he knows exactly what she's implying. The overwhelming strangeness of their positions must be as obvious to him as it is to her.

When he doesn't react, heat rises to Ada's cheeks. There goes her veneer of professionalism. Plenty of actors work with costars they once dated, were married to, slept with, cheated with, and God knows what else. She doubts they make such requests of one another. Because professionals never let their personal lives interfere.

Before she can revoke her suggestion and pray he forgets she ever made it, he nods. "If we have to do it eventually, we might as well."

Did he have to make kissing her sound like such a chore? Still, he's proving her point; if they can ease this tension between them, it will prevent her—both of them—from being distracted in the future. This will be best for the film.

As if preparing for a scene, Vince passes a hand through his thick chestnut locks, mussing them—which will be to the dismay of the hair department—then beckons her with a crook of his finger.

Once she's standing in front of him, her heart slams inexplicably against her chest. Their last kiss was after a romantic dinner in downtown Los Angeles. Some nosy journalist snapped a picture of the moment, and the next day's papers discussed their relationship. Nothing about her upcoming projects, her aspirations, her career, only that she was with Hollywood's favorite leading man.

She wanted to be more than an accessory. So she ended things without explanation. And now here they are. No cameras, nothing but themselves, their past, and a film relying on their performances.

"Shall I take the lead?" he asks. "A quick peck, something more like old times, or in between?"

"Surprise me."

Vince nods, then he leans closer. She doesn't reach for him, nor does he wrap his arms around her, so she keeps her arms pinned to her sides and lifts her chin to meet him.

He touches his lips to hers. Barely a brush, then he steps aside to clear her path to the door. Not *bad*—no kiss of his could ever be bad— just . . . brief. Chaste. Cautious. Nothing like the way he used to kiss her.

Her heart flutters, reconciling what she anticipated with what she experienced. She didn't *want* him to kiss her like before, when the de- sire pulsing between them left every touch searching for the next. Still, a bit more than this offering wouldn't have been entirely unwelcome either.

It's done, though. Future takes will be easier now, surely.

Ada gives a brisk nod. "Right, this has all been immensely helpful." She steps past him toward the door. "Let's get back to—"

Then she feels his grasp on her arm, pulling her around with such ease and speed. All at once his mouth is against hers, swallowing her words, and she forgets everything she was going to say.

Well, there's the man she remembers.

His lips rough, his arms strong and secure, his touch prompting her heartbeat to ache in her chest as she presses into him. One deep, linger- ing kiss, then Vince pulls away, leaving both gasping before he smirks.

"You told me to surprise you."

Ada looks from the spark in his eyes to the vibrant smear of her lipstick on his mouth, then his lips find hers again, desperate and ur- gent as if theirs is a reunion rather than two doing what they must for the work. Only for the work. She knows that, of course she does. As does he, certainly, even as he kisses her again and again, grips her body tighter against his, tangles a hand through her hair. She offers him her neck, gasping when his lips meet her skin.

This is exactly what she wanted.

Except they have a job to do.

Her voice emerges in a rasp. "Vince . . . *Vince*, the scene . . ."

He freezes. They remain centimeters apart, breathing heavily, and for a moment Ada dares to believe he will kiss her once more, just once more. Gently, she brushes a finger over his lips, wiping the bright mark of lipstick. Hair and makeup will be cursing them when they return to set.

His is no longer the look of indifference she has come to expect. Something else is there, something raw and honest that she has no time to decipher before he blinks and releases her.

Wordlessly she smooths her hair while he dons his jacket. And when they leave the dressing room, a small cluster of extras dissolves into titters. She bites her tongue to keep from ordering them to mind their own business.

Yet as she follows Vince back to set, she doesn't miss his straight-backed stride a few paces ahead of her, the way the hand that was tangled in her hair briefly clenches and unclenches. The same way she looks ahead rather than at anyone they pass, refrains from smoothing her hair again even as she still feels his fingers locked in it, bites her cheek against the lasting tingle in her lips.

Her brilliant plan to make filming easier is going to make this next take impossible.

CHAPTER 22

Washington, DC, 20 December 1946

INGRID

After returning from California in October, Ingrid's circumstances in the office have not changed. True, she gathered plenty of information to assist J. Edgar Hoover and the FBI with HUAC's investigation. True, she proved Crenshaw's doubts wrong by carrying out a successful assignment. Yet while her report is processed and she awaits confirmation that the investigation into Ada is closed, each day is no different from those prior to her time in Hollywood. So she waits, aching for responsibilities that won't come until her success is acknowledged.

"The 80th Congress will be sworn in next month," Crenshaw says at today's meeting while Ingrid sits in her usual seat, taking notes. "With Republicans holding a majority, the FBI has already notified me of HUAC's intentions to increase investigations, so when the time comes, I'll be sending some of you on assignment."

Ingrid sits taller. An opportunity for her to return to California, perhaps? Archie, too, leans forward in his chair, clearly eager for the same possibility. The Communist threat has not dissipated as she initially hoped after returning from her investigation; it has only worsened, judging by newspaper articles, talk among her colleagues, and the increase in investigations Crenshaw just mentioned. Even if Ada's views have been clarified, perhaps Ingrid will be assigned to someone else and can spend more time with her sister. Not the relaxing vacation she wanted for her next visit, but nevertheless an opportunity to see Ada.

"Mrs. Van Essen, a word," Crenshaw says after the meeting.

Anticipation courses through her veins, although it's too soon to allow her hopes to rise. This might not have anything to do with California. Tempering her expectations, she follows Crenshaw to his office, then waits while he closes the door and sits behind his desk.

"Stieber wants me to send you back to Hollywood to resume your investigation into Ada Worthington-Fox."

Slowly, Ingrid takes the seat across from him—even though he didn't extend the invitation—and folds her hands as they shake with unrestrained excitement. Stieber requested her. Even all this time after turning in her report and hearing no news from him or Crenshaw, nothing about whether they were pleased or dissatisfied. It seems he was indeed pleased. Except . . . what did her employer say?

Her throat runs dry, making words difficult. "To resume my investigation? Was my report not satisfactory?"

He taps his spectacles against the desk. "No, no, it was decent."

Decent is the closest thing to a compliment she's ever received from him. Between that and Agent Stieber requesting her, she should be satisfied. Instead, all Ingrid hears are her increasing heartbeats and the steady tap of his spectacles against the wooden desk. She had provided everything necessary to prove Ada's position and more. What else could he possibly need?

"Sir, I don't understand. Miss Worthington-Fox gave her exclusive, and the evidence I provided—"

"Does not prove the Star Society is not a front, despite her claims.

Even if she is not a Communist, she has Communist friends and, according to your report and others, a Communist agent, so she might be sympathetic to the cause. Until we have confirmation of the group's purpose, we can't rule out the possibility." Crenshaw arches a brow. "You've spent all this time pestering me for more opportunities, and I'm offering you one. Should I offer it to someone who will be grateful for it?"

"No, no, of course I appreciate it . . . I'm happy to resume my investigation." Even though she isn't certain she understands his reasoning. Still, if Ada needs her again, she must help.

Crenshaw leans across the desk. "Confirm Worthington-Fox's political views and the status of her organization. One mistake, or failure to give me or Stieber what we ask for, and we will remove you from the investigation. You are replaceable. Don't forget it."

Ingrid merely nods while he waves her out, so she returns to her desk and sits, too stupefied and unsettled to sort out what just happened. Why everything she gathered about Ada was decent yet not enough.

A slam startles her into focus. She blinks and stares at a thick file, then looks up at Archie, who stands above her.

"Your report," he says, nodding to the folder. "Crenshaw wants us to spend the next month reviewing materials and developing a new plan of action prior to our return."

Our return, meaning he will be going with her again. She clenches her jaw.

"What's your assignment this time?"

"Ada Worthington-Fox." He winks while Ingrid stiffens, then he laughs. "I'm kidding. You shouldn't make it so much fun to annoy you. I made some contacts last time who have been useful in identifying possible subversives, so I'll be working with them to gather more names." He taps the file. "Get to work."

Back to California with Archie. Maybe her leverage over him due to his past dalliance with Communism has kept him from interfering with her pursuits, but she still has no desire to work with him again.

Once he's gone, her mind is too clouded to review her work, so instead she calls Hattie.

"Who am I investigating this time?" Hattie teases following Ingrid's greeting; she knows her too well.

"Gregor Dietrich, Schutzstaffel und Polizeiführer in Arnhem, Holland."

"Bloody hell," Hattie mutters, her voice low to prevent eavesdropping. "SS and . . . Police Leader, is that correct? Meaning a role in security, suppressing resistance, that sort of thing?" Then she gasps. "Wait, you said Arnhem? Where you grew up? Ingrid, did he . . . Were you—?"

"I can't talk about it," Ingrid interrupts, keeping her voice low. "But, to reassure you, no, he has not done anything to me." Except he has, in a sense, because he tormented her sister, which hurts Ingrid far worse than anything he might have done to her directly had she ever encountered him. "I don't know if he's alive or not, but I need whatever you have on him, if anything."

Hattie sighs. "I'll see what I can find."

After thanking her friend, Ingrid hangs up. Ada will be finished with filming in the next few weeks, meaning her exclusive will be published soon. Once it is, if Dietrich really is looking for her, they must be ready. Until then, it seems Ingrid has an investigation to resume.

* * *

When she returns home, Ingrid leaves the file in her bag. She will begin her review soon enough, but the sight of it leaves a pit in her stomach. She had been so certain it was enough to help Ada, and apparently she failed.

She is still sitting on the sofa, brooding and staring at the briefcase containing the offending file, when the door opens.

"Busy day?" Lars asks as he enters and notices her pursed lips. "Any difficulty with Crenshaw?"

"Would you believe he was very nearly complimentary?" Lars grunts an indiscernible response, indicating he most certainly does not believe it. "Honestly, he was," she insists as she rises from the sofa and proceeds into the kitchen to start dinner. "Although I'm not certain if we'll ever progress beyond that. 'Very nearly' just about did him in."

Lars chuckles as he joins her. When his arms encircle her waist and his lips find her neck, a little shiver pulses down her spine. Somehow that gesture always makes her feel like a lovestruck girl again. She turns to face him and speaks in Dutch.

"Did you miss me today?"

"Shall I show you how much?"

He kisses her lips, then her neck. Yet, despite efforts to lose herself in his touch, the unsettled feeling in her chest returns, interfering until she avoids his next kiss and sidesteps him.

Silence falls. Normally, she would playfully push him away or order him to stop distracting her, or to put on an apron and help if he insists on being in the kitchen. Right now she can't say anything, certainly can't explain matters she doesn't understand. But for her husband's sake, she must try to explain as much as permitted.

"I have to leave. On assignment. I don't know when yet."

"Again? For how long?" When she says nothing, indicating she doesn't know the answer, he starts over. "Well, this is good, isn't it? If Crenshaw is giving you more responsibilities, he must be pleased with your work on the last assignment."

If only that were the reason.

"You're happy, aren't you?" Lars ventures when she stays quiet. "You've been wanting assignments for years, and now—"

"You know I can't talk about it."

Too cross, too short, too late to soften the undeserved blow even though she wishes she could. Ingrid doesn't need to look at Lars to know he's startled, confused, frustrated. The only sound is running water as she washes vegetables for dinner, then she sighs and dries her hands.

"I'm sorry, I don't mean to be irritable; it's just—" So many things, few of which she can admit. Her sister is not as protected as she thought, and she doesn't know what else to do when she already did all she could. And she does not understand why it was not enough. Now she has to leave Lars again for an indeterminable amount of time. "It's complicated," she finishes while Lars kisses her cheek in reassurance.

As she tries to push the matter aside, the evening proceeds normally until Lars retires for bed. Ingrid promises to join him momentarily, then she extracts the file from her briefcase and sets it on the coffee table.

A detailed, thorough report proving Ada is not a Communist. But somehow still not good enough.

Sighing, Ingrid pulls out the thick stack of documents, notes, articles, photographs, and recording transcripts. Then she begins her review.

HOLLYWOOD'S VIXEN: VERIFIED OR VINDICATED?

by Minnie Musgrave

No, my dear readers, you're not hallucinating. The time has come. An exclusive glimpse into who the most private actress in Hollywood really is.

Hollywood's Vixen herself, Ada Worthington-Fox, joins me in my office, wearing a shirtwaist dress with a palm tree print that is belted at her slim waist. Her hair is styled in her usual waves, her makeup minimal, her demeanor unusually sober.

Readers, you must think I talked her into this—and while I appreciate your faith in my powers of persuasion, I did not. Miss Worthington-Fox herself expressed a desire to make a statement. Which brings me to my first question and, likely, yours: Why? Why, after all this time of avoiding personal matters, does she want to address the public?

"Don't expect this to be a common occurrence," she says with a faint smile. "Hollywood is experiencing a time of difficulty, speculation, and concern, so I thought it best to make myself heard."

By this, of course, she means Communist influences in the industry. Her upcoming film, Hendrix Productions' *Lady Bella Donna*, is directed by Communist Abe Sternberg. Since Miss Worthington-Fox has never been forthright about her own views, naturally the public has questions.

"It is not my place to speak for anyone else, nor do I feel public pressure should demand private information or, conversely, demand silence, but those are not the reasons I've chosen to address this matter. I am doing this for me, no one else." She pauses to light a cigarette and takes a slow drag. "My silence has always been for my own protection, and while I still wish to maintain my privacy, I also wish to use my voice. Something I have not done enough lately. But I'll have more to say in that regard some other time."

Miss Worthington-Fox falls quiet again. Throughout our conversation, she has been open and forthright, not cleverly sidestepping topics she wishes to avoid. So when I ask her the question on all our minds, she looks directly at me and gives me her answer.

"I am not a Communist. The Star Society is not a front organization. And I do not believe that the entertainment industry is being used to advance anti-American causes. Even if such attempts were made, industry professionals who uphold American values would not allow the promotion of anti-American causes. So I would like to reassure the public and caution against allowing speculation or fear to cause damage that might have lasting impacts."

Confirmation at last. Beneath the actress who captured hearts and captivated attention is a woman not so different from the rest of us. A woman with values, a woman with a passion for her career, a woman asking to be heard.

My thanks to Ada Worthington-Fox for this open and candid exclusive. There is so much more we have yet to learn, but if this pattern of sudden willingness continues from Hollywood's enigmatic Vixen, I'm here to listen. Until next time, dolls, be patient, but don't be good. Life is too short to behave yourself.

CHAPTER 23

Hollywood, 31 January 1947

ADA

On the last day of filming, Ada and Vince must kiss on camera. One single, brilliant take is all they need. Ada can manage that. Then they never have to do this again.

As they begin the first take, they stand in a large, open room, facing a table displaying evidence uncovered in a previous scene. Evidence pointing to Stella's remaining sister as the culprit, for which she blames the detective, certain he has framed the only sibling she has left.

Both Ada and her character know this feeling: the loss of a sister. Something neither Stella nor Ada could bear once, certainly not a second time, and certainly not like this. A sister's death is a tragedy; a sister's betrayal is a choice. It cannot be true, so she blames the detective—but what if she's wrong?

The scene proceeds as their argument erupts, then Ada seizes Vince's collar. "Tell me the truth! Tell me you framed her, that this is your doing—"

"Accusing me won't bring us answers. And once we know the truth—whatever it is—you can either face it or make it go away. Isn't that what you do with all your problems, destroy them so they can't destroy you?"

That last line is not in the script, yet every part of it resonates through her—*well done, Vince*. Ada raises a hand to strike him. He catches her wrist before she can land the blow.

A tear slips from her cheek, though it was not in the script for her to cry in this moment. Next, Vince is supposed to kiss her. Instead, he does nothing.

This is *the* take; she can feel it. And without the kiss it will be ruined.

Ada jerks him closer and kisses him, this man who has voiced her character's deepest struggles, this man her character has come to respect and now doubts, so perhaps this is the only way to uncover true honesty from him. And from herself.

All part of the scene. Yet a small, deeply buried part of Ada awakens to the roughness of his lips, the tension in the palm pressed to the small of her back, the way he angles her toward slightly more prominence for the camera, the sharp breaths joined as one when they pull apart.

In the script, the kiss meant to lead her to clarity only leaves Stella more uncertain. Indeed, Ada's grip on Vince's collar does not loosen, does not permit him to draw back. Nor has he relaxed the hand holding her against him. This must be the take; Ada cannot film another, because kissing him is not like it was when they were together. Now it is more intense, sharpened by the reality that they are not Ada and Vince anymore, even though it is easy, far too easy, to feel like Ada and Vince again.

"Cut! A bit off script, but we got it," Mr. Sternberg announces. "Ladies and gentlemen, that's a wrap!"

Amid cheers and applause, Ada shakes outstretched hands and accepts congratulatory kisses on the cheek and pats on the back. Every nerve buzzes with energy, and not simply from the scene. The film is complete, but her work has only just begun. Interviews, press, mingling with the public—all of it awaits. All of it will determine if this film is destined to be everything she believes it can be.

"Am I allowed to say well done?" Vince asks.

"Just this once," she replies with a half smile. "Since when does Vince Hart freeze on set?"

He chuckles. "Thank God you salvaged the take."

Yet the look in his eyes is the one from her dressing room several weeks ago, indicative of something she has no time to examine before it disappears. Whatever it is prompts warmth to bloom against her cheeks.

"It's been a pleasure working with you, Vince, and I mean that with utmost sincerity." She kisses his cheek, then takes his hand. "Years ago, you offered kindness and encouragement to an aspiring actress, and I've never forgotten it."

"That's right, I did say you would see your face in the papers some-day." He kisses her cheek in return. "Get ready, Miss Worthington-Fox, because that day has come."

Heat lingers on her cheek from his touch and his breath against her ear. Her face in the papers.

It's what she's wanted ever since she began this journey—to perform, to entertain, to help people escape. And the closer she comes to being a star, the more she can use her position to leave a positive impact. Perhaps even to uncover the fate of a particular escaped Nazi who, at her core, she feels certain is alive. She has no proof, really, other than the feeling she's carried even before the notes began. Now, by using her position, her voice, the possibility of drawing him out is stronger than ever. Either he will emerge to silence her, or she won't rest until she finds him.

"Miss Worthington-Fox!"

The bellow reverberates around the room, so loud Ada jumps while extras, assistants, and crew members abruptly cease chattering. Mr. Hendrix barges through the crowd, clutching a paper, his face aflame.

A copy of *The Dish*, and Ada feels quite certain she knows what it contains. The exclusive. Earlier this week, Ada had notified Minnie Musgrave of her final day of filming, reminding her that the exclusive could run once it was completed, which the gossip columnist apparently interpreted as permission to proceed. Never mind that Ada had stressed the exclusive should not run until filming ended—and, knowing Mrs. Musgrave, she would argue it *is* over as of today, therefore she has not violated their agreement.

At Mr. Hendrix's outburst, Vince steps closer to Ada while a crowd lingers, eager to hear about whatever sin the film's leading lady has committed.

"What the hell is the meaning of this?" Mr. Hendrix brandishes the paper. "After I gave you strict instructions, after I plucked you from obscurity—"

"She was my idea, not yours," Mr. Sternberg says, so the studio head rounds on him.

"Stay out of this! I've already had to reassure countless investors and executives that this film is not tainted by your politics—"

"No director would alter a film into propaganda and expect to get away with it," Mr. Sternberg scoffs. "I'm not one to sabotage my own career, Hendrix, and you and your investors should know that."

"Be that as it may, I don't need my actress spouting her opinions."

"Mr. Hendrix," Ada interrupts through her teeth, not bothering with a tone that might placate him, because there will be no placating him. "I apologize for upsetting you, but extenuating circumstances required something different from my standard approach."

"Contributing to all this nonsense will only make it linger. Had you kept your mouth shut, you would have avoided getting caught up in it, but now you've destroyed everything you're supposed to be. Ada Worthington-Fox is charming, alluring, uncomplicated. Not this." He shoves the paper into Ada's hands. "This is not who you are, not who I want, and not who your fans want."

"Sir, I—"

"Not another word about this, *any* of this, while involved with my company and my film, or I will ruin you."

Mr. Hendrix barrels past Ada and storms off set. Quiet lingers like the moments after an earthquake, then cast and crew slowly move along now that the spectacle has ended. When a familiar hand covers Ada's, she blinks and looks at Vince, who gently takes the paper from her.

"Too bad the cameras weren't rolling. That was a better scene than any in our film," she says with a weak smile.

His blue eyes are alight with anger as he stares after Mr. Hendrix. Then he opens the article and reads while Ada waits, her heart suddenly racing in anticipation of his thoughts. Once finished, he looks at her.

"This is an excellent piece—not divisive or accusatory or portraying yourself, the film, or anyone in a negative light. Mr. Hendrix should be thanking you for it."

"It's not something I would normally do, therefore not what he wants from me, so he thinks the public won't approve either. Take away the mystery, take away the intrigue." She gives a half-hearted shrug, then flashes a teasing smile. "If I hadn't been so aloof and evasive, would Vince Hart have been interested in me?"

"Nothing would have made me disinterested in you, Ada."

He does not match her lighthearted tone, and her cheeks warm even as their eyes meet before shifting away. Once again, they have returned to that place. To recalling what they were, leaving them with the stark reality of what they are.

At last, Vince clears his throat. "You're all right?"

"Fine. Thank you," she murmurs, touching his arm briefly before stepping away.

As she goes, though, she feels him staring after her. She cannot determine if her heart is still racing from the conversation with Mr. Hendrix or the one with Vince.

Back in her dressing room, Ada changes out of her costume and notices a small parcel on her dressing table. A congratulatory gift from Gordon or Ingrid, perhaps, which must have arrived during filming. She unwraps the package—no card, only a small box. And when she opens it, a gasping cry catches in her throat.

The gift is a silver brooch in the shape of an ornate key. A skeleton key.

Ada presses a palm to her pounding heart, to the scar on her chest, to everything inside her that knows who sent this. The only person who would have chosen this symbol.

He is alive. And he has found her.

CHAPTER 24

Washington, DC, 31 January 1947

INGRID

S now crunches beneath their feet as Ingrid and Hattie leave the café's warmth, having met for coffee after work. Time together was a welcome respite, considering Ingrid has spent this last month reviewing her report over and over, meeting with Archie and others in the office, and awaiting orders. Today she learned they would be returning to California in May in accordance with HUAC's developing plans to conduct hearings in Los Angeles.

Hearings. Why it has come to hearings, Ingrid does not know, but it shouldn't take her long to satisfy Crenshaw and Stieber's demands, so hopefully Ada will avoid something so unnecessary. As they step out into the chilly January evening, she tugs her coat around her while Hattie tucks a loose brown curl behind her ear and exhales, her breath forming a hazy cloud.

"Call me once your fellow takes you to dinner," Ingrid says, since their conversation over coffee involved an FBI agent Hattie has been getting to know recently. "You really should accept his invitation."

"I know, I know. It's just so strange to think of another man that way, even though it's been nearly six years since I lost my husband. But the fellow from work really is kind, and Ian would want me to be happy."

"He would, and so do I." Ingrid gives her friend a reassuring squeeze, then checks her wristwatch. "Well, I should get home. Tomorrow, if I call after lunch, will you—?"

"You're going to call me to ask about Dietrich again, aren't you?"

"I'm hardly that predictable, am I?" Her friend's pointed silence communicates the answer. "Check again, please. You're an absolute dear," she adds with a smile.

"And don't you forget it."

After thanking Hattie, Ingrid bids her friend goodbye and continues on her way, biting back her frustration. Hattie has yet to find any information on Gregor Dietrich's fate, but information must be somewhere.

When Ingrid returns to the apartment, Lars is not home. His law office usually keeps him late, so she cracks open a window to welcome the chilly winter air and lights a cigarette, then the telephone rings—Lars, probably, saying he's going to be later than usual. When she answers, the urgency of the other voice—Ada's voice—brings immediate tension to her chest.

"It was him. At work. It was him, I know it was, and—"

"Slow down, what are you talking about?"

"*Him.*" A fragile breath. "Dietrich. The exclusive published today, and I received a gift on set—a silver brooch shaped like a skeleton key. Nothing else, no note, nothing. That key is part of his family crest, remember?" Her voice sounds the way it did the morning after the Star Society party, when she spoke of her experiences. The sound of memories, of suffering, of everything Ingrid can't bear to hear. "If this was from him, the cryptic messages have been too. I'm sure of it. He wants the evidence, he's trying to frighten me so I'll give it up, and—"

"Listen to me, listen to me," Ingrid interrupts, the words coming so fast she hardly knows what she's saying, overcome by a singular, aching need to ease the horror in her sister's voice. "We expected this, didn't we? It's like you told me: If he knows where you are, but he hasn't come for the evidence yet, there's a reason he's taking his time."

"Why? What reason?"

"Maybe just to taunt you like you said, but whatever it is, it's keeping you safe, and this proves your theory. He probably saw the exclusive this morning, so he sent the brooch—targeting you again like you thought he would following provocation. For whatever reason, he hasn't contacted you directly yet, but now we know if you keep this up, it might draw him out once he's had enough. The plan is working."

Silence follows while Ingrid can't breathe, can't fold her sister into her arms, can't reassure her. She listens, seeing only a broken, frightened, lonely girl haunted by her past, fighting for survival now as she was then.

"Provoking him was my idea, wasn't it?" Ada asks softly. Another moment of quiet, then a weak laugh. "God, you must think I've gone completely mad."

Quiet settles while Ingrid fumbles for a cigarette. She takes a long draw before Ada's murmur comes again.

"This is how it's going to be for the rest of my life, isn't it? Even if we find him and get justice. Even if considering him makes no logical sense. He will always be my first thought." More silence. Ingrid twists the phone cord around her finger, searching for a suggestion, a solution, anything to take away the fear, then Ada speaks with slightly more assurance. "Well, since the plan seems to be working, I'll encourage Gordon to have Paul build the gate around the property, and I could always hire security. If for no other reason than peace of mind."

"Yes, do both. Call the moment we hang up. Especially with your career advancing, security is a wise investment anyway, and I'll feel better knowing you feel better." Security. Of course. Why didn't she think of that? "And don't do anything more for now. Let Dietrich think he's successfully subdued you so Hattie will have more time to find information, if it exists, and you can get security in place and wait for me to come back before we try anything else."

Silence on the other line, then Ada's voice, gentle and hopeful. "You're coming back?"

"Your premiere is in May, isn't it? I wouldn't miss it. And I'm sure you'll need an assistant in the weeks leading up to it," she teases, to which Ada gives a faint chuckle. "Well done on finishing your shoot, by the way. How do you feel?"

"Utterly exhausted, though never too exhausted for a post-filming party." She sounds more like her usual self, thank God. Ingrid has little trouble picturing the extravagance that will certainly be taking place at Gordon's house this evening.

"I'm so proud of you, Leidje, and so sorry I'm not there to celebrate."

"I wish you were coming tonight. Jimmy will be here—Stewart, one of Vince's friends who enlisted—so I'm excited to meet him and glad he's working again. From the way Vince talks about him, I think you'd like him too."

The name is familiar, and Ingrid tries to focus on it, on anything other than the anxiety refusing to settle. "Was he in a Christmas film that released recently? Lars and I saw one a few weeks ago, *It's a Wonderful Life*."

"Yes, James Stewart, that's Jimmy. See, I knew you'd like him."

They carry on a light conversation while Ingrid fidgets, guilt and worry and concern vibrating through her. Soon she will be back in Los Angeles. Present for Ada, able to help and reassure her.

As she finishes her cigarette, the door swings open, so she bids her sister goodbye.

"Sorry I'm late. Was that Aleida?" Lars asks as he enters the apartment.

"Yes, she's finished filming."

She couldn't tell him about her initial investigation—confidentiality, after all—but she did tell him that she saw an advertisement about the actress and realized her sister survived, so after her work assignment, she took a trip to visit Ada before coming home. He glances at her, a look that makes Ingrid curse her own thoughtlessness. She didn't even attempt to control her tone, and now it's betrayed the tension fraying every nerve.

"Did something happen between you?" he asks as he hangs up his hat and coat.

This time her reply is more relaxed, though she's aching to light another cigarette. "No, we're fine. I'm just tired. How was your day?"

After they talk, Lars disappears into their bedroom to change clothes. In the ensuing silence, the conversation with Ada cycles through Ingrid's mind.

Dietrich is growing bolder. It's what they wanted, what they expected, what they needed. Except if he takes her evidence and disappears again, they will be exactly where they are now. Building a case, if only they could find the culprit.

CHAPTER 25

Los Angeles, 10 March 1947

ADA

Early press has become routine over the last week, then it will cease until closer to the film premiere. When Ada and Vince exit a studio following a radio interview, a group of young people notice them and nudge one another, clearly recognizing the actors—attention that will grow tiresome eventually, Ada supposes, but for now, makes her feel like a star. They appear to be of university age, she supposes, though she pretends not to notice them following her and Vince toward their car.

"Vince Hart?" one girl squeals. "I've seen all your pictures, and yours, Miss Worthington-Fox, and I read your recent exclusive."

Before Ada or Vince can acknowledge the fan, one of the young men leers at Ada. "How about a private meeting, Miss Worthington-Fox? I'll let you give me an exclusive."

"Mind your manners, sir," she chides amid whistles and shouts of assent from the other fellows. Must they make everything suggestive? Then she flashes a smile that falls between an invitation and a warning. "Is there to be another exclusive? If so, I'm afraid you've done a poor job of convincing me to grant it to you, darling."

Few things will ever be more satisfying than wiping a smug grin off a man's face. By now they've reached their car, so Vince steps back to allow Ada inside while a question from another man follows on their heels.

"Was your statement true? Or are you a member of the Communist Party?"

And then Ada forgets the whistles, the catcalls, these brazen questions. As expected, her statement changed little. People will ask what they wish to ask no matter how many times she answers.

"Why arrange a statement only to lie?" She arches a brow. "Every word was true, I assure you, including those regarding my views."

Then she precedes Vince into the car, and their driver takes them down the busy street toward Hollywood Hills.

Everything about Vince has shifted—his jaw tight, his winning smile gone. No longer beloved actor Vince Hart, instead a tense—even angry—young man. Once she would have loosened his tie, hooked a finger through the loop, and pulled him close, murmuring that all he needed to do was say the word and she would erase that look. For a moment she nearly does.

Instead she clasps her hands in her lap.

"You handle them well," he says after a moment. "Those questions. I'm just sorry you have to endure people who have no respect for you or your word."

"Welcome to being a woman," she replies dryly, though she briefly places an appreciative hand over his.

Silence descends over them. She glances at Vince—no longer tense or angry, simply that same indifferent look to which she's grown so accustomed. One so far removed. A knot forms in her throat while he shifts and passes a hand through his hair.

Ada runs her finger over a small tear in the seat's leather upholstery. "At least our interviews have been civilized so far, although we've only been at this for a short time. They're probably waiting until some good pictures end up in the papers before they really start speculating about us."

"Should we give them a good picture?" Vince asks, his brow quirking in slight amusement.

"Such as you sweeping me off my feet and leaving a big kiss right on my lips?" she replies while his laugh joins hers. How she's missed laughing like this with him.

"It's like we agreed before we started filming. Focus on the work. Anything else will only encourage them."

Something about the way he says it brings a dullness to the pleasant brightness of their conversation. Perhaps the reminder of how things are between them will always hold such power. The ability to take two people and keep them suspended in a liminal space between comfort and discomfort, ease and tension, familiarity and unfamiliarity. Because what they had before is not what they have now. Even if neither one wants what they once had, loss remains a painful ache.

After years apart and months working together, perhaps her reluctance to address that loss is what has kept them in this place of in-between. As the car stops in front of Gordon's house, Ada doesn't step out right away.

"Will you come inside for a drink?"

The question leaves her mouth before she can lose the courage to ask it, prompted by something she has kept buried for so long. She should have done this years ago when she left him, rather than once again succumbing to silence.

Gordon is out, and Sowerby greets them before retreating to the chaise longue in Ada's office, his favorite place to nap. The bar cart in the library is always supplied with a selection of libations, but Ada finds what she needs in the kitchen bar cabinet. She pours cognac for Vince, mixes a martini for herself—gin, a touch of vermouth, plenty of ice, stirred and strained into a chilled glass and garnished with a lemon peel, just as she likes it. Then she joins him in the library, surrounded by wood, leather, and the comforting smell of old books.

When they sit in caramel-colored leather armchairs, Ada can almost feel the tension beyond Vince's relaxed exterior, can almost sense him crushing down everything he wants to say because he knows she will never give him the explanation he seeks.

Not until now.

Ada has not rehearsed this speech, has not prepared, has done nothing in anticipation of this moment. For once, she wants to speak freely.

"I wanted to succeed on my own. That's why I ended things. Because I wanted to earn my place, not have it granted as an extension of your fame or anyone else's."

Maybe he expected this discussion, maybe not. Vince sits straighter, a slight edge sharpening his words. "You didn't think I wanted the same for you?"

"What either of us wanted didn't matter, not when the press knew me as Vince Hart's lady. Nothing more. I wanted them to know me first as Ada, then as Vince's." Her voice falls. "And you as Vince, then as mine."

He visibly winces, as if she's struck a nerve, then the muscle along his jaw ripples. "What's your point, Ada? To make yourself feel better? Because I know you're not saying any of this for my benefit, not after you let me spend the last few years thinking I'd done something wrong." This time it's her turn to wince as he finishes his drink in one gulp and stands. "Why now? Why explain yourself now?"

"Because you deserve the truth."

"And I didn't then?"

Silence has always damned her, by choice or otherwise. Silence to protect her resistance work, silence about the life she had, silence to Vince because she thought it was easier when, in fact, it caused far more damage than the truth.

Yet silence has also protected her in ways he will never understand. Ways she can never explain. Right now, though, she cannot allow silence to hurt him any more than it already has.

Ada sets down her drink and crosses to meet him. "What should I have said, Vince? I'm leaving you despite how I feel about you?"

"Finally, some honesty." He passes a hand over his jaw the way he always does when upset. "I thought we were happy. I thought *you* were happy. And then I thought I'd ruined the best goddamned thing that ever happened to me."

"Do you think it was easy, realizing I had to choose between my career and the man I loved?"

Deathly silence falls. She never admitted as much to him, even to herself. *Loved.*

Complete and total honesty, for once in her life.

They stand close together, chests rising and falling, both the drink and her admission rushing hot through Ada's veins. His words echo with each of her thudding heartbeats. *The best goddamned thing.*

Then she reaches for Vince and takes his face between her palms while his fingers tangle in her hair, and suddenly it's him. Only him. His lips tasting of cognac and charged with the tension still heating her skin, with everything she can never tell him, with the distance of these last years, with the last months of being together while being apart.

Now, perhaps, they can escape the clutches of the liminal space.

The air rushes from her lungs with a little gasp when he presses her back to the bookshelves, and she is aware of every part of her, every part of him. The tension in his fingers against her waist, the rumble of approval in his chest when she brings his lips to hers, the nearly tangible, insatiable craving for each other exacerbated by time, by this moment.

"I'm sorry. For all of it." She has little time for more before another kiss leaves her breathless.

"So am I." He punctuates each sentence with kisses to her neck. "Because if I'd known how you felt, I would have done anything. Walked away if that was what you really wanted. Staged a public separation and continued seeing you in private. Anything." He lifts his head to meet her eyes. "You deserve your career, and you deserve to be happy. Not to give up one for the other."

She loosens his tie, hooks a finger through the loop, and draws him closer, as she longed to do on their way here, as she once did so often—slowly, never breaking his gaze. Then he kisses her until the wall of heavy books behind her and the pressure of his body against hers are the only things keeping her upright. When they break apart, his voice is a rasp.

"Damn it, Ada, it's you. Still."

That word again.

Still.

Heat thrums through her stomach, marring her ability to ascertain anything other than an unmasked awareness of exactly what she wants: more. And from the way his lips remain inches from hers, the way his hand grips her skirt, the way he leans in, she senses he wants the same.

Except he doesn't give it to her.

Instead Vince releases her. He steps back without another word, another look, another touch. Moments later, she hears the front door close behind him, leaving her in the library, breaths sharp, heart beating too fast, heat spinning through her body. Anticipating a *more* that did not come, and likely never will.

* * *

After a few days and no word from Vince, Ada resigns herself to one conclusion: Their conversation in the library led to a moment of weakness. Nothing more.

What they want remains unchanged: a successful film. Not each other. Attraction is not worth shifting focus from the work.

But those kisses were far from stage kisses.

The attraction between them was never the trouble; that part has always been far too easy. Everyone is permitted a weak moment. She will be mindful to refuse herself another, that's all.

"If you and Vince get together, wait until closer to release," Gordon advises her a few nights later when she tells him about the incident over dinner. "The press is enjoying the will-they-won't-they, so leave your audience in suspense awhile longer."

"We are not getting together," she reminds him—not for the first time—but Gordon is already rubbing a hand thoughtfully over his mustache.

"Closer to release, have dinner at Musso and Frank Grill, and I'll hire a journalist to snap a few photos of you two. Let your audience wonder—are the rumors of a reunion true? Viewers will flock to the theaters during the first week to assess your on-screen chemistry and make their predictions. Then give your audience their happily-ever-after." He spreads his hands, as if showcasing a headline. "'A Love Story Fit for Screen: How Vince Hart and Ada Worthington-Fox Fell in and out of Love, and in Love Again.'"

"You should ask Minnie Musgrave for lessons on snappy headlines, darling, because that one is awful." While he grumbles about the gossip columnist, Ada shakes her head. "That's not how I want to make a name for myself."

Nor does she want to toy with Vince's feelings—or her own. Even if they agreed to excite the press with staged outings or a fake relationship, those feelings are too easily stirred. As proven by their kisses.

"You know I'd never tell you to do anything you don't want to do, kid," Gordon says as he takes their dirty dishes to the sink. "But it's my job to help you build your career. Gossip sells."

Of course it does. Gossip will sell enough without her and Vince contributing to the rumors.

"As long as you're happy, I'm happy. Just because my only relationship is with work, it doesn't mean yours should be," he concludes once they move into the living room, where he takes his favorite gold satin chair. "Get back together with Vince, or don't. Either way, you're a damn good actress. Nothing will change that."

She places a hand on his arm in gratitude before accepting a cigarette, turning on the television, and stretching out on the elegantly carved sofa with its emerald velvet cushions. Gossip might encourage interest, but it can't improve a poor film. That responsibility lies with those who made it.

"Another option," Gordon muses. "Invite Vince over and take him upstairs. None of the press and all of the fun."

"If I were considering any of these options, that one would have already crossed my mind."

Despite her teasing smile and Gordon's suggestive wink, she can almost feel the old scar burning. She glances down, though of course her clothing covers it. She takes a drag of her cigarette to push the sensation away and pats Sowerby as he nestles beside her.

God willing, there will be no more moments of weakness with a man Ada does not want.

Even if she can't get his words out of her head. Even if she can't forget the feeling of his lips against hers. Even if she can't stop recalling the way their kisses in her dressing room made her feel so *wanted*. The same way their kisses in the library did.

She doesn't have to see him again until press continues. And when that time comes, she will not be alone with him, will not do anything to lead to another possible moment of weakness. She will focus on the film. Only the film.

Over the next few months, she does precisely that. No encounters with Vince, no mysterious messages from men who are likely Dietrich, no provocations that might goad him or divert her attention from the upcoming release. Instead, Ada maintains her usual privacy as she awaits Ingrid's return. Once they are together again, Ada's film will premiere, then perhaps she will give another exclusive. Maybe one about escaped war criminals, encouraging the public to look for a particular officer who was stationed in Arnhem.

If that does not encourage Dietrich to steal the evidence back, nothing will. Then perhaps Ingrid can enlist Hattie's aid to send an FBI contact who might take him into custody.

* * *

On a pleasant morning in early May, Gordon leaves for a meeting while Ada prepares for Ingrid's arrival. Ada had insisted she stay at Gordon's rather than the Biltmore, so she tidies the house, making sure everything is in order, then gets dressed.

As she finishes styling her hair, the doorbell rings. Ingrid, here already? Her flight wasn't supposed to arrive until this afternoon. The anticipation of seeing her sister hastens every footstep until she throws open the door—and gasps.

Not Ingrid. An older woman.

Suddenly her grip on the doorknob is the only thing keeping Ada on her feet.

The woman's hair in her tight bun is as dark as Ada remembers, the lines around her eyes slightly more pronounced, the level, gray-eyed stare unwavering. And then comes her voice, clear and refined and thick with emotion.

"Oh, my darling girl."

Nothing could have prepared Ada for the way she would feel upon hearing that voice again. She can hardly think, and she hardly manages a breathless reply.

"Hello, Mother."

CHAPTER 26

Hollywood Hills, 6 May 1947

ADA

Constance de Vos enters Gordon Sharpe's home as if she's never belonged anywhere else. The same rigid posture, the same scrupulous gaze, a few more fine lines across her face. The war has left its mark on her as it has on so many others.

Mother is here, alive, leaving Ada no time to process the realization before Mother suddenly berates her, every barbed word driving deeper.

"After all I did to protect you, none of it mattered. *I* didn't matter. You left without a word, Aleida, without a single indication you were alive despite how difficult it was for us when Ingrid—" Then her voice breaks and she pulls Ada close.

Something within Ada shatters as she clings to Mother and fights her own tremulous breaths amid Mother's choked sobs.

"How could you? How could you let me endure such a terrible ordeal a second time? To lose both my daughters, my darling little girls..."

Every part of Ada prickles with heat—shame, guilt, relief, and uncertainty all at once.

"I'm sorry . . ." The words fall away, partially because Ada can't find them, partially because she doesn't know what to say.

She has so many questions, ones she was never permitted to ask. Because she was told simply to trust Mother and keep quiet. Once Mother has calmed, Ada draws back.

"How did you find me?"

"I've looked for both of you ever since the war ended. I came to America and hoped you might be here, or perhaps England, then I saw a film advertisement, and there you were. So here I am." Gently, Mother cups Ada's cheeks, her eyes welling with more tears before she regains her composure. "Might you have any tea? This is all rather overwhelming."

Ada leads her into the kitchen, where she sits while Ada brews tea, fetches two cups, and rummages through Gordon's cabinets. Crackers and sliced cheese will have to do.

When Sowerby pads into the room, the intrepid little fellow approaches Mother despite her discouraging frown. She never was one for pets. Ada calls to him, so he remains underfoot while she works in silence. Once the tea is served, Ada takes her seat. Then she can keep silent no longer.

"Tell me the truth, Mother. I have to know." Already she feels it—the scar on her breast, burning and aching as if fresh. She fights to voice his name. "Did Dietrich force you to be with him? Or was it your choice?"

Ada does not know which she expects, or which would be worse to hear. A shadow passes over Mother's face—sorrow, regret, or something else, Ada cannot tell.

"Being associated with your grandfather put us in enough danger, considering he was publicly anti-Nazi. We needed protection. When I think of what those men might have done to us, to you—" Mother stares into her teacup, swallowing hard. "I met Dietrich one day when I was out shopping. He took an interest in me, and when I learned he was such a high-ranking officer, I thought I could pretend for a little while. To keep us safe. No, he did not force me, nor did I want to give him or anyone else the opportunity. So I chose to be willing instead."

A choice, yet not a choice. Ada stares into her own teacup, a sour taste filling her mouth.

"I couldn't admit the truth to anyone, not even you, because it was safer for us both." Her voice breaks, so Ada meets her eyes. "How could you truly believe my actions were sincere?"

Ada had not known what to believe—at times fully convinced it was all real yet praying she was wrong and it was an act. Hearing the truth now gives her slight relief, even though her next question is tight.

"What happened to him?"

"A few days before Germany's surrender, I woke up and found he had fled."

Dietrich survived, then. Unless he was arrested or killed later. If he is alive, Ada's chance for justice remains, yet the realization brings little reassurance even though it's what she wants, what his victims deserve. Whether he is alive or dead, condemned or acquitted, this unsettled feeling will never leave her. He will never leave her.

"Darling, I realize how difficult those times must have been for you. How confusing. How frightening." Mother covers Ada's hand with her own, her gaze clear and earnest. "Every choice I made was for our protection. *Your* protection. All I ask is that you try to understand."

A ray of hope blossoms in Ada's chest. If Mother is telling the truth, she was simply a woman in an occupied country faced with an impossible choice. So she made the one that she thought might aid in her family's survival, wrong though it was to align herself with the enemy. Still, maybe she is not the dedicated fascist Ingrid fears her to be.

Perhaps they can start again.

"The war couldn't have been easy for you either."

"I did my best for you. And for Ingrid." When her voice breaks, she

pinches the bridge of her nose. "Such a stubborn girl, that one." A fragile breath, leaving Ada's heart tightening. "For years, every day has been
agony. And I've tried to accept it, I have, but how can I accept never
knowing what happened to my little girl?"

"No, please don't worry, Mother. Ingrid is all right, she's alive, she's—"

And then Ada can't quite comprehend what she's done. What she's
said. Ingrid might not want to be found, and Ada blurted out the information without her sister's permission.

Mother looks up, eyes bright. "You've found her? Oh, thank God."
She places a hand on her chest, closes her eyes to resist tears. "Please,
you must convince her to meet with me."

Ada is not certain Ingrid will be convinced, but she nods. Perhaps
Ingrid will surprise her; maybe she will set aside her mistrust long
enough to hear Mother's explanation.

Mother's chair scrapes across the floor as she stands. "I'll do whatever I must to prove myself to both of you. To earn your understanding
and forgiveness. To erase the past. All of it."

Despite the reassurance of her willingness, a chill settles over Ada's
skin. If only it were so easy. Forgetting.

Ada will never forget. Dietrich made certain of that.

"I know you took evidence, Aleida. Evidence against him. And
against me."

The quiet statement is not critical; rather, it is so anguished, Ada
can't meet Mother's gaze. Because she is right. Ada has held evidence
against her own mother all this time. Even if it was a choice made to
protect them, Mother betrayed innocent people. Can Ada forgive her
for something so terrible?

"Do you know what happened to Dutch women accused of collaborating?" Mother presses. "Their heads were shaved. I was spared only
because I fled right after Dietrich did. With help from a few officers
under his command who escaped with me, I got out of Arnhem, but

I saw what was happening. Those women were publicly shamed, humiliated, left with a visible reminder of their treachery. Perhaps some collaborated out of genuine support. Perhaps others were falsely condemned. Still others might have felt they had no other choice, or they were coerced, forced, threatened, assaulted, God knows what. And yet, no matter the reason, each woman was mocked and ridiculed just the same."

The disturbing images fill Ada's head, and she struggles to suppress them while Mother continues.

"Would you wish the same fate upon me? Because as long as you cling to your evidence, you cling to the past. To your mistrust. I can explain myself over and over, but I can't force you to believe me. All I ask is that you allow me time to earn your trust. To be your mother." A hand brushes a sudden escaped tear from Ada's cheek. "We can be a family again."

Despite the confusion and uncertainty swirling inside her, the words settle Ada slightly. It's all she wants too—for Mother to be a mother. Not a Nazi supporter, a mistress, a collaborator.

"I think time will be good for us," she agrees softly. "Gordon has a guesthouse near the rose garden, if you'd like to stay."

Mother offers a little smile. "I'd like nothing more."

Ada shows her the way and helps her settle into the little cottage, then she returns to the main house, her heart pounding.

Ingrid will be here soon. And Ada has invited both her and Mother to stay here. A notion Ingrid will certainly reject when she finds out.

How Ada is going to explain any of this to Ingrid, she does not know. She cannot lose her sister a second time.

CHAPTER 27

Hollywood Hills, 6 May 1947

INGRID

The prospect of seeing her sister leaves Ingrid's skin as warm as if she were relaxing in the sunshine by Gordon's pool. She's in California for work, true. This time, though, perhaps a little more play.

When she reaches the white brick mansion, both Sowerby and Ada greet her at the door. She scoops up the terrier, who seems pleased to see her again, then sets him free and looks to her sister.

"Why don't I see a security guard or a gate around the property?"

Ada frowns. "Due to existing commitments, Mr. Williams can't begin construction until the end of the year, and security comes at night. Must you criticize me before you've even said hello?"

"I was asking, not criticizing," Ingrid replies pointedly, but Ada is glancing toward the back door and clearly not paying attention. Ingrid follows the quick look, her pulse hastening. If Ada is jittery and sensitive, something has happened. "What's the matter?"

"Nothing . . . I'm sorry for snapping at you." An edge of tension remains in her tone, leaving concern lodged in Ingrid's chest.

Whatever is troubling her, clearly Ada is not going to say more. Stress due to the upcoming premiere, perhaps. If it were something worrisome, she would tell Ingrid, so Ingrid does her best to let the matter go.

"I brought this for you."

She reaches into her luggage and pulls out a small pistol that, until now, she kept tucked in her nightstand drawer at home. When they left Arnhem, Lars had given it to her and taught her how to use it throughout the long, arduous journey to America. She never needed it.

God willing, Ada won't either.

When Ingrid left for her first assignment, Lars had suggested she travel with the gun for additional safety. Even a few fellows in her office had recommended similar means of protection. But she had not wanted to be reminded of the last time she had carried this gun, so she had left it behind. For her sister's safety, though, not even the past was enough to make her hesitate, and she had promptly tucked the weapon into her luggage.

At the sight of the gun, Ada steps back. "For God's sake, where did you—how did you—?" Then her wary stare transforms into a frown. "Security isn't enough, then? Now you think I need one of those?"

"Keep it for my peace of mind. Please." She offers the gun to Ada, who makes no move to accept it. "You intend to speak out again about Dietrich, don't you? Even if I call Hattie and ask her to send the FBI to arrest him the moment he emerges, he might find a way to get to you first. You said he won't be predictable, so you've got to protect yourself."

With a frustrated exhale, Ada gingerly accepts the weapon, then the ammunition Ingrid produces next. She listens and reluctantly practices as Ingrid advises her on how to use it, then carries the gun into the library. Ingrid follows, watching as Ada tucks it into a decorative cigar box on the mantel. So long as she has it, that's enough.

When they return to the living room, Ingrid hears the back door open—Gordon coming in from the pool, most likely.

"Is Gordon here? I thought you said he had meetings all day." Ingrid neither waits for an answer nor listens as Ada stammers something. She's already on her way to greet him and thank him for allowing her to stay here.

As she goes, she hears a voice—not Gordon's. A woman's, bringing Ingrid to an immediate halt.

"Aleida, does the guesthouse have any—?"

The question abruptly stops when the speaker rounds the corner, and Ingrid is face-to-face with Constance de Vos.

"Ingrid?" The incredulous gasp is followed by a sob, then Mother's arms are around her.

Tears prick Ingrid's own eyes, so confused and twisted she can't make sense of them. Relief that Mother wasn't killed, shock that she is here, aversion to her touch, fury that the war is now rushing back, overwhelming her, prompting her to pull free from Mother's grasp.

The hurt over the rejection is visible on Mother's face even as her fiercely critical gaze scrapes over Ingrid, absorbing every inch of her.

"How could you abandon your own mother? Your sister? All for your own selfish pursuits, political beliefs, and him."

The pressure builds in Ingrid's temples like it did that evening in 1938 when she brought Lars to dinner after Mother expressed interest in meeting him. A kind man from a good Dutch family, a military man, a man falling in love with her, and she with him. Not even Mother could find fault.

Except she did. Of course she did. The disapproving clicks of her tongue, the pitying glances, the dismayed sighs. *Darling, I know you think me unreasonable, but in time you will be grateful. I want better for you. This infatuation will fade, so there's no use in putting off the inevitable. End it with him.*

Mother's disappointment should no longer cut so deeply. Ingrid is not a girl anymore. She's a woman, a married, working woman. Yet she cannot subject herself to this again.

As Ada joins them, her face the picture of abject horror, Ingrid gives her sister no time to speak. "I couldn't stay, Mother. Not when Lars would have been forced to fight for them. I can't expect you to understand when you never tried then and certainly won't now."

Mother sighs, as though she too realizes exactly where this is going. Back to their usual arguments. "Darling, we can't recover from the war unless we give each other a fair chance." Her eyes are bright, her voice soft, intensifying the discomfort rippling through Ingrid's body. "All I want is my girls. I found Aleida, and you can't imagine my relief when she told me you were alive too, and here you are."

Every nerve inside Ingrid is on the verge of severing. She cannot do this, cannot accept Mother's entreaty—and she has so much to say to her sister. Because Ada did not warn Ingrid, did not prepare her, and now Mother is here. The woman whose political beliefs Ingrid has never trusted, whose favor Ingrid could never earn. The woman who shared a bed with the man who tortured her own daughter without her knowledge.

"Get out." The command is low, threatening, then Ingrid's voice rises as every nerve shatters. "Get out, get out, get *out!*"

Ada attempts to say something Ingrid fails to hear, but Mother has already stepped back with an unsteady breath.

She hurries out the way she came, through the back door, while Ada stares from her to Ingrid, visibly torn, then rushes after Mother. When she's gone, Ingrid slams the door behind her and locks it.

Her sister has just made a choice. She might have stayed with Ingrid and let Constance go. Instead, she walked out.

Ingrid can't understand why, can't sort out what to do, whether to apologize and give Mother a chance or to trust this feeling she has always had, the feeling that they cannot, will not ever reconcile. All she knows are her own shaking hands and shuddering breaths until she hears the door failing to open. Through the glass, Ingrid watches as Ada realizes it's locked before she meets Ingrid's gaze, scowling while her muffled voice comes from the other side.

"Let me in. You can't lock me out of my own house."

"*Gordon's* house."

"*Ingrid.*" Although Ingrid finally unlocks the door, she doesn't soften her glare as Ada's defense comes out in a rush. "I'm sorry. I didn't mean for this to happen."

"You didn't mean to lie to me? Because that feels like a rather deliberate decision."

"She arrived unexpectedly—and it wasn't a lie; I just didn't know how to tell you."

"You might have tried 'Mother is here.'" Ingrid's scowl deepens as she crosses her arms. "Instead you deliberately chose not to say anything, and you told Mother I was alive."

"She was upset, worried about you, it just . . . slipped out. No mother deserves to live like that, never knowing what happened to her daughter."

"When I'm the daughter in question, that is my decision," Ingrid retorts. "And you thought I didn't need to know she would be staying here too? Or did you intend to talk to me, talk to her, make it all better?"

"She's the only parent we've got, so until we know her position with certainty, we owe it to ourselves and to her to put forth our best efforts."

"We don't owe her a goddamn thing! She's not the mother you want her to be, Aleida. She never will be."

Ada winces. But she must know it's true, even if Constance de Vos is a better mother to Ada than she is to Ingrid. Even so, at some point fantasy must give way to reality.

Ingrid returns to the foyer and picks up her bags. "I'll be staying at the Biltmore."

Ada grabs her forearm. "Don't, please. Mother is in the guesthouse, and you're upstairs, so you don't have to be near one another." Her voice wavers. "Please don't leave."

The request is almost enough to make Ingrid concede. The deafening quiet magnifies their unsteady breaths, both matched as they once were in a small bedroom in Arnhem. Then Ingrid breaks Ada's hold and lets the door close behind her.

THE G-MEN, THE GLITTERATI, AND THE GOSSIP
by Minnie Musgrave

All red-blooded Americans can agree on one thing: There's a different shade of red threatening to wash away our stars and stripes. Communist influences are infiltrating everywhere, even our own entertainment industry: That's where J. Edgar Hoover and his G-men come in.

We can count on the FBI to defend American freedom and protect American values, and rumor has it that government agents have been spotted around some of Hollywood's hottest haunts—men in suits don't exactly blend in around here. These men are dedicated to protecting the entertainment industry from those seeking to insert damaging influences. What does this mean, my fellow Americans? Well, I'll tell you: Thanks to their efforts, we can go to the movies with a clear conscience.

Beginning May 9, Chairman Thomas himself will hold hearings at the Biltmore Hotel—closed to the public and disappointingly hush-hush, but I hear these will mostly involve minor union members rather than our stars. Thomas has promised to keep us members of the press updated, but if you have an inside connection, well, you know what to do. Tip line below, dolls.

As for the glitterati, none seem particularly bothered by the impending hearings or government agents on their turf. Bogey and Bacall were spotted with a group of friends at the Formosa Café while other stars were recently caught engaging in far less innocent practices.

On the set of *Lady Bella Donna* last November, the two leads were seen emerging from Miss Worthington-Fox's dressing room. Last November! Shame on all of you for keeping such a titillating tidbit from me until now. What were Hollywood's Hartthrob and his past love doing behind closed doors between takes? According to my sources, by the looks of them, let's just say if their on-screen chemistry sizzles, there might be a good explanation for it.

What do we think, film fans? Is the couple back together, or were they simply enjoying some workplace perks? *Lady Bella Donna* premieres this month, so we might soon find out.

CHAPTER 28

Los Angeles, 9 May 1947

INGRID

Well, Mother's presence introduces a terrible complication into Ingrid's investigation.

Ingrid had planned to stay at Gordon's, to go to Ada's premiere, to immerse herself in Ada's world even more fully, to uncover something to close this investigation. How is she supposed to accomplish her work if Mother is there? Discretion will be impossible, and Ingrid will never be able to focus, knowing she might be interrupted at any moment.

Only a few days have passed since their encounter, and already Ingrid feels Mother over her shoulder at every turn. She will have to return to Gordon's eventually, but for now she steps into Minnie Musgrave's office.

"Come to arrange Miss Worthington-Fox's next exclusive?" Mrs. Musgrave asks in greeting.

"A different proposition, actually. I can share inside information from the hearings. Beyond what Chairman Thomas reveals—and, as you know from the last story I proposed to you, I will keep my word."

Ingrid's offer has its desired effect. A greedy light appears in Mrs. Musgrave's eyes. "To do so, I need an assurance from you in exchange."

"How much?" She snatches her handbag, to which Ingrid shakes her head. "No money? A deal, then?" Mrs. Musgrave smirks and crosses her arms. "Do tell."

Ingrid draws a breath. This had better work. Until she finds something she can use to satisfy Crenshaw and Stieber, she's out of ideas and can't have anything unexpected contributing to their mistrust of Ada. She produces a folded paper.

"To prove I'm telling the truth, this contains information from the first round of hearings this morning." She shows it to Mrs. Musgrave long enough to let her confirm its validity; she will not be handing it over before their deal is finalized. "If you receive any tips about Ada Worthington-Fox, allow me to help you verify the information prior to publication so you can avoid spreading anything false about her."

Mrs. Musgrave clicks her tongue. "Not how this works, doll. I will spin any narrative however you want—favorably, unfavorably, give Ada an affair, an unwanted pregnancy, a broken heart, a feud with another actress, anything. Alter an entire line of celebrity gossip about a woman whose film is soon to hit the silver screen—one where she stars opposite her former and possibly current lover—to include verified facts alone, just to fit your desires? Off limits."

"Then I'm afraid so are the hearings, thus limiting you to the same information every other publication will receive, because I highly doubt your existing sources can access what I can access." Ingrid rises from her chair until she's standing over the other woman. "This offer will last until I leave this room. Best make up your mind in five . . . four . . ."

"You don't strike me as the type to give a damn about a shallow actress."

"Shallow? You published her exclusive, so you know she's far more than that."

Mrs. Musgrave gnaws on her lip, eyeing Ingrid as if she's just uncovered something beneficial. "A celebrity's assistant claiming access to the hearings? Does Ada know she hired a Communist hunter?"

Exposing a connection to the hearings had been a risk, of course. A risk necessary to take for Ada. Now the knowledge is in Mrs. Musgrave's hands, and Ingrid can't revoke it or convincingly deny it. But private investigation is all about gaining the upper hand, and sometimes the way to do so is to allow another to believe the upper hand is theirs.

She lifts a brow in feigned surprise. "I beg your pardon?"

Mrs. Musgrave lights a cigarette and takes a thoughtful drag. "'Hunting Hollywood's Vixen' might do . . . Catchy, isn't it? About a dirty government agent who won her way into the Star Society and is determined to prove the up-and-coming actress has Communist ties. All the politics, drama, and betrayal of an Academy Award–winning film."

Even if Mrs. Musgrave publishes such lies, Ada will believe her sister over a gossip columnist, surely. Her efforts are to help Ada, not to condemn her. Still, if Ingrid is exposed and the investigation is ruined, Crenshaw will never forgive her, and she can't let him find out she supplied Mrs. Musgrave with information from the hearings.

She replies through her teeth. "Are you threatening me, Mrs. Musgrave? After I got you the exclusive proving she doesn't have Communist ties?"

"'The Huntress of Hollywood . . .' God, it's too tempting."

"Very well, you've made your point. What do you want?"

"Information about the Commies, of course—HUAC, the investigations, all of it. And to write whatever the hell I please. Provide what I want, and I keep you out of my paper. And because you're annoying me even more than usual, I want to schedule another exclusive with Miss Worthington-Fox."

A second exclusive sooner rather than later might not be a terrible idea. With the hearings starting, it will be best for Ada to reassure the public with her newfound reputation for occasional openness.

Mrs. Musgrave extends a hand. Ingrid accepts it, nearly gasping at the tight grip before the elder woman lowers her voice.

"Law and order don't exist in Hollywood. Don't leave your world if you're not ready for ours, doll."

Ingrid doesn't falter. "I will speak to Miss Worthington-Fox regarding the exclusive, but if you write anything I don't like about either of us, all information about the hearings will cease, and the exclusive will be off. If I have connections to these hearings, best to consider what other connections I might have within our government. Ones you might not want in your path. Do keep that in mind."

As Mrs. Musgrave's satisfied smirk disappears, Ingrid jerks her hand free and departs, leaving the woman sitting behind her typewriter in a cloud of cigarette smoke. People really should stop attempting to hold leverage over her. She can just as easily do the same to them.

* * *

Ingrid's next errand takes her to Melrose Avenue and Windsor Street, where lush shrubs and palms surround a two-story white Spanish-style building and a prominent sign indicates Lucey's Restaurant. Inside, she spots a young waitress—Beverly Tolbert. Just the woman Ingrid was hoping to find.

The restaurant is quiet, so after asking Beverly for a private word, Ingrid follows her to a secluded table.

"I'm in town for Ada's premiere, and since you're her friend, I was hoping you could help me," Ingrid begins. "You are aware of concerns regarding Communist influences in your industry, I presume?"

Beverly stiffens. "I am *not* a Communist. Why? What have you heard?" When Ingrid says nothing, waiting for her to continue, she passes a hand over her face. "God, it's because I'm represented by Gordon, isn't it? His damn political views have nothing to do with me. Did Ada tell you he's more than just a Communist? He's—" She lowers her voice to a whisper. "Different."

"Different," Ingrid repeats slowly. "Meaning . . . ?"

"Meaning your young, charming, absolutely gorgeous cousin lives with him and spends hours half naked by his pool, and the man has never once given her a second glance." Beverly raises an eyebrow, prompting Ingrid to understand.

"You think Gordon is attracted to men."

"Have I seen him with anyone? Technically, no." She shrugs. "He's a private person regarding certain matters and perpetually absorbed in work, so that doesn't mean anything."

Not quite the sort of subversive behavior Ingrid was expecting to uncover. Still, a combination of prioritizing privacy and having no interest in Ada—who is half his age, she suspects—is hardly grounds for such speculations.

"Haven't you heard about the G-men all over the place? Wait until they find out I have a Communist, homosexual agent." Though the words are low and sharp, Beverly looks around as if to ensure no one overheard. "They'll think I'm subversive too, and then my career will be destroyed before it's even had a real chance to begin. No one will want to hire me, and no studio will protect me because I'm a nobody in this industry— unlike that charming little Brit Gordon decided to make a star."

A flash of what can only be jealousy and anger sparks in her eyes, accompanying the cynical remark. She would do well to remember she's speaking to that charming little Brit's blood. A talent agent knows talent when he sees it. Before Ingrid can remind her of this, Beverly lets out a shaky breath.

"The government might be starting with the unions, but they won't finish there. Most actors aren't worried, and maybe I'm overreacting, but at least I'm being cautious. I don't want to lose my career."

"All you have to do is cooperate. These measures are being taken for protection, not harm, so if you're honest, that's not a reason to condemn you, is it?"

She considers, then nods vigorously. "You're right, of course you're right. This won't reflect poorly on me unless I allow it."

How this conversation developed into one about Beverly, Ingrid can't quite figure out. As she prepares to redirect back to Ada, the restaurant door opens, announcing new patrons. Beverly pulls a tube of red Max Factor lipstick from an apron pocket, reapplies it, and excuses herself, so Ingrid lets the matter go and exits the restaurant.

As she takes a cab back to the Biltmore, she jots down notes from her errands, ruminating on Beverly's confirmation of Ingrid's fears. Some actors are paying attention to what's occurring; others are not. Some are associated with Communists by choice or otherwise; others are not.

Ingrid bites her lip as the ink on the page runs together in her mind. All will be well. The hearings at the Biltmore this week will remain quiet and, ideally, identify subversives before they have a chance to reflect poorly on people like her sister. Then this will be over.

After finishing her notes, Ingrid tucks them into her briefcase while the cab lets her out at the Biltmore. As she makes her way through the hotel, Beverly's remarks about Gordon remain prominent in her mind. He is a kind man. Good to her sister. Communist in the past, but he has since reconsidered his political affiliations. As for Beverly's remarks about him never attempting to coerce Ada into bed, despite living with her, it seems like a rather extreme reason to accuse him of being homosexual. Regardless, Gordon's personal preferences are not what Ingrid is here to identify.

When she reaches the conference room where the afternoon's hearings will take place, suited men are everywhere. She offers her identification to the security guard stationed at the door, then slips inside and finds a table in a far corner, away from Archie and everyone else. As the room is called to order, Ingrid settles back to take notes, even though she can't focus.

If she's going to finish her investigation, and if she and Ada are going to move forward with their war crimes case against Dietrich, Ingrid has to go back to Gordon's. Where Mother is. And the longer she delays, the more time she wastes.

What if Ada has already told Mother everything about their plans to locate Dietrich? Such knowledge cannot be safe with her, not until they know where her loyalties lie. Maybe Ada is prepared to believe her, but Ingrid is not. Not yet, if ever. Certainly not while Mother's former lover is targeting Ada.

The thought brings a new one to Ingrid's mind, so clear, so obvious. She stops taking notes and sits up straighter.

Of course. Mother.

* * *

When the hearings end, Ingrid rushes to her hotel room to put away her work, then hails a cab and goes straight to Gordon's. There, Ada answers the door, her eyes brightening hopefully at the sight of Ingrid before dulling once again, as if wary of the purpose of this unplanned visit.

"Where is she?" Ingrid demands.

"The guesthouse."

Ingrid grabs Ada's arm and pulls her upstairs. Maybe Mother is in a separate building, but she will feel better with more distance and more privacy. Once in Ada's bedroom, she closes the door and releases her.

"What if it's never been Dietrich? What if it's someone who knows him well enough to impersonate him, who wants you to think he's found you? Someone who wants you to forfeit the evidence."

"Who else would want me to . . . ?" Ada trails off as she understands. But of course she will not say it, so Ingrid will.

"Mother. It's been her all along."

The woman who was sleeping with Dietrich. Who knows his family crest. Who wants the opportunity to start over with her children, to forget everything the war did to them. Maybe she has been back in Ada's life for far longer than Ada realized. Watching, carefully orchestrating, making her demands, and she will continue the charade until Ada succumbs.

Just when Ingrid thought she couldn't resent that woman more. Now she's tormenting her own daughter. All to ensure she will never be held accountable for collaborating with the SS and Police Leader.

"Why would Mother do such a thing when she could talk to me outright, exactly as she did the other day? She wouldn't have spent all these months knowing I was alive and avoiding me."

"She would if she's been impersonating Dietrich. And now she's here to find out if you've been suitably frightened enough to let the past go." When Ada protests again, Ingrid holds up a hand. "Promise me you won't tell her about the war crimes case. Until we know her true loyalties, we can't trust her."

Ada sighs. "Fine. But please talk to her. I can't do this without you."

Her sister has a point. Ingrid cannot determine who Constance de Vos really is by avoiding her. A conversation might give her some insight. Best not to put it off, then.

Every step Ingrid takes toward the guesthouse is heavier than the last. Not even the fragrant air of the rose garden is enough to settle the impulse twisting inside her, warning her to turn back. But she presses on. She must do this for herself and her sister. Once there, she gathers her strength, then knocks on the door.

When it swings open, Mother regards her in silence. Ingrid had expected something—a relieved sigh, an entreaty, a frown of displeasure, anything. Maybe the lack of reaction is hurtful, maybe not. Ingrid can't discern anything beyond the anxiety coiling inside her.

The guesthouse is a quaint little cottage with a small bedroom, bathroom, kitchen, and living room. A bouquet of freshly cut roses is displayed on a small table, doing little to settle Ingrid as she faces Mother, uncertain what to say.

"There's a reason I fell in love with your father," Mother says softly. "Because his spirit was so incredibly fierce, exactly like yours. When he left, you girls were not even a year old, and as you grew, any reminders of him were too painful for me. So when you became so much like him, I didn't know what to do. Maybe I sensed I was doing everything wrong, but I didn't know how to do anything differently."

Ingrid drives her fingernails into her palms, unsure if she should accept or reject the excuse, the apology, whatever this is. She was never jealous of how much Mother favored Aleida, never unaware of the ways Papa's absence had affected each of them. She simply wanted to be recognized for who she was and who she had become, not to be held accountable for wounds she had not inflicted.

"I needed you, Mother."

When Aleida lost one parent, Ingrid lost both. Truth is such a stark, unsightly thing.

A single tear slips down Mother's cheek. "It should not have taken losing you to make me realize how unfair I was to you."

Hearing the admission is salve upon a wound—not healing it entirely, but easing the pain a little. Not enough to make Ingrid accept the apology, but enough to allow Mother to brush a tear from Ingrid's cheek. Not encouraging Ingrid to trust her completely, but convincing her to step into Mother's arms and embrace her in return.

She doesn't know how long they stay there, the quiet broken by their shuddering breaths. At last, Ingrid releases her.

"I will try if you will," she says, to which Mother kisses her cheek, too overcome to reply.

Ingrid doesn't know if she's entirely prepared to try at all. There is no part of her relationship with Mother that does not require repair. Yet perhaps if she puts forth an effort, it will help her determine if her theories are correct.

She doesn't want to be right. She doesn't want Mother to be a fascist, to have chosen Dietrich, to be the one harassing Ada. But at one time Mother had wanted so desperately for Ingrid to see someone other than Lars that she refused to listen to Ingrid's entreaties on his behalf, made no efforts to get to know him beyond their initial introduction, forbade his presence in their home, and threatened all manner of punishments if Ingrid disobeyed her.

All to force Ingrid to give him up. To get what she wanted. And now she wants her daughters to give her a second chance.

When it comes to getting what she wants, Constance de Vos will do whatever it takes.

CHAPTER 29

Los Angeles, 13 May 1947

ADA

Since resuming publicity for *Lady Bella Donna*, Ada's schedule has included interviews, events, articles, all involving her alone. Until today. Today she has an interview on a radio program with Vince.

The man she has not seen since they kissed in the library.

After an assistant directs her to the recording room, Ada clutches her handbag and matches her breaths to her steps. Vince won't be fretting over this interview. When she sees him, he will be as relaxed as always. As if their moment of weakness never happened.

Her stomach should not tighten at the thought. At how easily he can forget. And her breaths should not hasten when she sees him approaching the recording room from the opposite end of the hall.

As she walks, she opens her handbag, avoiding the tiny pistol tucked inside—brought along to satisfy Ingrid—and pushes a few items around her bag, as if looking for something. Surely Vince didn't notice her noticing him.

"Message for you, miss."

Ada pauses. An errand boy of perhaps fourteen offers her an envelope. "From whom?" she asks, though a chill is already prickling across her skin.

"Dunno. The receptionist said she found it on her desk a few days ago." He flashes a lopsided smile. "So many folks come in and out, it's hard to say who left it."

A few days. Meaning whoever left this message was aware she would be in studio today. Masking her concern, Ada accepts the envelope, then the boy disappears. Ada ducks into the nearest door, a small break room, drops her belongings onto the sofa, and extracts the typewritten paper.

> Congratulations on your upcoming film. I hope you received my gift, and remember: When I want to find you, I will.

She presses a hand to her chest above the scar. The gift. The brooch shaped like a key.

A chill overtakes her. Whatever Ingrid believes about the messages, about Mother being the one sending them, she is wrong. Mother has no reason to harass Ada like this, not when Ada has always been obedient and compliant. She would simply win back Ada's trust, the same as she's trying to do now. She would not resort to these measures. Dietrich would.

A sound breaks through Ada's unsteady breaths. Footsteps getting louder, closer.

When I want to find you, I will.

He knows her schedule, where she is, when she'll be there, and he's chosen his time—now, this moment, even though she has not done anything to provoke him since the exclusive. Ada drops the note, snatches the gun from her bag, and whirls, pointing it directly at the man who appears in the doorway.

"Don't come any closer!"

Except the man who abruptly halts while uttering a sharp "Jesus Christ!" is not Dietrich. It's Vince.

"It's not loaded, I swear it's not loaded." She quickly lowers the weapon and places it on the sofa, cheeks burning. How is she supposed to explain this? "It's . . . a precaution."

He's already slamming the door and approaching, his eyes on her, then the gun, then the slip of paper, stark white against the sofa's blue-and-green-striped upholstery. Before Ada can stop him, he picks up the note.

Well, now she has much more to explain than the gun.

She should have waited to read the message. There was no reason to read it here, not when she knew who surely sent it, what it would contain, how it would make her feel. And now that it has just made her jump to conclusions, it's in the hands of the man who does not need to be staring at it with such a deep crease in his brow. Not when she is no longer his to worry about, and he is no longer hers.

After what feels like an eternity, Vince holds up the note. "Who sent this?" His voice is close to a growl, infused with a rage Ada has never heard from him before. "Someone you've worked with? An obsessed fan? Someone you've been seeing? How long has he been harassing you?"

"I've got it under control, hence the precautions." Her voice is remarkably level, surprising even her. She snatches the paper. "It's nothing."

"Nothing. That's why you're carrying a goddamn gun."

"Let's not miss the interview." When he doesn't follow her, she places a hand on his arm, her voice soft. "I'm being overly cautious, that's all. You needn't worry."

She should assure him she's fine, that the situation is not nearly as severe as it seems. But she can only endure so many lies. This will have to do for now.

A gentleness resides in his gaze—open, honest, everything he once never withheld from her. Soon they will remember their places, and his look of indifference will return. Ada releases him. Watching the shift occur is never easy, and right now she can't bear it.

* * *

When Ada returns home, she hears raised voices from Gordon's office—his, followed by Beverly's.

"I wish your television pilot had developed into a series too, and I'm doing everything I can to book auditions for you. This industry is frustrating, I know, but if you expect the business to be fair—"

"Not the business, my agent. My *Communist* agent who should remember most people do not look kindly upon that fact. We're through, do you hear me?"

Ada holds Sowerby to her chest. His little body vibrates with suppressed growls, given his aversion to loud noise. The office door collides with the wall, then Beverly stomps into the foyer, ignores Ada, and slams the door behind her.

Ada shushes Sowerby while Gordon joins her in the foyer and picks up his suitcase. Though his flight leaves in a few hours, the profound heaviness filling this room makes her reluctant to permit him to go.

"Cancel your trip. Let's stay in, watch films, eat chocolate, and have a relaxing night all to ourselves."

He gives a wry smile. "Stop tempting me." With a heavy sigh, he smooths his mustache and kisses her cheek. "Don't work too hard while I'm gone."

Ada places a hand on his forearm in silent comfort, then opens the door for him and watches as he climbs into the waiting car. If these hearings don't destroy them first, everyone in Hollywood might very well destroy each other.

She glances at the clock. Odd that the security guard isn't here yet. She wanted to extend his presence for the duration of Gordon's absence, and she did notify him about Gordon's trip. Unless she forgot, which is possible given how busy she's been with publicity.

She pulls Ingrid's gun from her handbag and takes it into the library, where she keeps it hidden. Perhaps she should load it after all. Ignoring the discomfort rippling through her, she carefully pulls ammunition from the cigar box, loads the weapon, and closes the items inside.

A few hours of daylight remain, so Ada changes into a bikini and takes Sowerby into the backyard. After the day she's had, time by the pool will clear her mind. She can't be distracted when she has a film to premiere in less than two weeks. If *Lady Bella Donna* fails, Mr. Hendrix will never hire her again—punishment for failing to make him money and for making a statement against his wishes. A positive reception would afford her more protection and job security, although she's starting to wonder if either one really matters. Nothing and no one can protect her, really, and if these issues over politics escalate, will the entertainment industry hire anyone anymore?

When the sunlight wanes, there is still no sign of security. She pulls on a chenille beach jacket over her bikini and goes inside to call the guard, but there is no answer. She must have forgotten to notify him, after all, so he'll certainly arrive later for his usual evening shift.

In the kitchen, after Ada feeds Sowerby, a sound captures her attention. Rattling. Sowerby's ears perk, a sign she didn't imagine it. The noise comes again—distinct, near the back door. Something disturbing the knob.

Something. Or someone.

A high-pitched yap pulls a curse from Ada's mouth until she recognizes Sowerby's bark. She grabs him, preventing him from charging after the rattling sound. While he squirms against her hold, she peers toward the back door but does not approach.

"Mother?"

No answer. In the increasing darkness, she can't make anyone out through the glass. And Mother would knock after realizing the door is locked. Which means she is still in the guesthouse.

Silence. Perhaps it was nothing.

Ada is putting Sowerby down when the sound comes a third time, and she snatches him back into her chest when he resumes barking. Every breath comes faster while she retrieves the gun, then closes the little dog in her office, much to his dismay. Better than having whoever is out there find both of them.

She grips the pistol—loaded this time—and approaches the back door, step after cautious step. By now it's too dark to see outside. She stops. Listens. No signs of broken glass or forced entry, both of which she certainly would have heard, even over Sowerby's barking, so whoever it is cannot be in the house.

Ada tightens her grasp on the pistol as today's cryptic note echoes in her mind. Enough of these games. If he wants the documents, he won't hurt her, not before he gets ahold of them, so she flings the back door open.

"Have you decided to find me yet?" she shouts as she steps out. "Show yourself, you cowardly bastard!"

Silence greets her challenge while a faint breeze tugs the hair falling loose around her shoulders. Whoever was here has gone. Or is somewhere hiding, watching, waiting.

She could seek refuge with Mother, but the guesthouse is too far, out by the rose garden, and if he is out here, she can't risk Mother's safety. Ada is the one he wants. She does not lower the gun until she's returned inside and locked the door, then she puts away the weapon, frees a disgruntled Sowerby from his temporary prison, and only makes it a few steps down the hall before she presses her back to the wall and sinks to the floor.

He won't show himself until he's ready. Why he's waiting, she still doesn't know. Until then, he will terrorize her with notes, threats, the promise that he will come. Like the promise he made when his fingers were sticky with her own blood.

Every time you look in the mirror. Every time another man touches you. Every time you try to forget, you will remember: You belong to me.

She carries him with her in her mind and on her body. She doesn't belong to him, though. She belongs to no one, not even to herself. How can the girl whose soul died during the war or the woman whose life is built on lies belong to anyone?

Sowerby paces, agitated by her distress, so Ada gathers his warm little body against her chest. Not even his usual comfort is enough. Since Arnhem, she can't be alone. Because when she is, she returns. To the war, to the house, to her sister's absence, to the Oranjehotel.

Ada releases Sowerby, who runs off while she finds the telephone. She calls the Biltmore, fighting to steady her breaths. "Ingrid van Essen's room," she says when the receptionist answers. "This is Ada Worthington-Fox. Tell her it's urgent."

Ada waits, flinching when sudden movement proves to be Sowerby scurrying into the room. All will be well when Ingrid gets here. When she's no longer by herself.

"Miss Worthington-Fox?" the receptionist prompts. "I'm sorry, Mrs. Van Essen didn't answer."

The sinking feeling that accompanies those words is almost too much. Ada barely hears as the receptionist offers to take a message; she mumbles a refusal and hangs up. Ingrid must be out, perhaps having dinner somewhere.

Security isn't here; neither is Gordon or Ingrid. Mother is all the way across the property. Ada can't be here without company, not feeling like this. Because, while there's a chance the rattling was caused by a small earthquake, by the wind blowing or the house settling, by something entirely harmless, there's also a chance it wasn't.

She could call the police—and say what? *I'm hunting a Nazi war criminal, and I believe he's hunting me as well. I heard a noise that might have been anything, so would you kindly look around the property for him?* That story would certainly find its way into the papers.

No, she can't do that. Instead she places a different call. This time, she receives an answer.

"Ada? Is something wrong?"

Vince's familiar timbre settles the shake in her hands, the tension in her fingers gripping the phone cord, the clench in her jaw.

"No," she replies quietly. "Everything's fine."

It's all she wanted. To hear his voice. One that always makes her feel like she's not so alone.

His voice comes again, steady, assured. "I'm coming over."

She can't ask that of him, not with the way things are between them, not when it's her own fault for letting her worries put her in this state. Neither does she want to refuse.

A quick visit will be all right, won't it? Just enough to settle herself. And for those blessed few minutes, she will not be alone.

*   *   *

When Ada answers the door for Vince, one look at her deepens the crease in his brow. Likely his mind is on the note she received this afternoon coupled with Gordon's absence, which she had mentioned earlier when leaving their radio appearance. She can't bring herself to say more, though. Not even after he's come. Because one explanation might lead to another.

Instead she clears her throat and proceeds to the living room. "Please come in and—" She breaks off when she senses his firm grasp on her wrist, then he pulls her around to face him.

And then all formality is gone, the liminal space is gone, cast aside by the fierceness in his grip, the concern in his eyes, in his voice.

"Are you all right?"

That look steals her ability to reply. So she nods.

Then he blinks and it's gone, banished as usual. He releases her and looks her over, still clad in her bikini and beach jacket, and smirks.

"You didn't tell me there was a dress code."

Normally she would laugh; he's always known how to lighten her mood. Instead, as his eyes spark with humor, something inside drives her toward him, then she kisses his cheek.

"You really shouldn't have come, Vince. But I'm delighted you did."

The look overtakes him while the feeling overtakes her, the ones they always suppress, the ones that drove them together in the library, and all at once they are dangerously, dangerously close to another moment of weakness.

Ada mutters something about changing and invites him to help himself to the wine she selected from the wine cellar, then retreats upstairs. Has she no common sense, no self-control? Did she not resolve to keep such moments from happening again? He came as a favor to her, and if they aren't careful, the distance between them might become worse than it has ever been. No need to let that happen, not when they are perfectly capable of being friends and professionals.

Once dressed in shorts and a striped bolero top that ties at her bust, Ada rejoins Vince, who sits in the living room with two glasses of wine and an array of papers spread on the coffee table. When Sowerby jumps on the sofa next to him, he offers the first page to Ada. One with Vince's name on it.

"Do a reading with me? Tell me if it's any good?"

"Is this one of your scripts?" she asks. "What's the premise?"

"A man is accused of murdering his wife, but he has no memory of the night it occurred, so he's trying to determine why he can't remember and if he really is responsible."

"Sounds thrilling." She sits beside him and eagerly accepts the paper. "You play the main character, and I'll play everyone else."

Vince passes a hand along his jaw and takes a long sip of his wine. Then they begin. Once they reach the end, the wineglasses are empty and, for a moment, Ada is too impressed to find adequate words.

"It's wonderful, Vince, really. How have you not sold a script when you write like this?"

"Because acting doesn't scare me as much as scriptwriting does," he says with a wry smile. "I never would have pursued it as a career if you hadn't encouraged me. Since then, I've worked on a few projects, including this one, but I haven't tried to sell any."

"You must. If this script came across Gordon's desk, I would beg him to put me up for it."

"Not bad for a kid from the Midwest who played sports, wrote stories, and auditioned for his school play—anything to avoid his homework. Although I still hate watching myself in a picture or hearing my work read aloud."

She lets out an incredulous laugh. "Then why did we just read your entire script aloud?"

"This job is about the audience, not me. If my work can entertain them, move them, distract them from their worries, then it's worth it."

He puts the script away, avoiding her gaze, prompting her to realize what he's not directly saying. This was for her sake. To take her mind off her reason for calling him. Because the man she once loved has always known what she needs, even now when they are nothing more than friends, and she wishes she could find the words to express what such a gesture means to her.

Suddenly she is acutely aware of how alone they are, of the lack of distance between them as they sit too close, of the way he could easily tangle his hand in her hair, pull her lips to his. She would not be entirely opposed if he did.

Except she has promised herself no more moments of weakness.

He has succeeded, though. He has taken her mind off her fears. Nothing has been amiss since he arrived, so when he goes, perhaps she will take Sowerby and stay in the guesthouse with Mother, citing loneliness as her reason for seeking company. For now, as he refills their wineglasses and leans back against the sofa, the silence that falls over them is not charged, not tense. It's a silence that might nearly be called comfortable.

CHAPTER 30

Hollywood Hills, 14 May 1947

INGRID

When Ada called to invite Ingrid to join her and Mother for dinner, every reservation had told Ingrid to refuse. But, as she has reminded herself countless times, any evidence that the Star Society is not a front will likely be at Gordon's, so she has little choice. If she must endure Mother's company, so be it.

In the kitchen, where Ada has given Gordon's cook the night off, she boils potatoes, carrots, and onions, then combines them with spices, butter, and cream until smooth to make *hutspot* while Ingrid prepares the sausages. Not rookworst, but it'll do. Neither has had a proper Dutch meal in far too long. Mother settles in the living room with wine, stating her inexperience with Dutch cooking will hinder the girls, which is perfectly fine with Ingrid. She would rather cook with her sister anyway.

This was a meal their grandmother taught them to make prior to her death, and they often prepared it for Opa in memory of his late wife. She can almost envision Opa's warm blue eyes, almost hear the faint rumble of approval in his chest as he takes the first bite and compliments his granddaughters.

As they work, Ingrid peers down the hall to ensure Mother is occupied, then she steps to Ada's side and lowers her voice.

"Minnie Musgrave wants another exclusive, which would reassure your fans amid these hearings and help us determine if Mother is behind the threats. Now that she's here, it might be easier to catch her leaving the next note."

"You really mustn't be so quick to accuse her," Ada replies, matching Ingrid's tone. Any response Ingrid makes will only provoke argument, so she stays quiet. "After the premiere, I can capitalize on the attention from the film with my next statement, then once I've named Dietrich, we can turn in the evidence. That should encourage the FBI to explore the matter."

After further discussion, they agree Ada will give the interview now if Mrs. Musgrave will agree to run it after the premiere. Ingrid promises to set it up for later this week. Perhaps while Ada is occupied, Ingrid will wait at Gordon's and explore her office for more evidence of the Star Society's innocence.

Assuming Mother is not here to interfere.

While Ada calls Mother in from the living room, Ingrid proceeds into the dining room and sits. The meal looks just as it did when they made it at home in Arnhem, bringing both warmth and an ache to her chest.

Ada joins her, then Mother enters, holding an old edition of *The Dish*.

"You gave an exclusive to the press, Aleida? Mentioning politics? I should think that would be of interest to Ingrid, not you."

"Well, she did encourage me," Ada replies with a knowing smile. "I thought I might as well speak freely."

"'My silence has always been for my own protection . . . but I'll have more to say in that regard some other time,'" Mother quotes, reading aloud before she sets the gossip rag down and sits with a sigh. "Darling, no one could speak freely then, and no one wants to be reminded of those times."

"And no one wants to feel silenced," Ingrid counters.

"Which is why I'll be giving another exclusive, to—"

"Clarify a few things," Ingrid interrupts, silencing Ada with a kick to the ankle beneath the table. What did she tell her about not sharing their plans with Mother? Nothing can stop Mother from reading the piece, but then it will be too late for her to interfere.

"Right," Ada replies tightly even as she returns the kick out of indignation. "Because all this trouble over Communism is increasing, isn't it, Inge? With the hearings?"

"What, that fuss? No need to trouble yourselves over such nonsense." Mother scoops a forkful of dinner into her mouth and gives an approving nod. "Lovely. Well done, you two."

An effort to change the subject. Ingrid will not let the matter go so easily.

"Media frenzy creates fuss and noise, which runs the risk of transforming a concerning issue into a farce. Such possibilities don't make the matter any less serious," she says. "Communism threatens democracy, and if such issues have been identified in the entertainment industry, the government will address them without permitting the innocent to fall victim. So I think it's best if we make our positions clear, then leave them to it."

While Ingrid takes a bite of her meal, she watches Mother, seeking a reaction. Mother sips her wine—perhaps carrying on with dinner, perhaps avoiding Ingrid's probing gaze.

"But hearings?" Ada presses. "You don't find it concerning? The way the government has decided when it should be allowed to question someone over how they vote?"

Ingrid sighs. "Well, that's another issue entirely. These methods are . . . unconventional. It's quite early, so I don't know enough to know how I feel. Part of attempting to understand is to avoid drawing hasty conclusions." Then Ingrid looks across the table. "But to avoid confusion or potential repercussions, it's wise to clarify one's position, isn't it, Mother?"

"Certainly."

A little glimmer of anticipation rises unbidden in Ingrid's chest. Is she actually going to explain her views, to satisfy the curiosity that's been plaguing Ingrid all these years?

"But clarifying one's position should not be done at the expense of one's happiness," Mother continues, meeting Ingrid's gaze. "The time of war and politics is behind us. We put forth so much effort to build new lives, so why sully them?"

The glimmer dies. Ingrid is starting to wonder if Mother is choosing to be vague simply to irritate her. Or maybe she is like Ada once was, believing such things are not necessary to address. Whatever the reason, it gives Ingrid no more confidence in her.

Once the meal concludes, Ada suggests sitting by the pool for dessert, so Ingrid volunteers to slice the flourless chocolate cake Ada made this morning. The conversation over dinner has left her even more anxious to find something beyond Ada's word to satisfy Crenshaw and Stieber, so she can seize the alone time to slip into Ada's office. A hearing is nothing of concern, but if Ingrid can close this investigation, then there is no need to put Ada through one.

Mother places a restraining hand on Ingrid. "Go outside and relax. I was no help with dinner, so let me prepare dessert."

"And a splash of Scotch," Ada calls as she gestures for Ingrid to accompany her. "It's delightful with a cigarette in the evenings."

Ingrid reluctantly follows Ada toward the pool, her jaw already tightening. Mother is alone in the house, where Ingrid was hoping to be. More importantly, where Ada's evidence is hidden.

When Ada notices Ingrid's furrowed brow, she sighs. "How are you supposed to make peace with Mother when you won't stop being so suspicious? We don't know if she's behind the messages, and she's just being helpful."

"Is she, or was she trying to get rid of us? You trust her far too readily."

"Contrary to what you seem to believe, I'm not entirely gullible. I know we can't be certain of anything yet. I'm just trying to give her the opportunity to earn my trust. And you could do the same."

Maybe Ingrid should try harder with Mother, but not at the cost of her sister's safety. She glances toward the house. *Sowerby*. If she goes inside to let the terrier out, it's the perfect excuse to thwart Mother if she's prying.

After sharing her intentions to get the dog—although Ada will surely see through her motives—Ingrid rushes back toward the house before Ada can stop her. Once inside, she goes immediately to the kitchen.

Three slices of decadent cake rest on three small plates. And Mother is gone.

Ingrid knew it; of course Mother is up to no good. She must be looking for the evidence, or perhaps she's preparing the next threatening note to send to Ada now that she knows Ada will be giving another exclusive. Quietly so as not to alert her, Ingrid continues down the hall, where she notices the library door is ajar.

The library. Where Ada keeps the evidence.

Her heartbeat picks up speed as she nears, then she peers around the corner. Mother's back is to Ingrid—no doubt she is examining the shelves for clues, or maybe she suspects the documents are in this room and she has only to find them.

"I don't recall the cake being in here," Ingrid says loudly. She wants

Mother to be caught, to face her, to admit that her reasons for reconnecting with Ada are not as innocent as Ada might think.

Indeed, Mother steps back and turns, her brow lined with confusion. "No, not cake . . ." She gestures with the empty crystal glass in her hand, indicating the bar cart near the edge of the sofa, which her original position had blocked from Ingrid's view. "Scotch. For your sister." She picks up a second empty glass. "And for you, if you'd like?"

Heat flushes Ingrid's neck. She shakes her head, muttering her excuse about letting the dog out. Mother fills a glass of amber liquid for Ada, then leads the way from the library. Ingrid calls to Sowerby, then they follow her outside.

The night is comfortable and warm, yet between the dinner conversation about the hearings and her concerns over Mother, a weight remains in her chest. Maybe Ada is right; maybe Ingrid is far too suspicious. And she will continue to be suspicious until she has a reason not to be.

* * *

A couple of days later, Ingrid makes her way to the Biltmore Hotel conference room for the final day of hearings, every step light with a relief that might be premature but she hopes is not. After today, HUAC will surely have all the information it needs, subversives will be dealt with accordingly, and this threat of Communism will cease. And with Ada meeting with Mrs. Musgrave today to give the next exclusive, which will publish after her premiere next Friday, everything Ingrid has set into motion is shaping up rather nicely.

Ingrid is about to enter the conference room when a young woman approaches. A familiar woman.

Beverly Tolbert.

The actress doesn't notice Ingrid as she speaks with a few men gathered around the door before disappearing inside. What is she doing at the hearings? And more importantly, what does she intend to share?

That charming little Brit, she had sneered about Ada. If ever there was an opportunity to remove her competition by accusing the more successful actress of being a Communist, this is it. And Ingrid has no doubt Beverly will seize her chance.

Another familiar figure is approaching the conference room—Archie—so Ingrid grabs his arm and pulls him away from the crowd.

"That woman who just entered the room is one of Ada's friends," she says in a low voice. "You met her at the party, then again at Schwab's, remember? I can't risk her recognizing me, but you'll blend in more easily, so will you go in there and stay out of sight? I need to know everything she says. Especially if she says anything about Ada."

"This sounds awfully similar to a favor, and a risky one since I might be noticed and recognized, which means you owe me something in exchange." He crosses his arms, as if pondering. "Do I want information? Another invitation to a Star Society party? A romantic evening with—?"

"I'll buy you a drink. Now go." There is no time for this nonsense. She shoves him toward the door. He obeys, strolling toward the room while listing his terms.

"A strong drink—no, two strong drinks. From Ciro's. And a third drink after the hearings move home."

Ingrid's breath catches, and she hurries after him. "More hearings at home? HUAC doesn't have enough?"

He laughs. "Far from it. We're only just getting started."

Archie disappears into the hearing room while Ingrid stares at the closed door, her heartbeat pounding in her ears. Hearings at home. Her earlier relief was indeed premature.

This is not the end of matters as she hoped. It's only the beginning.

CHAPTER 31

Hollywood Hills, 23 May 1947

ADA

Stop making a fuss, Inge. You're coming to my premiere, and I won't hear another word against it." Ada cradles the telephone receiver against her shoulder and refills her coffee cup. "I've already sent a dress to your hotel, and a tailor to ensure it fits—and you *are* wearing it, so don't tell me you're not."

"You know how I feel about you inviting Mother."

"It's my premiere. You don't want to disappoint me on the biggest night of my life, do you?"

"Must you be so insufferable?" Ingrid huffs, though Ada hears the smile behind the words. "Of course I want to be there for you."

"Matters between you and Mother will never improve if you avoid her, and I can't leave her out, certainly not when our theories remain speculation. But I understand if it makes you too uncomfortable." Silence while Ada sips the fresh coffee. "Please? It won't feel right without you there."

Ingrid sighs. "Fine." Then her voice softens. "And I am terribly proud of you."

Ada smiles, then bids her goodbye. Nearly time to get ready. A shiver of excitement collides with the warmth of the coffee spreading through her insides. Her premiere, watching *Lady Bella Donna* on the silver screen, seeing herself in the lead.

Attending the event on Vince's arm.

The thought overtakes her before she can subdue it. They will be expected to pose for pictures, to sit together throughout the film. Then he will come to her party tonight. Even though his name will appear above hers in the billing, since he is more successful, tonight is about what they have achieved together. The hearings at the Biltmore are over, and they can focus on the film industry, not political disputes.

She draws a breath. She will not think about this eager flutter in her stomach. About kissing Vince in this very house not so long ago. Otherwise, at tonight's premiere, she might be unable to stop herself from bringing her lips to his just to feel that way again.

The press would certainly delight in that.

* * *

When the limousine reaches Grauman's Chinese Theater, Ada checks her reflection in a compact mirror one last time. Outside, she can already hear voices clamoring and glimpse flashing bulbs.

They are waiting for her film. For her.

With trembling hands, she tucks her lipstick into her clutch and glances at Gordon beside her. He smooths his waxed mustache, adjusts his bow tie, tugs on his tuxedo jacket.

"Are you this fidgety at all premieres?" she asks with a chuckle.

He flushes, then clears his throat. "No, no, I'm fine, it's nothing. Nerves mean you care," he adds with a wink.

Something in his tone makes Ada feel as if he's not being entirely forthright. Then again, she's never been with him at a premiere of this magnitude before. Now is not the time to question him, only to thank him for taking a chance on a young Broadway dancer. For his unshakable faith in her. For his unwavering kindness. She kisses his cheek; it's all she wants to say and more.

Gordon places a hand over hers. "Enjoy it, kid. Every minute of it." Warmth and pride fill his gaze before he nods to the waiting press. "Now get out there."

When the chauffeur opens her door, the pulse of energy on the other side practically pulls her from the car and onto the red carpet.

Amid the shouts and flashes, Ada poses for photographs and looks across the crowd, glimpsing red hair. Too many people to confirm the face. Still, the thought of Ingrid out there somewhere settles her pounding heartbeat.

Gordon poses with her, then they make their way toward the theater. Before going inside, Ada pauses.

The marquee. She hasn't even looked at it yet. Suddenly she can't lift her eyes; doing so might prove none of this is real, that she is still a girl fighting for a position she will never achieve. For tonight, however, she must give that girl permission to be proud of herself.

With her heart pounding and her breaths sharp, Ada looks up.

Lady Bella Donna, Starring Ada Worthington-Fox and Vince Hart.

Her name is listed first. Above his.

Someone will be in quite a bit of trouble for that mistake. By this time tomorrow, it will likely be remedied. Until then, it's as if no one else is on this carpet. No one around her, no one clamoring for her photograph, no one cheering, simply Ada and her own name in lights. A moment that is hers and hers alone.

"This would be quite the opening scene for a film, wouldn't it? A gorgeous actress arriving at her premiere."

The familiar voice brings an immediate smile to Ada's face as she looks at him. Another sight that nearly takes her breath away. His tailored tuxedo, his hair neatly combed and styled, his bright blue eyes absorbing every inch of her—from her elegant updo to her dove-gray satin gown with its full skirt, then to her eyes.

Vince offers her a hand, so she takes it. He spins her around slowly, much to the delight of their onlookers, then wraps his arm around her waist and kisses her cheek.

"You always draw every eye in the room," he murmurs, the words low, meant for her alone.

"You never have much difficulty doing so yourself." She kisses his cheek in return—again, to the delight of the photographers—before he releases her and steps to Mr. Sternberg's side, allowing the press to photograph her individually.

In these careers that demand certain amounts of selfishness, of attention-seeking, of competition, he has forfeited the attention to her. A gesture that leaves Ada staring after him a moment too long, hoping he will look back.

At last she urges Vince to join her, then they indulge the flashing cameras. Part of her expected this encounter to feel no different than their encounters these last months. As if they remain trapped in a liminal space, one they can't move beyond. Instead, being here with him feels—well, like it did when they were together.

A thought that is, perhaps, not entirely disturbing.

Following the photographs, they proceed indoors to watch the film. Despite her fascination with watching herself on camera, the opportunity has never presented itself in much capacity. A silent part in this film, a line or two of dialogue in that one. This time, she's in nearly every scene. An odd experience, yet somehow Ada separates herself from her character, watching not as a critic but as a spectator.

Beside her, Vince is calm and attentive. Not betraying his aversion to seeing his own work. After the first few scenes, Ada gives his forearm a reassuring squeeze. He places a hand briefly over hers in gratitude before they release one another.

They make excellent scene partners. He is good, too good, as is she. As is their film. A fast-paced, powerful, moving film. A *good* film.

When it ends, the theater erupts in applause. Ada stays seated, uncertain if she's laughing or crying or simply numb, residing in a moment she never wants to move beyond. To her right, Gordon dabs a handkerchief to his eyes and kisses her cheek. To her left, she feels Vince's touch on her shoulder before he stands and shakes Gordon's hand.

After offering congratulations and accepting them in return, they exit the theater, where a flash of white and red catches Ada's eye. Vince moves in front of her while Gordon flanks her, both clearly attempting to block her view. Too late; she's already seen what they're trying to hide.

A small group of men sends indiscernible shouts toward them while they hold up white posters bearing red messages. *Boycott Sternberg* and *Hollywood Is Red* and *Get the Commies Out of America!* Security ushers the protesters away while Ada pushes aside the ripple of tension in her stomach.

The display will not ruin this night. She will not allow it.

Still, Ada was a fool to believe the hearings that took place at the Biltmore would be the end. More likely, those hearings were just the start.

* * *

Despite the protesters casting a pall over the premiere, the pall lifts the moment the party at Gordon's begins. And the moment Ada gets home, Ingrid is there, beaming with pride and pulling her into an embrace.

Ada's eyes well with tears. For so long, every time she envisioned her career successes, this was what she saw. Her sister. Except she'd thought her sister was gone, making the vision an impossibility. Ada had accepted that nothing in her life would ever feel quite right again. Now Ingrid is here and everything is right, will always be right.

"Absolutely brilliant!" Ingrid exclaims. "The film was spectacular, truly, and you were marvelous."

"Speaking of marvelous . . ." Ada appraises Ingrid in the dress she selected—cobalt-blue taffeta with a fitted bodice and ruffled straps. "You really must allow me to contribute to your wardrobe more often."

"Enjoy it this once, because I nearly sent it right back to whatever designer it came from." Ingrid shakes her head despite a slight smile. "Utterly ridiculous."

"Utterly gorgeous." Ada grins as the door opens. When Vince steps inside, his brows lift, his eyes darting between the two women. "Vince Hart, allow me to introduce my cousin, Ingrid van Essen."

"Well, that explains the family resemblance."

"Yes, we're told we favor," Ingrid says as they shake hands, though the sly smile she offers Ada nearly makes her laugh.

The door opens again, this time revealing Mother, wearing a simple yet elegant burgundy gown. She introduces herself to Vince as Ingrid's mother, and hers only. Prior to this evening, Mother agreed to keep her relation to Ada more distant, as Ingrid is, so as not to encourage the press to pry should they find out about her.

Following introductions, Ada invites Mother to accompany her for a drink. As they go, a familiar urge wells inside her, a longing to ask Mother's opinion regarding the film. A need for the approval she always sought as a girl. Before she can decide between voicing it or swallowing it down, Mother kisses her cheek.

"You were wonderful, darling. I'm so proud of you, and I'm delighted to share in your success."

Without awaiting a reply, Mother slips into the crowd while Ingrid's voice fills Ada's head, whispering that the words were only Mother's attempt to earn Ada's favor. Maybe Ingrid is right; maybe Ada is trusting Mother too easily, if not completely yet. Still, she allows the praise to fill her, to feel as genuine as she wants it to feel. For tonight, she will be selfish, foolish, naive, and believe what she wants to believe. For tonight, she can pretend.

The celebration proceeds while Ada mingles with her guests. If those who were at the premiere noticed the protesters, it seems everyone has long forgotten the incident. A live band plays, the drinks flow, and someone will certainly jump into the pool before this night is over.

After filling two champagne glasses, Ada returns indoors. No doubt Ingrid has escaped to somewhere quieter, or else somewhere far from Mother. She really must do a better job of keeping up with her sister at these events. The library seems like the most likely place she would go, so Ada makes her way there, leaving the music and laughter behind, taking the glasses of champagne with her so she can offer one to her sister.

In the darkened room, she doesn't find Ingrid; she finds Vince. He strolls slowly before the bookshelves, examining titles illuminated by golden lamplight. Ada lingers in the doorway, reluctant to disturb him. The bond between the writer and the written word is a sacred one.

"Seeking inspiration?" she asks at last.

"What writer can resist a library? Although there's plenty of inspiration to be found out there." He nods in the general direction of the party. "These events of yours could make a fine plot for a romantic comedy, a film noir . . . just about anything."

"Again, I'm delighted to be your muse and expect to be cast as the lead once you develop that award-winning script."

Vince accepts the extra glass of champagne, then they drink. The bubbles in her glass sparkle like the lights on the marquee. Like Vince's eyes when they met hers on the red carpet. Like they might be now, if the sudden heat in Ada's cheeks weren't preventing her from meeting his gaze.

She clears her throat. "Did you notice they put our names in the improper order on the marquee? Quite a mistake."

Vince shakes his head. "Not a mistake."

"Of course it was. The newcomer's name is never placed before the seasoned actor's, if it's included at all. Mr. Hendrix must have been livid . . . Someone is probably correcting it as we speak."

He doesn't respond, nor does he look at her. A harmless fault, true, but a fault nonetheless. Perhaps he's loath to discuss it because he fears Ada will be disappointed when the correction is made—and she will be, of course, though he's not to blame for that.

Shadows obscure his features. When he lifts his champagne to his mouth, lamplight reflects in both the golden liquid and his quick sidelong glance.

"Vince, what are you not telling me?"

Whatever has shifted between them prompts Ada to press her palm against the satin sheen of her gown, if only to prevent herself from reaching for him.

"When Mr. Sternberg and Mr. Hendrix offered me the role, I told them I'd accept if your name received top billing. The condition was written into my contract terms. And not because I think you need my help to establish yourself," he adds quickly. "I didn't tell you because I didn't want you to misunderstand my intentions."

Not a mistake, then. Vince's doing. Slowly, Ada takes his glass, then sets both down. Still, he studies the books. She swallows hard, seeking her voice.

"Why would you do that for me?"

"Because nobody should give a damn about who has been working longer or has more accolades to their name. This film is primarily about her, not him. You deserve to be credited properly."

A swell catches in her throat. "Why do you care if I receive credit or success? Especially after everything that happened between us?"

"Because everything that happened between us was a result of your willingness to give up anything, even your own happiness, to succeed. And because when you left, I was too confused, too busy trying to understand how I'd driven you away, that I never stopped to think about it from your perspective. If I had, I might have realized what you were doing and why. By the time I was offered this part, I was no closer to understanding what happened between us, but our past has nothing to do with giving you proper recognition."

"I never intended to make you feel like it was your fault. Certainly not for all this time," she says softly. "You were never anything but wonderful to me. And I'm sorry I didn't explain myself sooner."

At last Vince looks at her—his eyes bright like the last time they found themselves in this library. "You don't have to give up anything. No one will ever stand in the way of your career. You won't let them."

Perhaps he's right. And perhaps she was so afraid to lose the career she was working to build that she was also afraid to allow herself to be content.

"We agreed to focus on the work . . . Why did you kiss me the way you did?" Every instance rushes over her—in her dressing room, in their scene, in this library. And he could easily ask her the same question.

"Maybe I spent two years waiting to kiss you again. Maybe I wanted you to regret losing me as much as I regret losing you. Maybe I know you well enough to know how you like to be kissed." Then his hand finds the back of her neck while his thumb presses her chin higher, his voice tight, tense. "Maybe I thought if this is the last time I'm ever going to kiss her, then by God, I'm not going to disappoint her."

Ada grips his tuxedo jacket. His eyes gleaming in the lamplight, his hair slashed in shadow, his ragged breath matching hers, his touch sending sparks across her skin—all of him known to her, always known to her, whether in light or shadow, on the silver screen for the world to see or in this darkened library for her eyes alone.

It's you. Still, he said not so terribly long ago.

Perhaps it is still him for her too.

Vince's jaw clenches, as if he is forcibly extracting himself from this moment. From her. He cannot turn aside, must not; they have spent long enough this way. *She* has spent long enough this way, robbing them of one another. When he releases her, she presses her hands to his face, urges him closer.

He catches her wrists. "Don't, Ada. Don't do it." He pulls her hands away but maintains his firm hold on them. "Not unless you can swear to me that this is what you want—and not simply for this time, or this moment, or this night. Because I cannot do this with you again."

The flame in his eyes is the desire she's come to recognize mingled with deeply held hurt. Damage she put there. Her heart clenches. "Darling, I never stopped wanting you for so much more than this time, or this moment, or this night."

Then she kisses him and wraps her arms around him, pressing her heart to his, letting it communicate every reassurance that she will never break it again.

Vince grips her waist, pulls her against him, presses her back to the bookshelves with such force that the books might have fallen if the solid wooden structure weren't secured to the wall. Ada dissolves into his touch, the vibrance of the champagne on his lips, the faint notes of his cologne, spice and citrus. It's a party; no one will be coming into this library. They are alone. She can be with him, truly be with him as she has never allowed herself to be.

Yet the burning sensation has already found her breast, the place where another man took his time intricately carving while she stood before him for hours, naked and helpless. She kisses Vince more deeply and threads her fingers through his hair. She will fight it, ignore it, will not let it interfere this time.

But when Vince caresses her breast, over that same hidden place, the sensation intensifies. She arches her back to combat it, tightens her hold on his hair—two gestures he interprets as encouragement, considering he lifts her skirt.

She doesn't protest, doesn't want to protest, has no reason to protest, not when he won't see anything. In here, she has to keep the damn dress on, for God's sake. Even if she takes him upstairs, she can find a reason to leave her brassiere in place.

He won't see anything, feel anything, notice anything. He won't.

But she will not be present for herself or for him. She will feel nothing other than the mark Dietrich left upon her skin. Already her back is against a prison wall, not a bookshelf, as the sharp blade presses into her flesh.

She turns aside, breaking their kiss, and catches the hand seeking her undergarments. "Stop, please stop, I can't!"

Vince obeys. This is hardly the first time she's stopped him. When they were together, she got quite good at it, actually. Often with casual excuses, never reaching the point where he might feel as if he did something to upset her. Rarely did she forget herself or attempt to push beyond the moment when the feeling overtook her. Because every time she tried, it never worked. Instead her breaths quickened and her voice found this frantic place over which she has no control.

The place it has found now, prompting concerned lines across Vince's forehead.

Though her heart thuds, she clears her throat. "It's just . . . Well, it won't do for the hostess to be absent from her own party, will it?"

Ada smooths her skirt, then she forces herself to look at him. Vince regards her with no disappointment, no animosity, nothing beyond his usual steadfast gaze.

She brushes her thumb across his cheek and leaves a gentle kiss on his lips to assuage any worries. It is not him. Never him. Then they take their champagne glasses and exit the library while the burning sensation on her chest joins the one wrapping around her heart.

Before Vince, she knew only one other man this way. A young man in the resistance—just once, nothing more than respite for two lonely individuals until, a mere week later, he was arrested and she never heard what became of him. Then she herself was caught. After that there was no one, no matter how she tried or how many men sought her affections.

Since Vince, she has wanted him, always him. The trouble is, she can't permit herself to have him.

ROLL OUT THE RED CARPET!
by Minnie Musgrave

On Friday night, the cast and crew of *Lady Bella Donna* gathered for the premiere at Grauman's Chinese Theater—and some of those involved are as red as the carpet.

Protesters stood outside the theater, expressing their disapproval of Communists in the entertainment industry. Namely, of director Abe Sternberg, self-proclaimed Red. Judging by the rave reviews of his film, he kept his views from tainting the picture, but it does make the viewer wonder: If Mr. Sternberg is a Communist, does Hendrix Productions employ other Communists?

In the past, leading man Vince Hart has expressed disapproval of Communist views and acted in military training films to support our boys on the front, so one can reasonably conclude that his involvement in Sternberg's project was never politically motivated. As for leading lady Ada Worthington-Fox, her recent exclusive clarified her views more than ever before, but there is so much we don't know about her.

Will Miss Worthington-Fox elaborate further regarding her private life, as promised? She reached out with her comments, saying, "Another exclusive? Is that what you want, readers? My, my, aren't you curious . . . Patience will be rewarded, darlings."

Whatever has gotten into our secretive starlet, let's hope it's here to stay.

Miss Worthington-Fox threw one of her Star Society gatherings for the afterparty at the home of her agent, Mr. Gordon Sharpe. Mr. Sternberg and many others attended, including famed architect Paul Revere Williams, Screen Actors

Guild president Ronald Reagan, actresses Bette Davis and Ginger Rogers, actor Gary Cooper, director and producer William Wyler, and, of course, Hollywood's Hartthrob. As for how much of a good time Miss Worthington-Fox showed her guests, well, let's just say Mr. Hart was spotted leaving Mr. Sharpe's home early Saturday morning.

Quite early. Dawn, to be precise.

Brava to our siren. It seems Hollywood's Vixen has caught a Hart—again.

Alas, our lovers might be star-crossed if their director's views impact their film, even their careers. Red is no one's color in Hollywood. America wants to know she can trust her stars, so for all the celebrities reading this, if you haven't taken a stand, now is the time. Your fans and your careers will thank you.

To my readers: If you think the G-men are finished with the glitterati, think again.

CHAPTER 32

Los Angeles, 27 May 1947

INGRID

A few days after the Star Society party, Ingrid wishes she were at Lucey's—her usual spot, given the number of stars who frequent the restaurant, making it ideal for eavesdropping on idle gossip—instead of the small diner Agent Stieber selected. It's for the best, though, so she won't risk an encounter with Beverly if Ada's friend is working today. Beverly would certainly tell Ada about Ingrid's clandestine meeting with a strange man, then Ada would ask for answers Ingrid cannot give.

While she waits for her handler, she reads a recent copy of *The Dish*, rolling her eyes at Mrs. Musgrave's comment implying Vince spent the night with Ada after the film premiere when, in fact, the celebration lasted all night, so no one left Gordon's before dawn. Not even Ingrid.

When Stieber joins her, they order lunch, then he steeples his fingers together. "Your initial report was thorough, Mrs. Van Essen, which is exactly what I asked of you. However, we asked you to resume this case because we still have lingering concerns regarding the actress and her colleagues, many of whom have questionable associations."

Never has Ingrid felt so exposed, hearing him discuss her report. All those names. That's the purpose of this, though, isn't it? To protect the country from subversives. To protect subversives from themselves before they do something they regret. So often people are misguided, swayed by pretty words or seemingly convincing actions, unable to recognize lies and manipulation until it's too late. This work—her work—and the hearings are meant to help those people. To caution those who need cautioning.

She forces herself to meet his gaze. "Sir, Miss Worthington-Fox's associates include everyone from registered Communists to members of the Motion Picture Alliance for the Preservation of American Ideals. She, like most Americans, has friends who are left wing, right wing, liberal, conservative—"

"Have you located her Communist Party card number? Evidence of support of Communist causes? Confirmed her front organization?" His light blue eyes meet Ingrid's. "She is a Red, is she not?"

Stieber is strict, meticulous, determined. Never this harsh, this critical, this . . . frightening. He looks as if he might close his hands around Ingrid's neck if her answer is unsatisfactory. The charged silence fills the space. She holds his unblinking gaze, keeps her response neutral and professional even as she fights the urge to flee.

"No, sir, Miss Worthington-Fox is not a Communist. As noted in my report, she told me herself and made her public statement, and I haven't uncovered evidence to the contrary."

"Only a subversive would agree to star in a film directed by a Communist Jew." At such vitriol, Ingrid nearly winces. "The hearings in Washington will take place in a few months, and I need evidence before then."

Under the table, she presses her palms into her seat. Something crosses his face too quickly for her to determine what it is before it disappears. Why does something about this discussion feel like it's tarnishing the nature of her investigation? Her own frustrations are impacting her interpretation of the conversation, she supposes. The dignity of their work remains intact; he is simply convinced Ada is subversive and believes proof is there, even though Ingrid has failed to find it.

"Did you confirm the front organization at the Star Society event following her film premiere?"

Why is he so insistent on confirmation of the front when disproving it is just as likely? From her briefcase, Ingrid extracts the guest list, which includes stars of all political affiliations, then a recording and a transcript.

"Any political talk was no different from the other documentation I've submitted to you, sir. Talk of Communism is related to industry discussions, not discussions one would expect at a front meeting. And I've looked all over the house and found no evidence she or her agent are spies or anything other than honest."

Stieber accepts the transcript, and Ingrid sits while he reads, remembering the two unknown men in conversation before Ada interrupted.

Do you know anyone caught up in these hearings?

A friend was subpoenaed, but he wants to cooperate.

Well, I simply won't stand for this! An empty glass at my party? Come along, darling, let's get you a refill.

Two men remarking on industry circumstances before Ada apparently noticed the empty glasses and approached. Harmless, innocent conversation. Similar ones took place all night. The next day, Ingrid spent hours painstakingly transcribing to have it all finished before this meeting. At last, Agent Stieber nods and returns the paper.

"Miss Worthington-Fox has also given another exclusive to further reassure the public of her openness and honesty," Ingrid adds. "It will publish next week."

His expression remains impossible to read, then he nods again. "Get me a copy of the exclusive and gather as much information as you can prior to the hearings in Washington. If you're correct about her, we must be certain."

At least he's willing to consider the possibility that Ingrid's original findings were accurate—because they were. All she must do is convince him. Which is proving far more difficult than anticipated.

* * *

When Ingrid returns to the Biltmore, she opens her hotel room door to find an envelope on the ground. She freezes, heart racing, staring at it. No name, no markings, nothing.

Someone must have pushed it beneath the door, or else forced their way inside and left it. She skirts the envelope and looks around, ensuring nothing is missing and no one is hiding, before picking it up. Inside she finds a couple of documents along with a letter in a script that brings immediate warmth to her chest.

> My darling friend,
>
> Don't be angry: Remember the agent I've been seeing from work? Since secretaries don't have access to everything, I enlisted his help in finding information on Gregor Dietrich. I didn't think you'd mind if I shared your request with him since I needed the help, and I can't exactly ask you for permission right now, can I? We've been busy with HUAC and the hearings, so we haven't had much time for research, but we did find this.
>
> My fellow is part of the same assignment as you and is traveling there this week—don't worry, he kept everything confidential—so he offered to deliver our findings when he arrives. I thought you should see them sooner rather than later.

I'll keep looking, and so will he when he's able. Call me if you're permitted, should you want to talk.

And, Ingrid? I don't really know what to say, except I'm so terribly sorry.

xx,

Hattie

With hands that suddenly shake, Ingrid extracts the first document and sinks onto the bed to read.

Everything is in German, of which she knows very little, but it appears to be orders of some sort. Across the bottom is a signature that sends a chill across Ingrid's skin: Gregor Dietrich. Whatever this is, it's something he authorized.

The second document is a translation of the report—God bless Hattie. Ingrid places the two side by side. An order from the Ordnungspolizei dated 1942, listing prominent Dutchmen and intellectuals being held hostage in retaliation for resistance activities, followed by orders for their execution.

Ingrid can hardly read through her blurry vision: The men were taken to a forest, ordered to dig their own graves, tied to stakes, and shot, then their bodies hastily buried and their graves left unmarked. She must continue until she finds the name she knows she will find, because Hattie's closing and this terrible feeling in her chest indicate it will be here. She will find it because she owes it to him. To his bravery, his sacrifice, his unwavering commitment to his beliefs even to the point of death.

At last, she moves the papers aside to avoid staining them with her tears. She has found it. The final name listed among those executed: her grandfather, Bernard de Vos.

The tears steal her strength, her breath, her will to do anything except curl onto the bed and sob. She never told him she went to

America, never even told him goodbye before she left Arnhem. And now he's gone. Taken by the same man who invaded her childhood home and her mother's bed.

Not only did Gregor Dietrich torture her sister. He authorized her grandfather's murder.

CHAPTER 33

Hollywood Hills, 27 May 1947

ADA

The late May sun warms Ada's skin as she and Ingrid sit in chairs on the edge of the tennis court, far from the house, the pool, the guesthouse, anyone who might interrupt them. The pleasant day is marred by the sharp ache in Ada's chest and the tears she brushes aside following the news Ingrid brought from Hattie.

Opa was murdered. Ada had left late that same year, after the order was enforced. He was already dead, and she had been unaware.

"Did Mother know?" Ingrid asks at last.

"Dietrich never spoke of his work. I can't imagine he would have told her, or that she would have kept it from me."

Ingrid's dubious look indicates she does not necessarily agree. "Well, with this and your evidence, we have further proof of his war crimes. Can I hand everything over to the FBI now?"

"The FBI probably gets thousands of complaints about war criminals. They won't concern themselves with Dietrich until I make him a more prominent figure. Wait until I've named him publicly—which Mrs. Musgrave refused to allow yet so she could get a third exclusive out of me. Once I've done all I can to hold him accountable, I'll let the authorities handle the rest and pray they do the right thing if they locate him."

Of course Ada could submit everything to those with the power to do something about it, but she must exercise her own power first and garner attention so hopefully the FBI will prioritize the case. Then, no matter what comes of it, she can be at peace knowing she did her best.

Ingrid is quiet, and Ada recognizes this look. Knows what Ingrid is about to say.

"Leidje, the more this develops, the more I don't think he's the one targeting you. I don't mean to diminish your concerns, but Mother is the logical conclusion. She found you, she was afraid you would use the evidence against her, she impersonated Dietrich to scare you into getting rid of it, and when that didn't work, she came forward to convince you herself."

When Ada says nothing, Ingrid places a comforting hand over hers. Then she stands, picks up a tennis racket, drags a basket of balls into the center of the court, and begins hitting them across the net while Ada watches.

Perhaps Ingrid is right; perhaps Mother makes more sense. Dietrich would be more likely to confront her right away, or perhaps he's not afraid of her evidence. Even if Ada submits it to the authorities, he could make a deal with the government, like Ingrid said other escaped Nazis have done. But Ada trusts this feeling in her chest, and there is one way to test their differing opinions.

"I'm going to give Mother the evidence."

Ingrid stops with her racket in the air, and the ball she tossed drops uselessly to the ground. "Have you gone absolutely mad? I won't let you."

"It's not your choice." Ada stands before Ingrid can continue naming the many reasons this is a terrible idea. "You think the threats have been from Mother. I think they're from Dietrich. My next exclusive is publishing soon, so if I give Mother the evidence and don't receive another threat, we'll know it was her sending them. If another message comes despite her having what she wants, we'll know they're from Dietrich."

Ingrid clenches her jaw, then she goes back to hitting tennis balls—for once, not arguing, yet the force behind each blow makes her feelings clear enough.

"You have copies of everything, remember? Keep those and the information Hattie provided, and I'll keep the negatives with all the original photographs. We aren't losing anything, just testing a theory." Ada places a hand on the racket to interrupt the next hit, so Ingrid finally stops, her chest rising from exertion or from whatever it is preventing her from meeting Ada's gaze. "Everything will be fine."

"No, it won't, because I don't want to be right, and I don't want you to be right either. One means our own mother is responsible. The other means a murderer is hunting you." Ingrid draws a sharp breath, her voice unsteady. "I know we need to find out the truth, and we've been aware of both possibilities, but if something happens to you—"

Ada shakes her head, stopping her. No use in dwelling on such fears. There is little either one can do to prevent the risk, so they might as well focus on what they can control.

With a small sigh, Ingrid begins to gather the scattered tennis balls and return them to the basket, so Ada assists. They change the subject to lighter topics, then Ingrid picks up the final ball and offers Ada a tennis racket.

"May I beat you before I go?"

"You may lose to me before you go," she counters, to which Ingrid flashes a competitive grin.

After two games—one win apiece—Ingrid departs for the Biltmore. Despite Ada's efforts, she has not conceded to staying at Gordon's while Mother is here. Which does not stop Ada from trying to convince her.

Inside the house, vases filled with vibrant bouquets cover almost every table and surface, all sent in congratulations from various actors, friends, and members of her cast. Some beginning to wilt, others still flourishing. The spray of tulips from Ingrid is her favorite, though. A reminder of their home in Arnhem. Gently, Ada brushes a finger over the soft petals while the discovery of Opa's fate crashes over her again. More damage to her family. More crimes committed by Dietrich. More reasons to hold him accountable.

When the telephone rings, Ada pushes the thoughts aside and picks it up.

"Is Gordon in?" comes Beverly's clipped voice. "I need him to send some information to my new agent."

"He's swimming—I'll have him call you later, but it's lovely to hear from you. Everyone missed you terribly on Friday night." Ada waits, though her friend says nothing. She clears her throat. "Fancy a lunch tomorrow?"

"I can't. I'm tied up at the Biltmore."

"What's at the Biltmore? A party? A date?" Then the teasing edge leaves Ada's voice. "You haven't been caught up in those hearings, have you? Aren't they over?"

"There's no need to be afraid of the hearings unless you have something to hide." Her tone is unusually snide, even accusatory. "I'd advise talking to the G-men before they talk to you."

Without awaiting a reply, Beverly hangs up. Ada stares at the receiver. Were her statements not enough? Could there still be doubts about her views? Maybe there are benefits to speaking to the G-men, as Beverly believes, even though she's made her position clear. Perhaps she should ask Ingrid. The protesters outside her premiere were a clear indication that the turmoil over Communism is far from over.

She hurries to Gordon's office to leave Beverly's message. His desk is tidy and organized, and she's looking through a stack of papers, seeking a notepad, when a pink slip falls loose from the pile. Ada picks it up to return it, then pauses when she notices the capital letters splayed across the top.

BY AUTHORITY OF THE HOUSE OF REPRESENTATIVES OF THE CONGRESS OF THE UNITED STATES OF AMERICA

Her heart slams faster with every word as she reads on. A subpoena delivered this past Friday, the same day as her premiere, summoning Gordon Sharpe before the House Un-American Activities Committee. Tomorrow.

A hearing she knows nothing about involving the man insistent on keeping no secrets from her. After the hearings were supposed to be over.

With Sowerby charging after her, eager to be included in the excitement, she hurries through the house. She will drag Gordon from the pool if she must. Whatever it takes to get an explanation.

By the time she reaches the kitchen, he's already stepping inside, rubbing a towel over his water-studded skin, then his eyes fall to the pink document. A cross between guilt and disgust passes over his face, a look that makes Ada's chest tighten even more.

"You should have told me." She holds it up, unable to keep her voice steady. "For God's sake, Gordon, why didn't you tell me?"

"And ruin your premiere for both of us?"

"That was days ago. You've had plenty of opportunities to mention it." When he reaches for the document, she holds it aside. "How did you intend to have me find out, then? When the FBI bursts through the door to drag you off before Chairman Thomas? And I thought you had reconsidered your views."

"I'm still a card-carrying member, which I assume they finally found out. And it won't come to the FBI or Chairman Thomas or any the-atrics." He places a hand on her shoulder in attempted consolation, though she steps back. "It's not for you to worry about."

"Of course it's for me to worry about. You're my agent. My friend." Blinking hard, she pushes back tears. "Cancel everything I have sched-uled for tomorrow."

"It's a closed hearing, Ada. What are you going to do, sit outside the conference room when I could just as easily tell you about it at home?" Gently, he takes her shoulders. "The best thing you can do for me is promote your film."

She says nothing; then he takes the pink slip and disappears down the hall. She lost her father, and for a time, her sister and her mother, and now her grandfather. Lost her own name and who she was to a life that forced her to seek a new one. She will not lose him too.

* * *

The next morning, after an interview alongside Vince, Ada tells him of her planned errand at the Biltmore. Together, they pull up to the hotel in the middle of Gordon's scheduled hearing. Good—he'll already be inside, so he won't see Ada or attempt to order her away.

Before exiting the car, Ada looks to Vince. "Are you certain you want to accompany me?"

A journalist could easily photograph them, write some article specu-lating about their reasons for being in the same building as the hearings, so she will understand if Vince doesn't want to be tasked with settling any potential rumors.

"My politics are clear, so if confusion arises, I'll clarify if needed." He passes a hand across his jaw and looks to the hotel door, then to Ada. "If something happens, I want to be there for you. I don't know how the government is approaching these hearings, but I hope the purpose is to identify clear threats rather than acting without reason or making decisions based on speculation, because God knows where that might lead. Maybe Gordon was summoned simply because he's a Communist Party member, or maybe because of something you and I don't know about."

Perhaps Gordon is someone living a lie, the same as Ada has been. Holding one belief while professing—or concealing—another. Maybe Vince is right and there is something more to the reasons for this hearing.

Or maybe this has little to do with Gordon himself and more to do with someone else mentioning him. Naming names, as the exposé she read last August stated. In Arnhem, a mere accusation was all it took to lead to arrest or worse. Ada lived through those times. What if these times come to that, to neighbor turning against neighbor based on speculation and nothing else?

In response to her silence, Vince takes her hand. "My point is, it might be nothing, or a misunderstanding, but until Gordon tells us more, we don't know because we aren't in that room. Be prepared for anything. That's all I'm saying."

Preparation has little to do with it. In Arnhem, every day she was prepared to be accused, betrayed, caught. Or she thought she was, until it actually happened. Then she learned how nothing could have prepared her for what awaited, nor could anticipation of every possibility have prepared her for what occurred in her own home. For living with a Nazi and witnessing her mother's support of the regime, fabricated or not.

No, preparation could not have helped her then, and it won't now. She simply must face whatever is to come.

Inside, they find the hotel conference room where the hearing is taking place. Once there, they only have a few minutes to wait before the conference room doors swing open. Gordon emerges, looking not at all surprised to see them. Still, the lines on his forehead soften despite the rebuke that follows.

"You weren't supposed to come."

"Don't pretend you expected otherwise." She threads her arm through his and kisses his cheek before dropping her voice. "All right, then?"

"The gist of it? Yes, I'm a registered member of the Communist Party. No, I'm not a spy. Recently, I've come to reconsider my political views. Thoughts and opinions change, and I've always been open to learning more and challenging my beliefs. Encouragement from a trusted source doesn't hurt either." He smiles, prompting Ada's in return, then lowers his voice. "No questions about anything else."

For Gordon's sake, Ada offers him a relieved smile—and of course she's relieved nothing worse happened, but she can't shake the feeling that relief might be premature. Matters can always escalate. Even Dietrich's visits began with simple dinners.

She can only hope Vince and Ingrid are right, the hearings are being carried out properly, and her concerns are rooted only in her own experiences under an oppressive regime. For now, Gordon is safe.

For now.

HOLLYWOOD'S VIXEN: ON THE HUNT
by Minnie Musgrave

Here's an idea: Use the tip line below to express your over-whelming gratitude to me for this, your next exclusive with the one and only Ada Worthington-Fox. Once again, the silver screen siren joins me in my office, wearing simple gray trousers and a sleeveless red-and-white-striped blouse, her hair in its usual style, a cigarette in her hand.

Lady Bella Donna was released last month and has been favorably received, with reviews praising its leading lady for her nuanced and memorable performance. The woman who sits before me is not the actress, though. Simply Ada.

"The character I played in my recent film was fully aware of the power she held and was unafraid to use it," she explains. "I'd like to do the same."

When I ask if she, like her character, intends to break laws or scheme against handsome detectives, Miss Worthington-Fox laughs.

"No, I won't take up those particular methods. But now I more fully recognize the uniqueness of my position: I have a wonderful career, and fans all across America welcome me onto their screens. It seems foolish to have such a role and not recognize the good I can do through it."

Here, Miss Worthington-Fox finishes her cigarette and lights another. She is quiet and reserved, and for a long moment I wonder if she will go on. Then, softly but resolutely, she does.

"No one speaks of the war, but I must, because the war took something from all of us. From me, it was everything. My loved ones. My freedom. My ability to speak my mind.

My safety and security. And ever since, I have lived as I did under occupation. In fear."

This was news to me and, I expect, news to you, readers. We've all heard from the accent that Miss Worthington-Fox is not American, but never before has she stated when she came here. I, like most of you, assumed it was prior to the war. Instead she lived under occupation but came onto our screens a few years ago. Which can only mean she got out somehow, in the middle of it all.

She does not speak on any of this, though, when she continues.

"Words hold the power to harm, to condemn, but also to empower and liberate. I spent so long living in fear, so accustomed to the damage, that I forgot to find strength. To find myself. A man from my past took those things from me, so I'm taking them back. Many war criminals escaped without punishment, so if he is alive, I intend to do everything I can to ensure he is held responsible."

A war criminal! A quest for justice! An actress out for blood! God, all you screenwriters wish you had thought of that script. Maybe Hollywood's Hartthrob will secure the rights to his lady's story, since I hear the two are back together, and Vince Hart is rumored to be dabbling in screenwriting—but I digress. More on this second chance for Hollywood's favorite couple another time.

This is where I must leave you, on this Oscar-worthy cliffhanger in Miss Worthington-Fox's story—and I can hear you swearing at me from here. Don't worry, dolls, I won't leave you in suspense too long. There's plenty more to come. What happened, how it happened, why it happened, and who is responsible for taking this bold young woman and forming her into our secretive starlet. Into the woman who is now standing up to him, asserting herself, and demanding justice.

All this and more in the next exclusive with Ada Worthington-Fox.

And that war criminal she mentioned? Next time, she's promised me a name.

CHAPTER 34

Hollywood Hills, 16 June 1947

INGRID

The day Ada's second exclusive publishes is the day Ingrid and Ada have chosen to give Mother the evidence. A plan that still leaves Ingrid feeling much too unsettled, but Ada is right. This might determine who is sending the threats.

When Ingrid arrives at Gordon's, she brings the latest issue of *The Dish*, as if stopping by to discuss it with Ada, which will ensure Mother sees it as well. Gordon answers and permits her inside, where he, Ada, and Mother have just finished breakfast.

"Don't discuss all the good gossip without me," Gordon calls over his shoulder as he lets himself and Sowerby into the backyard.

He seems well, to Ingrid's relief. Following the initial round of hearings, a few others were conducted locally, then future hearings will take place in Washington, DC. When Ada told her of Gordon's, she couldn't help feeling responsible. Others might have named Gordon a Communist, but her report certainly did, even if she also reported evidence of his changed views. Maybe he wasn't spared a hearing, but it seems the committee was satisfied with the discussion, so all is well.

After greetings and small talk, Ingrid holds up her copy of *The Dish*. "Wonderful piece, Leidje. I thought you might like to see it in print."

"Is that the next exclusive? It published today, then?" Ada eagerly reaches for it—playing her role perfectly, as always—then sits beside Mother so they can read together.

While they do so, Ingrid pours herself a cup of coffee, discreetly watching Mother's face. Her expression remains neutral, yet Ingrid detects the faint pursing of her lips and creasing of her brow.

"For God's sake, Aleida, must you persist with this?" she asks once they finish and rise from the table. "Why must you speak on such matters?"

"Because he's a war criminal," Ada says. Ingrid has a mind to elaborate, but she stays quiet. "I need to know what happened to him, to get justice for all his victims. Which includes you, Mother."

"I have my justice." Mother wraps her arms around their waists, drawing them close. "This. My girls. You are all I want."

Ingrid resists the urge to pull away. Mother has not criticized her at all recently. The reprieve is welcome, of course, but this version of her almost makes Ingrid more uncomfortable. Mother does not dote on Ingrid like this. She is critical and perpetually disappointed. She did promise to try to be better, so Ingrid should be grateful, yet nothing about this feels natural when the mother she knows is so different.

Mother's next breath is unsteady as she releases them. "You will never forgive me, will you? Is that why you intend to hold everyone accountable? Even me?"

She looks so hurt, so defeated, nearly prompting Ingrid to extend a hand or offer a reassuring word. Perhaps Ingrid's perception is due to her own inability to move beyond her mistrust, making Mother's efforts seem unnatural when the problem truly lies with Ingrid.

"Speaking of her experiences doesn't mean Aleida will mention your involvement, or that she won't forgive you. Nor does it mean I won't, either, in time." At this, Mother meets her gaze. They did agree to put forth more effort with one another, so Ingrid presses forward with words that feel unusual on her tongue, but she tries to form them anyway. "You have been hard on me all my life, Mother. But I have been hard on you too."

If they are able to make peace, Ingrid will try to be better. Assuming Mother truly recognizes and regrets her past mistakes and is not the one who has been manipulating Ada all this time. For now, though, and for the purposes of this conversation, Ingrid will push her suspicions aside.

Mother takes Ingrid's hand, seeming too overcome to speak. Ada is silent, as if pondering something, then she departs without a word. Ingrid knows exactly where she's going, but she simply sips her coffee, listening as Ada climbs the stairs—clever girl, moving the evidence from the library to her bedroom so Mother won't know where the negatives are hidden.

When Ada returns, she presents Mother with an unmarked envelope. "Few choices made during the war were made freely. Yours were to protect me, and I can't imagine what you suffered. I don't wish to contribute to further suffering."

Mother accepts the envelope, opens it, and peers inside. When she glimpses the documents and photographs, her breath catches, then she kisses her daughters' cheeks. Ada returns the kiss, and after a moment's hesitation, so does Ingrid. Everything about Mother seems entirely sincere, yet Ingrid's concerns linger and do not allow her to fully accept this display.

After another hour of casual conversation, Mother returns to the guesthouse, taking the envelope with her. Ingrid watches her through the back door as she crosses the beautifully manicured lawn.

"Does Mother know you took film? Will she realize you still have the negatives?"

"I doubt Dietrich gave her an itemized list. He probably just told her I stole materials against them both." Ada steps to Ingrid's side, watching Mother's retreating figure. "And now we wait."

Last time an exclusive published, Ada was threatened the same day. Now, as Ingrid glances at her sister, she sees the tension in her rigid spine, the anticipation encircling her and, in turn, constricting Ingrid's heart.

Perhaps it is due to the threat they await. Or the thought of Mother across the property, in possession of the evidence. No number of copies could ever make Ingrid comfortable with that.

* * *

The days pass without another note appearing. Which could mean nothing. As Ada said, Dietrich is not predictable. Or nothing has happened because Ada gave Mother the evidence. Which means Ingrid is right and no more threats will come.

The next exclusive is not scheduled to take place for a few months, so there is time for the culprit to make a threat, but one will not come. Ingrid is certain of it.

Because Mother has done this.

Mother, who claimed she wanted to be better—an opportunity Ingrid was trying to permit. Mother, who was so worried about being held accountable for her choices during the war, she used her own daughter's fears against her.

"I can't explain how I know, but I do," Ada insists when they discuss the matter in Ingrid's hotel room a couple weeks later. "I know it's not her."

"It *is*. You can't dismiss the test just because you don't like the outcome."

"Fine, let's say you're right. She was afraid I would expose her, so maybe she acted out of fear to protect herself, the same as she did during the war—which doesn't make it right, but am I supposed to hold it against her for the rest of our lives?"

Why Ada insists on giving Mother chance after chance, Ingrid does not know. Still, Ingrid senses how unnerved Ada is by the prospect of Mother being responsible, yet how desperately she does not want it to be Dietrich.

How can Ingrid focus on her investigation when it means going back to Gordon's with Mother there? She has tolerated her over these last weeks of attempted improvement in their relationship, but now Mother has proven herself to be the woman Ingrid has always known her to be: a manipulative liar. And Ingrid cannot bear to be around her, nor can she bear the thought of Ada associating with her.

Since her last meeting with Agent Stieber, Ingrid has turned in a copy of Ada's second exclusive and provided reports of conversations and materials to reinforce her initial findings, but she must keep working until she's called back home. How is she supposed to continue when it requires going to that house?

Where Mother is. And Mother cannot be trusted.

CHAPTER 35

Los Angeles, 23 July 1947

ADA

The purpose of an intimate evening in Vince's downtown Los Angeles apartment was to help each other prepare for upcoming roles. Instead, so far they have cooked and eaten penne alla vodka, talked, laughed, kissed—quite a lot—and have not glanced at a single page of either script.

At last, they agree to rehearse one scene each. Better than nothing. While Vince refills their wineglasses, Ada stretches her legs along the sofa and examines his part.

"A western?" she asks as he joins her, picks up her legs, sits, and lowers her crossed ankles into his lap. "You haven't worked on a western before, have you?"

"No, ma'am, I reckon I haven't." He tips an imaginary cowboy hat while she chuckles, then he drops the Southern accent. "I was cast for one during the war, but the project was canceled. Most of those involved left to join the service."

Something bitter touches the words. She and Vince have never talked about the war. He removes her leather pumps and runs his fingers along her nylons before gently massaging the cramps from her feet and calves.

"You didn't serve, did you?" she asks.

His jaw clenches, then he shakes his head. "I volunteered. They turned me away—due to 'mechanical problems' or some such bullshit. Sure, I broke my ankle playing football as a kid, and it's a little weak, but I could have fought just as well as the next man."

She knows a similar sentiment, feeling frustrated with her circumstances. Maybe she was part of the resistance—what some might call a double agent, in a sense. But living among fascists meant voicing neither outright support nor outright opposition so she could best serve the work. Meanwhile countless others were vocal, heedless of the consequences. And many suffered those consequences.

For so long she stayed quiet. First with fascism, next with Communism or anything that might expose her to conflict, to difficulty, to harm. Then, to protect her work; now, to protect herself. Except now she has taken a public position. Silence is not the protection she always believed it to be. One can be condemned for silence as much as for action. Maybe there is a time for both, a use for both, and it's simply a matter of knowing which is needed and having the courage to choose it.

Vince leans back, staring into the distance. "As the months wore on, I expected to be drafted. Other men had genuine reasons preventing them from serving; mine was nothing. I did everything I could to convince someone to take me."

"Sending you to the front might have been unnecessarily reckless, and the role you fulfilled was important in a different way."

"People were dying, Ada." His eyes sharpen along with his tone. "My sister lost her husband to Pearl Harbor, and where was I? Sitting in the comfort of my own home, entertaining my fellow Americans, raising funds, acting in military training films, boosting morale, cheering for our boys while they went through hell."

"It was hell for everyone," she counters while he stands and turns away from her. "Every soldier on the front, every resistance member, every Jew subjected to persecution, every person living under occupation, everyone at home wondering if or when their loved ones would return. All of them suffered, and all of them were important. And you feel like you weren't important enough because you weren't shot at or bombed or killed?"

She, too, stands and turns aside even as he faces her again, likely prompted by the catch in her voice. By the tears it's too late to prevent. She already sees the haunted look in every soldier's eyes when he returned from the battlefront following Germany's triumph over the Dutch Army. Hears the soldiers' jackboots marching down the street. Feels the terror and helplessness passing between herself and Madame Bellamy in the Oranjehotel interrogation room.

As Vince's gentle hand finds her forearm, she presses into him, lets him hold her close until she looks up. "You contributed and supported your country. Be proud of that." She brushes a lock of hair from his forehead. "What happened does not make you a coward."

He searches her gaze, no doubt wondering if the past she mentioned in her last exclusive has contributed to her reaction. Now is not the time to discuss such things, so she brings his mouth to hers, tastes the crisp Chardonnay they shared on this warm summer evening. Then she obeys the subtle yet increasingly insistent prompting that always awakens in response to him. The one her mind always warns her to silence.

She hooks her fingers through his suspenders, draws him closer, slips them from his shoulders. Next she reaches for his shirt, unfastening one button, then another.

Vince looks from her fingers to her, the unspoken question clear. Not since their film's afterparty have they attempted to be together in this way. Over these last two months, she has thought about it, longed for it. This time, *this* time, they will know one another completely.

Ada dips her head in assurance, then pulls his shirt off before he catches her in a fierce hold, and suddenly they are kissing, touching, staggering into his bedroom.

Clothes fall away with frantic intensity—Vince's undershirt, then Ada's skirt, then Vince's trousers. His touch renders everything else insignificant. She wills it to sweep her away, to erase everything except her gasping breaths, her pounding heartbeat, her hands against his sculpted chest, then seeking his hips, pulling him nearer. Soon they will be too absorbed in one another for him to notice what she never wants him to see. It will not interfere, not this time.

Vince pulls off Ada's blouse, leaving both in undergarments as they collapse onto the bed. She knows only the heat of his skin, the energy pulsing through her body, their eagerness for one another.

Until she feels him unfastening her brassiere.

At once it seizes her, the adversary she can never overcome, then she's turning away from his next kiss, shoving against his chest, writhing beneath him.

"Stop! Stop, get off me!"

Vince's weight lifts immediately. "I'm sorry, what did I—?"

Ada hears no more. She moves to the far edge of the bed, snatches a blanket, and holds it across her chest. Against her thudding heart. Aside from her shuddering breaths, no sound disturbs the quiet. Her bra hangs on by one hook, yet she feels the scar cutting into her flesh. An ache almost as fierce as the one coursing through her body, urging her to tear this mark from her skin, to go back to Vince, to assure him he's done nothing wrong.

Her entire body is aflame; she cannot keep doing this to herself. To him.

"I'm sorry, I thought I . . ." Her voice dies. She makes no effort to revive it.

"Talk to me," he murmurs. "Tell me what you want."

You, she answers silently. *I want you so desperately, Vince Hart.*

What she wants she cannot have, no matter how hard she tries. This night has proven it to her—perhaps also to Vince.

That place and that man will take from her for the rest of her life. First her freedom, then her home, now the man she loves. *Loves*. She knows it with each of her aching heartbeats. Someday she might be able to trust him with every part of her—both who she was and who she is. Or perhaps this will always remain between them.

This scar is a reminder of that moment when her life belonged to Dietrich. Now she is the one permitting him to retain that power.

She has permitted it long enough. He will not silence her, nor will his actions define her.

"May I show you?" she asks quietly.

A momentary flicker of surprise or perhaps confusion crosses Vince's face, then he nods. Ada stands with her back to him and, with some effort, leaves the blanket on the bed.

With hands that now tremble, she unfastens the final hook and removes her bra. The single lamp on his bedside table washes her body in golden light. The scar is there, clearly visible, but if she does not turn to face Vince, then Dietrich wins again.

Before, she was not ready. Now, she is.

She closes her eyes. Takes a slow breath. Then she turns.

Gradually, he rises from the bed, then he is standing in his shorts, his chest rising and falling, his blue eyes clear and warm in the light as he looks first at her face, with her dark hair draped over her shoulders, then to her exposed breasts. The moment will come; she will know when it does.

And there it is—his eyes narrowing in scrutiny as he notices, then his jaw flickering as it clenches. Each of her heartbeats comes faster than the last. Still, she does not turn away, does not close her eyes. She watches him.

His eyes are bright and sharp, his voice gruff, each word measured with slow, steady rage.

"Ada, who did this to you?"

She shakes her head. Someday she will answer questions. Not today.

"I've wanted to tell you, to explain why I . . ." She draws a steadying breath before finishing more softly. "It's not you, Vince. It's never been you."

He passes a hand across his jaw, yet upon her reassurance, the tension in his shoulders lessens slightly. He reaches for her but waits, seeking permission. After she dips her head, he brushes his thumb across the scar—a single, slow stroke. A gesture that doesn't prompt it to ache as it usually does.

It prompts a different ache entirely—an ache for him, stronger than ever, yet steadying, calming.

"You are safe with me. Always."

That, she has never doubted. She presses her hands to his, holding his open palm to her chest, where each heartbeat speaks of her gratitude.

There is more to tell. Much more. Not today, though. Today there are only two joined heartbeats echoing their love for one another.

Vince picks up his white cotton undershirt and slips it over her head. The fabric is light and soft against her skin, the straps slim, the scoop neck covering her so the mark is no longer exposed. She draws a deep breath smelling of him, aromatic and comforting.

"However long you need. It's all right."

His gentle murmur settles the last of Ada's lingering nerves as he kisses her forehead. Of course she knows him, knows he will never pressure her. Yet the reminder is everything she needs to hear. Tension no longer seizes her so fiercely despite standing here before him, more exposed and more herself than she has been in so long.

"Do you mind if I stay with you?" she asks softly.

In response, Vince returns to his bed and beckons her, so she settles beside him. They do not touch, allowing one another's presence to be enough. And soon the idea of being seen, touched, loved is not so overwhelming. So Ada shifts closer to Vince and slips her arm across his firm waist. He draws her closer and kisses the top of her head. Breaths and heartbeats match as one in stillness, in silence, in comfort and security.

Someday, perhaps more will be attainable. For now, she is here, safe with him, and it is perfectly enough.

* * *

The next morning, sunlight slips through the partially open curtain, its beams falling over Ada's arm draped across Vince's bare chest. She blinks away sleep, listening to his deep breaths.

She is wearing Vince's shirt, sleeping in his bed, waking next to him. Something that seemed impossible a mere few days ago.

After a moment, he stirs, so she kisses his cheek. His eyes flutter open, as bright blue as the morning sky, while a drowsy half smile cocks the corner of his mouth. She brushes the hair from his forehead and kisses him slowly, deeply, pouring all her affection and appreciation into the gesture. Then she rises, dresses, and slips out, filled with more peace than she's felt in a long time.

When she arrives at Gordon's, she steps onto the motor court, where an unfamiliar voice chases away her lingering ease.

"Excuse me, miss, are you Ada Worthington-Fox?"

Two suited men approach. Beyond them, a black car is parked a short distance from the house.

G-men. Ada can manage fans or journalists—make a small acknowledgment to appease them, then ignore them if they grow more persistent. The G-men, she fears, will not be so easily appeased.

Neither one is looking at her with ill intent, which does not make her any more comfortable when she considers the many reasons they might be here. Gordon already went to a hearing, and she gave her statement. What else could they possibly need to know? She bites her lip hard as the men reach her.

One tips his hat in greeting, then hands her a sealed envelope. "Have a nice day, miss."

Nice day, indeed. As if a sealed envelope from the government wouldn't ruin it entirely.

There is no name on the envelope, but if they were waiting outside Gordon Sharpe's home and knew her name, they must know she, too, lives here. Maybe this is her mail to open, maybe not. Either way, when the men drive away, Ada breaks the seal and eases the envelope open to glimpse what's inside.

A pink slip of paper.

They must want to see Gordon again. He is the registered Communist, and she clarified her views. She doesn't pull the paper out, not wanting to see the official statement, the summons, the demand for a hearing. Not again. Was once not enough?

Her walk to the front door takes twice as long as usual. Once she gives Gordon this envelope, she can no longer pretend it isn't real.

Inside, a kettle whistles from the kitchen, so she follows the sound, each step more difficult than the last. Sowerby greets her with excited yet indignant yaps, clearly offended that she left him overnight.

"Well, if it isn't America's favorite vixen," Gordon greets her without looking up as he pours his tea. "Tell me, does Hollywood's Hartthrob perform as well in the bedroom as he does on the silver screen?"

The teasing grin disappears immediately when he reads the fear that is surely reflected on her face. He opens his mouth, then his eyes fall to the envelope.

Slowly, Ada offers it to him. Perhaps she can't change the contents, but she can stay with him while he reads the summons. And this time she will find her way into the hearing room. This time, he will not endure it alone.

Gordon extracts the pink slip. He reads without expression, then something changes in his face, impossible for Ada to decipher. He passes a hand over his mustache.

"Not mine, kid."

Her relieved exhale catches in her throat. Not his. But there is only one other person living in this house.

With a trembling hand, she accepts the document and reads.

The same as the previous one—a summons to a hearing, this time in Washington, DC. This time, not summoning Gordon Sharpe.

This pink slip is a subpoena for Ada Worthington-Fox.

CHAPTER 36

Los Angeles, 24 July 1947

INGRID

Insistent, aggressive pounding on her hotel room door startles Ingrid awake. She listens, staring into the darkness—so dark it must not yet be dawn. Some intoxicated fellow staggering back to his accommodations, most likely; he'll move along to the proper room soon enough.

The knocking persists. "Rise and shine, Holland."

God, not him.

Sighing, she tugs on her dressing gown and switches on her bedside table lamp before stumbling to the closed door.

"May I help you?" she asks dryly.

"Downstairs. Ten minutes. Stieber is picking us up."

Heedless of her dressing gown, bare face, and the silk headscarf keeping her pin curls contained, Ingrid flings the door open. "What? Ten minutes?"

Archie is fully dressed, luggage in hand, and checks his wristwatch. "Nine now. Less talking, more packing."

"What the hell is going on?"

"Last night, Stieber told me we're closing our investigations for now and asked me to relay the message to you along with the plans for our departure, which I had no intention of doing, because after you threatened me with that Communist rally I attended in New York, why shouldn't I let Stieber believe you failed to follow orders? You're welcome for my change of heart."

A change of heart ten minutes before her handler expects her to be ready to travel home? Ingrid pinches the bridge of her nose. "Archie Stribling, you absolute bastard." Further raging will have to wait.

After closing the door, she shoves her files and equipment into one valise and her clothes into another. Then she takes down her hair, pulls on a dress, shoes, earrings, and a necklace, slaps a fascinator atop her head, applies lipstick, powder, and blush, tosses the last of her belongings into her valise, and is out the door, shoving past Archie and leading the way to meet Agent Stieber.

A whistle sounds behind her as he follows. "Impressive."

"Shut up before I slam this bag into your shins."

She's wide awake now. Irritation has a way of doing that. Withholding direct orders over his own wounded ego. Of all the petty, childish methods of retaliation.

Downstairs, Agent Stieber is already waiting. No one speaks as they climb into the black car chauffeuring them to the airport, so Ingrid can't tell if he's satisfied or not. Still, he hasn't professed further concerns regarding Ada's loyalties or the Star Society's purpose, so perhaps she did her job properly this time.

* * *

After a long day of travel, when the taxicab reaches her apartment, Ingrid feels sudden tears spring to her eyes. Home. Nearly three months away, and she is home.

Once inside, she opens the curtains to permit the dwindling afternoon light to wash over the space, quickly unpacks her luggage, then calls Gordon's. Moments later, Ada picks up.

"Where the hell are you? I've been calling the bloody Biltmore all day, and they keep telling me you've checked out."

"My boss needed me back in the office unexpectedly. It was urgent, so I left early this morning and didn't have time to call."

"Do you really mean to tell me you went home? You might have said goodbye." As Ingrid starts to apologize, Ada huffs and cuts her off. "Never mind, I need to talk to you. I've been subpoenaed."

Ingrid's blood runs cold. "By HUAC?" What a ridiculous question. Who else? Yet confusion prevents her from thinking clearly, so she doesn't bother to correct herself.

"I don't understand—I clarified my views. Is this because of Gordon's hearing?" She hesitates. "There are other reasons I think HUAC might consider him subversive . . . reasons I can't specify, not because I don't trust you, but because it's not my . . . Well, do you understand?"

Indeed she does.

"I understand," Ingrid replies softly. "You have nothing to worry about, Leidje. Answer honestly and clarify whatever it is they want to know. That's what Gordon did, and he turned out all right, didn't he?"

"Did he? With the way the papers have been talking, those involved in the hearings are being ostracized regardless of the findings, so what does that mean for him, for me, for our careers? Mrs. Musgrave already found out somehow and called to postpone the final exclusive until further notice, and if I try to pursue a war crimes case, will the FBI even listen to me if I've been caught up in this mess?" Before Ingrid can find a reply, she hears the faint sound of a door opening in the background, then Ada lowers her voice. "Listen, Gordon is coming inside, and he's already driving himself mad with worry, so I'll call you another time."

After hanging up, Ingrid stays in her seat, her heart pounding. Her own sister has been subpoenaed. The purpose of these hearings is to identify concerning individuals, to guide them to better ways, to clarify confusion. Why speak with Ada when nothing in Ingrid's investigation pointed to a need? Unless that is exactly why this happened: because Ada is not a Communist, but those around her are, so HUAC wants information from her.

Or perhaps this has nothing to do with Ingrid's findings. Someone might have called Ada into question—for authentic concerns or simply to cause trouble, leading to doubts and a need for clarification since the information will conflict with Ingrid's report. Someone like Beverly Tolbert. The actress knows Ada, knows Gordon, is jealous of their relationship. This might be her doing.

And, by extension, Ingrid's doing.

This won't reflect poorly on me unless I allow it.

At the time, Ingrid thought nothing of the conversation they had at Lucey's or of Beverly's assertion. All she did was assuage the other woman's fears and advise her on what to do if HUAC contacted her. And then Ingrid saw her at the Biltmore. What if Beverly took Ingrid's counsel to mean she should take matters into her own hands? What if she went to HUAC and seized the opportunity to damage Gordon and the actress she views as competition?

What if she named names?

Damn it all.

Ingrid has no more time to speculate before the door opens. Despite the weight pressing on her chest, pleasant warmth fills her when Lars enters and nearly drops his briefcase at the unexpected sight of his wife.

"Hello, darling," she says, and she's hardly on her feet before he wraps her in his arms.

Even as she clings to him, she can't help the pang of resentment curling within her core. Why did Ada have to be subpoenaed at all, and why did the news have to come on her first day back home? After so long away, all she wants is a comfortable night with her husband. Instead, it's been spoiled, because now she can't focus on anything except the impending hearing.

Lars presses his mouth eagerly to hers. "Welcome home, *schatje*," he murmurs against her lips. When he releases her, his chuckle is tinged with uneasiness. "Aren't you excited to be back?"

She sighs. "Of course I am. The trip was long, that's all."

"Is that all?"

Uncertainty touches his words, but she lacks the capacity to address it. Instead she will do her best to settle into normalcy, to banish the worry plaguing her. She's about to change the subject when the corners of his mouth dip slightly. He takes her left hand.

"Where is your wedding ring? Did you lose it?"

Bile rises to Ingrid's throat, threatening to spill over. In her haste to call Ada after unpacking, she forgot to put the most essential item back on.

"No, no, of course not." She breaks free, wipes sweaty palms on her dress, and hears him following her to their bedroom. "On my vanity, just there . . ." She grabs it, nearly drops it as she fumbles with it, keeping her back to him.

She knows it's not the lack of jewelry concerning him; it's not as if she's never removed her ring for any number of harmless reasons. But she is not this person, this woman who forgets about her wedding ring and fails to push her worries aside enough to focus on the man she loves. Now she can almost feel the distance stretching between them, because of course he senses her discomfort, which will make him wonder why something so insignificant has made her pull away. And the only way to ease his mind is to tell him what's distracting her.

Yet the truth requires an explanation regarding everything she's been doing these last months. Everything she can't reveal.

"Ingrid, look at me." His voice is painfully quiet, achingly calm, speaking to a confusion that is far more difficult to bear than suspicion or even accusations. Her heart thuds in her chest as she turns. "What is troubling you?"

When she opens her mouth, words catch, but she must try to explain as much as possible. "The ring. I've had it off all this time. For work. But it was never my idea, never what I wanted—"

"What kind of investigation requires you to pretend you aren't married?" The words sharpen along with the tension cutting across his jawline.

"No, it wasn't like it sounds." Even if she did reveal her reasons, it might not make a difference. Not with the way he's looking at her.

"Tell me where you've been."

"On assignment."

Suddenly she can say no more, because she realizes exactly where this line of questioning is going. What he's thinking. Except she can't let him think that, because it's wrong, completely and entirely wrong. He knows it's not true, knows *her*. Doesn't he?

She should explain everything now, confidentiality be damned. Instead, when she swallows hard, she can only manage one question. "Lars, do you trust me?"

"Should I not? Are you having an affair?"

Maybe she expected the question, but nothing prepares her for how fiercely it pummels her. Part of her wants to rage at him for suspecting her of something so terrible. Another part cannot move beyond a deep, aching sorrow unlike any she's ever experienced. Every tremble in his voice cuts far more deeply than the conclusion he's drawn, than everything she's kept from him.

"For God's sake, Ingrid, just tell me the truth! All this time when you said you were working, have you been with someone else?"

"Darling, of course not." She grabs his forearms, clings to him despite how he stiffens, and when the tears start, she can't stop them. "I love you with my entire heart, and I have never been unfaithful—not now, not ever." She tightens her hold. "Please. You must believe me."

He is Lars, her Lars, honest and gentle and unshakable. Her husband. A man she was once in danger of losing to war but never thought she would be in danger of losing to her own actions. A man who would never hurt her, certainly not as she has hurt him.

Slowly, he steps away, then he proceeds to the door. Leaving. She will lose him the same way she lost her father, her grandfather, her sister for a time, and the mother she never had from the start.

"Hollywood! I've been in Hollywood—twice, for both trips. Crenshaw thought a woman who appeared unmarried would be more approachable for the celebrities, less interesting to the gossips. That's all it was—an effort to help me do my job and keep my name out of the papers. Nothing happened, *nothing*, I swear to God. It's not someone else, it's . . . it's my sister." Even if she can't explain everything, she must tell him who has taken up so much of her time these last months.

When she finally takes a breath, the blood rushes in her ears. She has never betrayed the strict regulations of her career, not even for him. Not even when hiding so much of her life from him has kept her awake most nights, longing to hear his voice, to feel his touch, to share everything.

He knows nothing about her assignment, only that she has been away for work. Nothing about the war crimes case. Nothing about Mother. Nothing about her sister, only that Aleida survived the war and became an actress, so Ingrid visited her and they have kept in touch. Some matters she cannot share even if she had been permitted to call him. Others she will share in time, when she can find the strength.

From her briefcase she produces an article—a recent edition of *The Dish*, one of Minnie Musgrave's latest writings about the hearings. She places it on the bed, hoping it will lead Lars to the conclusions she cannot state herself. Investigations into Communism have resulted in hearings, her sister is an actress, and Ingrid has been in Hollywood. Surely he will understand this is what she's been doing: investigating the entertainment industry and trying to protect Ada.

He stares at the article for a long time. The silence is unbearable. At last, understanding ripples across his features, which does not lessen the tension in her chest, because he still does not acknowledge her.

"Lars, please say something. Please look at me."

When he does, his voice is so quiet she hardly hears over her shuddering breaths. "I trust you, Ingrid, but it's not about that. It's the way you've been acting ever since you started this assignment. Like you have something to be ashamed of."

Maybe he's right. She's ashamed of failing her sister, of forgetting herself and her marriage so much that her husband suspected her of infidelity. Ashamed of knowing her work is important, honest, so she has no reason to be plagued by this reoccurring feeling of doubt. A feeling that tells her something is quite wrong.

CHAPTER 37

Hollywood Hills, 23 August 1947

ADA

If Gordon doesn't stop swimming laps, Ada will drag him out of the pool herself. It's practically all he's done since her subpoena, as if he can't look at her without imagining that dreadful pink slip.

Sighing, she tosses her magazine aside, rises from her chair, and sits on the edge of the pool. When he passes, she stretches her leg as far as it can reach, far enough to tap her foot against his shoulder. He stops, breathing heavily and scowling.

"Don't interrupt me."

"Then stop ignoring me. Must I remind you that this is not your fault?"

"No? My job is to protect my clients—their images, their careers, and *them* most of all." He wipes the water droplets from his face. "I should have mentioned my changed views sooner, never should have believed my hearing would be the end of it. Of course they'll come for all of you next."

Why she was called to a hearing, Ada still can't understand. Nor does she like the way it's provoked memories of the last time she was questioned by authorities—entirely different circumstances, perhaps, considering last time was under occupation by an oppressive regime, but such rationalizations do little to assuage her. She will soon find out the reason, though. She leaves tomorrow, and her hearing is Monday morning.

Gordon emerges from the pool, sighing. "Is it better or worse if I offer to go with you?"

"Better, of course." Ada stands and kisses his cheek, which does little to erase his dubious frown. "But I want you to be safe, and Sowerby will be much happier if he's with you while I'm gone, so it's best if you stay."

Despite her reassurances, the prospect of traveling leaves Ada's skin prickling. Appearing before HUAC in Washington, DC, seems far more undesirable than doing it here, in the comfort of her own city. There, everything is unfamiliar, everyone unknown to her.

Except Ingrid. Thank God she will have her sister. Ingrid told her not to worry, but Ada's nerves won't settle until her twin is by her side and this is all over.

The back door opens and Vince emerges, wearing swim trunks and carrying a tray with the three martinis he prepared. Gordon accepts his with a nod of thanks, wraps a towel around his waist, scoops up Sowerby, and disappears inside. Giving the couple privacy or, more likely, fleeing from Ada's presence.

Vince watches him go. "Still blaming himself?"

"Naturally."

Not even Sowerby's company has been enough to settle Gordon over these last weeks. The thought of leaving him like this makes Ada's heart ache as she accepts her drink and returns to her chair.

"He'll be all right," Vince says, likely guessing her thoughts. "And even better after you come home."

He stretches onto the lounge chair beside Ada's, the muscles across his chest and stomach rippling as he settles. She rolls onto her side to face him.

"You think it'll be all right, then?"

"How could it not be? You're not a Communist. Maybe you've worked with some, but who hasn't?" He brushes a lock of hair from her face—a touch that almost makes her forget her concerns. "They must want confirmation of your views to assuage any remaining concerns."

"Then why must it involve a hearing when I've already given multiple statements?" She sighs. "This is all so dreadfully extreme."

Vince chuckles. "Now there's a suitable slogan for HUAC: 'Dreadfully extreme.'"

One hearing on Monday, hopefully time for a quick visit with Ingrid, then Ada will come home, Gordon will stop worrying, and they can forget this ever happened. Until then, she'll have Vince by her side. Upon hearing about her subpoena, he immediately volunteered to accompany her. An offer she couldn't resist.

He glances at her with the look of concern she's noticed ever since he caught her with a gun and a mysterious note, but he says nothing. Since the radio program, they haven't spoken of those messages or who sent them; to Vince's credit, he hasn't pressured her for details. Ada has simply allowed him to infer what he wants to infer. And technically, the messages have stopped.

As for whether Ingrid is right and they stopped due to Mother taking possession of the evidence, Ada does not know. It's the most logical conclusion, yet it still doesn't feel right.

When the glasses are empty, she climbs onto his chair, straddling him, bringing an immediate spark to his bright blue eyes. She takes his face in her hands and kisses him deeply, tasting gin, vermouth, brine from the olives he added to his own beverage, salt from the droplets of sweat left by the August sun. For a moment, just a moment, she can forget everything to come and lose herself in him.

But they have an early flight and Ada still needs to pack, so with a final kiss and a promise to meet her at the airport in the morning, Vince bids her farewell. Once he's gone, Ada continues barefoot across the lawn, enjoying the soft grass beneath her feet, and knocks on the guest-house door.

"I'm leaving before dawn, so I wanted to tell you goodbye," she says when Mother answers.

"You're certain you don't want me to accompany you?"

Ada shakes her head even as a pang of confusion and hurt and un-certainty constricts in her chest, one she hasn't been able to let go. Would a mother who had threatened her daughter be concerned about supporting her through a difficult time? Although Mother has not be-haved any differently since the last exclusive, Ada must know.

"Did you send them?" she asks quietly. "The messages."

Mother's brow furrows. "Messages?"

"To discourage me from pursuing a war crimes case."

"Are you still considering such things? Darling, you must let it go. You're worrying me. Why did you give me the evidence if you still in-tend to use it?"

"Because I intend to use it against him, not against you. Once the hearing is behind me, I need to know what happened to him."

Mother's confusion and concern are evident. The reaction Ada ex-pected because Dietrich is certainly responsible for the messages, even if Ingrid does not agree. Why he hasn't threatened her since the last exclusive, she does not know, but it's giving her time to get through her hearing. Then she'll tell Ingrid to move forward with the FBI.

When Ada returns to the house, noise down the hall catches her attention. She follows the sound. Gordon is in his office on the telephone—his voice getting louder, harsher.

"You know I'm right, and if you don't believe me, believe the fans who couldn't get enough of her last film. I'm not asking you, Hendrix; I'm telling you: Sign her."

She pauses near the closed door, her heart pounding. He's on the phone with Mr. Hendrix, having a conversation that is presumably about her. And clearly not going well. Recently there was talk of signing her on to an upcoming romantic drama from Hendrix Productions, so that must be what this is about.

Footsteps sound across his floor, then the pacing stops.

"You begged me to keep Ada's schedule open for this project, and this is the thanks I get?" A pause, then: "Who told you she was going before HUAC? And until she's condemned for something, you can't drop her just because of— Hello?" The clang and ding of the receiver as he slams it down, then a heavy sigh and a muttered "goddamnit."

Without making noise, Ada retreats. Word of her pink slip has reached Mr. Hendrix, apparently. If he's already decided not to hire her for anything else, other studio heads will surely hold the same opinions, and then what of her career?

Except she hasn't been accused of anything. Summoned, nothing more. Ada fights the tension in her stomach. The public knows she is not a Communist, yet negative impacts to her career are already coming to fruition.

All over a hearing. All when Ingrid said there is nothing to worry about.

Maybe there is still time for Ingrid to be right. Maybe when the hearing is over, those worried about associating with her will realize their concerns were unnecessary.

Or maybe the outcome doesn't matter, not when this will follow her. Even if the outcome is favorable, people will whisper about her, will wonder what sort of secrets Ada Worthington-Fox harbors to have been brought before HUAC.

And once it starts—the talk, the whispers, the rumors—there will be no stopping it. No undoing the damage. A simple suspicion is all it takes to irrevocably alter a life.

Something Ada knows far too well.

* * *

When Monday morning comes, stifling in its August heat, Ada and Vince stand before the imposing white marble and limestone colonnade, entablature, and balustrade of the Cannon House Office Building in Washington, DC, where the hearing is to take place. Spectators and journalists surround them, but Ada can't hear anything they say. She can only thread her arm through Vince's, lift her head with the confidence that she looks both marvelous and professional in the dress she chose for the occasion, and walk inside.

There, the shuttering cameras and bellowing voices fade. The quiet is almost unnerving.

With the quiet come memories of booted footsteps, forceful thuds of heavy objects against bodies, desperate pleas and sobs as guards ushered her down the halls of the Oranjehotel. She bites her lip, needing the pain to keep her present, grounded, focused. This is not the war. Not the same as last time. She is not under arrest, not facing torture, not alone.

Outside the Caucus Room, more people eagerly await photographs and information. Some spectators even approach Ada and Vince, asking for autographs, until a young woman who looks like an assistant ushers the actors into another room, instructing them to wait until summoned.

They take their seats. Ada keeps her hand in Vince's, his strong, assured grasp slowing her pounding heart. After a few minutes, the door opens, followed by the same woman's voice.

"Miss Worthington-Fox, the committee is ready for you."

Except then the woman's voice is overtaken by the German one echoing around Ada's mind: *On your feet, Aleida de Vos.*

She closes her eyes against a shudder. She can do this, must do this. This is not a Gestapo interrogation; this is a hearing. Only a hearing.

Once they reach the Caucus Room, the doors open to welcome them into a massive space glittering with crystal chandeliers and grand marble pillars, thick with heat from the crowds packed inside and the klieg lights alongside the newsreel cameras. Ada draws a deep breath, channeling not the actress she portrays but the woman she is, the one she allowed the world to see in her exclusives. Herself, honest and open, because only that woman has the power to assuage whatever concerns will be presented today.

"Mr. Hart, you may sit there, and Miss Worthington-Fox, follow me."

A man's voice. One Ada recognizes.

After Vince kisses her cheek and departs, Ada doesn't move. The dark-haired man now grinning at her is none other than Archie Stribling.

What a fool she is. She never trusted this man after he inserted himself into her world, although she never fully explored her suspicions, perhaps too afraid of where they might lead.

"It was you. My agent, me, these hearings, you're responsible for all of it."

"All of it?" He laughs. "You give me too much credit, doll. If I had been responsible for you, you and I would have gotten much better acquainted."

He offers a salacious wink, then gestures for her to accompany him, but she doesn't.

"Why am I here? If not because of you, who is responsible?"

Mr. Stribling won't reveal that answer even if he knows it, a realization almost as infuriating as the arm he offers her. Glaring, Ada refuses and turns toward the seat he indicated: a table, a chair, and a small microphone in a stand, facing the chairman. She only takes a few steps before she stops.

A woman stands at the far end of the room, engaged in a fervent conversation with another man. Ada cannot tear her gaze off the woman, the one wearing a neat, tailored skirt and jacket with her red hair pulled back into a tight bun. The woman who doesn't notice Ada until the man walks away. Then she stares with wide, piercing blue eyes while everything inside Ada turns too delicate, too fragile, preparing to shatter completely.

From across the Caucus Room floor, Ada stares at Ingrid, who stands among countless men in suits—members of the FBI, without a doubt, and the House Un-American Activities Committee.

CHAPTER 38

Washington, DC, 25 August 1947

INGRID

The night before Ada's scheduled hearing, Ingrid hardly sleeps, then she wakes long before dawn, mentally rehearsing what to say to her superior when she sees him. Crenshaw has been mostly out of the office, so ever since learning about her sister's subpoena, Ingrid's efforts to speak with him about it have come to naught.

She will make the time, though, before the intended hearing. It might be happening today, but so are countless other hearings. Ingrid will find Crenshaw and encourage him to call the whole thing off—a plan that has little chance of succeeding, but all she's got for now. If she has to recount her entire report to convince him this is unnecessary, she will. Ada's position is already abundantly clear.

She leaves for the hearing before Lars rises. Typically, she would rouse him long enough to kiss him goodbye, or the night before he would remind her to wake him if she leaves early. They have not done either since their argument.

Despite the lump that lodges in her throat, Ingrid pushes the thought deliberately from her mind as she hurries to the Cannon House Office

Building. The stately government buildings have always brought her comfort, symbols of freedom and justice and everything she came to this country to find. Everything she hopes to ensure for her sister.

This is her investigation. And yet no one bothered to consult her about the plan to subpoena Ada. Ever since the news of the hearing, a strange feeling has settled in her chest, one that grows stronger every time she considers why she was not included in the decision. It makes no sense, not when she was the one assigned to uncover Ada's loyalties. If there is something she does not know, something that was not in her report or that came from another source and led to this, someone should have told her.

Outside the Caucus Room, throngs have already gathered, as they have ever since the public learned celebrities would be appearing before the committee. Ingrid doesn't notice Ada. Either she's not here yet, or she's already inside. She pushes through the crowd. No sign of her sister in the Caucus Room either. Ingrid lets out her breath. She has time.

Shoving down the coil of tension in her chest, Ingrid hurries to the front of the room where her employer lingers. Crenshaw is here; Ada is not. Ingrid will convince him that this hearing is unnecessary, and then her sister will be told there's been a mistake and she isn't needed after all.

"Mr. Crenshaw, speaking with Ada Worthington-Fox today is unnecessary. I spent months with her, sir; she doesn't know anything beyond what we already know, and she is not a Communist. As you know from my report. We should call off the hearing and allow the committee to put its time to better use—unless there's something you know that I don't, in which case I'd like to be informed, because I found no reason to subpoena her."

"Who receives a subpoena is not your decision, Mrs. Van Essen, and I don't give a damn about what you think is or isn't necessary. We've worked too long to secure this hearing."

Ingrid stares; he can't mean that the way it sounded. "To secure this hearing?"

Crenshaw scoffs. "Do you think Stieber and I give a damn about the actress or her private life? She's a cautionary tale—influential enough, questionable enough, easy enough to be an example to her industry. All we needed was a convincing case and someone willing to build it: you."

"No, I didn't. I never— Sir, our job is to seek the truth, not to tarnish the integrity of the work through lies or manipulation, not to use innocent people." Ingrid nearly loses her voice to the tremble that overtakes it. "My findings did not warrant this."

She has been committed to this job, to justice. She is a fascist's daughter dedicated to democracy—not because it is within her power to atone for her mother's views, but because she can take a stand against them. And despite it all, her efforts have led to this.

A cautionary tale. An example. A convincing case.

"The entertainment industry won't miss another vapid actress, nor will I miss an easily replaceable woman if I need someone to blame— because the report, therefore the responsibility, is yours." He lets the threat remain there. "Sit down, shut up, and do your fucking job. Or you are finished here."

Without awaiting her response, he storms away.

Her urge to protest feels empty, useless, so incredibly stupid. This was the plan all along. To plant evidence against Ada if needed, whatever it took to bring her before the committee, to condemn her. To use her.

To use Ingrid.

And if anyone finds out Ada was set up, all Crenshaw has to do is blame Ingrid. He has her report. She has no idea what he's done to it. If the findings have not been reported honestly, she has no way of proving he tampered with them. It will look like Ingrid developed the falsified account herself to portray Ada as subversive, as a Communist, as whatever she is about to become when this hearing begins. Or if Ingrid herself disputes the hearing, she will be contradicting her own supposed findings and, once again, condemned for allegedly submitting false information.

The urge to scream, or else to sob, nearly overtakes Ingrid before she pushes it down. She will not let this end poorly. Ada isn't here yet. She'll intercept her, explain everything, and advise her on how to get through this hearing unscathed—if doing so is even possible at this point. But she must cling to hope because they have nothing else.

Before she can slip into the hall, suddenly everything around Ingrid disappears. Everything except the elegant dark-haired woman standing near the door. A woman in a pale pink dress that cinches at her waist, delicate and feminine, with hair styled in her signature bold waves. A woman regarding Ingrid as never before, with a look combining understanding, fury, betrayal, and heartbreak.

Ingrid is too late. Ada is already here.

And by the looks of it, she has drawn her own conclusions regarding why.

CHAPTER 39

Washington, DC, 25 August 1947

ADA

Mr. Stribling must take her arm, though Ada can't feel him. Nor can she tell if she's placing one foot in front of the other or if the cameras around her are flashing. Nothing is happening, no one fills this cavernous room, only her and her sister.

Her *sister*.

Ada has misunderstood, surely. Ingrid must be here to support her—although if that were true, wouldn't she be sitting among the spectators? She will explain, will ease the constriction closing around Ada with every aching beat of her heart. Except something deep inside Ada rejects the notion, pummels her with the truth standing before her.

Finding her way back to Ingrid made it worthwhile—the war, the suffering, all of it. Ingrid has always been home, comfort, acceptance. Until now. The one constant familiarity in her life is unfamiliar. What was it all for if she's the same abandoned, rejected soul now that she was then? Aleida, Ada, whoever she is.

She lost her sister to war, to separation, to time. She cannot lose her to betrayal.

When Ada reaches her seat, Ingrid finds her own. Not a step toward Ada, not a second look, nothing further. She might as well have marched across the room and shoved Ada into her chair, given the way Ada's legs no longer support her.

"Mr. Stribling," she manages, "do you know Mrs. Van Essen personally?"

"She's my coworker. A private investigator." A devilish grin pulls at his lips. "A relative of yours, isn't she?"

That smirk gives her every confirmation regarding who is responsible for Ada being here. The nausea in her stomach threatens to overtake her.

Ingrid van Essen, a private investigator.

She could have refused the assignment, warned Ada, anything. Instead she carried it out, so here they are.

No time to dwell on distractions. She must get through this hearing, then she can concentrate on Ingrid.

Once settled, she glances at Vince. His jaw is set as he stares at the committee; if he's noticed Ingrid, he gives no indication. He meets Ada's gaze and offers an encouraging nod. The simple gesture instills her with the comfort she needs. She pushes aside the ache twisting her heart and faces the men before her.

Maybe she no longer has Ingrid, but she's not as entirely alone as a girl in Arnhem once was.

First are the formalities—who she is, where she's from, how she started in the industry, when she began working with Gordon. Chairman Thomas regards her the way so many in her industry do. As if sitting before him is a young woman he can use to his advantage. But he, like the others, will learn she's not so naive when it comes to encounters with powerful men.

When it comes to encounters with her own sister, well, Ada cannot say the same.

"During the war, you were offered a part in a film portraying a soldier's wife, encouraging Americans to stay American: not fascist, not

Communist, but democratic. An opportunity for a woman like yourself, an immigrant who found refuge in this country, to express her gratitude and patriotism. Instead, you turned it down. Why?"

Ada fights to draw a calming breath. This is really happening, then. She must defend a choice she made years ago to this group of strangers seeking to demonize her for it.

"My decision was not politically motivated." Her voice is clear, level. "My experiences during the war were too recent for me to be comfortable playing a soldier's wife, that's all."

Ada keeps her head forward, yet the flare of red hair is a beacon in her peripheral vision. She shifts her gaze to Ingrid. Her sister scribbles in a notepad with alarming speed.

"Your Star Society parties are well attended by those in the entertainment industry, including union members and confirmed Communists. Are you now or have you ever been a member of the Communist Party? Is that why you refused to partake in aiding the war effort and why you host a Communist front organization?"

A front organization? Her insides churn, as if she's been violated but can't quite make out how.

Aside from the obvious violation of her own sister's betrayal, of course. All this time, Ingrid has encouraged her to make a statement, to clarify her views. She did, and as she feared, what she says or does not say never seems to matter. Silence and statements can both be powerful, both damning. Both useless now.

"With all due respect, Mr. Thomas and the esteemed members of this committee, the parties I host are simply parties."

A paper rustles, then Chairman Thomas brandishes a document. "I have a transcript from a conversation between you and a guest at one of your recent gatherings. The guest stated, and I quote: 'A friend was subpoenaed, but he wants to cooperate.' To which you replied: 'Well, I simply won't stand for this.'" The chairman looks up. "You claim your parties are innocent, yet you were discouraging cooperation with these proceedings?"

Ada can hardly speak and glances briefly at Ingrid, who is also staring with a look that might be shock or confusion, but Ada doesn't evaluate her long enough to decipher it. This is nonsense, all nonsense. Ada vaguely remembers making such a remark in reference to a guest's empty glass. Not about politics. She hadn't even known what the men were talking about when she stumbled upon them, and now her words have been taken and twisted to serve this purpose.

"Sir, I never discouraged cooperation! Am I not here cooperating with you?"

"Known Communists have also been photographed at these events, gathered together in conversation." He holds up a collection of images she can't make out from her distance. "Given the example previously stated, it's reasonable to conclude the nature of such conversations."

Photographs at her private party? Those would have come from a guest, then—Ingrid, surely, even as the thought makes beads of sweat form along her brow. Everything Ingrid witnessed—every innocent interaction, every conversation, every party attendee—she turned into a weapon for her case.

"You reside with your agent, Gordon Sharpe, in Hollywood Hills?"

This change in tactic does nothing to ease the knots twisting her stomach. To ask about her politics is one matter; if they ask about Gordon's, what right does she have to answer such questions?

"Yes, sir. I was tired of boardinghouses."

"Has Mr. Sharpe ever made advances toward you?"

"Of course not." Ada does not bother keeping the ire from her voice. Were these sorts of questions posed to everyone at these hearings, or simply to women?

"You mean to tell me this man lives with you, a beautiful young woman, and has never attempted to entice you into his bed?"

"Men are quite capable of maintaining professional relationships, of treating women with respect, of controlling themselves. Thank God for the decent ones who do so. All you've proven is that Mr. Sharpe is a gentleman."

"Is Gordon Sharpe a homosexual and a member of the Communist Party?" the chairman presses, his face and neck flaring red.

Ada flattens her palms against her skirt to keep her hands from shaking, uncertain if an answer would help her and Gordon or condemn them. "Sir, is this hearing about me or about my agent? Please don't ask me to speak to anyone else's views or thoughts or opinions."

"Watch your mouth, miss, or I'll hold you in contempt." Chairman Thomas lets the threat sink in. "I'll make this easy for you. Tell me about the Communists who attend your gatherings and answer in regard to Mr. Sharpe, then we will be finished here."

The air in her lungs turns shallow. All her life, she has played whatever part has been required of her. This is a part she cannot, will not play. Again, he demands her compliance. She hardly hears him, unable to focus on anything other than the ache squeezing tighter and tighter in her chest.

She is here because of Ingrid. Because of her own flesh and blood.

And suddenly the pain is too great. She springs to her feet and snatches the small microphone and stand, bringing it close to her mouth to be heard over the banging of the chairman's gavel and the orders for her removal.

"I am not a Communist, and I do not run a Communist front organization! Ask me or anyone who knows me, read the exclusives I've given to the press—these accusations are baseless, the results of lies or fabricated evidence or whatever it is you used to justify bringing me here. And I will leave, Chairman Thomas, but first I have a question for one of your private investigators, Ingrid van Essen. My sister."

The banging gavel stills, the shouts stop, the bailiff surging toward her freezes, and Ingrid stares at Ada in utter shock.

The microphone trembles in her hand, matching the shake in Ada's voice as she holds Ingrid's gaze.

"How could you do this?"

The shutters and flashes of the cameras are the only sound as Ada places the microphone back on the table. Her vision blurs so much she can hardly see as she steps away from the small table. She walks past the bailiff, past Mr. Stribling, even past Vince, who is on his feet and pushing through the crowd toward her.

Nothing will make Ingrid understand the gravity of what she's done. Not a statement, not a declaration of their blood relation, not even a question of her loyalty.

Ingrid might be standing in this room, and Ada might have spent this last year believing she found her sister again. But the sister Ada knew no longer exists.

CHAPTER 40

Washington, DC, 25 August 1947

INGRID

My sister echoes with each of Ingrid's pounding heartbeats. With each of Ada's deliberate footsteps away from her. With each shuddering breath. Then the door closes behind Ada, and the silent room erupts.

This has gone so horrifically wrong. The questions, the transcripts with information deliberately removed to frame Ada's supposedly Communist leanings, the photographs, all of it. Everything she gathered to prove her sister is harmless, now twisted to condemn her.

A tight grip finds Ingrid's arm. "A conflict of interest?"

She returns Crenshaw's glare with her own. "You and Stieber altered my report so HUAC would subpoena her, didn't you?"

"We used what we needed. And you're lucky we can blame any discrepancies on you trying to protect your sister; otherwise you would be out of a job."

"I don't want a job. I don't want any part of this." Ingrid shoves his hand off her. "My career is not worth my integrity."

The chatter and flashing cameras fade as she rushes out the nearest door. Ada can't leave, not like this. Not until she's heard Ingrid's explanation.

Down the hall, Ingrid spots the lone woman strolling away from the Caucus Room—her gait elegant, poised, neither hasty nor leisurely, simply intentional steps to take her from this place that, Ingrid is certain, she never wants to see again.

She follows and catches Ada's forearm. "This was not my intention, I swear it. But you couldn't have talked to me privately instead of blurting out that we're related in the middle of a bloody hearing? Do you realize how much damage you've done?"

"Let's not compare who has caused the most damage," Ada retorts as she jerks her arm free. "That's the only reason you reconnected with me, isn't it? Not because you cared that I was alive, but because you saw an opportunity."

"Don't be ridiculous." Even as she says it, Ingrid feels heat rising to her cheeks. "I was trying to protect you, not hurt you."

"By lying to me and using me and my friends to further your own career?" Ada crosses her arms. "That's all you care about. The politics. Fighting Communism even if it means sacrificing your own sister."

"I was trying to prove you weren't one of them, and to keep those who are from damaging your work and image."

"The entertainment industry is the problem, then?" Ada asks with a dubious laugh. "All the actors, writers, directors—men and women trying to make a living when really they're all liars, schemers, menaces to society. Subversives, every one of us."

"Don't twist my words. You know I don't mean you or Gordon or—"
"Or yourself?"

The accusation makes Ingrid's breath catch in her throat. The thunderous gray in Ada's eyes deepens while voices sound down the hall, coming closer. A sign everyone else has emerged from the Caucus Room. If Ada notices, though, she doesn't tear her eyes from Ingrid's.

"Like it or not, you're in show business too. The media is your silver screen, the courtroom is your stage, the committee is your crew, and you are the actor. The biggest fraud of them all."

Ada lets a beat of silence fall, as if challenging Ingrid to dispute her. Even if she wanted to argue, the constriction around Ingrid's throat prevents her from speaking.

Her purpose was always to defend her country, her beliefs, her family. Not for her efforts to lead to this, to the destruction of lives and livelihoods. To drive away the sister she lost once and cannot lose again.

Before the crowds can reach them, Ingrid takes Ada's hand. She stiffens but doesn't pull away. There is no time to explain everything—the way Ingrid, too, was used, the way none of this was supposed to happen. So she can only say the most important thing.

"I will make it right, Leidje. And I'm so sorry."

"I don't want an apology. I don't want empty promises about making it right when you can't. I don't want anything from you ever again."

She cannot mean it, not when reuniting was supposed to ensure they would never part. This cannot be the way they lose each other again.

The hurt in Ada's eyes is too overwhelming as she pulls her hand free, leaving Ingrid clinging to nothing. Then she steps back.

"Goodbye, Ingrid."

Goodbye. Somehow it feels final.

* * *

Hours later, when Lars comes home, Ingrid is sitting in the living room with a half-empty bottle of wine and a cigarette. Finding her like this, he will know something is wrong, but she can't bring herself to look at him when he sits across from her. He extends a hand, so she passes him the pack of cigarettes. After a few quick puffs to light one, he takes a deep inhale.

"Do you want to talk about it?"

Of course she doesn't. But she must.

"When I went to Hollywood, I was investigating Communism. Specifically, Aleida. I didn't want anyone else on the job, because I thought I could advise her away from Communist leanings—if she held them—so such views wouldn't reflect poorly on her or her career. Not because I thought it would come to hearings or ostracization or anything negative, simply because I wanted to help. I convinced her to clarify her views, which she did, and she isn't Communist, never was, except . . ." She takes another drag of the cigarette before a tear slips free. "Except it's all gone so terribly wrong."

Now she has neither sister nor career. She told Ada she would make it right, but she's not certain she can.

No, perhaps that's not entirely true. Even if she can't remedy the situation entirely, she can try to help Ada rehabilitate her public image after this, because the truth remains: She is not subversive. Perhaps Ingrid has a way to prevent Crenshaw's efforts from destroying her sister's career. Through the one thing Ingrid hasn't ruined yet.

She goes to her bedroom and searches through her briefcase until she finds them—her copies of Ada's documents, of which Mother has the originals.

This case. Maybe Ada will never speak to Ingrid again, but she asked for her help, and Ingrid agreed to give it. A war crimes case can't change what happened at the hearing, but it can reaffirm Ada's commitment to justice. To the truth.

Maybe there is still time to prove who Ada Worthington-Fox is— and who Ingrid van Essen is. Because Ingrid van Essen will be damned if she'll allow herself or her sister to be defined by corruption, by lies, by manipulation.

Something in these documents will lead to determining whatever happened to Gregor Dietrich. All Ingrid has to do is find it.

CHAPTER 41

Hollywood Hills, 26 August 1947

ADA

The return trip to California is spent in overwhelming silence. If Ada doesn't speak of it, not even to Vince, she can pretend nothing is different: not her life, not her career, not her sister. Not herself.

Pretending will not return everything she's lost.

Moments like this are when she longs for her sister's guidance, her comfort, her support. She doesn't have her anymore. Perhaps she never will again after the things Ingrid has done, the things Ada said to her. When did they become two people who deliberately hurt one another?

"Your sister. Not your cousin," Vince says when the car takes them from the airport to Gordon's. When she doesn't reply, he runs a hand across his jaw. "Right, who was I to think we could have a conversation?"

"Don't make it sound as if I'm the one being difficult when you're the one pressuring me."

"I'm not pressuring you, Ada. I'm trying to understand why you lied. Why can't you trust me?"

If she could reassure him with her touch, her words, she would. If accepting his safety and security were as simple as that, she would. Instead, acceptance is too easily overwhelmed by brokenness, fear, everything that leaves her unable to entrust every part of herself to him. Even after all this time. Even as much as she wishes she could.

When she says nothing, Vince averts his gaze to the window. The silence forces them apart, further and further, until Ada is certain she will lose him completely. She sidles closer, weaves her arm through his, and nestles her head against his shoulder. All she can offer by way of reassurance, of how much she wishes she could bring herself to explain everything.

"We're twins. We lost touch during the war," she murmurs at last. "For the sake of privacy, we agreed to say we were cousins rather than siblings as a way to explain our resemblance. Then I gave my exclusives, and sharing more about myself might have led to eventually sharing more about Ingrid with those close to me, but I suppose part of me wanted the truth to be ours alone. To keep my sister to myself. Until I learned none of it was real." Hearing the words aloud brings tears to Ada's eyes, so she forces them down. "Darling, please don't make me dwell on it anymore."

Vince rests his hand on her thigh in consolation, then kisses the top of her head. Dear, patient Vince. Soon she will share everything with him, once all this is over and they can simply be. No concern for their careers, no buried pasts, simply the life they create together.

Assuming theirs will be a life they create together after what's happened, and after he knows the entire truth about who she is—sister to a private investigator for HUAC, daughter of a former fascist.

When they reach Gordon's house, she leaves Vince with a long, lingering kiss, pouring all her love and appreciation into the gesture. For accompanying her to the hearing, for his understanding, for being who he is.

Inside, she coddles Sowerby, then proceeds through the empty house. If the papers haven't already reported what happened at her hearing, she must tell Gordon before the news breaks. She finds him by the pool with an empty bottle of champagne and a second one in an ice bucket, a half-empty glass, and a newspaper.

Suddenly Ada can't approach, can't bring herself to look at the article he's reading. But she must. She steps to his side. The image is from the Caucus Room—first a picture of Ada on her feet and gripping the microphone, then a picture of Ingrid's horrified reaction. She doesn't need to read the headline to know what it describes.

As her shaky breaths break the quiet, Gordon doesn't look up. "No secrets, kid. A sister working for HUAC is a pretty damn big one."

"I should have told you we were siblings. I *wanted* to tell you. I—" She falters. "I swear I didn't know she was an investigator."

"You brought her into our lives. You brought *this*"—he waves the paper—"into our lives, and now it's bad. Really bad, and getting worse, judging by the phone calls I've received this week alone, pulling jobs from both of us." He throws the paper down and stands. "Did you tell Ingrid everything she wanted to know? Name names with or without proof? Not that it really matters, since I'm sure she's already given the committee plenty."

"Of course I didn't. She built a false case against me with false evidence, never told me her real purpose for being here, and if I'd known—" She grips his forearms, though the scowl he gives her is worse than if he had refused to meet her gaze. "You know I would never intentionally hurt you."

Except hurting him is exactly what she's done.

Gordon turns his back. Walking away. Or, rather, being driven away. It should not ache as it does; she should expect it by now. It's what she's done to nearly everyone in her life: forced them away somehow or another. First Ingrid, then Vince, now Gordon.

"Please tell me what I can do." She swallows hard. "Do you want me to leave?"

"I don't really give a damn." Then he gives a cynical laugh. "Actually, no, that's not true, is it? I'm not going to throw you out of my house, or let the media crucify you, or tell you and your witch-hunting sister to go straight to hell." He picks up the bottle of champagne from the ice bucket. "Even after all these lies and everything you've caused, I still give a damn about you, Ada. And that's what I hate the most."

As does she. That these people—good, kind people—care when she and Ingrid have proven their incapability of caring in return. Two women who come from destruction can try to escape, to move forward, to become different people, but in the end they will create what they come from, what they know, what they are.

A faint breeze chills the moisture on her cheeks long after the door closes behind Gordon. He is right, of course. She caused this, and she will fix it—or at least control the damage. Even if she's left with no one in the end, regardless of her efforts.

She might know a way, though. Ada and Vince aren't the only non-Communists in the entertainment industry who are dissatisfied with the way HUAC is handling these hearings. Maybe if they come together, they can do something about it.

* * *

Over the next few weeks, more members of the entertainment industry are subpoenaed. Meanwhile, Ada goes through her list of Star Society attendees, contacting anyone who might be interested in joining her and Vince to take a stand against HUAC's methods. As luck would have it, screenwriter Philip Dunne, actress Myrna Loy, and directors John Huston and William Wyler had the same idea. And thus the Committee for the First Amendment was born.

Maybe Gordon is hardly speaking to her. Maybe Ada hasn't spoken to Ingrid since the hearing. But now she has a committee to raise a voice against the way HUAC is handling these proceedings and to support the Hollywood Ten, a group of men refusing to testify. At least she has a purpose.

One evening, Ada slips into an empty table at Lucey's. When Beverly notices her, she hesitates, then gives a curt nod. Ada pushes her menu aside, indicating she's not here to order.

"Come to our meeting—the Committee for the First Amendment. With all this confusion and concern over HUAC and the trials—"

"Stop, stop it!" Beverly interrupts in a hiss, glancing around. "Why would I want to join a Communist group, and why would you ask me about it in my workplace? Go, before you get me fired."

"No, you don't understand. It's me, Vince, and others who feel like HUAC is overstepping. These concerns over Communism are valid, of course, but the attack on the entertainment industry has gone too far, and shouldn't these hearings be based on fact rather than speculation? That's the point we're trying to make. The group is not Communist, nor does it contain a single Communist member," she concludes for emphasis.

Beverly falters. "You mean you're not . . . ? The Star Society isn't . . . ?"

"No, I'm not, and I'm not operating a bloody front organization." And if she'd bothered to read Ada's statements or ask her directly, Beverly would have known as much. With some effort, Ada softens her tone. "Think about it. We might travel to Washington in October to protest the hearings, so if you want to learn more, you're welcome to attend the next meeting."

Beverly appears too stricken to respond, and it's nearly time to close, so Ada excuses herself. Outside, she lights a cigarette, enjoying the quiet evening. Whatever Beverly's decision, at least Ada has assured her that rumors of the Star Society being a subversive group are false.

Ada has just stubbed out her cigarette when she hears the door to Lucey's open, then she notices Beverly hurrying down the street toward a parked black automobile. One similar to those Ada often notices lurking outside Gordon's house. She swallows the sour taste in her mouth. Beverly is climbing into the back seat beside a second figure, then the door closes.

Streetlamps illuminate her path as Ada approaches, eyes narrowed to make out the faint silhouettes. If either has noticed her, they make no indication—and as she nears, one climbs onto the other's lap.

So that's what this is.

Beverly straddles a man while he hitches her skirt and grips her thighs. Ada can't see his face—buried in Beverly's neck—so before they can proceed, she slaps an open palm against the roof of the car. The loud clang is disruptive enough. They look up, chests heaving. Beverly, as expected, and Archie Stribling.

Ada simply can't get rid of him.

He opens the door and pushes a messy lock of hair from his eyes. "Hop in, doll, we've got room for one more."

By the looks of her scowl, Beverly appreciates that invitation as much as Ada does. She doesn't give him the courtesy of a reply and instead glares at her friend.

"You're working with the G-men?"

"Some of us don't book as many acting jobs as others," she replies pointedly, buttoning her blouse as she steps out, followed by Mr. Stribling. "Selling gossip pays my bills, and working with Archie protects my reputation."

She's hardly the first in Hollywood to sell gossip, yet upon her second admission, Ada grabs her shoulders. "Did you give my name to the committee? And Gordon's?"

"All I did was tell the truth." Glaring, Beverly pulls out of Ada's grasp. "Maybe I don't have much of a career yet, but I still don't want it ruined."

An informant among her own circle of friends. How have they

fallen this far? To use one another, betray one another, all to protect themselves.

Exposing Beverly's collaboration to everyone in Hollywood is not worth the potential repercussions, though allowing her to continue might be just as disastrous. But Ada doesn't want to condemn Beverly if it means others might ostracize her—a feeling Ada is beginning to know. They are not on opposite sides. They are simply two people whose industry is facing challenges, ones no one knows how to approach. They know only confusion and fear as they search for solutions that may or may not be the right ones.

"Excuse us," she says pointedly to Archie, who settles into the back seat. After he closes the door, Ada leads Beverly a few steps away. "You and Archie? How long?"

"Since your party. Just sex until I told him I was worried about the industry, then he told me about his real job and said we could help each other."

Ada swallows hard, her voice quiet. "We've been friends ever since Gordon introduced us. If you were worried about my parties being a front, why didn't you talk to me?"

"Because I didn't want to speak with anyone except a government official, and I didn't want anyone to falsely accuse me of Communist sympathies." A moment of tense silence, then Beverly sighs. "Look, I didn't expect it to get so out of hand. I asked Archie to set up a meeting for me, and when the investigator asked if I knew any confirmed or suspected Communists, I gave my honest thoughts. I read your exclusives, but I wasn't sure what to believe, so I wanted to be thorough, especially given my own involvement with the Star Society, so I . . . I guess I panicked and named anyone I could think of." She swallows hard and looks down. "And now I realize I did to you exactly what I didn't want done to me."

If Beverly named Gordon and Ada, then Ingrid is not solely responsible—an idea that is somehow deeply unsettling and strangely comforting. They would have been summoned to hearings regardless. Despite Beverly's false assumptions about Ada's position, Ada doesn't fault her for taking precautions. She places a hand on her arm, and her friend offers a rueful smile.

Beverly is not the only one who wishes she had handled matters differently.

CHAPTER 42

Hollywood Hills, 1 October 1947

ADA

Reporters crowd outside Gordon's house—not unusual since Ada's hearing—but when someone knocks on the door, Ada hesitates. Journalists are usually not so bold, but if that's who it is, she might as well find out what he wants. When she opens the door, though, she finds a man in a suit who shoves an envelope into her hands.

This time, she knows better than to assume it's not for her. A second summons? She shouldn't be surprised; it's not as if anyone believed anything she said.

She tears open the envelope and reads the official document addressed to her.

Not a hearing. A citation for contempt, ordering her to appear for trial.

She reads it again, willing the words to change. This is far more severe. Far more damaging. The job offers have already slowed considerably. After this, no one will endanger their reputations to work with her. Mother was already upset over the disastrous hearing, and maybe the future of her relationship with Ingrid remains uncertain, but Ingrid certainly won't associate with her after a citation for contempt, nor will anyone seeking to protect themselves from suspicion. Everyone in her life is at risk. A realization that overtakes her like a physical assault until her lungs are too tight, her body too weak.

"What's wrong?"

Vince.

Vince.

As he joins her in the foyer, likely wondering why she hasn't returned to the living room after answering the door, Ada can't look at him, at this man who cares for her with such honesty and intentionality, who does not deserve to lose his acting or screenwriting because of her.

She hands him the citation.

Vince reads it, his jaw tight, then he takes her hands. "You can fight this."

"No, I can't. How can I fight this any better than I fought the hearing?"

Nothing can protect her—not silence, not speaking her mind, not action. She's at the mercy of those in power, and all she can do is protect those who matter to her even if she can't protect herself.

She wraps her arms around his neck, allows the warmth of his blue eyes to draw her into him, then she kisses him. As he once said, if this is to be the last time, then, by God, she will make it count. She wants to do anything except walk away. This time, though, the decision is so much greater than what both would choose if they had a real choice.

"Please go, Vince." She fights to say the words aloud. "Go and don't come back. I won't do this to you."

His eyes darken. "We didn't change anything after your hearing. Why should we do it now?"

"Because a citation is far more serious. No one will approve of me or anyone associated with me after this. I won't be the reason you lose everything."

"You don't get to decide what's important to me." Despite the cutting words, his voice is strained as he takes her shoulders. "If you don't want to be the reason I lose everything, then don't ask me to lose you."

Gently, she takes his face in her hands, searches the depths of his gaze, holds him until every part of him is seared into her memory. "Darling, please do this for me, and let me do this for you. If you love me, lose me."

She does not have to conjure tears or anger or pain; she must simply harness them, redirect them, and convince the masses outside. Giving Vince no time to react, she throws the door open, shouting loud enough for the reporters as she shoves him across the threshold.

"Go on, then, if that's how you feel! Get out!"

Cameras flash, capturing the apparent dispute, while Vince looks back at her—agonized, furious, confused. A look for her eyes alone.

Ada slams the door. The reporters have seen and heard enough, and she can't look at Vince a moment longer. She presses her forehead to the door as a final sob rips through her chest, this one not for the cameras or anyone but herself.

She will make herself forget him, like last time. She will try, anyway. For now, she goes to the library. To the place that will always remind her of eager, champagne-soaked kisses, of the desire sparked in every touch, of the foolish belief that this time she would never drive him away.

Gently, she passes her fingers across the worn, cracked spines until she reaches the shelf where her novel is hidden. She picks up the little robin figurine from Ingrid. Tonight, she will retreat into *The Secret Garden*—though perhaps even the story has lost its magic.

Before she can return the figurine, she feels what must be a crack near the small hole in its hollow base. It can't be broken—unless someone knocked it off the shelf and fixed it, hoping she wouldn't notice. She turns it over.

Indeed, a faint crack betrays a repair—a thin line indicative of a clean cut rather than a break. Ada turns on a lamp and holds the bird beneath the light for closer inspection. Inside the hole, she notices something long and thin.

A wire.

She shakes the figure; no sound. Whatever it is has been secured in place, perhaps to avoid detection. And now, as she stares at the wire inside this gift from private investigator Ingrid van Essen, recalling the transcripts presented during her hearing, she knows what this must be.

A listening device.

She raises her arm to throw the figure and shatter it, but she stops. She can't bear to destroy it, even if preserving it means the wire will remain. The robin still reminds her of the little bird who befriended Mary Lennox when the child had no one else.

Let Ingrid listen. There's nothing to hear anymore.

Instead Ada puts the robin back and goes to her office to use the telephone.

"What have you got for me, love?" Minnie Musgrave asks when she answers the tip line.

Ada puts on her giddiest, most American accent. "All the dish, Mrs. Musgrave: Vince Hart just ended his relationship with Ada Worthington-Fox because she was cited for contempt due to her refusal to cooperate with HUAC—and thank God he came to his senses. Why sacrifice himself or his career over a silly love affair?"

"Quite a week for our vixen, isn't it?" comes the smug reply. "You're a doll." Then the line disconnects, leaving Ada staring at the receiver.

Quite a week? What did she mean? Ada's name hasn't been in the gossip rags at all this week.

Except she has not seen today's edition of *The Dish*.

Everything inside her stills.

Gordon keeps the magazines and papers in the library. When she gets there, the latest issue of *The Dish* is lying in his favorite armchair—an indication he has already read it, even though she failed to notice it a moment ago. The paper is neatly folded, allowing Ada to clearly see the featured article across the front page. With an unsteady grasp, she picks it up and sinks into the chair.

HOLLYWOOD'S VIXEN: FRAUD, FABRICATOR, AND FASCIST
by Minnie Musgrave

Have I got all the dish on one of Hollywood's favorite dishes—or former favorite, I should say, considering opinions might change after this. Pour yourself a stiff one, have a seat, and listen up: Hollywood's Vixen herself, Ada Worthington-Fox, is the star of today's exclusive interview with Constance de Vos, Miss Worthington-Fox's mother.

You heard me—but be patient, dolls, we'll get to that.

Allow me to remind you of August, when Miss Worthington-Fox appeared before HUAC and announced that one of the private investigators, Ingrid van Essen, is her sister. A few weeks after this shocking revelation, Mrs. De Vos approached me to give us the whole story—we'll need a family tree momentarily to keep it all straight.

"My ex-husband was in London on business, where we met and married before moving to his family home in Arnhem," explains Mrs. De Vos. "After our twins, Ingrid and Aleida, were born, he abandoned us, so I raised my girls alone."

Many celebrities change their names, so this is hardly unusual. One wonders if Miss Worthington-Fox, known for her privacy, maintained such privacy about everything, even her birth name, for a reason.

Mrs. De Vos has the answers. She sits across from me in my office, hands folded primly in her lap.

"I confess I am not proud of my past. In the 1930s, I, like many, was captivated by Adolf Hitler—his charm, his promises, his confidence. Eventually I realized the truth of Nazi ideology, and after Arnhem fell, Ingrid fled—to America, we learned later." One tremulous breath cracks her resolve. "Remember, I was a woman with a daughter to protect, living alone in an occupied country. While this may be no excuse, allow me to humbly ask for your understanding as I tell you the rest."

Imagine my shock, readers. Our beloved actress is the daughter of an admitted fascist.

"We lived alone—no ability to defend ourselves, no family except my father-in-law, who was vocally anti-Nazi, which endangered us even more. I don't have to explain the risks we faced, the brutal things men do to women, especially during war. My Aleida, my beautiful girl, she was hardly eighteen—" Her voice breaks; she closes her eyes, gathers herself. "How else was I to keep her safe? I became an SS officer's mistress and publicly supported the Third Reich by hosting the soldiers in our home, hoping to endear them to us. Yet each day we lived in terror, and each day I begged God for my efforts to be enough so those men would not harm my daughter."

There you have it: During the war, Ada Worthington-Fox entertained Nazis in her own home. Maybe she's not a Commie but a Hitlerite.

"I told no one the true reasons for my actions, not even Aleida," Mrs. De Vos continues. "I could accept her resentment, even her hatred, if it meant she didn't have to feel guilty, to feel as if her very existence forced me into the choices I made and what I suffered. Now, despite knowing the truth, she has never forgiven me. Instead she dramatizes her past, speaks of hunting war criminals, all for attention and sympathy. And if you indulge her, you encourage her to linger in resentment. My wish is for her to live a good life—the life I did everything to give her, even if she will always hold my choices against me. All because I acted as any mother would to protect her child."

Let me be the first to say I'll be damned. Who is the real Ada Worthington-Fox? Will we ever know? My thanks to Constance de Vos for her openness and honesty in this exclusive interview.

It's no wonder Miss Worthington-Fox is such a skilled actress; she's been putting on a show ever since she came to Tinseltown.

Ada grips the paper, fights the urge to weep for Aleida, for Ada, for whomever she has become, and for all those she has driven away. And then, as she reads the piece again—portraying her as resentful, bitter, unreliable—all grief is driven away by a fierce, pulsing anger, sending her to the guesthouse, where she pounds her fist against the door until it opens.

"Why, Mother? Why did you do this?"

For so long, Ada has accepted her mother's efforts, has not questioned her changed loyalties, perhaps because she fears the truth. She fears Ingrid is right, has always been right. Whatever the truth is, it's time Ada faced it.

Mother glances at the article in Ada's hand. "After that scene at your hearing, how else was I supposed to encourage the public to overlook your transgressions? Now at least they know your mother is willing to be honest. And since you insist on pursuing this war crimes case, I had to put a stop to it. No one will listen to a girl desperate for attention, and if that's what it takes to encourage you to forget about all this, then it's my responsibility to help you do so."

She stands in the doorway, regarding Ada with a steely frown, not bothering to invite her inside. And suddenly Ada has no idea what is true and what is not. During the war, perhaps Mother did what Ada had done: acted. Or perhaps she was never a repentant fascist, simply a fascist.

"We could have fled, joined the resistance, anything that didn't require aligning ourselves with the enemy. You didn't have to become his mistress to protect us."

"How does one determine which choice is the right one? *Is* there a right one? Or is there only survival?" Mother places her hands on Ada's shoulders. "A mother only has one choice, a choice that defies reason: to protect her child. Survival is not rational. It simply must be done."

The article is published; Ada can't change that. And here, standing outside the guesthouse, she can't comprehend anything—who her mother really is, why she did what she did, why she gave this exclusive to damage Ada's credibility. If she wants to reconcile with her daughters, this is not the way.

"I've done all I can to rebuild this family, and now you and your sister will make peace and forget this nonsense about hearings and trials and war crimes cases. Or shall I tell Ingrid of how you resented her for leaving Arnhem, therefore you discarded every letter she sent to the ballet school? Assuring you of her safety, desperate to know of yours, imploring you to write back . . . yet you never did."

Why would Mother tell Ingrid such lies? Then, as understanding crashes over her, Ada can't speak. Mother didn't; she couldn't have. Upon their reunion, Ingrid insisted she had written—letters that, they concluded, never reached Ada.

Or perhaps she simply never received them.

"All those years, you knew Ingrid was alive? You took the letters she sent me?"

"You helped her run off with that boy, then lied about it. I had to teach you both a lesson." Her scowl shifts into a pitying scoff. "Honestly, dear, Gregor was the SS and Police Leader. Mail is simple enough to intercept. Did you really expect to deceive me?"

Suddenly Ada feels as she once did when dancing center stage, when the music's crescendo overtakes her as she pushes her body to its limits, smiles despite how every jump and turn pummels her muscles, unites her pain with the beauty of movement. Then, after she takes her final curtsy, she is left with the ugliness the beauty has left behind. The sore muscles, the bloody, blistered, calloused feet, the mental and emotional fatigue.

Once again, the pain and emotion unite inside her and emerge through movement. Through her hand delivering a single, precise, hard slap across her mother's porcelain cheek.

The smack of palm against flesh gives way to Mother's startled cry as she takes an unstable step back, then Ada is shouting, furious and desperate and unable to be anything except what she is: a girl who lost the most important person in her life when neither was truly lost at all.

"You knew and never told me, never told her! Your own daughters, how could you?" Then she sinks to her knees as her shrieks give way to sobs. "I thought she was dead . . . I thought she was dead . . ."

Dietrich had contacts everywhere, of course. Mother probably had him looking for anything connected to Ada, to the dance school, to whatever might lead her to Ingrid. Because of course she suspected Ada's involvement, given how close the twins were.

A closeness that was ripped away for six long years. Mother made sure of that.

A cool breeze sweeps over them, chilling the moisture on Ada's cheeks. Mother takes her chin. Ada blinks past her blurred vision, stares from the flaming mark on Mother's cheek to the cold steadiness of her gaze.

"Make amends with your sister and pull yourselves together. We must work toward the betterment of our future, darling, and I can't be the only one putting forth an effort."

This woman is not the mother Ada wanted, not the mother she thought she had; this woman is the mother Ingrid had, and so much worse. The urge to be sick nearly overtakes her as Mother maintains her firm grip a moment longer, then releases her and slams the door. Ada stays on her knees in the grass, unable to move. All this time she has been wrong, fooled. Utterly fooled.

As for making amends with Ingrid, after the way they turned on each other, what if it's not possible?

The betterment of our future, Mother said.

Right now, the only thing in Ada's future is a trial.

CHAPTER 43

Washington, DC, 2 October 1947

INGRID

Over the last few weeks since the hearing, Ingrid and Ada haven't spoken. Neither has Ingrid heard news of her being called to a second hearing, or worse. She must keep her faith in that.

One cool October afternoon, the smell of stale coffee greets Ingrid when she enters the FBI offices in the Department of Justice building, finds Hattie's desk, and is met with a frown.

"Some friend you are." Hattie's scowl deepens, silencing Ingrid's attempted explanation. "I didn't need to know you were investigating your sister. I didn't even need to know she became an actress with a new name. But the three of us spent years together at boarding school, and when you came to America, I missed her, worried for her, prayed she would answer your letters, comforted you every time she didn't. Aleida was your sister, but she was my friend. You should have told me she was alive."

Ingrid drops her gaze, unable to bear the hurt shining in Hattie's. Somehow she has become a woman who can't do anything except hurt those closest to her. "You're right, I'm sorry. I've been terribly unfair to you and an even worse friend."

"On that we can agree. And I'm not helping you with anything else—not that Nazi, not your sister, not her citation—"

"Citation?" Ingrid nearly chokes on the word. "She received a citation?"

"For contempt. I figured you knew—and if you want details, you're not getting them from me."

Rehabilitating Ada's image after the hearing will be difficult enough. If she's been cited for contempt, there will be a trial, if only to continue using her as a scare tactic. After this, a war crimes case might not be enough to encourage the public to overlook the image HUAC is crafting for her.

"A few coworkers just returned from Hollywood and brought back some gossip rags, so this has been circulating around the office." Hattie produces a copy of *The Dish* and shoves it toward Ingrid. "Enjoy."

Ingrid barely notices the sarcasm as she stares at the article headline. "Hollywood's Vixen: Fraud, Fabricator, and Fascist." And then, in the first paragraph: Constance de Vos.

Damn it all.

Ingrid reads quickly, then shoves the paper into her handbag and fights the quaver in her voice. "Hattie, let me say this, and then I'll go. My findings were manipulated without my knowledge and used to portray her as someone she is not. My sister is not subversive, and she is not lying about her war crimes case like my mother's article says. All I want is to show the public she's a good person trying to do the right thing. I don't expect you to keep helping me, but if—"

"Right this way, Mrs. Van Essen."

The new voice makes Ingrid press her mouth into a hard line. She is here because Agent Stieber summoned her to a meeting, but she wants nothing to do with him. Not after the way he deceived her. She came only to find out what he wants since it likely involves Ada.

Wordlessly, she follows him to his office, where they sit across from one another—he as impossible to read as always, she not bothering to hide her frown.

"I'd like to discuss Miss Worthington-Fox's efforts to pursue a war crimes case, as mentioned in her statements and addressed in a recent exclusive from your mother. Such claims must be taken seriously, fabricated or not. You were assisting her, I presume? Without permission while on a separate assignment?"

"Do you intend to manipulate this case too?"

He doesn't react to the jab, nor does Ingrid regret making it. After the way Stieber and Crenshaw used her, she has no desire to answer any questions or placate him with politeness.

"You are dissatisfied with the approach taken regarding Miss Worthington-Fox and HUAC's proceedings, but this matter of war crimes is greater than your personal feelings. I am a German with regrets. Even though I was not involved in the crimes perpetrated by so many of my countrymen, I, like many others, joined the party to survive. Help me atone by allowing me to help your sister."

Accepting his help might move the case forward, but the evidence is not Ingrid's to submit. Not without Ada's permission.

And she cannot receive Ada's permission until her sister speaks to her again. When she finally does, the evidence must be given to someone committed to honesty, and Ingrid no longer believes that man is Stieber.

"The case is hers to make, not mine," she says at last.

"You don't believe she's lying for attention? Did she give you a name? Proof?"

Ingrid says nothing; he is not her handler anymore. She does not have to explain herself to him.

After a moment, Stieber sighs. "Very well, then. When she's ready, you know where to find me."

Ingrid simply nods, rises, and doesn't wait for him to follow before she exits the office, her heart racing, although she can't explain why. Only that it's the same feeling she experienced throughout her assignment, warning her something is wrong.

* * *

A few weeks later, Ingrid has had no luck contacting Ada. She has called countless times, and her sister still won't speak to her or return her messages. But she will keep trying and will continue reviewing her copies of the documents Ada took from Arnhem. Hattie has provided nothing new, and Ingrid has gone over the materials so much she's practically memorized them, but she keeps looking in case there's something she missed.

This evening, she conducts her daily review to no avail. When her eyes are too tired to read anymore, she leaves the materials on her bed for a final look later tonight, makes dinner for one since Lars is out for a work dinner, then slips into a dressing gown and runs a bath. Ada's trial is tomorrow, so she'd best turn in early.

She might not be allowed to attend, but she will find a way, will be there, will make things right. She must.

Once the bath is prepared and she turns off the water, a sound captures her attention—the bedroom floorboard that always creaks.

"Home early, darling?" she calls out. "Feel free to join me, then."

Not that he will. Since her return from California more than two months ago, nothing is as it was—not their conversations, their lovemaking, *them*. As they gradually cross the bridge to complete reconciliation, sometimes she fears it will collapse beneath their weight.

His footsteps approach, a promising sound that sends a flutter through her chest. She stacks an extra towel atop her own, teetering on the edge of the small sink, then the bathroom door creaks open.

"Shall we talk, Mrs. Van Essen?"

Not her husband's voice. A German-accented one.

Ingrid whirls to face a man standing in the doorway. A familiar man in a neatly pressed black suit with a small pistol glinting at his hip.

Agent Stieber.

There must be some mistake. Some explanation regarding how and why he is in her home, why this discussion couldn't wait until work hours, why the look on his face says his request for a conversation is not a request but an order.

As she clutches the gown's gap at her chest, he steps back, giving her space to exit the bathroom.

He's an FBI agent, her former handler. And he is in her home, without permission, holding a stack of documents. *Her* documents. The copies of Ada's materials and the execution order Hattie uncovered.

Slowly, Ingrid steps into the bedroom until she faces him—her bare feet against the wooden floor, her back to the wall, acutely aware of the lamp aglow on her nightstand, of the bed steps away. Of her naked body beneath this dressing gown.

"Is this everything?" Stieber holds up the documents. "All your materials for the war crimes case?"

That's what this is about? He regards her with an unusual look, one she can't discern. Unnerving for reasons she can't identify.

"What are you doing here?" she asks at last. "Those materials are mine."

"Evidence of this nature belongs to the FBI. You have no right to withhold it, and this is now a government case, so you are forbidden from pursuing it further. Is this everything?" he asks again, more forcefully this time.

"Yes, but—"

The protest dies when he opens his own briefcase and tucks the documents inside.

Is he really seizing her work? This is her case, the proof she needs to help her sister, and suddenly she forgets his gun and yields to fury as she closes the distance between them.

"Give me my materials and get out."

When she reaches him, he does not react. Then her pulse quickens while Stieber sets down his briefcase and loosens his necktie, as though weary, before sighing.

"I wanted to do this the polite way. It seems you require more clarity."

Sudden pain sparks across Ingrid's vision while she gasps to recapture the air escaping her lungs, and only then does she realize he has just driven his fist into her stomach.

She reaches for support to keep herself upright, doesn't find any, but before she can hit the floor, a grip finds her shoulders. Everything is too quick, too painful, too shocking. She feels her back colliding with what must be the solid bedroom wall, writhes futilely until more flares of agony announce a second strike, a third, her cries muffled by the large hand secured over her mouth.

Everything stills, leaving only the pain pulsing through her body, the strong grip holding her in place, the hand smothering her, then transferring to her chin, forcing her head up as she coughs and gasps.

"Stop your investigation. If you persist, I will discourage you through Lars or Ada."

"Stay away from them." She bites off each word, glaring, straining to break free until another blow ends her struggle.

Spasms of pain and nausea ripple through her. Then, when her next bout of coughing ceases, Stieber tugs the knot at her waist, unfastening the dressing gown so it falls open.

Acrid bile rises to Ingrid's throat as he evaluates every exposed part of her. Not this. His gun glints in the lamplight—a warning not to struggle. She holds impossibly still, every painful, whimpering breath enhancing the agony coursing through her.

"Stop your investigation. Or I will pay that lovely sister of yours a visit."

"No, please . . ." How she hates that he knows the threat will subdue her. "I'll stop, I swear I'll stop . . . Please don't hurt her."

His eyes return to her exposed chest while the nausea in her stomach threatens to overtake her. Then he brushes his thumb across her right breast, just above her nipple. Deliberate, the way one might clear a speck of debris from a canvas, leaving it pristine and prepared.

The firm grip prevents her from pulling away while the gesture prompts her toward something she cannot entirely recall, not now with his cold touch against her skin or the terror twisting her insides. She will not concede to whatever is next—or perhaps she has no alternative, because if she fights him, what of Lars and Ada?

A muscle clenches along Stieber's jaw while something in his gaze shifts, distant yet concentrated. Then he blinks and lifts his head.

"I trust we won't need to have this conversation again. Good night, Mrs. Van Essen."

When he releases her, Ingrid moves only to cover herself, though controlling her shaking hands enough to tie the gown is nearly impossible, while Stieber picks up his briefcase and leaves the room. Moments later, the apartment door clicks shut.

The sound prompts her unsteady legs to carry her to the door, which she locks, though it hardly matters because it was locked in the first place. If he wants to come back, nothing will stop him. Then she stumbles into the living room, sinks onto the sofa, and buries her head in her hands, awaiting a sob or a scream or something beyond her shaking breaths.

He confiscated her materials. Attacked her in her own home. Threatened her husband and sister. This is not the way to seize evidence, not even if she has no right to possess it as he claimed. During their meeting, he was a man eager to help; here, he was a threat. This is wrong, entirely wrong—yet if she pursues the case, he will target Ada next.

After an indiscernible amount of time, something jostles the lock on the apartment door. Ingrid springs to her feet, darts toward her bedroom for her pistol—except Ada has it. She pivots toward the kitchen for a knife, but before she gets there, the door opens and a man enters—Lars.

"Goddamnit, don't do that! It's late—you can't barge inside with no consideration for anyone."

"You're attacking me for opening the door?"

One hand finds her chest to combat her unsteady breaths while she tidies the newspaper on the coffee table and listens as he hangs his hat on the hat stand and sets down his briefcase. Another night, another argument. Never in all their years together have they been so perpetually short with one another as these last weeks. Gingerly, she touches the stomach that will no doubt be painted with bruises tomorrow. Such effortless, precise blows. Stieber must have done this before—many times, from the feel of it. She senses Lars looking at her, at his wife who is not normally on the verge of tears after one meaningless spat.

"Ingrid? What's upset you?"

How she longs to press into his steadiness, his comfort, everything she's missed for so long because none of it has been as it usually is. He's her husband, for God's sake. Is she really going to let silence and secrets do this to her, to him, to their marriage?

When he reaches her, she throws her arms around him, forgetting the throb still pulsing through her until his grip applies pressure to those places where a man's fist collided with her body. Pain tears across her midsection, and she staggers with a gasping cry.

He loosens at once, takes her shoulders, meets the tears welling in her eyes. Then his voice nearly trembles with urgency and terror. "What's wrong? What happened?"

For a moment she fights the swell in her throat. "My handler."

"Here? Tonight? He's hurt you?"

She places a gentle hand on his cheek, silencing the influx of questions. She's not under orders of confidentiality anymore. So she tells him everything—about her sister's life during the war, Opa's death, Mother's presence in Hollywood, Ingrid's investigation, the war crimes case, and Stieber's confrontation this evening to deter her from pursuing it. She omits her handler's name or anything that might endanger Lars, but she shares what she's withheld all this time.

Once finished, she is unburdened and her body still aches, but she is better. Not all right yet, but she will be. And she hopes they will be too.

Yet moments later, as she lies awake next to Lars, she tenses against another man's fingers on her body, envisions his head as it lifted to meet her gaze. The way the lamplight fell across him, illuminating the skin exposed by his loosened tie.

As a chill overtakes her, Ingrid closes her eyes, but it's all she can see: that long, thin scar stretching across Agent Stieber's neck.

CHAPTER 44

Washington, DC, 28 October 1947

ADA

The morning of her trial finds Ada in her hotel room, alone with this odd version of herself. Not the resistance member defending her country, not the glamorous actress protecting her past, but this woman the public has vilified. She should have traveled with the Committee for the First Amendment yesterday, on their way to protest the hearings. Instead she's preparing for her own trial.

Once dressed, Ada sits on the bed. Suddenly she's in her childhood bedroom in Arnhem, alone for the first of many mornings. Awaiting whatever is to come. Facing it without her sister.

She picks up the telephone, then hangs up without placing a call. Something she's done often since receiving her citation. Telling her sister about it means involving her in a situation that could lead to terrible repercussions for both of them. Ada sent Ingrid away once for safety; this time, she must keep her away as best she can.

They have caused enough harm to one another. Even if she still hasn't returned her sister's calls. Even if the urge to share this experience with Ingrid battles against her lingering reluctance to speak to her.

A knock sounds on the door. Gordon, most likely, coming to fetch her so they can leave. Instead, when she answers, Ada finds Ingrid.

Unsurprising, really. Ingrid always does her research. Still, a knot forms in Ada's chest as she steps aside, permitting her to enter, then they face each other in silence. Much like they did little more than a year ago. A reunion of sisters. Since then, they have clung to an unbreakable bond tested by distance, time, confusion, yet never severed. Except, now, perhaps it has been. Perhaps their own actions have destroyed everything.

"If you don't want me to attend the trial, then you'll just have to alert security and hope they manage to stop me, because telling me to stay away won't work." Ingrid removes her headscarf, reading glasses, and a small badge identifying her as a member of what Ada suspects is a fictional publication. She places the items on the bed. "So much of this is my fault. I don't expect that to be forgotten or forgiven. But please let me say this, and then you can go on hating me if you want."

Ada does not want to concede. She heard enough of Ingrid's excuses at her hearing. But the pain is not so acute anymore, and she doesn't want to dwell in anger or resentment. She stays quiet, granting unspoken permission.

"A few corrupt men took my findings and built the case they wanted to build, despite all evidence to the contrary, to convince the committee you were a threat. They used you. And I let them use me too, even though I wasn't aware of their intentions. None of which is an excuse, because I still lied to the person who should always be able to trust me." A tear slips free as she holds Ada's gaze. "No job is worth losing you."

The admission softens the lingering ache in Ada's chest. Ingrid was used too. It does not absolve her entirely, but it means the sister Ada thought she knew is still there after all.

"Others named me, so if the plan was to use me, it would have come to that with or without you. And you encouraged me to find my voice again, so that much was worth it. As was finding you." She offers Ingrid a faint reassuring smile. "You can't lose me again that easily."

Both are at fault for so many things. The time to forgive those things will come, gradual and unhurried. For now, her sister is here, and that is enough.

She pulls Ingrid into an embrace until her sister makes the smallest sound, a tiny squeak indicative of a pain she's attempting to mask. At once, Ada pulls back.

"You're hurt."

It's not a question, because it doesn't need to be.

"Not terribly." Her wince indicates otherwise. "There's a bit of a problem with our war crimes case—meaning I was encouraged to desist."

A rancid taste fills Ada's mouth as she studies the creases across Ingrid's brow, the way she shifts from foot to foot, the agitation that has never been present in her conscientious, sensible sister. Ada lived it, for God's sake. She never should have involved Ingrid, should have known this was bound to lead to danger, especially when Ada herself was threatened numerous times. Of course the threats eventually extended to Ingrid.

"Someone confronted you?"

"Klaus Stieber—my former handler. He called me into his office a few weeks ago to ask about the war crimes case you claimed to be building and offered to help with it—but he's one of the men involved in your investigation, so I don't trust him anymore. Then last night, he broke into my apartment and seized the evidence, claiming it was a government matter so I was no longer permitted to have it."

"And he attacked you?"

Ingrid flinches. "Perhaps that was the most unusual part: Stieber knew Lars was out, so he had the time and opportunity to do worse. Much worse. He untied my dressing gown, for God's sake, then he just . . . *looked* at me." She clenches her jaw, visibly fighting to push the memory aside, then takes a breath. "He's a former Nazi. Hattie read his file—just desk work, but I'm sure he knew men who committed war crimes. Maybe he doesn't regret his former political allegiances as much as he claims, so he's trying to prevent others from being held accountable." She looks at Ada. "Might he know Dietrich? Did a man named Klaus Stieber ever attend one of Mother's gatherings?"

"Klaus Stieber . . ." After pondering for a moment, Ada shakes her head. "If so, I don't remember him, but there were too many for me to remember them all. Either way, if Stieber is trying to stop us, perhaps that's a sign we should move forward, so he'll be too late. Is there an agent you trust to take the negatives?"

Ingrid nods. "Hattie is seeing a fellow who has been helpful. After your trial, we can give the negatives to him."

With their plan established, they have no more time to delay before the trial, so they go downstairs, where Gordon is waiting. When he notices Ingrid, he tenses, but before Ada can reassure him, Ingrid steps forward.

"When we have time, I will give you a detailed explanation and a thorough apology. No one was fully honest with me about the work I was doing, but I was not fully honest with you either. You have been so good to me and my sister, and I'm so sorry for betraying your kindness and trust, and for how appallingly you've been treated."

Gordon looks from Ingrid to Ada, the crease in his brow softening in understanding. He gives Ingrid's shoulder a reassuring squeeze, then they follow him into the waiting car. Yet throughout the drive, the tension in Ada's stomach is not due to whatever awaits her in the courtroom. It's due to the man who attacked her sister, the war crimes case they started and must finish. But if Agent Stieber is trying to stop them, how many more former Nazis working for the FBI will support his efforts?

Upon reaching their destination, her concerns are abruptly pushed aside when Gordon goes ahead to find his seat and Ada is moments away from entering the courtroom, where a handful of suited men linger by the doors. One face drags Ada back to a cold cell in the Oranjehotel, and she is that girl again, threatened and stripped and tormented and surrounded by men. She can't tell if she's still walking, if terror is etched on her face, if she's gasping or staying quiet, until a tight grip on her forearm drags her around a corner and out of sight, followed by Ingrid's urgent whisper.

"Oh God, he's here. My handler. That's Agent Stieber, right over there."

Ada does not need to ask which man, but she must be entirely certain. "Ingrid . . . does Stieber have any defining marks? Such as—" Ada can't say it, *must* say it. "Such as a scar?"

Ingrid pales. "A long, horizontal scar across his neck. How did you know that?" The look in her eyes says she already knows the answer.

All this time, he's been right there. All this time, she hasn't known.

"It's him . . . Your handler, it's *him*. Klaus Stieber is Gregor Dietrich."

Ingrid is already pacing, hands pressed to her temples. "Damn it all . . . He's got my bloody files, for God's sake." She stops abruptly. "He knows everything."

Perhaps he's known all along. If Dietrich has been sending messages to Ada, he's been watching them, perhaps suspected that Ingrid had copies of the documents Ada handed over to Mother, likely noticed the missing negatives were not among the surrendered materials. Which means he will be looking for the negatives and any remaining copies that might still exist. For more evidence that needs destroying.

Except Mother said they lost touch after the war. She might not know Dietrich has been watching them. They might not be working together. Dietrich becoming Ingrid's assigned handler and Mother reconnecting with Ada to recover the documents might be merely coincidence.

But Mother has been known to lie.

"Maybe that's why he never came for the evidence . . . because of my hearing, because I would have recognized him and we would have realized who your handler was. He had to wait until the case was complete. And now that it is—"

"He's not hiding anymore," Ingrid finishes, the words tight, then she steals a discreet glance around the corner. "You can't go over there."

"I have no choice. Stay here. I'll be fine—they're just waiting to take me inside," she says, cutting off Ingrid's protests. "If Dietrich sees you, he might try to keep you out."

Ingrid scowls in clear disapproval of the plan, but she nods. "You'll be all right."

Feeble reassurance, but Ada is grateful for it anyway. Then, drawing a breath, she proceeds, walking to meet Dietrich because she must. She keeps her expression neutral, but he will notice the tremble in her clenched fists, will know the sight of him is enough to conjure every word, every touch, every horrible moment of those years under occupation.

"Miss Worthington-Fox." Dietrich meets her gaze levelly and gestures through the door. "Right this way."

She proceeds without a word, then his grip finds her elbow. A gesture the spectators will take as gentlemanly, yet the tension is nearly enough to make her wince. She does not react, though, not even when he lowers his voice.

"A person of interest regarding an investigation into Communism, and a person of interest to me. How convenient it was when your file came across my desk. But then you had to complicate matters." His grip tightens. "You should have kept your mouth shut."

Ada does not respond. There are many things she should have done. Keeping her mouth shut is not one of them.

* * *

In the courtroom, Ada sits before a judge, jury, and committee members. Men who have already decided her fate, she expects, so this
sham of a trial is hardly necessary. She finds it impossible to focus
when every man in this room becomes Dietrich and every woman
becomes Mother.

How easily they have toyed with her all this time.

Among the spectators she finds Gordon, wearing an impeccably
tailored navy pinstriped suit coupled with a burgundy and gold bow
tie. A sight that reminds Ada of the first time she spotted him in a
crowd. She was a Broadway showgirl then and noticed the audience
member sitting a few rows from the stage. A man with kind eyes and a
thick handlebar mustache—such extravagant facial hair was impossible
to miss. After the performance, he came backstage to introduce himself.
He hasn't missed her in a production since that day.

Even if today's production is not the sort either will enjoy.

The trial begins—formalities, a review of her hearing, then questions.
So many questions. About her work, life during the war, her behavior at
the hearing. Nothing helps her pay attention, although she must. Until
this is over, she and Ingrid can't discuss how they intend to proceed
now that the war crimes case has been compromised and Dietrich is
here in this room.

"There you have it," the prosecutor concludes at last. "The daughter
of a fascist who mingles with Communists through her work, her Star
Society, nearly every aspect of her life. As for Miss Worthington-Fox's
personal politics, the only conclusion is this: She might be fascist. She
might be Communist. She might be neither. What she most certainly is
not, as demonstrated by these proceedings, is an American patriot. And
if anything she says tempts you to believe otherwise, may I remind you
she is an actress."

The contempt in the final statement almost makes Ada shout an objection, as her lawyer has been doing. To them, she is someone who pretends for a living. Therefore she cannot be trusted.

Her lawyer gestures for her to deliver her statement, so she stands, finding Gordon in the crowd. *Let them admire you*, she can almost hear him say. Except, despite the cameras, the advice does not apply to this instance. This is no performance, no press event, no publicity stunt.

"I've learned art is not something we choose; it chooses us. And when it does, we choose to accept it in return—no matter the struggles, the triumphs, the joys, the sorrows. We choose it over and over, because we must. To create art without honesty is impossible." Ada takes a breath, then looks to the jury. "That's why I've come before you today: to be honest. To clarify that I have no association with Communism or fascism. And to ask you to be honest in return. In our country's efforts to preserve democracy, I hope proceedings will be based in law, truth, and fact—not rumor, not speculation. I lived under an oppressive government, where accusations destroyed lives and people were not free. I chose America for its liberties. Those who understand the privileges we appreciate here will defend and uphold the values of our great nation. Have faith in the American people—those born in this country, and those who chose it."

Silence follows, then Ada is dismissed. She exits the room, walking slowly in a failed effort to settle her nerves. Whether she helped or hurt her trial, she hasn't been offered a job in months, and the Star Society was her idea. If she has failed to prove the group is not a Communist front, those who attend her gatherings will be at risk.

In a private room, she sits with Gordon, awaiting summons for the verdict. Silence fills the space. Words won't erase the lines of worry across his face or ease the tension in her chest.

"You were honest with me from the start," she says quietly. "I'm sorry I never gave the same to you."

"You weren't ready. I can understand that better than most." He gives her knee an affectionate pat. "We'll still throw a party the moment we get home."

She leans back in her chair and closes her eyes. Home. A tentative shadow of comfort and security amid the glaring lights of politics that would all too eagerly chase it away.

The door swings open, then a voice calls Ada back for the verdict. Back into that place of harshness and noise and theatrics so like what she does for a living, yet entirely the opposite.

She reaches for Gordon, who takes her hand. Neither moves. They simply cling to the quiet, to the comfort of home.

When they stand, he looks at her for a long moment—a look Ada might have wanted her father to give her, had he cared enough to remain in their lives. Then he wraps her in an embrace and kisses the top of her head. She holds tight to him while her shuddering breaths match his.

At last, she pulls back to find his eyes bright.

"I'm proud of you, kid. Even if we never work again."

"We made decent money together; we'll spend it together until it runs out," she replies with a rueful smile. "And we'll find work eventually. Even if the only job I can book requires dancing half nude in a sideshow at some seedy downtown theater for the most unsavory of patrons."

The jest wins a small smile before she kisses his cheek and threads her arm through his. Together, they return to the courtroom.

All she can do is pray she's right. That the work will return someday, and that she's done enough to convince this jury she is not the threat they fear she is. They already used her hearing to demonstrate what happens to subversives. Do they really need to convict her of contempt too?

A chill settles over her as she finds her seat. She glances briefly toward the members of the press. Ingrid is there somewhere, hiding among them. A few more minutes until this is over, then Ada will go home, give Ingrid her negatives for the FBI, and divert Dietrich's attention from her sister however she must. She finds him in the crowd, his eyes on her; she stares back, though her heartbeat races in her ears.

"On the charge of contempt of Congress, we find the defendant, Ada Worthington-Fox, guilty."

The declaration snaps Ada back into focus, though she hardly listens while the judge sentences her—a fine and three months in a women's prison. A fine she can accept, but prison? All because she refused to answer questions to the chairman's satisfaction, and because it seems they have chosen to condemn her to the fullest extent.

The role as HUAC's sacrificial lamb is not one she agreed to play.

Three months, the judge said. Three months during which Mother and Dietrich could disappear.

CHAPTER 45

Washington, DC, 28 October 1947

INGRID

uilty. Her sister has been found guilty.

Condemned to three months in prison for contempt because she refused to speak about anyone except herself. Ingrid bites her lip to contain a protest, her eyes never leaving Ada.

Ada is always composed, always what she should be for her audience. Except, as the sentence is declared, her face is white, her usual poise absent as she takes a faltering step toward the bailiff awaiting her. A momentary lapse. Then she visibly gathers herself before looking in Gordon's direction, then Ingrid's, and disappearing from the courtroom.

A sham trial just to make an example of her? Was the hearing not enough of an example?

Ingrid pushes through the throngs of reporters and spectators until she emerges into the quiet hall, where she presses her palms against her bruised stomach. How did her efforts to serve her country and protect her sister amount to this? The job she accepted with integrity and pride reduced to lies and manipulation, and to her own inability to realize it until it was too late.

"Nice work, Holland."

She closes her eyes as the remaining energy drains from her body. "For once, will you not patronize me?"

"I'm not, I'm not. I mean it, really." Archie tosses a cigarette butt into an ashtray. "Even though she's your sister and the truth isn't what you hoped it would be, you still did your job."

"No, I didn't, because none of this was the truth. Crenshaw and Stieber used us to make a point." When Archie's brows lift in what might be surprise or the start of an argument, Ingrid steps closer. "Do not trust them. And if Agent Stieber says anything about me or Ada, tell me. Please. As your former coworker and your friend, if we can call ourselves that."

She doesn't await a reply and proceeds down the hall, away from the emerging crowd. Moments later, she pauses, seeking one face until she finds it. Her handler. She has worked for the man who tortured her sister.

The realization is too revolting to process as she feels him following her down a secluded hallway until they are alone.

"You knew we were sisters all along, didn't you? You sent those messages and knew Aleida's schedule, in part thanks to me keeping you informed. Did you also send Mother to recover the evidence?"

"Your sister was becoming unruly with all those statements you kept encouraging her to give. Beyond the planned hearing, I needed her credibility hindered. Now, if she pursues a war crimes case, she's a subversive caught in her lies, holding a grudge against her mother, seeking revenge against the FBI agent who worked her case by accusing him of being a war criminal despite a lack of evidence."

Ingrid digs her fingernails into her palms, wishing she could do something, say something, but it's useless. He planned this expertly. With Mother's exclusive, a lack of suitable evidence to contradict Dietrich's falsified history, and now a conviction, Ada will not be taken seriously and Dietrich can argue his way out of a war crimes case.

Except, despite losing the execution orders Hattie uncovered, they still have the negatives, which document similar crimes. If they can keep him from taking the materials, and if they can prove Stieber and Dietrich are the same man, they might have a chance.

When he steps closer, she takes an immediate step back, hates the faint smirk of satisfaction it brings to his lips.

"Behave yourself over the next three months. I'll be watching you both. Then I'll take what belongs to me and we can put all this behind us."

"Mother is of no use to you, then?" Ingrid presses, because the only thing she can think to do is put doubts in his mind. "Why wait three months when you could have her looking for what you want, if Aleida really does have more information against you?"

"Because I don't want it from anyone else. I want it from her."

A chill courses down Ingrid's spine, then he strolls unhurriedly down the hall, leaving her alone with her unsteady breaths. She's got a war crimes case to build and three months to do it—assuming she can do it without Dietrich realizing he failed to deter her. And assuming he doesn't change his mind about waiting for Ada to forfeit the negatives herself, because if he starts looking for them, three months is far too much time for him to find them.

* * *

The next morning, after Lars leaves for work, a knock sounds on the apartment door.

Ingrid's blood runs cold—although Dietrich didn't knock last time, which is her only consolation. Cautiously, she answers to find Hattie, who hasn't spoken to her since their encounter prior to Ingrid's meeting at the FBI. Before she can pull Hattie into a relieved embrace, her friend marches inside without looking at her.

"Lest you get the wrong idea, I'm still mad at you." Hattie plops into an armchair and extends an expectant hand until Ingrid provides her with a cup of coffee. "But maybe I kept looking into your case."

Ingrid sits across from her. "And?"

"And you're not going to believe this." A pause as she adds sugar and cream. "That man you asked me to look for, Gregor Dietrich? I found him. Except he's got a new name."

"Klaus Stieber."

Her friend's face falls. So much for her dramatic reveal.

"Well, if you knew he was your handler, then why the hell did I bother coming over? His agent file is under his new name, which is why I didn't make the connection initially, then I found some old paperwork documenting the changes when he entered the country. Except the file under his original name matches the information listed under the name Stieber. Dietrich claims he was in the military working in finance, and he never left Germany. Which doesn't match the paperwork I found about Dietrich authorizing your grandfather's execution."

"He was cleared to work for the FBI, I suppose?"

"Right." Hattie's jaw is set in contemplation, incredulity, as she attempts to make sense of it all. "He lied, didn't he? Meaning Stieber really is Dietrich? And a murderer? But he's so dull, so quiet, so . . . normal."

Ingrid scarcely keeps her penmanship legible as she jots down the claims in his files, all of them entirely different from the evidence Dietrich has been destroying. Evidence confirming he is exactly who Ada says he is.

"Dietrich is not the man presented in those files. He was in Arnhem suppressing resistance and persecuting Jews. He must not have known the execution orders you found still existed; otherwise I'm certain he would have erased the evidence the same way he erased his past." When

Hattie opens her mouth to reply, Ingrid leans closer—then winces and pulls back when pain flares in her midsection. "You read my mother's exclusive, didn't you? Did you also read my sister's?"

Hattie nods, although her lips remain pursed in confusion before she claps a hand to her forehead. "After the hearing when I realized Ada was Aleida, I read all the exclusives, and I didn't even make the connection. That's your war crimes case. The man your sister mentioned."

Ingrid nods. "She has proof. And I know I don't have a right to ask for your help, but if you can keep watch from the inside, ensure the evidence stays in trustworthy hands—"

"Of course I'll help." Hattie no longer regards her with the hostility from their last meeting. She glances at the newspapers on the coffee table, open to articles Ingrid was reading about Ada's trial. "I heard about the conviction," she says quietly. "Aleida was always the one keeping our spirits up at boarding school. I wish we could do the same for her through this."

There is so much Ingrid wishes she could do. For now, she places a hand briefly over Hattie's.

"Might the three of us have dinner together the next time Aleida is in town? She would be delighted to see you. In three months," she adds bitterly.

"Sounds lovely. By then, I'll be slightly less mad at you," her friend replies with a slight, teasing smile, to which Ingrid smiles in return.

Soon they will spend an evening together, just like old times. But not until this is over. A little spark of hope blooms in Ingrid's chest, although she doesn't dare indulge it too much yet. Still, with the information from Hattie, she has proof that Dietrich's FBI file does not match the documents Ada took from Arnhem. Meaning Dietrich lied to the government.

Meaning Ingrid and Ada might have a case.

CHAPTER 46

California Institution for Women, 13 November 1947

ADA

Following the trial, Ada is paraded past the press without being permitted so much as a goodbye to Gordon, Ingrid, anyone. From beloved actress to cautionary tale.

Maybe it will be nice to avoid the press, the stories, the gossip for a few months. Even if she must do so behind bars at the California Institution for Women.

When she's placed in a small cell, her racing heart acknowledges nothing beyond what it experienced the last time she was imprisoned. Except this is not the Oranjehotel. Her captors are not the Gestapo. She will be permitted visits. She is not awaiting interrogation or torture. Even if such truths are ones her mind cannot entirely trust.

And when her first visitor comes a couple weeks later, it is Mother.

Ada waits at a small table in an otherwise empty cell while the guard opens the door for Constance, who murmurs something, then presses a few bills into his palm. After the door closes and locks, he walks away.

Mother doesn't want eavesdroppers, then. A realization that makes Ada feel no better about this visit.

She wears a smart pair of trousers, a blouse, and an elegant cloche resting atop neatly styled hair. A sharp contrast to Ada's unsightly prison garb. Constance looks her daughter over with obvious disapproval before sitting down.

"Really, darling, it did not need to come to this—although contempt is a fitting sentence, considering the contempt you and your sister both held toward my efforts to guide you, to protect you, to raise you better than this."

In the past, Ada has glimpsed all sides of Mother—the harsh critic, the disciplinarian, the woman who praised her, loved her. Mothered her. Beneath those facets was always the woman Ada had never seen, not until recently. One whose chosen punishment for her children was to cut them off from each other entirely.

"I did my best," Ada replies simply, because if Mother is still with Dietrich, anything Ada says might be reported back to him, might endanger herself or Ingrid.

"Your best? No, you let yourself be swayed by your sister, by your obsession with this war crimes nonsense, by anything except reason, just like when you were a girl. Even after the measures I took in Arnhem, you haven't learned. Should I have left you imprisoned for months instead of days? Would that have taught you better?"

The measures she took in Arnhem? Last time, Ada was imprisoned following Gestapo arrest. Nothing to do with Mother.

Or perhaps everything to do with Mother.

As her challenge settles over the room, Ada can't speak. Mother knew Ada helped Ingrid escape, and she confiscated Ingrid's letters. Perhaps she knew much more about Ada's life under occupation. Enough to orchestrate her daughter's arrest.

Surely not. Yet the thought is all too easy to believe, as much as it prompts a deep ache in Ada's heart. She has learned the twisted nature of her mother's love all too well.

"The Oranjehotel . . . That was your doing?"

"No, that was *your* doing. You and your resistance, your Jewish dance instructor, your meddling where you didn't belong." Mother's eyes flash, dangerous and threatening, before she draws a steadying breath. "Fortunately, I cared for you enough to put a stop to it."

Ada presses shaking hands to the table as heat sears every part of her body. "You had Dietrich arrest me?"

"Not a real arrest, of course; I was quite clear that no harm should come to you. After I found that note around your hairpin, Gregor and I discussed our suspicions and concerns regarding your activities, so I asked him to frighten you a little, nothing more. To leave you imprisoned for a few days without explanation, then make it appear as if his men had mistakenly arrested the wrong girl. Had you continued making such poor decisions, eventually you would have been arrested without my intervention, then God knows what might have happened."

As if Ada never understood the dangers posed by resistance work. As if she was an impressionable girl influenced by her subversive Jewish dance instructor. As if she was not a young woman who made her own decisions to defend her country and help the oppressed, all with complete awareness of what might happen if she were caught.

Mother places a hand over Ada's. "You were never in any real danger at the Oranjehotel; it was simply a teaching tactic. I kept you safe, my darling."

Arrested by order of her own mother who was foolish enough to believe her instructions would be followed. Tortured without her knowledge or consent. Then freed by her entreaty, although that was merely an act.

Ada stands and steps back. "Shall I show you how well you protected me?"

With shaking fingers, she finds the buttons at her chest. Unfastens one, then another, her speed increasing until the movements match her breaths while Mother stares in blatant confusion. A trance that breaks only when Ada removes her blouse.

"What are you doing?" When Ada grabs her undergarments, Mother's chair nearly topples in her haste to get up, then she catches Ada's wrist. "Enough, that is quite enough! I said stop!"

"So did I! Not at first, I tried not to say anything at first, but by the end it was all I could say. Stop. Please stop." Holding Mother's gaze, she takes off her brassiere. "He didn't listen to me. He didn't listen to you either."

Suddenly this cell is as cold as the one in the Oranjehotel, where the only heat came from the terror rushing through her veins, the tears escaping down her cheeks, the blood seeping from her skin. She watches Mother's eyes fall to her breasts. To the scar. To the key symbolic of Dietrich's crest.

Stunned silence, then a sob. "Oh, my darling girl . . ."

Their matching unsteady breaths cut through the quiet as Mother sinks into her chair, motionless, her eyes glassy and glazed. As if she's not entirely present. Ada's heartbeats throb in her chest as she waits for an apology, an expression of concern or regret, anything to acknowledge what she's done and the nature of the man she brought into their lives.

Somewhere down the hall, a muffled voice breaks the stillness, prompting Mother to spring to her feet. "For God's sake, cover yourself. This is most inappropriate."

Ada doesn't oblige. Mother is already snatching her clothes, dressing her, muttering to herself.

"I should have removed you from that ballet school. Then you never would have been coerced into such reckless behavior and this would have been avoided."

Not another glance at her scar, not an embrace, nothing more.

Because Constance will never be the mother Ada wants her to be, only the mother she is.

Once Ada is dressed, Mother takes her shoulders. "When your father left, then Ingrid, then you, I found no solace in resenting what I couldn't change. Each time, difficult though it was, I realized I had to move forward. To forgive. So must you." She tightens her hold. "Leave the past where it belongs."

If Ada had found a way to forget, she would have done so long ago.

Clinging to pain serves no purpose; neither can it be entirely left behind. Pain shifts and eases but always remains.

"You wanted to be with him, didn't you?" she asks through her teeth. "It was never due to fear for our safety. And you never lost touch with him."

"You wouldn't have understood, not when both your sister and your dance teacher corrupted your politics. So I gave you a version of events you would accept. Few can entirely fault a desperate parent doing what she must." Mother arches a brow in a slight challenge. "Life is acting, darling. You know that."

Those words drive the dagger into Ada's final remaining hope the same way a dagger once sliced through her flesh. She presses her palms to her stomach, suppressing the urge to wail, to sob, to sink to her knees and lament her own foolishness. Ingrid was right, has always been right. Their mother has never been a woman capable of learning, of changing, of being anything other than the manipulator and liar she has proven herself to be. Despite Ada giving her chance after undeserved chance to be something different.

"Eventually I was going to tell you Gregor and I stayed together. You might have disputed me at first, but you would have accepted it soon enough. Appeasing your sister has always been impossible, but you are far more gracious."

All along, he's been here with Mother and supervising her sister. But Mother is wrong; Ada was willing to accept repentance, to extend forgiveness. She will never condone the fascist beliefs Mother pretended to renounce, will never accept her relationship.

Ada has not been gracious. She has been too gullible, too trusting, too foolishly hopeful.

"Don't be stubborn, Aleida. Gregor works for the FBI. Do you expect to make a convincing case against him? Give up the negatives and any additional copies of the documents. I know you have them. I looked everywhere for them. Let them go so we can move on with our lives."

Mother has been in Gordon's house, looking for Ada's evidence, all while Ada thought Ingrid was being far too suspicious. She wants to order Mother to get out, to never return. Except, if she leaves before Ada has conceded to her wishes, she might use Ingrid as a perverted teaching tactic to encourage Ada's cooperation.

There is only one way to protect herself. To protect Ingrid. She must be the gracious daughter Mother expects, even though these will be the most difficult lines she's ever had to deliver.

"I don't wish to dwell in the past," Ada says quietly. "But without Ingrid, we can't be a family."

That word, that single word certain to win Mother over. Her expression doesn't change, but a slight softening occurs around the corners of her eyes. An indication Ada's approach is working.

"Once I'm released, Gordon will throw a party to celebrate, so perhaps we can speak to Ingrid privately there? If you help me, I'll give you my remaining evidence. We can put all this behind us."

A little smile of approval, then Mother kisses her cheek. "What a lovely idea."

Returning the kiss is perhaps more difficult than spinning her story. Only once Mother is gone does Ada realize how tightly she's digging her fingernails into her palms.

She convinced Mother to agree. Next she will convince Ingrid the moment she visits, which will be soon, of course; she's probably as eager to talk as Ada is. She's going to hate what Ada has in mind.

When the guard gestures for Ada to exit, she obliges. "Sir, might I make a call?"

"No calls permitted."

"Then will you do me a favor? My sister should be scheduling a visit soon, and I'd like to know the moment she does so I'll know when to expect her. Please, it's quite important. Her name is—"

"Do you think this is a movie set where you expect everyone to do your bidding?" His mouth twists with apparent disdain. "You're not a celebrity here. You're no one." Then he shoves her down the hall, so she swallows a retort and walks dutifully back to her cell. She'll just have to wait to hear from Ingrid.

Yet over the next three months, she hears from no one. Not Mother, not Gordon, not Vince, not Ingrid. Ada is alone with herself, her fellow inmates, and the plan she needs to implement the moment she's released. One she can't fulfill without her sister.

The person who has not contacted her at all.

Maybe Ingrid's visit and their reconciliation was an act. Ingrid has deceived her before.

Had Ada kept her mouth shut at the hearing, Ingrid might not have been exposed as her relation. For that, perhaps Ada had not been as forgiven as she thought. Perhaps Ingrid was only trying to get more information about the war crimes case to pursue Dietrich herself, win acclaim once he's caught, and secure another job in government.

It wouldn't be the first time Ingrid used Ada to advance her own career.

No, it can't be true. She knows Ingrid, trusts her. Even though she has not come.

On a crisp January morning when Ada is released from the California Institution for Women, it is not Gordon or Ingrid who picks her up, but Mother.

"Come along, darling," Mother says without preamble, gesturing for Ada to get into the car. "You've got a party to attend."

* * *

The drive from the prison to Hollywood Hills is spent in overwhelming silence.

A party awaits—one Gordon planned, apparently, despite never visiting. Mother will not let Ada out of her sight until she hands over the negatives, which means she's likely prepared to fulfill Ada's request to speak to Ingrid. Except Ada only made that request because she thought she and Ingrid would have time to discuss what Ada has in mind. Instead Ingrid never contacted her. Now Ada can either forgo her plan or trust that her sister still intends to help her and hope to God they manage.

Which is the only choice she has, really. Otherwise, Mother and Dietrich will take her negatives and disappear.

When they reach Gordon's house, Ada hurries ahead—both to crush him in an embrace and to send him on an errand, tell him she'd rather spend some time alone with Mother, anything to get him away before Dietrich gets here. If he's not here already.

"Gordon? Sowerby, come here, my darling boy!"

Neither the sound of footsteps nor the scrabble of tiny paws on the parquet floors. Quiet. Then, at last, footsteps on the living room carpet. With a relieved breath, Ada rushes in their direction.

"Darling, I missed you so—"

She stops. The man in the living room is not Gordon, and there is not a terrier anywhere in sight.

His condescending stare leaves her skin prickling; the scar across his neck leaves her own scar aching. She can't endure seeing him again, but she has no choice. She developed this plan and dragged her sister into it. God willing, together, they can get out.

Ada doesn't flinch as Dietrich approaches her, or when he takes her hand.

"Always a pleasure, Fräulein."

Before he can bring her hand to his lips, she snatches it away. "What have you done with him? And my dog?"

"Manners," Mother chides, joining them. "Gordon probably took the little beast on a walk."

He would not be taking the time for a leisurely stroll, not even for Sowerby. A quick jaunt down the street and back, maybe, but no more when party preparations take precedence.

Ada sucks in a sharp breath, already considering all the terrible possibilities, when a car pulls onto the motor court. A man with a handlebar mustache steps out, followed by a Yorkshire terrier.

Gordon hasn't made it halfway to the door before Ada is outside and throwing her arms around him, then crushing Sowerby to her chest, blinking past tears as she kisses both.

"Your mother insisted on picking you up, so Sowerby and I went to pick up the dress I ordered for you." He indicates the garment bag in his hand, then nods to the dog. Questions about Mother and the man she brought with her will certainly follow, but they have no time for those.

Without loosening her embrace, Ada keeps her voice low. "When Ingrid gets here—" Then she stops, feeling Mother's hand on her forearm—then Sowerby's little body vibrating with a growl.

"Run along, darling. Make yourself presentable."

Continuing her explanation is not worth the risk of Mother overhearing, so Ada swallows back everything she wanted to say and scratches beneath Sowerby's chin while Gordon leads the way. Yet tension coils in her stomach. Resolving this will be even more difficult to do discreetly once guests arrive.

After getting ready under Mother's supervision—Dietrich's orders to watch her, probably—Ada closes Sowerby into her bedroom, keeping him safe despite his dissatisfaction with being left behind. Downstairs, music fills the house while the usual chatter and revelry take place around the pool. Gordon selected a gown of ivory satin for her, which she adorns with pearls. Perhaps she can slip away from Mother long enough to tell him how to help. She doesn't want him involved, but she might not have a choice.

Gordon waits at the bottom of the stairs, then he offers Ada his arm. "Shall we?"

"Mother and I would like to wait for Ingrid. Tell everyone I'll be along shortly." She kisses his cheek and squeezes his arm to reassure him.

Gordon says nothing, then nods. His eyes stay on Mother as she gestures for Ada to lead the way.

Already, Ada's heart is thudding. Mother won't leave her side. She will have no time to communicate a plan to Ingrid, to do anything but forfeit the evidence she can't allow Dietrich to have. She manages a few steps before she pauses and whirls to face Gordon.

"Oh, I forgot to thank you. A few months ago, before my trial, I noticed you fixed my little robin in the library, the one Sowerby broke." She shakes her head, chuckling. "The one time I took it off the shelf, and after I told him to stay away from it . . . Perhaps someday that little rascal will listen to me."

She guides Mother away before Gordon's furrowed brow can betray the lie. He will understand the message; he must. The bird is from Ingrid, and Ada mentioned listening for a reason. If she can't intercept Ingrid, perhaps Gordon can. Then Ingrid can tell him how to tap into the device and catch Mother and Dietrich in the confession Ada hopes to extract—a plan she has had no time to prepare given the lack of communication with her sister. Without Gordon's understanding, the device that could be of so much use to them will be of none at all.

In the library, they take their seats while the sounds of the party fade. To Ada's right, the little robin sits on its shelf—eyes bright, head cocked to one side. Listening.

Now to wait for Ingrid.

Ada focuses on her breathing and the heartbeat thrumming in her ears, absorbs the addictive rush that precedes stepping onto the stage or in front of the camera, focuses on her role. She has always been a performer. Tonight, convincing her audience will require all her skill. And even that might not be enough.

CHAPTER 47

Los Angeles, 13 January 1948

INGRID

I n DC on a chilly January afternoon, snow might be falling. In California, the sun burns bright as Ingrid pulls aside her hotel curtains at the Biltmore. She and Lars have come for Gordon's party to celebrate Ada's homecoming. Despite the occasion, unease has consumed Ingrid these last months like a distant storm looming ever closer, leaving her unable to concentrate on anything else.

While Lars sits in bed with the morning paper, Ingrid calls the California Institution for Women, as she's done every day since Ada was incarcerated. "Good morning, I'd like to speak with Ada Worthington-Fox regarding an urgent matter."

The other woman lets out an aggravated huff. "No calls or visits are permitted; no, do not come to California to ask in person because you will be turned away; no, you may not speak to anyone else because you won't get a different answer; no, the restrictions will not be changing. And as I'm sure you know, Miss Worthington-Fox is being released today, so for the last time, *goodbye*, Mrs. Van Essen."

The line clicks. After all these calls, Ingrid never did learn that irritable old crone's name.

Sighing, she returns to the window and observes the bustling street traffic below, battling the apprehension in her chest. Her efforts to contact Ada over these last months have been met with silence. Whether Ada truly isn't permitted to communicate or simply doesn't want to speak with her, Ingrid has never been told.

The uncertainty has left Ingrid tossing and turning nightly. Although they made peace before the trial, the sentencing shocked everyone and perhaps fueled Ada's resentment toward Ingrid for her role in the events leading to it. Perhaps Ingrid was not as forgiven as she thought.

Despite her sister's silence, they will see one another this evening, so Ingrid takes solace in that. She even bought a new dress for tonight—navy, long sleeves, buttoned bodice, soft pleated skirt, and a high neck cinched with a ribbon. Not as extravagant as one Ada would have chosen, but it'll do.

As the time for the party nears, Ingrid is tying the bow at the base of her throat when a knock against the door reveals Archie—expressionless, professional, giving Ingrid no indication of why he's come.

"Mrs. Van Essen, due to your personal and familial ties to Ada Worthington-Fox, concerns have been raised about the effects of her subversive influence; therefore you and Mr. Van Essen are required to answer a few questions prior to engaging with her this evening."

Lars scoffs, muttering that this is ridiculous while he dons his suit jacket. Agitation creeps across the back of Ingrid's neck. This feels wrong. Quite wrong. As for who issued such nonsensical orders, she's certain she knows. Neither Dietrich nor Crenshaw will keep her away, so they will answer Archie's questions quickly and go to her sister.

Except, once they reach the lobby, Ingrid glimpses a parked car through the glass door. Leaning against it is a man dressed in trousers, a jacket, and a button-down shirt with an open collar. The exposed scar stretches across his neck.

Just as she thought: Something is quite wrong. Archie is not conducting this inquiry.

She comes to an abrupt halt, desperately pushing the nerves from her voice. "Lars was never involved. You don't need to question him."

Archie nods to the door. "Please join Agent Stieber. Mr. Van Essen and I will talk separately."

A small mercy; Dietrich has no interest in Lars, who is already frowning at the mention of their separation. And if Dietrich intends to keep her from her sister, Ada will need someone else's help.

"Listen," she says to Lars in Dutch. "At Gordon's house—" She stops when Archie grabs her arm.

"English. Don't make this difficult."

Lars breaks Archie's hold. "Do not touch my wife."

Ingrid regards Archie with a silent entreaty—everything she can't say, not without endangering her husband. The look in Archie's eyes indicates he hasn't forgotten the warning she issued about Stieber. Then he gestures to the door.

The sinking sensation in her stomach almost roots her in place. Nothing she does will ever encourage Archie to trust her.

Lars has never let her down, though; today is not the day to start.

She places a hand on his arm. "I need you to *listen*," she urges, this time in English. Surely he will understand what she's trying to tell him, will find a way to help no matter how Archie interferes. Then she draws a breath and proceeds.

Even if Ada hasn't forgiven her, they have a war crimes case to complete. To do so, Ingrid needs those negatives.

* * *

Ingrid could run, scream, flee back into the hotel. There's no shortage of people to assist her if she causes a fuss. Yet the gun against Dietrich's hip is clearly visible when he straightens and opens his palm. She surrenders her handbag, which he searches—presumably for weapons—before tossing it into the back seat, then he pushes her forward until she braces herself against the shiny black automobile.

Her stomach tightens, and she almost drives her elbow into his ribs while his hands travel down her arms, along her legs, under and over her breasts, across the stomach he bruised. Seeking the weapon she certainly would have brought if Ada didn't have her gun.

Once satisfied, he nods for her to sit, then he follows.

The chauffeur takes them to their destination for this interrogation that will be nothing like Archie has apparently been led to believe. As for what Dietrich intends to do with her, she will soon find out. Her heart keeps time with the trees, mountains, and roadside racing past in blurs of color. A route she soon recognizes. They are on their way to Gordon's mansion—precisely where Ingrid needs to go, although it makes Dietrich's purpose no clearer.

When they arrive, she steps onto the motor court. Judging by the vehicles parked along the street and faint voices and music as they approach the front door, the party has already started.

Hope and fear wrestle for control as Ingrid walks. Surely Ada is here. Or perhaps that would be worse. If she's absent, she might be somewhere safe. Or Dietrich might have already gotten her out of his way, if he's already obtained the evidence from her.

Inside, the house is quiet compared to the noise from the open back door. Gordon is nowhere in sight. Neither is her sister. Ingrid silences all the possibilities swirling in her mind, refrains from springing at Dietrich to demand to know what he wants, why she's here, where Ada is. She must not panic. Her sister must be here, must be safe.

Dietrich nods down the hall toward the library, so she continues. There, amid the darkened bookshelves, Mother sits in an armchair. Beside her, thinner than Ingrid recalls yet no less poised and elegant, is Ada. Unharmed. Ingrid could nearly collapse from relief, and this room sparks a tiny flame of hope in her chest. The library. The listening device.

Ada must know about it, must want them in this room for the same reasons Ingrid does—except the stiff, reserved frown Ada gives her sends a chill across Ingrid's skin. Her sister has never looked at her like this.

"Well, if it isn't the witch hunter herself."

Ada's statement is so cutting it makes Ingrid flinch. This can't be, not after they made peace. Her sister can't have turned against her, even though they haven't spoken in months. And as Ingrid casts an uncertain glance from Ada to Mother, she sees no tension in Ada's posture, nothing that indicates she is here under duress or wishing to be anywhere except at Mother's side. She can't be cooperating with the two who made her life hell all those years ago. The seed of uncertainty is planted deep in Ingrid's core, choking everything else, except she can't let it. Not after everything they endured together.

As Dietrich directs Ingrid farther into the room and closes the door, Ada regards her with a cold stare. So much like Mother. Then Ada looks her up and down, lips pursed, chin lifted. So much like Mother.

So much like when they were girls, when Ada imitated Mother to make Ingrid laugh.

The thought sends a sudden spark of energy through Ingrid's veins. Her imitations, her mannerisms, all to amuse Ingrid. Her stories she developed to fool Mother when Ingrid slipped away to be with Lars, preventing Ingrid from getting caught.

Keeping her safe.

Perhaps Ada is intentionally hoping to provoke such memories; perhaps this, too, is all an act. She can't tell. There's a reason her sister belongs on the stage and screen.

As Ingrid's heart thuds and she looks from Dietrich to Mother to Ada, it's Ada she knows. Ada she trusts. Such trust has never been misplaced before; surely it won't be now.

CHAPTER 48

Hollywood Hills, 13 January 1948

ADA

After greeting her sister with criticism as their mother often does, Ada looks at Ingrid, only Ingrid, regards her with her best imitation of Mother's judgmental frown even as her heart thuds.

All Ada can do is play her part. Subtly this time, not the somewhat exaggerated caricature of her youth. Just enough so Ingrid will understand, because even though they were unable to prepare this plan, surely she will recognize that this is an act and Ada needs her help.

Ingrid stares as if she can't quite comprehend what's occurring. Then Ada catches it, the slightest shift when Ingrid's eyes return to hers—curiosity, uncertainty, then something dangerously close to hope.

Clever girl.

Still, the pit in Ada's stomach tightens. Ingrid entered with Dietrich, meaning she probably had no time to speak with Gordon or anyone else. Meaning the message Ada gave Gordon will yield nothing. The little robin on the shelf is listening and has no one to tell its secrets.

But they have one more asset in this room: a gun. Surely Ingrid will remember its hiding place inside the empty cigar box on the mantel. If needed, Ada can distract Dietrich, allowing Ingrid time to recover it.

"Sit down, darling," Mother says, but Ingrid does not. Before Mother can insist, Ada draws a breath, as if letting her fury go.

"Can't we forget all this, Inge? It's in the past—the war, the hearing, everything you and I have done to one another." Now for the most unbearable line of all, certain to make Ingrid recoil. Ada stands, reaching out to grip Ingrid's shoulders, hoping Ingrid will trust her eyes, not her words. "We must stop pursuing the war crimes case."

Heavy silence fills the room. Even if Ingrid concedes, Ada is not certain Dietrich will permit them to leave here alive.

They might have a chance, though, if only they can seize it. She tightens her grip on Ingrid before releasing her, willing her to understand. Both stand by the fireplace. By the cigar box containing the gun.

Dietrich's scoff breaks the quiet. "You can't build a convincing case even if you try."

"Your FBI file and the documents are proof." Ingrid glares at him, moves slowly toward the chair Mother offered, away from the mantel. Distracting him. Giving Ada the opening she needs. "Do you think the American government will show mercy to someone who deceived them? You're a murderer who lied to enter this country, and I will see you held accountable."

The moment she finishes, Ada grabs the box, opens it, reaches inside, closes her fingers around—nothing. Emptiness. She stares in horrified silence, then looks to Dietrich.

He holds up the small pistol, shows her it's empty, and tosses it into a chair. He is always thorough, meticulous; of course he searched the room. Ingrid returns to Ada's side, and they glance at each other for the answer neither has. They have no defense, no weapon, nothing.

His hand moves to his hip, then there is only Mother's deafening silence, Ingrid's gasp, and Ada's sudden desire to change everything about this night, anything to keep her sister away. Because now both stand before Dietrich's pistol.

Beside her, Ingrid grabs Ada's arm, as if her grip could prevent him from firing. He holds the gun level at Ada, then his eyes fall briefly to her chest, nearly prompting her to flinch. She won't allow him to conjure those memories, to distract her, to maintain the hold she's finally managed to break.

"Darling, this isn't necessary," Mother says with the slightest edge of concern as she steps to the twins' side. "Aleida has agreed to cooperate, has she not?"

"I'm not risking the lives we built on the word of a frivolous girl who just tried to use her own weapon against me. Until she fulfills her end of the bargain, she can't be trusted." He focuses on Mother, keeps the weapon steady. "Get out of the way, Constance."

Behind Mother, Ada grips Ingrid's hand, holds tight. Maybe her sister has always been right; maybe Mother will never be the parent Ada wants her to be. Yet this time, for once, she dares to hope, to believe, to pray Mother will choose her daughters.

With a small sigh, as though this is all quite exasperating, Mother steps aside.

The sorrow that slices through Ada's core is almost enough to bring her to her knees.

"First I find a gun." Dietrich watches Ada for the reaction she does not give, though her next breath skips in anticipation of what comes next. "What else might you be hiding?"

He knows exactly what was missing from the materials she surrendered to Mother. If he's searched the room, he's likely found them. He's probably destroyed them already, meaning he's right. She and Ingrid have no case, and now they're trapped here.

"Are you going to return my property, or shall I encourage you?"

Ada keeps her eyes on the barrel of Dietrich's gun. He might know where the evidence is. He might not. It makes no difference. Last time he used her dance instructor to force her compliance; this time, he will use her sister. The only way to protect Ingrid is to do what he wants.

"Without my testimony or the evidence, there is no case for Ingrid or anyone else to pursue, so you don't need her." Ada fights to speak calmly, reasonably, anything to prevent him from turning the gun toward Ingrid. "I'll do as you say, but let her and Mother—"

And then Dietrich's eyes never leave hers as he applies pressure to the trigger, squeezing. Firing.

A collective shriek rises as she and Ingrid push and pull, each simultaneously fighting to spare the other, awaiting the bang, the agony, someone's cry of pain.

A snap, paralyzing and gruesome, then nothing. Ada feels nothing, smells no metallic blood, no gunsmoke. First she meets Ingrid's stunned gaze, confirms she's unharmed. Then she looks to Mother, who remains frozen, her face pale.

Dietrich cocks the pistol again. "There was only one empty chamber. Next will be a bullet."

Mother appears too startled to speak, while Ada's pounding heart refuses to slow. He is tired of bargaining, of wasting time, of delaying. Before she can act, Ada feels a light squeeze on her hand, then Ingrid releases her.

"Keep the gun on me, Agent Stieber—pardon, Herr Dietrich." She steps aside, showing her palms to prove her compliance. "If you keep it on me, Aleida will cooperate."

Then she looks to Ada. A look that says *Trust me.*

Ada does.

Outside are so many who might help, none of whom know to do so. None of whom she wants involved. And the one she wants involved least of all now has a gun pointed at her.

Ingrid moves away, step by cautious step, until she reaches Dietrich's side. She is calm, focused, although Ada can almost feel how desperately Ingrid wishes to be far from the man who attacked her, harmed both of them. Dietrich adjusts his grip on the gun, watching as Ingrid's eyes follow.

"Face your sister. Get on your knees. And do not move."

Ingrid obeys while Ada's breaths sharpen, then she looks to Mother—still pale yet her gaze stubbornly set, as if this is all simply for show to encourage cooperation and obedience. No real threats, no real danger, no different from Ada's Gestapo arrest.

Except Mother refuses to accept how real the danger was then and is now. How this man does nothing for show.

Dietrich touches the gun to the back of Ingrid's head; she tenses as the rise and fall of her chest hastens. "You said she'll cooperate, Mrs. Van Essen. Prove it."

Ingrid swallows hard. "Please, Leidje . . . Please give him the negatives."

The look in her eyes speaks far more than the unsteadiness in her voice, communicating the trust they can place nowhere but in each other. Ada clings to that look as she proceeds to the bookshelves, moves the stack of books and the robin figurine, and reveals her worn copy of *The Secret Garden*.

With gentle reverence, she picks it up. The novel that saw her through long days at a boarding school in Kent, lonely nights through a war in Arnhem, and an arduous journey to America. Now it must see her through this.

She opens to the correct page and finds the negatives just as she left them. Soon to be destroyed once they fall into Dietrich's hands. And once he has them, he will pull the trigger on Ingrid, then on Ada. Of that, she is certain. He will never be held accountable for anything.

She trusts Ingrid; God willing, Ingrid will trust Ada. Whatever it takes to get the gun off her sister. Then she channels her role and descends into the memories—the war, Mother's parties, the Oranjehotel. Every moment overcomes and overwhelms her until he extends a hand. She gasps and presses into the bookshelves, unable to hear Dietrich's order over her own sobbing wail, then she feels an insistent grasp on her arm—Mother.

"Really, that is quite enough. Settle down and hand me the—"

"You trusted him, Mother! Every lie about the importance of his work, every promise not to hurt me, all lies. Every one of them." Ada pulls the book and negatives to her chest as tears streak down her cheeks. "Please trust Ingrid, trust *me*. Not him."

Something shifts, something that Ada can only pray indicates understanding. Then Mother blinks and the look disappears.

Before either says more, Mother gasps as something knocks her aside, then a forceful shove pins Ada's back against the bookshelves and Dietrich is centimeters from her—his face blood red, his grip on her wrist like a vise. His other hand pointing the gun at her.

One sister in front, the other behind. Out of his sight. Ingrid must go for help, for safety, for anything, because in seconds Dietrich will pull the trigger again. And this time there will be a bullet.

She draws away from him with another sob. "Don't, please! I won't say anything, won't pursue a case. I—"

"No, you will not. Neither of you will." Dietrich plucks the negatives from her grasp while Ada cowers, then he grabs her chin. "Eyes open. Watch your sister die."

She can't feel anything except his fingers on her skin and his gun at her chest, can't see Ingrid, Mother, anyone. Only him and the silver scar across his neck flaring red in the lamplight.

Then, as another sob racks Ada's body, he removes the gun. The moment he rotates to direct it at Ingrid, Ada ends her supposed fit and snatches the robin figurine from the shelf. The movement recaptures

Dietrich's attention, and as he turns back to Ada, she glimpses Ingrid on her feet, moving toward them, toward Dietrich's turned back. Toward the pistol that, for this instant of chaos and confusion, is not pointed at either sister.

Ada's eyes lock with Ingrid's for only a moment before Ada lunges for the gun and swings the figurine toward Dietrich's throat, feels the tiny pointed beak make contact even as he prevents her from snatching the weapon. Amid his furious shout, Ada loses sight of Ingrid, of his weapon, of everything when his hand closes around her neck, gripping tight before his eyes cloud with something close to surprise and he begins to turn toward where Ingrid must be. A deafening clap pierces the air and a woman screams.

No, not this, not Ingrid. He can't have shot Ingrid.

Another cry mingles with the first, harsher and deeper, except Ada can't see around him, can't see who was shot, can see only Dietrich as he staggers with something crimson pouring from his neck and shoulder—blood. She shoves him away, breaking his hold and sucking in painful breaths, yet his eyes never leave hers, bright and furious as he lunges toward her, teeters, collapses. His head strikes the coffee table with a dull thud. Then he sprawls across the floor and lies still, blood seeping from his head and shoulder and trickling from the old scar.

Within every performance lies rawness and truth—honest, emotional, uninhibited. And when it concludes, the lines between reality and performance blur, too real and overwhelming to separate when both exist fully within the performer. Now, as Ada's ears ring and she stares at Dietrich's limp form, she can't distinguish which is which.

He fired. She heard him fire the gun while Ingrid was rushing to help Ada, to save her rather than herself. He did not shoot Ada, so he must have shot Ingrid, yet the weapon has disappeared from his clutches.

"Don't move, Mother."

At Ingrid's command, a wave of lightheadedness crashes over Ada.

That voice, strong and assured and not in pain. She looks to her sister—unharmed, standing with the gun she apparently snatched from Dietrich during Ada's efforts to distract him, pointing it at Mother.

"Girls, what have you done?"

Neither acknowledges Mother's cry. Ingrid's chest heaves as she holds the weapon level while Ada kneels by Dietrich—unmoving, surrounded by blood. Bile rises to her throat as she presses her fingers to his neck. There will be a pulse, must be; they can't have gone through all this to end with a body. He's got a trial to withstand.

Centimeters from the scar, she finds a faint thrum.

"He's alive."

Amid Mother's relieved breath, Ingrid's knuckles remain white as she grips the pistol. "Do you realize what he's done? To so many during the war, to Aleida, to me? Or do you simply not care, you heartless, wretched—"

"Inge, look at me."

The gentle prompting silences her, breaks the trance; she blinks and obeys, her eyes glassy, her hands shaking. Ada touches Ingrid's forearm, guiding her as, together, they slowly lower the gun.

"You're certain I . . . I didn't . . . ?" Ingrid looks at Dietrich, supplying the unspoken.

Before Ada can reply, the door bursts open and three men enter—first Gordon, then Lars, then Archie Stribling, of all people.

Perhaps the little robin relayed the messages it overheard in this room, after all.

"I'll take it from here." Archie gestures to Mother, who responds with a fierce scowl. "Mrs. De Vos, if you would—"

"This is between me and my children, and this is all a misunderstanding." Then her voice is high, shrill. "Please, my girls, my darling, beautiful girls—"

"Enough!" When Constance closes her mouth, eyes bright with

sudden, imploring tears, Ada doesn't flinch. "No more, Mother. Not now or ever."

Ada vaguely senses Gordon's gentle touch on her forearm while Lars steps to Ingrid's side, yet she keeps her eyes forward, as does Ingrid, on Constance. The woman who might have been everything Ada always wanted in a parent, if she had ever cared enough to try.

As suddenly as her tears nearly spill, Mother clears her throat and draws herself up. Her stony gaze shifts between her daughters and Dietrich before she ignores Archie entirely and exits the room. Gordon quickly pursues her, leaving Lars and Archie to contend with Dietrich's bloody, unconscious form, which they heft between them and drag out. Then the library is empty of all except endless worlds contained within the pages lining the shelves, two sisters, and the secrets they have carried for so long. A burden now imparted on this room, hidden among the figurines, tomes, and drops of blood.

Lamplight falls across a floor bruised with bloodstains while the distant sounds of music and laughter settle the thudding of Ada's heart. If anyone heard the gunshot, Ada will have to explain it somehow. Perhaps she will give the simplest explanation of all: the truth. Beside her, Ingrid's breaths remain shallow.

"Honestly, Inge, you bugged my bird?"

She lets out a faint laugh. "And I'm not going to apologize. That little fellow was just the help we needed."

Indeed it was. Ada finds the figurine on the floor where she must have dropped it and picks it up—intact, with the wire inside still in place. Quite a resilient little thing.

When Ada takes Ingrid's hand, the remaining tremble she finds there eases slightly. Then Ada pulls her close, their breaths sharpening in unison as they cling to one another. Dear, infuriating, brilliant Ingrid. The sister she lost once and will never lose again.

When they release each other, Ada nods to the door.

"Shall we?"

She still has a party to host.

* * *

By the time Ada and Ingrid step onto the motor court, Mother and Dietrich are already inside the black car. Out of sight. Still, something in Ada won't settle until she glimpses them for herself. She steps closer, as does Ingrid, whose tight jaw mirrors Ada's. When they can make out the two silhouettes of Mother and Dietrich, the turmoil inside Ada settles a little, despite the feelings swirling inside her and the strangeness of this night. While Lars stands guard over the vehicle, Archie leads Ada and Ingrid a few steps away.

"I've got an FBI contact waiting to hear from me, so I'll transfer them," he says.

"How did you and Lars know to help?" Ada asks. "Did Gordon give you my message?"

"He did, confirming my suspicions that something was wrong." Archie glances at the two shadowy figures in the back seat. "Early in our investigation, Agent Stieber gave me a sealed message with instructions to plant it at the Star Society party—a test for Ingrid, he said, to see how she dealt with your reaction since this was her first assignment. I thought nothing of it until after your trial when Ingrid warned me about Stieber. Then today he told me he needed to question her."

A chill overtakes Ada. Dietrich really was behind the messages all along. Never Mother.

Archie looks to Ingrid. "I couldn't defy orders without him getting suspicious, but I had no intention of leaving you with him. I told Lars, and he told me what you said about Gordon's house and listening, so we assumed that meant you had planted a listening device. We followed you to the house, then Gordon took us upstairs to use our equipment privately to record your conversation."

Quite similar to the plan Ada had hoped to devise, if she and Ingrid would have had time to discuss it. Despite ignoring her ever since the trial, somehow Ingrid hadn't lost her willingness to help with the war crimes case. They made each other a promise, after all.

"Listen carefully, because you will never hear these words from me again." Ingrid's teasing smile fades as she extends a hand to Archie. "Thank you."

"God, that was painful for you, wasn't it?" He smirks as he clasps her hand. "I'm sure our paths will cross again, so until then, don't let anyone aggravate you too much. That's my job—and you're actually not so bad at yours."

She flashes an appreciative smile. "I do hope that was painful for you."

"Agony."

After nodding to Ada, Archie returns to the car. She stays with Ingrid, watching him go. Taking their mother with him. Heaviness settles in Ada's chest while Lars insists on cleaning the library himself, so she and Ingrid proceed to the backyard until they stand far from the pool, the entertainment, the noise. Neither speaks as they stare at the night sky, dark aside from a sliver of moonlight.

"Why did you not allow me to speak with you these last months?" Ingrid asks softly.

"Not allow you? No one tried. I never received a call, word of your efforts, nothing from anyone except—" The words stop in Ada's throat. "Except Mother."

The mother who confiscated Ingrid's letters to keep her daughters apart. The mother with a powerful FBI contact who likely held the ability to set boundaries and restrictions for Ada Worthington-Fox.

"Except Mother," Ingrid repeats, the words bitter. And yet, like Ada, she resigns herself to the understanding they have come to know too well.

Perhaps Ada should feel something more. More shock, more guilt, more anger, more than this odd emptiness that has overtaken her. Constance will be held accountable for her role in Dietrich's war crimes, yet she is still their mother. Then again, she is not. A mother in name does not a true mother make.

When she feels a gentle hand on her cheek, brushing away the moisture she didn't realize was there, she sighs unsteadily. "How could I have been so foolish, to believe the better of her?"

"Not foolish; optimistic. Not ready to accept the truth. Willing to see the best in others—something I should do a bit more." Ingrid gives a rueful smile before she sobers. "You can't change someone who has no desire to change. But I wish things were different too."

Mother's actions were never those of a woman aspiring to care, nurture, or support. If they had been, she would have been exactly who Ada always longed for her to be.

Ingrid's giggle breaks the quiet. "I must say, I've missed your impression of her."

"Shall I regale you with it more often? Or why don't I practice one of you to expand my repertoire?"

"The pool is just over there, Leidje, and I will have absolutely no regrets about pushing you in. Even if Gordon kills me for ruining your dress."

As Ada laughs, the sound of Ingrid's name reaches their ears. Lars approaches, so Ada nods her sister along. Seconds later, Ingrid captures him in her arms. Warmth spreads across Ada's skin as she watches them kiss, then Lars holds her against his chest. The man who loves Ingrid as she deserves to be loved.

How Ada wishes she would allow herself to be loved similarly. As a twinge of longing flickers in her chest, she stifles it. The love she shared with Vince was indeed similar. Which is precisely why she can't be with him. Loving him is not worth ruining him.

As Ingrid and Lars return to the party, Ada stays where she is, gazing skyward, and she's not sure how much time has passed when footsteps approach, rapid and urgent. A sure sign something is wrong. Ada whirls, and there he is, his eyes bright and blazing.

"I had no intention of coming tonight, not after that bullshit story you gave the press about me leaving you, and not when I thought you wouldn't want me here anyway. But somehow I can't stay away from you even though I should, and Gordon just told me about you nearly getting killed and—"

Ada throws her arms around him, and his words cease. Vince clings to her, his grip too tight, his breaths too sharp; then, just as abruptly, he releases her. Because she is not his to lose anymore. Ada's throat tightens. An embrace is only an embrace, words only words, except not when both conjure every feeling and memory she's fought to forget.

Silence weighs down every second. She can't allow herself to look at him, to change her mind, so she steps back.

"I thought I had moved past my feelings for you," he says quietly. "But when I saw you again at the announcement party . . . How can I ever want anyone else when I know what it's like to have you?"

His voice, deep and smooth and everything her heart has missed for so long. Even as his words send fire through her core, a sharp ache follows.

"It's too complicated."

"If having a relationship with you, attending your Star Society parties, and being a member of the Committee for the First Amendment haven't ruined me yet, I'll be fine." Despite the sardonic remark, he clears his throat. "After the committee's purpose got misconstrued, most of us recanted anyway. But if any of those things were destined to ruin my career, shouldn't I decide if I'm willing to take those risks?"

This is her opportunity to fight for him as he has never stopped fighting for her. But when she glances at him, he's already resigned to that look—indifference. As if they are destined to be what, once again, they have become: two who were and are no longer.

She swallows hard. "I should have—"

"Don't, Ada. We're finished. You're one of the bravest people I've ever known and somehow still a coward when it comes to us."

"Is it cowardice to fear hurting the people you love?"

"Only if that fear prevents you from loving as fully as you might." He steps closer, doesn't break her gaze. "Once I said no one would stand in your way because you wouldn't let them, but I was wrong. You stand in your own way."

Vince leaves her there, the darkness swallowing him with every step. Soon he will be out of sight, gone, never to return. They have tried and failed too many times to endure another failure. Except, this time, perhaps they won't fail.

"Maybe I do stand in my own way," she calls out to him. "Maybe you aren't willing to give your heart to anyone unless it won't be hurt, except it's impossible because love will inevitably hurt at times. And maybe we'll both have to be all right with that."

He tenses before facing her. No longer the look of indifference; this time, his expression reveals the same fears and hopes wrestling inside her. Slowly, cautiously, she approaches until she's standing before him.

It's all right to be scared or uncertain or concerned, to choose happiness in spite of those things, to face them together should they come. A choice that should be so simple, yet is not. Choosing happiness, true happiness, is the choice she has always failed to make.

If she were to claim such a choice for her own, she would choose this—herself, her decisions, her work, her life, the people within it. Him. It's him. Still.

"When I came to this country, all I wanted was to become someone else. I tried and failed, and I'm all right with that—with who I am and who I've become. And through it all I have never stopped loving you."

A cool breeze tousles his hair while the moonlight sparks in his eyes, darkening them to the deepest blue.

"I made choices for us that we should have made together. I gave up on what we had because I thought it would be best for you, for both of us. And I shouldn't ask you to love me in return." She presses a hand to his cheek, urging him to see into the deepest parts of her. "I shouldn't. But I will."

"And I shouldn't go through this with you, not when I can't love you if there's a possibility of losing you." He slips a finger beneath her chin. "But there's also a possibility, however small, of keeping you. For that, you just might have convinced me."

"Good, because there's only one way we can do this properly: together."

She guides him nearer while his thumb brushes over her lips, then his kiss settles the thud of her heart, the tension in her veins, every lingering wonder and worry. Serenaded by her party's distant merriment and illuminated by the faint moonlight overhead, she lets the heat of his touch and spicy notes of his cologne pull her into this time, this moment, this night.

Because it has always been him.

CHAPTER 49

Hollywood Hills, 15 January 1948

INGRID

T he war crimes case will be moving forward. This morning, Ingrid spoke with Hattie, who confirmed that the FBI is gathering evidence and said that Mother and Dietrich will likely be taken back to Europe for trial. This is what she always wanted out of a career in government: the opportunity to bring justice.

An opportunity she thought she was pursuing all along.

In a booth at Chasen's, a deep ache settles in Ingrid's chest as she looks to Lars, then Vince, Ada, and Gordon while the five enjoy lobster Newburg, prime rib, and breaded veal cutlets. Some of these brilliantly talented people might never work in film again, in part thanks to her.

She can still see Minnie Musgrave's recent headline: "The Huntress of Hollywood Surrenders Her Pitchfork." An article praising Ingrid and Ada for combining forces to bring a Nazi war criminal to justice, yes, but that doesn't change the moniker Mrs. Musgrave so gleefully attached to her.

Following dinner, they return to Gordon's, where the men retire to the living room, drinks in hand, followed by Sowerby—never one to be left out. Meanwhile, Ada leads Ingrid to the library. There, the little robin rests atop Ada's copy of *The Secret Garden*.

She pulls the negatives from the book, tucks them into an envelope, and offers them to Ingrid. "Will you give these to Hattie?"

"You're certain you want to testify, should it come to that?"

She nods and presses a hand to her chest, her next breath unsteady even as her jaw remains resolutely set. "How many women received this same brand and didn't live to tell of it? I've got to do it. For myself and for them."

Ingrid picks up the tattered copy of *The Secret Garden*. How Ada adored this story. How often Ingrid teased her, asking, *Are you reading that silly book again?* To which Ada's cheeky reply was usually, *No one likes boring old political tomes except you.* Ingrid smiles at the memories and opens the book.

"Can I convince you to read it this time?"

She chuckles. "I might consider it."

This novel is Ada's world, one of fairy tales and magic. So different from her own. Yet if Ada belongs here, perhaps Ingrid does too. Where one belongs, so does the other.

"About the case . . . these things take quite a while, so I can't say with certainty when anything more will happen." She closes the book. "The trial might not yield the results we want. Or, at the very least, the results might be unsatisfactory."

"I know," Ada says quietly. She picks up the robin figurine—no longer bugged, simply a decorative piece—and brushes a finger over its wing, then she sets it on the shelf. Ingrid recognizes this look from when they were girls, when Ada lost herself in a story or piece of music or dance, in the emotions the piece evoked.

"I never heard what happened to her. Madame Bellamy. She might have survived, or she might have been caught again." Ada's next breath trembles before she looks to Ingrid. "We've got to try our best for the sake of every victim who never received the justice they deserved. Even if our best is not enough."

If only Ingrid could assure Ada that it would be enough. If only one could profess with complete certainty that the law would hold true, justice would be achieved, the guilty would pay for every crime, and every victim would be honored. Yet in no world can one find complete certainty. One can only cling to the hope that justice will prevail, whether by magic or by law.

Perhaps their two worlds aren't so different, after all.

They will try their best. Except Ingrid's best can't give her more power, more ability to make a difference. Justice might fail.

But they will try, then she will move forward, this time with both her sister and her husband by her side. Then, wherever careers and life take them, maybe it won't be in accordance with Ingrid's carefully laid plans. And maybe that will be all right.

* * *

Later that evening, in Gordon's guest room, Ingrid adjusts the pillows propped against the headboard and finishes her chamomile tea without taking her eyes off the pages illuminated by the lamplight's soft glow. The bed creaks as Lars rolls over to face her.

"I hope you're enjoying your book more than I'm enjoying my attempts to sleep with your light on," he teases, then he props himself up to peer at the contents. "You're reading fiction? Willingly?"

"You're as irritating as Aleida," she says indignantly, to which he chuckles.

On Ada's insistence, she took *The Secret Garden* to bed with her, accompanied by strict instructions not to bend the pages. Never mind that it's been read countless times and spirited from one continent to another. The pages are already in pitiful condition. Still, Ingrid has decided to read a little, just to humor Ada in the morning when she will inevitably ask after Ingrid's progress.

"After I finish this chapter, I'll turn off the lamp," she says.

He mumbles in agreement before rolling over. Away from her. Away from the light, really, the rational part of herself clarifies. Except it wasn't so long ago that their nights were spent back-to-back with empty space stretching between them. Barely a word or touch, neither breaching the invisible barrier keeping them apart. She twirls the wedding ring on her finger and swallows the sudden lump in her throat.

"Lars?" She waits until he gives a little grunt of acknowledgment. "We're all right, aren't we?"

This time he sits up and looks at her for a long moment. "We're all right, *schatje*," he agrees softly.

She brushes her fingers through the thick blond locks and over the fine features that captured her heart years ago and hold it to this day. Then he draws her nearer until his lips find hers, and she settles into the comfort of every truth, every reassurance. He is the boy who once brought warmth to her cheeks, now the man who brings peace to her soul. They are all right.

When he settles again, he takes her hand, warm and secure as she reads the rest of her chapter. Once finished, she glances at Lars—eyes closed, his hand still in hers. If not asleep, convincingly faking. In which case he certainly won't mind if she reads a little longer.

CHAPTER 50

Hollywood, 23 January 1948

ADA

While attending her first film premiere since the one she shared with Vince, Ada isn't quite certain how to feel. Ashamed or embarrassed, perhaps, or like she doesn't belong. She's an outcast among most of these people. No one wants to hire her, none of the work she completed recently is moving forward, and any talk of accolades for *Lady Bella Donna* quickly fizzled out.

The industry she cherishes has turned its back on her.

Yet as she takes Vince's hand and steps from the car, none of those feelings overtake her. She is with him, celebrating him and his career. Maybe the papers will be full of gossip and criticism for her tomorrow even as they sing the praises of Hollywood's Hartthrob. None of it matters, really. This night is his. More importantly, it is theirs.

Vince leads her down the carpet. Past the shuttering cameras, a few hostile glares and shouts directed at her, and toward the theater, where his name is prominently displayed on the marquee. Then he sweeps her into a dip and leaves a long, lingering kiss on her lips amid the shouts, cheers, and clamors of the photographers. When he brings her upright, Ada matches his grin.

"One of the most sought-after actors in Hollywood arrives at his premiere with a convicted criminal on his arm and kisses her in front of everyone?" Ada grabs his tuxedo jacket by its lapels and kisses him once more. "Sounds like a brilliant opening for a film."

"I might know a fellow who can write the script."

With a sly wink, Vince threads her arm through his and they continue into the theater. If the gossip columnists didn't have enough to say about them before, they certainly will now.

Following the premiere and a splendid afterparty at the Chateau Marmont, the car takes them to Gordon's. Upstairs, Vince loosens her dress—since no one else is awake, he has promised to help her—and kisses her exposed shoulder.

His touch fills her with peace, with the longing she has held patiently and cautiously, allowing it time and space. Now, she turns, removes his tuxedo jacket, and unfastens each button on his shirt. Then she looks up at him.

"Stay with me."

He brushes his thumb along her jaw, sending a ripple of heat through her core. "Are you certain?"

Here, with him, with every reassurance, she knows only certainty.

"If it becomes too much, I'll say so." She takes his face between her palms, because in her eyes he will find every desire, every truth. "I trust you."

His eyes soften. "We'll go slowly, then."

He removes the dress from her shoulders. With each touch, she relaxes more fully into him, anticipation and desire building as she has never permitted before. She has always held back. This time, nothing interferes. She does not hold back. She exists entirely in the present—

not the past, not the future, this moment. It is all she knows, all she craves, all she has finally permitted herself to accept. Because, for all this time, and at last, it is him.

* * *

The next morning, when light spills through her bedroom window, Ada rubs the sleep from her eyes. Yawning, she grabs last night's half-finished glass of water from her nightstand and swallows the rest, easing her thirst. Beside her, Vince remains asleep, sunbeams streaking across his hair, turning it copper. Quietly so as not to disturb him, she gets up, finds his tuxedo shirt on the floor, and pulls it on—long enough to serve as a short nightdress, so it will do while she slips from the room to refill her glass. She reaches the door, then pauses when an approving voice, gruff with sleep, breaks the quiet.

"That looks far better on you than it ever does on me." Vince lies on his back, one arm behind his head as he regards her.

"Well, I'd hate to make you feel insecure the next time you wear it." She sets down the glass, flashing a suggestive smile. "Shall I take it off?"

"I'll do that myself." He throws the sheets aside, gets up, grabs her waist, and tosses her onto the bed, silencing her giggles with a kiss. "Stunning in your gown at the premiere, stunning in my wrinkled shirt the next morning. You never cease to impress, Miss Worthington-Fox."

When his hand slips beneath the shirt, across her stomach, and over her breasts, the old, familiar flash of tension seizes her—one that doesn't come as often anymore but finds her on occasion. At once, Vince draws back. She longs to keep her arms around him, to push beyond the feeling that no longer controls her but finds a hold at times. Instead she lets him withdraw. If the moment is going to pass, she must give it the space it needs.

They lie side by side while Ada slows the breaths threatening to hasten. When she feels ready, she faces Vince, whose gentle gaze searches hers.

She runs her fingers through his disheveled locks. "Is it odd for you, knowing my name isn't my birth name?"

He shrugs. "Odd? Not particularly. Do I wish you had trusted me with the truth? Selfishly. But that's not my decision, is it?"

For so long the truth was hers to share or withhold. Here in her bedroom, wearing this shirt that smells like him while the early morning sunlight skips across his bare chest and his eyes spark with life, she trusts him with every part of her.

"I chose Ada because it's similar to my given name. Worthington because—" She giggles. "Well, for no reason other than I thought it sounded delightfully pretentious. And Fox because it's the English translation of my Dutch surname."

"And together? Powerful. Intriguing. Effortlessly seductive. All of which you'd manage no matter what your name is." He presses his lips to the pulse at her wrist, prompting the usual spark left by his touch. "Call yourself whatever you like, so long as I get to call you mine."

Ada moves into his arms again, leaving kisses on his chest, his neck, his jaw, his lips, then pulls him on top of her. A shiver courses through her body as she arches against him, feels the little growl vibrating in his throat as his lips find her neck.

"Vince?" she prompts. "You've never said it. My name. My real one."

He removes the tuxedo shirt with deliberate ease. Then he kisses the scar on her breast while everything in her stills, slows, calms, even as she simultaneously pulses with life.

"You are safe with me, Aleida de Vos."

Safe. She can't recall the last time she felt entirely safe. For so long she's been hiding, disguising everything she couldn't bear to reveal. Now the lies have given way to the truth—every part of her, body and spirit, entrusted completely and entirely to him.

He is her safety, her choice. And she will choose him time and time again.

* * *

Tonight's Star Society gathering is the first since the one that led to Mother and Dietrich's arrest. Prior to sending invitations, Ada wasn't certain if anyone would come. Those who haven't been blacklisted have been largely avoiding those who are. Now that the time has come and the event is perhaps the largest gathering she's ever thrown, she can't resist giving Gordon a triumphant grin over the top of the champagne tower.

As usual, he insisted it was necessary.

Everyone gathers around the champagne, so Ada scoops Sowerby into her arms and accepts a glass from Vince. "Well, to those of us who have been part of the Star Society for some time, I'm thrilled to see you here. To those who are new, I'm delighted to have you. Who knew we were a Communist front organization?"

A collective laugh rises. They can't change what happened, so they might as well find the humor in it. When silence falls again, Ada clears her throat.

"This group is not, in fact, a political group or anything of the sort. It grew out of a simple wish, really. A Dutch girl's dream to make friends in America and find her way to the silver screen, and indeed that dream came true for me and many of you. And due to recent events, for many that dream has been crushed."

Stillness falls over the crowd as Ada observes her audience. Union members, Mr. Sternberg, Gordon, some claimed by the hearings, others who retain their careers, and even Beverly. Old friends and new.

"Most of us have friends on all sides of these disagreements. Most of us have made mistakes in dealing with these matters. Most of us have regrets. No matter what befalls our industry, the Star Society is a place that, I hope, everyone can call home." She looks to Ingrid and Lars, then Vince beside them. "And to those of us on the blacklist—well, they say black is everyone's color."

Laughter and cheers follow as she lifts her glass, to which the guests toast, then the music resumes and the party commences. Ada kisses Sowerby's silky head before freeing him, and he scampers away, likely to mingle with guests before retreating indoors to nap on the chaise longue in her office.

She converses with a few people before Vince reaches for her through the crowd, so she takes his hand. He leads her to the table where Gordon, Ingrid, and Lars await them.

"Quite a party, though I expected nothing less," Ingrid says as Ada sits beside her.

"Only the most proper sendoff for you, dear sister, though I'll be terribly sorry to see you go tomorrow."

"We're due for a long vacation," Lars says, his arm draped across the back of Ingrid's chair.

Suddenly Vince leans forward with an eagerness Ada recognizes; he has an idea for a script. "Two sisters—an actress and an investigator. Loosely inspired by you two, by what happened, working together to take down a larger player . . . Let me write it, and I'll let you approve it once I'm finished."

He settles back, thoughtful as the idea takes shape—which, Ada agrees, is a good one. She glances at Ingrid, who clears her throat.

"I suppose I haven't properly apologized to all of you, have I?"

"To hell with apologies," Gordon says with a scoff. "We've all been used as a means to an end or involved in something that got out of hand or that we didn't entirely understand. I was an impressionable young fellow when I joined the party, and I'll be the first to admit Communism isn't the practical idea it seemed. So if you'd reassure your friends at HUAC that I'm no threat, I'd like my career back." He winks, to which Ingrid smiles. "Let Vince write the script."

"If Ingrid and I can play ourselves," Ada says. Then, before Ingrid can protest, she mimics removing reading glasses and lifts an unamused brow in clear imitation. "I most certainly will not, Leidje, and if you pester me, I will throw you into the pool."

"No, no, no, you've got me all wrong." Ingrid shakes her head. "*If you pester me? You always pester me.*"

After more laughter, pleasant conversation, and refills of champagne, Ada pushes through the crowd until she overlooks the pool. She stands a few feet away, letting the vibrance of the party wash over her until arms encircle her waist, dragging her toward the edge. With a laughing protest, Ada struggles as she meets Ingrid's bright, challenging gaze, and only when Ada threatens to pull her in with her does she relent. They stand there, clinging to one another and dissolving into laughter while the water shimmers like the champagne flowing through their veins.

A band plays a lively tune while couples dance, so Ada and Ingrid release one another as Vince and Lars join them.

"Would you really want a blacklisted actress in your film?" Ada asks.

"Of course, and not simply because that blacklisted actress is you." He spins her under his arm, then pulls her close as his voice softens. "People are nervous, but it shouldn't last, God willing. Until then, whatever I can do to help."

Perhaps he can help; perhaps not. They can't force industry professionals to support a project, movie theaters to show it, or moviegoers to attend. Still, there must be a way they can aid those affected by what's happened. She looks around. Nearly everyone here is part of the entertainment industry. If they can come together for fun, why not for a shared endeavor?

"Maybe we can use the Star Society for more than just parties. We can help one another find work."

"An excellent idea. Once I'm established as a screenwriter, I'd be happy to lend my name as a front for blacklisted writers until all this is over." When the wind pulls a lock of hair into Ada's eyes, he brushes it aside. "And you? What do you want to do next?"

What, indeed? She hasn't thought of life after the blacklist—if there is to be one. She dismisses the bleak thought. Everything comes to an end, even if right now the end feels unreachable. As the song slows to "La Vie en Rose," she rests her head against Vince's chest, listening to the steady beat of his heart.

"Someday I'd like to perform in a ballet, either in film or onstage. It's what I did during the war, and I didn't think I'd ever be ready to do it again. Now I am, because . . . well, that's all I've ever wanted, really. To perform and to live."

Performing demands genuine authenticity by its very nature; only then can it feel real. Only then can the audience believe it. There is nothing more intimate, more personal, more honest. To create art is to bare the entire soul. Bestowing such a gift to others is both a responsibility and a privilege.

It's all she knows, all she is. For so many years, she's concealed her former self behind the woman she created. Now both are part of her, soul and spirit, as much a part of her as those who surround her on this night.

Across the dance floor, Ada meets Ingrid's gaze and returns her smile; then she finds Gordon among a circle of friends with a drink in one hand and Sowerby in the other; then she nestles into Vince, who kisses the top of her head. Her twin sister, her dear friends, the man she loves, all the greatest pieces of art in her life.

She closes her eyes to feel the music, to lose herself in the rhythm of her body in time with Vince's, in this art form she has known her entire life perhaps better than any other.

Someday, there won't be a blacklist. Someday, even if the job offers resume, they will cease again. And someday, she will look back on her life and ask herself if everything was worth it. If she was happy in spite of it all.

And someday, she hopes her answer will be as it is on this night: that she was, that she is. Even still.

A word of warning: Do not read further unless you've finished the book. Spoilers!

Once you've read the book, carry on. Or, if you choose to ignore this word of warning, sadly I can't stop you, but I tried my best.

I'd like to take this opportunity to share more about the history that inspired *The Star Society* and to express any liberties or fictionalizations I took, starting with my characters. Although my character Ada was heavily inspired by Audrey Hepburn, neither she nor this story is meant to be biographical fiction. I took plenty of liberties with Audrey's life and experiences, and as far as I know, she was never swept up in the Red Scare. This story, however, did begin with her.

Ever since I was a little girl, when my grandmother introduced me to her films, Audrey Hepburn has been my favorite actress. And maybe it's the historical author in me, but when I take an interest in something, I look up as much information as possible on the topic. Learning more about Audrey's life eventually led me to her early life, where I discovered something truly fascinating and unexpected: Audrey Hepburn spent her early life the Netherlands, pursuing her goal of becoming a professional ballerina and living under occupation during World War II. According to Audrey herself and to various sources, she aided the Dutch resistance during this time. Various factors, including the effects of malnutrition, impacted her dreams of dancing professionally, so she turned to acting instead.

What might it have been like to go from resistance member to Hollywood star? Growing up, I held on to this question and finally found the opportunity to explore it through this novel. *Dutch Girl: Audrey Hepburn and World War II* by Robert Matzen was an incredibly detailed account of Audrey's early life in Arnhem and Velp and was a tremendous help in shaping Ada's character, her family, and her experiences with the resistance, although I simplified and condensed my portrayal for story purposes. Many details, however, were fictionalized versions of true events. For example, Ada and Ingrid's grandfather is dismissed from government work when he refuses to name anti-Nazis, and this is exactly what happened to Audrey Hepburn's uncle, Otto. He was also among a group of prominent Dutchmen who were arrested, then ultimately executed in retaliation for resistance efforts, which is why the same tragic fate befalls Opa in the story.

I wanted to write this Audrey Hepburn–inspired idea as a story of sisters, and I was fascinated to learn that the House Un-American Activities Committee was dedicated to uncovering and combating Communist influences, which resulted in the Red Scare. In the 1940s, the entertainment industry was HUAC's primary target. I learned so much about these events from *Witch-Hunt in Hollywood: McCarthyism's War on Tinseltown* by Michael Freedland; *Show Trial: Hollywood, HUAC, and the Birth of the Blacklist* by Thomas Doherty; and *Naming Names* by Victor S. Navasky.

At first, those in the entertainment industry were not worried about rumors of Communist influences, investigations, or HUAC hearings. Due to the numerous stages of a film's production, most believed it would be nearly impossible for Communist influences—if inserted—to survive all the way to the final cut. Ronald Reagan, the Screen Actors Guild president at the time, expressed respect for HUAC's purpose in fighting Communism but cautioned against sacrificing democratic principles or civil rights to do so, because Americans could be trusted to defend democracy. Both conservatives and liberals approved of his remarks, as they summed up the opinions held by most, but fear continued to build, ultimately resulting in hearings, naming names, and the condemnation of the Hollywood Ten, who were put on trial for refusing to testify before HUAC.

I wondered what it might be like to have two people involved in the Red Scare, but in completely opposite ways: one dedicated to identifying Communists, another identified as possibly subversive. How easy might it have been to use and manipulate such people, and to turn an innocent into a cautionary tale? It seemed frighteningly simple.

This led me to Ingrid, Ada's twin, who is eager to defend democracy, protect her sister, and clarify Ada's position. I fictionalized and simplified Ingrid's work as a private investigator, the FBI's involvement in investigative efforts, aspects of HUAC's timeline and process, and the resulting legal proceedings, but I thought it would be easy for a few manipulative higher-ups to take an ambitious woman like Ingrid, send her to complete a task, and manipulate her findings. By concocting a specific story about Ada and sending her before HUAC, they could demonstrate what happens to those who are not explicitly clear about their views or who might be associated with subversive influences. Certain organizations were suspected of being Communist fronts, so Ada's private parties and her associations with Communists and others considered subversive— such as homosexuals—presented the perfect opportunity to make an example of her.

With the war and the Red Scare, I needed another element to more strongly connect the storylines. Postwar, most Nazis escaped punishment, but many were also blackmailed into serving other governments, including the American government, in roles such as combating Communism or aiding the Space Race. *The Nazis Next Door: How*

America Became a Safe Haven for Hitler's Men by Eric Lichtblau provided valuable insight into this process. This was the perfect way to connect my plotlines. Gregor Dietrich was inspired by Hanns Rauter, the Higher SS and Police Leader in the occupied Netherlands. I condensed and simplified Dietrich's role by assigning him as the SS and Police Leader overseeing the Gestapo and Ordnungspolizei, and then I brought him to America and back into Ada's life. Add in Constance de Vos, an incredibly manipulative mother and Nazi supporter, and I had everything I needed to disrupt Ada's and Ingrid's present with their past.

I could say so much more about the history, characters, and the Easter eggs I slipped into these pages as nods to Audrey Hepburn's life or characters she played, but then we would be here awhile. However, I'll leave you with one of my favorite tidbits: When Audrey Hepburn starred alongside Gregory Peck in *Roman Holiday*—her first American film—he was so impressed by her skill that he insisted that she receive equal billing, even though Audrey Hepburn was not an established Hollywood star yet. Peck was certain she would win an Academy Award for her performance, and he was right. In 1954, at the 26th Academy Awards, Audrey Hepburn won the Oscar for Best Actress for her performance. This is why I have an experienced actor, Vince, Ada's costar, insist on placing Ada's name most prominently on the billing for their film even though it's her first major role.

I hope this gives you some insight into the history behind the story, clarifies the liberties I took, and encourages you to learn more about the events portrayed. As always, thank you so much for reading. Any errors in historical fact or setting are entirely my own.

ACKNOWLEDGMENTS

First, the biggest and most heartfelt thank you to my agent, Kaitlyn Katsoupis, for never giving up on me. To my editors, Lizzie Poteet and Laura Wheeler, for supporting me, challenging me, and bringing out the best in my work. To the entire team at HarperCollins Focus, Harper Muse, and Harper Audio, and all those involved in publishing, design, editing, proofreading, marketing, publicity, production, and the many stages of placing a book on shelves, this book would not be possible without your tireless efforts. Thank you, thank you, thank you!

So many people deserve thanks, and I'm honored to call many of them my incredible friends. To Olesya Salnikova Gilmore, you've been by my side since the beginning, when we were just two hopeful writers with big dreams who became the best of friends. I can't thank you enough for always silencing my doubts and worries and sticking by me no matter what. You're the best, and I can't imagine doing this without you. To Vik Francis, the most selfless and loving friend: you inspire me in so many ways and have been such a constant source of encouragement and reassurance. I'm so grateful and so fortunate to have you by my side through the ups and downs. To Diana Giovinazzo and Rose de Guzman, for showing me around Los Angeles on my research trip and being such thoughtful, generous friends. To Bren and Tonny, for tirelessly answering my questions about Dutch and German language and culture. I'm so glad that this career led me to every single one of you.

To the readers, librarians, booksellers, and book lovers: you make my work possible. Thank you for spreading the word about books, championing authors, preordering, requesting from your local library, attending events, leaving reviews, and making me feel so loved. What you do truly makes a difference.

Finally, above all, to my family—my parents, siblings, grandparents, aunts, uncles, and all those who made me who I am today. A simple "thank you" is an understatement, but I'll say it anyway. How fortunate I am to have been raised by people who showed me the meaning of family, of faith, of love, of hard work, and of believing in yourself and your dreams. Thank you, and I love you with all my heart.

1. Prior to reading this book, what did you know about the Red Scare in America? Did you know about its impacts on the entertainment industry, such as the blacklist? Did you learn anything new from this book?

2. This novel discusses the concept of silence as a means of protection versus silence as the result of fear, particularly with Ada's outlook on life given her experiences. Do you think silence is helpful, hurtful, or both depending on the context? Had you been in Ada's position during the war or during the Red Scare, how would you have handled her circumstances? Did Ada's outlook change, and if so, how?

3. *The Secret Garden* by Frances Hodgson Burnett is Ada's favorite book. She relates very closely to the characters and symbols within it, and its story world has become a place of comfort, protection, and inspiration for her. Similarly, Ingrid turns to nonfiction, particularly to books about history and politics that make her feel close to her beloved grandfather. Can you think of a book that had a similar impact on your life? Is there a book that has stayed with

you ever since you first read it, or one you return to time and time again?

4. Ada processes the world through creativity and artistic expression, Ingrid through knowledge and facts. Which approach most closely matches how you adapt to change and the way you understand the world around you—one, the other, or a mixture of both?

5. Both Ada and Ingrid are strong personalities, and both make mistakes as a result of their differing approaches and worldviews. Through these mistakes, differences, and what ultimately comes from them, what do you think Ada learned from Ingrid, and what do you think Ingrid learned from Ada? Which sister surprised you more? Which do you relate to more?

6. Ada's manager, Gordon, begins the novel as a registered Communist. By the end, he has reconsidered his political beliefs. What do you think this says about him? If someone challenged your views—political or otherwise—would you listen to them with an open mind? Do you think people today are willing to be respectful and open-minded when it comes to these kinds of conversations with others who may or may not believe as they do?

7. Do you notice any similarities and/or differences between the Nazi occupation of the Netherlands and HUAC's investigation into Communism? Compare and contrast those similarities and/or differences.

8. The Star Society—Ada's exclusive group of friends who attend her lavish parties—is a key feature in the novel. Discuss the symbolism

of this social event, specifically in relation to Ada herself and to the impacts of the Red Scare on Hollywood.

9. Discuss Ada and Ingrid's relationship with Constance, their mother, and discuss your thoughts on Mother. Did your opinion of her change throughout the novel? Why do you think she parented the way she did and made the choices she made?

10. As women in the workplace, both Ada and Ingrid face challenges in their male-dominated fields. Neither one is treated with equality or fairness as compared to her male counterparts. Ada is often defined by her looks and her relationships with powerful men; Ingrid is overlooked and is considered inferior. Are these sorts of issues still prevalent in the workplace today? What are your thoughts on Archie's character arc, specifically in relation to his interactions with Ingrid? What about Vince's in relation to his professional interactions with Ada?

11. This book, particularly Ada's character and her life under Nazi occupation, is inspired by the actress Audrey Hepburn. Did you notice any references to Audrey Hepburn's life, her films, or characters she played? If so, discuss.

12. At the end of the novel, Mother's and Dietrich's fates are left unresolved. The reader learns that their cases will be moving forward, but not if they are found guilty at trial and punished for their misdeeds. What do you think ultimately happened to them? What do you think happened to Ada, Ingrid, Vince, Lars, and Gordon in terms of their lives, relationships, and careers?

ABOUT THE AUTHOR

Photo by Janie Long Photography

Gabriella Saab is an acclaimed author of historical fiction. Her first two novels, *The Last Checkmate* and *Daughters of Victory*, have been published in multiple languages and various countries. She graduated from Mississippi State University with a bachelor of business administration in marketing and lives in her hometown in Alabama.

* * *

Connect with her online at gabriellasaab.com
Instagram: @gabriellasaab_
Facebook: @GabriellaSaabAuthor
X: @GabriellaSaab_